Sign up for our newsletter to hear
about new and upcoming releases.

www.ylva-publishing.com

Other Books by Jae

Happily Ever After

Standalone Romances:
The Roommate Arrangement
Paper Love
Just for Show
Falling Hard
Heart Trouble
Under a Falling Star
Something in the Wine
Shaken to the Core

Fair Oaks Series:
Perfect Rhythm
Not the Marrying Kind

The Hollywood Series:
Departure from the Script
Damage Control
Just Physical
The Hollywood Collection (box set)

Portland Police Bureau Series:
Conflict of Interest
Next of Kin

The Vampire Diet Series:
Good Enough to Eat

The Oregon Series:
Backwards to Oregon
Beyond the Trail
Hidden Truths
The Complete Oregon series (box set)

The Shape-Shifter Series:
Second Nature
Natural Family Disasters
Manhattan Moon
True Nature

Wrong Number

Right Woman

Jae

Acknowledgments

A huge shout-out to my wonderful team of beta readers. Some have been working with me for years, while others joined the team to provide expertise on Portland, Oregon, where *Wrong Number, Right Woman* is set. Thanks so much to A.C., Anne-France, Caitlin, Chris Zett, Claire Jarrett, Danielle, Erin, Laure, Louisa, Maggie, Melanie, Tina, and Trish.

I'm also grateful to my sensitivity readers, Claire Anderson and Mey Rude, for taking the time to read the novel and making sure I portrayed Heather in a respectful and realistic way.

I'd also like to thank my editor, Alexa Bitsko, and the team at Ylva Publishing.

Thank you to all the people in my Facebook Reader Group, who provide great support and book recommendations, and especially to Nia, who suggested the name for the grocery store where Denny works.

Last but not least, thank you to my readers for letting me keep you up way beyond your bedtime with yet another novel.

Chapter 1

DENNY MADE IT TO THE bus stop with two minutes to spare. Right before the end of her shift, a customer had dropped a bottle of ketchup in aisle three, and Denny's boss had sent her to clean up the mess, making her late. How fitting for April Fools' Day!

Still in her Grocery Port uniform, with spatters of half-dried ketchup all over her shirt and pants, she huffed to a stop at the corner where the bus would drop off her niece. She bent over to catch her breath. Christ, she really needed to get back in shape.

Not that she had ever *been* in shape.

Her phone vibrated in her back pocket.

When she pulled it out, she wasn't surprised to see it was a text from her sister.

Did you do it?

Before she could ask for clarification, a new text bubble popped up beneath the first one. *You didn't, did you? Stop being such a chickenshit and ask her out already!*

Denny wiped the mistlike Portland drizzle off the small screen before typing, *Would you stop it? The bus isn't even here yet. Besides, who says I want to ask her out? Just because two women are gay doesn't mean they are interested in each other. If she even is gay.*

Her sister's reply was almost instant. *Oh, she is gay—and interested, trust me. I saw her smile at you the last time we dropped Bella off at the bus together.*

Denny stabbed at the keyboard on the phone screen as if that would finally make her sister listen. *I smile at customers all day long. It's called being friendly. Part of the job, nothing more.*

But what if it's more? Salem's predictable reply popped up within seconds. *Maybe she likes you.* She had added a row of kissy-face smileys.

Yeah, sure, Denny wrote back.

What have you got to lose? You haven't been on a single date since Bella was in first grade. That was more than four years ago, Denny!

Denny groaned and typed, *Thanks for keeping track.*

This time, it took a while before Salem's answer appeared. *I just worry about you. You're too amazing to end up alone.*

The last word made Denny grip the phone more tightly. She stared up at the overcast sky, then firmly shook her head. Bullshit. She wasn't alone, was she? She had her niece and her sister, as annoying as Salem could be. She was fine.

The big, yellow school bus rumbled around the corner, saving her from having to reply to Salem's text. It pulled up to the curb only steps from Denny, with its lights flashing and the stop sign extended.

When the bus door swung open, Denny sucked in her belly and plucked her shirt away from her hips, hoping to hide her love handles before she stepped up to the bus.

"Hi." The driver—Ms. Burkhart—smiled at her.

Denny froze, staring up at her. What was she supposed to say? Even if she wanted to go out with her, could she really ask the woman out while she was working, in front of about fifty kids? "Um, hi."

Two girls in the first row of seats nudged each other and giggled.

Sweat trickled down Denny's spine. She reached up to adjust her glasses.

The giggling got louder.

Shit, had she just smeared ketchup all over her face?

2

Ms. Burkhart's smile broadened. "Looks like you had quite the April Fools' Day."

"Uh, excuse me?"

Ms. Burkhart took one hand off the oversized steering wheel, ran it through her blonde locks, several shades lighter than Denny's sandy hair, and then pointed at Denny's ketchup-spattered shirt.

"Oh. Yeah. That. It's not blood—just ketchup," Denny blurted out. God, she was bad at this. So, so bad. It was almost as if she was watching herself from far away, witnessing the train wreck, but she still couldn't avoid making a fool of herself.

Bella bounded down the three steps and paused on the last one. "You're blocking the door."

"Oh, sorry." Denny stumbled back. It was a relief to have the eye contact between her and Ms. Burkhart interrupted.

Bella jumped out of the bus. "Bye, Ms. Burkhart," she called over her shoulder.

"Bye, Bella," Ms. Burkhart answered. "See you in the morning." She nodded at Denny and lifted her hand to press the button that would close the door.

It was now or never. Her sister's words echoed through Denny's mind. *What have you got to lose?* Ms. Burkhart seemed kind. Even if she wasn't interested in her, she wouldn't reject her too harshly... would she?

Denny gave herself a mental kick and opened her mouth to ask. "Um..."

"Yes?" Ms. Burkhart waited, her finger hovering over the button.

"Thanks for dropping her off safely," Denny finally got out. What? That wasn't what she had wanted to say!

Ms. Burkhart tipped an imaginary hat. "My pleasure."

A nod, then the door closed between them.

The red lights stopped flashing, and the bus pulled away and continued down the street.

Denny's shoulders slumped. Well, maybe it was better that way. Asking Ms. Burkhart out while she was at work might have gotten her in trouble. And even if she had said yes to having coffee with her, Denny probably would have ended up embarrassing herself even more.

"What's for dinner?" her niece asked from behind her. "I'm starving."

Denny laughed and shook off the feeling of defeat that had settled over her. She joined Bella and loosely wrapped one arm around her shoulders as they walked the three blocks toward home. "What else is new?"

Bella leaned into her half embrace—a moment of closeness that had become rarer since she'd become a tween—and directed a puppy-dog look at her. "Can we get French fries?"

"Nope. Your mom will be home from work in an hour. We'll have dinner then."

"Please?"

From the first moment Denny had held her newborn niece, she knew she would always have a hard time telling her no. But because Bella and her mom were living with her, Denny had taken on more of a parental role, not that of an aunt who saw her niece occasionally and could spoil her rotten. She knew she had to be firm. "No, Bella. Not today. Getting takeout is a treat, not something we can do all the time. Besides, the zucchini will go to waste if we don't eat them today."

"Ew. Zucchini." Bella wrinkled her nose.

She looked so much like the pouting three-year-old she had once been that Denny struggled not to laugh. "I'll tell you what. If you finish all your homework tonight and don't complain about dinner, I might pick up some ricotta cheesecake from your favorite Italian bakery after work tomorrow."

"Okay." Bella rushed ahead of Denny as if running would speed up the process of getting cheesecake.

Denny watched her with a fond grin. *Good old bribery. Works every time.* Now if only her moves were as successful when it came to charming women. Sighing, she followed Bella up the driveway to the two-story townhouse complex where they lived.

Half an hour later, Denny spooned the tomato sauce filling into the scooped-out zucchini and sprinkled shredded cheese and a bit of basil over them. Once the zucchini boats sizzled away in the oven, she dropped onto a chair next to Bella, who was doing her math homework at the dining room table. *Whew.* It felt good to be off her feet.

Just as she reached for her phone to see if she had beaten her personal record of walking twenty-five thousand steps at work, the device buzzed with an incoming text message.

"Yeah, yeah. Bawk, bawk, baawk. I'm a chicken. I know," Denny muttered. She tapped her messages icon to read her sister's inevitable admonition.

But the new message wasn't from Salem. Denny didn't recognize the number, but the area code was 503, the same as her own. Maybe one of her colleagues had a new phone or something. She opened the message to read it.

A red SOS emoji jumped out at her, along with: *Help! I'm hopelessly overthinking my first-date outfit.*

Denny chuckled. Someone was asking her of all people for advice on fashion and dating? Everyone who knew her was well aware that she had no interest in the former and no talent for the latter. Was this an April Fools' Day joke? Had Julie, her work wife, borrowed someone's phone to prank her?

Another message from the same unknown number popped up beneath the first one. *What do you think? This...?*

A photo appeared on her screen.

That was definitely not Julie. The selfie, shot in front of a closet with a mirrored door, showed a stranger. A cute stranger, Denny had to admit. The young woman's glossy chestnut hair was tucked behind one ear, while the other side grazed her shoulder. A pair of black skinny jeans hugged her narrow waist and slim hips, and an off-the-shoulder top revealed tantalizing hints of fair skin. Her lips quirked up in a self-deprecating grin, and her dark eyes twinkled as if she was poking fun at herself for obsessing over what to wear.

After a couple of minutes, a second picture arrived, along with the question: *Or this one?*

The photo showed the same woman in a different outfit. A tight top stretched across her small breasts, and a flowing skirt that ended above her knees made her look like a ballet dancer, lithe and graceful.

Denny's gaze trailed down the stranger's slender legs—then she burst out laughing.

Instead of the sensible yet sexy heels she'd been wearing in the first picture, a pair of canary-yellow sneakers now graced the woman's feet.

Bella looked up from where she was trying to multiply fractions. "What's that?" She craned her neck to catch a glimpse of what was on Denny's screen.

Denny hesitated. But why hide the messages from her niece? It wasn't as if the stranger had sent her nude pictures. She turned the phone so Bella could see the photos. "Someone is asking for fashion advice. I think she has the wrong number."

Bella giggled and pointed at the baggy sweatpants and the worn T-shirt Denny had put on after taking a shower. "If she's asking you for fashion advice, she's *clearly* got the wrong number."

"Hardy-har-har." Denny gave her a playful nudge that made Bella giggle even harder. "If you think I'm so fashion-challenged, maybe you should have someone else make your Halloween costume this year."

The giggling stopped abruptly, and Bella pretended to be focused on the phone. "So what are you going to tell her?"

Denny shrugged. "Sorry, wrong number?"

Bella looked back at her with wide eyes. "But she needs help."

Aww. Now that Bella was getting closer to puberty, she sometimes acted cool and aloof, but she couldn't hide her big heart. "Okay, then let's see if we can help her." Denny still wasn't sure how helpful she could be, though. Unlike her, the stranger clearly didn't shop in the men's section. She held out the phone to Bella and scrolled back and forth between the two images. "Which one?"

"Sneakers with a skirt?" Bella burst into giggles again.

Denny studied the photo once more. The canary-yellow sneakers made her smile. "I don't know. I kind of like it."

"Mm-hmm, me too. Just be yourself, right?"

It was what Denny and Salem had told her when she had come home crying a few years ago after someone at school had bullied her because she wasn't wearing the right brand of clothes. Apparently, their words had gotten through to Bella after all. Denny smiled and nodded. "Right."

A string of new messages appeared on the phone, moving the photo up the screen until all Denny could see was the yellow sneakers.

Heather???

Hello?

Which one?

Help me out here, please. I really don't want to give the wrong impression.

Denny pulled the phone closer to her. Without letting herself overthink it the way she usually did when she talked to women, she typed, *I'm not Heather, and as someone just reminded me, I'm not the best person to ask for fashion advice, but I'd definitely go with the second one.*

Several seconds ticked by. They bent their heads over the phone, waiting for a reply, but none came.

Bella reached over and tapped the screen as if that would encourage the stranger to answer.

Still nothing.

Bella shot her an accusatory look. "Oh no. I think you scared her off."

Yeah, apparently, she had that effect on women. Denny was about to put her phone away when a new message arrived after all.

Heather? Please tell me this is an April Fools' Day joke.

No, sorry, Denny typed back. *It's not a joke. You've got the wrong number.*

Again, there was a short pause before the reply came. *Oh shit. I'm so sorry. My friend just got a new phone. She must have given me the wrong number, or I put it in wrong.*

Don't worry about it, Denny replied.

She waited for a few more seconds, but no answer came. None was needed. She had gotten accidental text messages a time or two before, and the short back-and-forth always ended at this point. But unlike the other times, she found herself a little regretful. She wanted to know more about the woman with the yellow sneakers.

Bella nudged her. "Tell her you think the outfit is cute."

"I already told her to go with the sneaker one. Anything more would make me sound like a creep." When Bella reached for the phone, Denny pulled it away and stuffed it into the pocket of her sweatpants. "Come on. Your mom will be home soon. Let's set the table. You can finish your homework later."

Bella got the plates while Denny took knives and forks out of the drawer. When she placed the glasses on the table, her phone vibrated against her thigh.

"Ooh! Is it Sneaker Girl?" Bella rushed around the table to stand next to her.

"Sneaker *Woman.*" Denny wasn't great at guessing women's ages, but the stranger was probably at least ten years younger than her own forty-one, in her late twenties or early thirties.

"Yeah, yeah." Bella waved her hand. "Is it her? Check!"

Denny pulled out the phone.

Yes. It was a new text from Sneaker Woman.

So, she had written, *are you sure about that?*

That I'm not Heather? 100% positive. But I can check my ID to make sure, if you want. Denny added a grinning smiley face.

"Maybe you should send her a picture," said Bella, who had read the message along with her. "To prove that you're not Heather."

Denny shot her a no-way-in-hell look. "Remember what your mom and I told you about putting pictures of yourself online or sending them to strangers?"

"But she sent you photos of herself already," Bella pointed out.

"By accident."

Bella scrunched up her nose but gave up arguing and leaned closer to read the reply.

Sneaker Woman had answered with a rolling-on-the-floor-laughing emoji. *No, that's fine. I'll trust you to know your own name. I meant about the outfit.*

If you like wearing it, why not? Denny typed back. *You should wear whatever you feel comfortable in. If your date doesn't appreciate you the way you are, they're not worth your time.* She hesitated, but when Bella nudged her again, she added, *I, for one, would think it's cute if my date showed up dressed like that.*

They waited, but again no answer came.

"See?" Denny muttered. "Now we really scared her off."

"No, look, she's typing." Bella pointed at the three animated dots that had popped up on the screen.

A moment later, they disappeared, and Sneaker Woman's reply showed up beneath the other messages. *Thank you. That's good advice. I needed to hear that today. Despite your low opinion on your own fashion sense, I think you helped me more than Heather would have.*

Glad to help. Denny lowered her phone and glanced at her niece. She couldn't have kept her broad smile in check even if she had wanted. "What do you know? We helped her."

Bella poked at Denny's upper chest. "You're all puffed out. Like you're waiting for a medal." But she, too, was grinning proudly.

"Am not."

"Are too."

Denny poked her back. "Am not."

When the front door swung open and Salem stepped into the dining room, they were racing each other around the table, poking back and forth. Salem put her hands on her hips and regarded them with a shake of her head. "So this is what goes on here when you're the one who picks Bella up? And here I was thinking you were my older, more mature sister."

"Hi, Mom." Bella slid to a stop in front of her. "A woman texted Aunt Denny."

Salem let out a whistle and eyed Denny with an appreciative look. "Seems I underestimated you. Or my pep talk earlier really helped."

Before Denny could answer, Bella added, "By accident."

"Thanks a lot, kiddo," Denny murmured. "When you put it like that, it does wonders for my self-esteem. Some of the people who text me actually *want* to talk to me, you know?"

"I mean, this woman got her friend's number wrong," Bella said. "But we gave her great dating advice."

Salem opened her eyes comically wide. "Your aunt...giving dating advice?"

Denny shrugged. "Well, you know what they say. Those who can, do; those who can't, teach."

"So that means you didn't ask Ms. Burkhart out. You chickened out, didn't you?"

"You wanted to ask out my school bus driver?" Bella scrunched up her face. "Ew!"

Salem gave her a stern look. "Bella! I know I taught you better than that."

"Not because they're both girls...women," Bella said with a glance at Denny. "It's just that... That's like my aunt dating a teacher or something. My friends will make fun of me."

"She's right," Denny said. "It's not a good idea. It could get Ms. Burkhart in trouble with the school. That's why I didn't ask her out." Well, that and because she *had* chickened out. "Plus, like I told you repeatedly, I don't need to date anyone to be happy, so would you please stop meddling in my love life?"

"Nonexistent love life," Salem muttered. When Denny shot her an I'm-the-big-sister-and-I-know-where-you-sleep look, she held out one hand. "All right, all right." She lowered her gaze to the oversized purse she still held and examined it as if the battered old thing was about to spit out the winning lottery numbers. When she looked up again, the expression on her face was unusually timid.

A lump lodged in Denny's throat. She hadn't seen her confident, outspoken sister like this since she'd been a scared seventeen-year-old, confessing to their parents that she was pregnant.

Salem nibbled her bottom lip. "Um, what would you guys think if I did?"

"Did what?" Denny asked.

"Date someone," Salem said so softly that Denny had to strain to hear her.

Denny stared at her. Of course, her sister had dated every now and then in the eleven years she had lived with Denny. But she had always done so discreetly, without making it a topic of conversation in their everyday lives and without introducing Bella to the guy she was dating. But something seemed to be different this time. "Someone in particular?"

Salem nodded. "Matt has asked me to do a haunted pub tour with him next weekend."

"Matt?" Denny repeated to give her brain a chance to process the news. "You mean, your Matt...Matthew Kowalczyk?" Salem often mentioned her favorite colleague, and Denny had even met him a couple of times over the years, when there had been an open day at the garden center.

"He's not *my* Matt," Salem said. "But yes, *that* Matt."

"And you're going on a date? This time, it isn't just two colleagues grabbing a beer, right?"

"Right. It would be a date. I mean, if that's okay with the two of you." Salem looked back and forth between them, and her gaze ended up resting on her daughter.

A tiny wrinkle formed on Bella's brow. She seemed to think about it for a moment, then said, "As long as he doesn't think he can boss me around."

"He won't. It's not like we're getting married, honey. It's just one date." Salem sounded as if she was saying it as much for her own benefit as for Bella's.

The oven timer went off.

"Finally! I'm starving." In her sock-covered feet, Bella skidded into the kitchen and tore open the oven door, even though she had declared her hatred for zucchini not even an hour ago. A cloud of steam and the scent of sizzling tomato sauce and melted cheese wafted out.

"Careful. Don't burn yourself." Salem followed her.

Denny stayed behind for a moment, only half listening to Bella's protest about being treated like a baby. New people and new situations made her nervous, but she would deal with it for Salem's sake. Bella was no longer a little kid, as she reminded them nearly every day, so after years of focusing only on her, Salem deserved some kind of adult life.

Denny's phone dinged, jarring her out of her thoughts.

When she pulled it from her pocket, she discovered another message from Sneaker Woman. It was an upside-down photo of her navy skirt and the canary-yellow sneakers, as if she had pointed her phone down her body to take a quick snapshot. *My lucky sneakers and I are ready to head out*, the text said. *Thanks again and sorry to have bothered you.*

No problem, Denny replied. *Have fun on your date.* Without waiting for a response, she slid the phone back into her pocket. She didn't care if everyone and their dog were going on dates while she stayed home. Bella and she would gorge themselves on ricotta cheesecake while Salem made boring first-date small talk with Matthew Kowalczyk. Who needed a date if they could have cheesecake, right?

She gave herself a firm nod. Right.

Chapter 2

LATER THAT NIGHT, ELIZA SLID her key into the door and exhaled as she stepped into her studio apartment. Before she could close the door behind her, the one to the apartment across from hers swung open.

"Hey, you're home early," her friend Heather called. "How was the date?"

Eliza turned and leaned against the doorjamb. "Don't ask."

"That bad?" Heather bridged the space between them with two long-limbed, graceful steps. "Or are you just being picky again?"

"I'm not picky. I have standards." Eliza looked left and right. "Want to come in for a minute so I don't have to pour out my dating woes to every tenant in the building?"

"That depends."

"On?"

Heather laughed that deep, melodious chuckle that had made Eliza like her right away when they had first met five years ago. "On whether you have any of those yummy snickerdoodle cookies left."

"I do." Eliza waited until Heather had entered the apartment before she closed the door behind them and added, "Although come to think of it, I'm not sure you deserve any."

"Oh, come on, you can't let your best friend starve just because I made you go on one bad date."

Eliza snorted. "No one ever died from a lack of cookies, and you won't be the first." Despite her words, she detoured to the kitchenette, pulled the last package of snickerdoodle cookies out of the cabinet, and tossed them to Heather. "Here."

Humming, Heather settled on the colorful braided rug that covered the bamboo floor and ripped open the package.

Eliza sank into her easy chair—the one she and Heather had found at a flea market last summer and dragged home to her favorite spot in her tiny apartment, by the bay window overlooking the South Park Blocks. She kicked off her sneakers without untying them first and curled her feet under her.

Heather glanced up from her impromptu picnic and raised one perfectly shaped eyebrow—a talent Eliza had always envied. Despite one cheek already bulging with a cookie, she somehow managed to look elegant. "Sneakers with a skirt?" Heather tilted her head and seemed to consider the daring outfit choice for a second before declaring, "It's cute."

"That's what he said."

"See? If he complimented your outfit, your date couldn't have been that bad."

"You've got no idea. The entire date felt like one big April Fools' Day prank someone was playing on me. But I'm not talking about my date. I'm talking about the guy whose number you gave me."

Heather blinked. "I gave you a guy's phone number? When was that?"

"When you scribbled down your new phone number in that awful chicken scratch of yours."

"What?"

Eliza pulled up her contact list and held out her phone. "Is that your number?"

Heather leaned forward and studied the contact details while gobbling down another cookie. "Yes," she said with her mouth half full. "Oh. Wait." She swallowed the remainder of her cookie and pointed at the small screen. "That last number should be a nine, not an eight."

Eliza gave her a meaningful look. "And that's how I ended up asking a perfect stranger for fashion advice."

Heather burst out laughing, nearly spewing cookie crumbs all over the rug. "You sent a stranger one of your first-date panic texts?"

"Yeah. And pictures of my outfits. How embarrassing is that?" Eliza bent down and slapped Heather's knee. "Stop laughing."

Of course, that made Heather laugh even harder.

"And to think you drive a school bus full of innocent little kids for a living," Eliza muttered. "I hope you're nicer to them than you are to your poor best friend."

"Well, the transportation department frowns on drivers making fun of the kids, so I have to behave. I didn't even laugh when Butch Auntie showed up covered in ketchup today."

"Butch Auntie?" Eliza asked.

"Yeah, an aunt of one of the kids. Butch, kinda cute, and painfully shy. I told you about her, remember?"

"Oh, her. Right."

Heather eyed her. "What's up? You seem distracted. I hope the guy you accidentally texted wasn't an asshole about it."

"No, he was the perfect gentleman. He appreciated my style and encouraged me to be myself—which is more than I can say about my actual date."

"What did he do?"

"What didn't he do?" Eliza shot back. "He could write a handbook on 101 ways to mess up a date. Please tell me I don't have to go back out there again."

"What, and have me waste my hard-earned money on that online dating service I paid for?" Heather firmly shook her head, making her blonde locks fly. "You promised you'd give it six months, so that's what you're going to do. Just because the first one was a dud doesn't mean all the men on No More Frogs are going to be like that. The perfect guy for you is out there, I promise."

"From your mouth to the dating goddess's ears." Eliza rescued the last cookie from Heather and pressed the phone into her hand instead. "Now please put in your correct number before I end up bothering that unsuspecting stranger again."

Chuckling, Heather tapped the screen to edit her number.

Denny hated running the register. It wasn't the process of pulling the items over the scanner that she disliked, even though some of them were heavy. The pressure of being timed didn't bother her either. She had been doing this job for six years, so she could have scanned forty items per minute with one arm tied behind her back. The grocery store chain she worked for even allowed cashiers to sit at the register. But the constant interaction with customers often left her exhausted—especially if it was customers like the little old lady whose groceries she was ringing up right now.

Instead of swiping her card or handing Denny a bill, she was digging through her purse for the exact amount—eight dollars and ninety-three cents—while the line of waiting customers behind her got longer and longer.

There goes my ring speed. Denny resisted the urge to tap her foot and hurry her along.

Finally, the lady gave a triumphant cry and pressed the last cent into Denny's palm.

With a polite smile, Denny handed her the receipt.

Before she could start scanning the next customer's items, Julie walked over with her cash drawer. "I told the boss I'd cover your register so you can finally take your break."

As if on cue, Denny's stomach rumbled, reminding her that she hadn't eaten since before her shift had started at six. "Thanks. I knew you were my favorite colleague for a reason."

They switched out their cash drawers, and Denny watched with amusement as Julie pumped up the chair as high as it would go so she could reach the register. It wasn't that Denny was especially tall, but her colleague barely measured five feet.

"What?" Julie squeezed past Denny and slid onto the seat.

"Oh, nothing." Denny massaged her wrist, which had started to cramp after moving thousands of items across the scanner.

On her way to the back of the store, she grabbed a cheese twist and a chocolate croissant from the baked goods section. She dropped her cash drawer off in the office, where her boss would lock it in the safe, then headed to the break room.

It was empty. Unlike other supermarkets, the Grocery Port's retail operations used minimal staff, with each employee doing every job. There were no produce stockers or cleaning staff, so all of her colleagues were busy at the register or on the sales floor. At least the job paid better than most others in retail, and being busy made each shift fly by and left no time for small talk with customers, which Denny was grateful for.

She got her cell phone from her locker to see if Salem had texted her any last-minute items she needed Denny to bring home. A red dot on the messages icon indicated that she indeed had a new text. She sat at the table in the break room, took a big bite of her chocolate croissant, and opened the app to see what her sister wanted.

The message waiting for her wasn't Salem's shopping list, though. Denny paused mid-chew. She had another text from Sneaker Woman. Had she forgotten to edit her friend's contact?

Denny tapped on the message to read it.

Turns out my friend Heather is your number neighbor.

Denny sat stunned for a second. Sneaker Woman hadn't sent her another accidental text meant for someone else. She was actually talking to her! Denny had never understood how people could start a conversation with a total stranger. She usually tended to keep to herself, but now she surprised herself by setting down the croissant so she could type using both hands.

My what? she texted back.

It didn't take long for Sneaker Woman to answer. Maybe she was on her lunch break too. *Her number is the same as yours, just the last digit is one off.*

Number neighbor. Who had come up with that term? Denny shook her head. God, some days she felt old. *Ah, got it.* She hesitated, unsure how to continue the conversation, but knowing she wanted to. Finally, she typed, *So how did the date go last night? Did they appreciate your outfit?* She wasn't being nosy, right? Asking how her date had gone was the polite thing to do.

Looks like the sneakers weren't so lucky after all, Sneaker Woman answered. *He didn't even get to see them. I was already seated when he showed up twenty minutes late.*

Denny scoffed. What an ass! Sneaker Woman had put herself out there and agonized over what to wear, and he hadn't even cared enough to show up on time. Before she could think of an answer, another text bubble popped up.

With his neck covered in the biggest hickeys I've ever seen.

Denny stared at the screen. *You're messing with me.*

No, I swear. He then proceeded to talk about nothing but his ex for an hour.

What on earth...? Denny whistled through her teeth. Sometimes, she didn't understand people. *Um, if he's got hickeys the size of a small country, maybe the ex isn't that much of an ex after all.*

That's what I figured, Sneaker Woman replied. *So I told him we weren't a good fit and left. I'm too old for games like that.*

Denny nodded her approval. *Good for you. But forgive me for saying... I saw your pictures. You're...what? Late twenties? That's hardly old.*

Finally someone who knows how to compliment a woman! I'm thirty.

Denny snorted around another bite of her croissant. Then she paused and studied the screen. Was Sneaker Woman flirting? And was she seriously considering flirting back? Finally, she decided she was imagining things and typed back, *Ha! Spring chicken!*

Hardly. How old are you? Sneaker Woman asked.

Denny started to type: *Didn't your parents teach you not to ask a woman her age? No wonder you're single.* But then she shook her head. Sneaker Woman was dating guys. Chances were, she was straight, so her manners around women didn't affect her relationship status. Denny deleted both sentences and instead typed, *I'm forty-one.*

Oh, so I'm practically talking to a senior citizen. Sneaker Woman added three crying-from-laughing-so-hard emojis.

For a moment, Denny considered replying with a one-finger salute emoji, but then she reminded herself that Sneaker Woman was still a stranger, even though they had fallen into a surprisingly comfortable back-and-forth. Countering with an eye roll emoji was the safer option.

Before either of them could send another text, the store manager stuck her head into the break room. "Can you finish your break early? Apparently, the good people of the Portland metro area are preparing for an apocalypse. They are killing us out there. We need another person on checkout."

"Be right there." Denny shoved the remainder of her croissant into her mouth and hastily typed, *Sorry. This senior citizen needs to get back to work.*

The last thing she saw before she tossed her phone into her locker was, *Don't break a hip.*

For once, Denny grinned all the way to the register.

Chapter 3

ON FRIDAY EVENING OF THE next week, Denny sat on the edge of the bathtub and watched her sister put on makeup. She had never understood the need to use more than some lip balm, but the familiar ritual seemed to help Salem calm down. She had buzzed around the house all day, nervously anticipating her first date in ages, until Bella had rolled her eyes and disappeared upstairs, where she and Salem shared the upper level of the two-story townhouse.

Salem gave herself a once-over in the mirror above the sink, shook her head, and wiped off the lipstick before applying a different one that, to Denny, looked exactly like the first one.

Okay, maybe the ritual wasn't helping as much as Denny had hoped.

Her phone vibrated in her pocket, but she ignored it to address her sister. "Calm down. You look great."

"That's what you said when I was five and insisted on wearing those ugly pink rubber boots to school."

"But this time it's true. Matt better appreciate you. And if he doesn't, I can always beat him up for you." Denny flexed her biceps, which was pretty impressive from lifting all the canned goods at work, even though the muscles were hidden beneath a layer of chubbiness.

Salem giggled nervously. She lowered the lipstick and met Denny's gaze in the mirror. "Are you really okay with this? If you'd rather not watch Bella, I can stay home and—"

"Would you stop it? I've been watching her since the day she was born. Hell, I watched *you* since the day you were born! Why would I suddenly mind?" Denny got up from the edge of the tub and stepped up to her sister so she could study her. "What's going on?"

Salem exhaled a long breath and turned to face her. "I know I'm being silly. It's just... I think I'm freaking out a little."

Denny gave her an affectionate smile. "A little?"

Salem pinched her. "Do you think it was a mistake to say yes when he asked me to go out with him? Matt isn't some stranger that I never have to see again if we mess this up. We have to work together."

"He's probably aware of that, and that means he cares enough to take the risk. That has to count for something."

"Hmm." The wrinkle on Salem's forehead smoothed out. "It does." She looked down into Denny's eyes, and even though she had been taller than Denny since she'd been fifteen, it was still mildly annoying that she was able to do that. "Thank you."

"Any time, you know that." Denny returned the pinch. "Now go get ready. Your daughter and I have a ricotta cheesecake to devour, and I have a feeling she's hiding out in her room and won't come down until you're gone."

Chuckling, Salem turned back toward the mirror, and Denny returned to her place on the edge of the tub.

Her phone dinged again.

When she pulled it out of her pocket, she discovered two new messages from the now-familiar number.

The first one, sent several minutes ago, said: *Should I try my luck with the sneakers again or assume they are cursed and wear something else on my next date?*

Beneath it was a second text, which she had probably written when Denny hadn't replied: *Sorry. I don't know why I'm messaging you again. I promise my parents did have that stranger danger talk with me.*

Denny couldn't help grinning. If someone had asked her ten days ago, she would have said a stranger who kept contacting her

21

was a major annoyance, but for some reason, she wasn't bothered by it at all. *Well, I promise I'm not a serial killer, so it's fine,* she wrote back.

Hmm... Wouldn't you say the same even if you were?

Probably. But cutting up a body and hiding the pieces is too much work.

Sneaker Woman sent a wide-eyed emoji. *How do you know?*

I watch way too many crime shows.

Ah, so that's what kept you from answering. Central Precinct is on tonight, isn't it?

And you know that how? Denny typed, then paused with her finger over the *send* icon. Other than her sister and maybe Julie, she had never bantered back and forth with a woman like this. There was something freeing about having a conversation without knowing a lot about the other person. But now that she thought about it, her old self-consciousness returned, and she tapped the backspace symbol until the unsent message disappeared. Instead, she typed, *Sorry. I didn't mean to ignore you. I was busy calming down my sister's first-date jitters.*

Wow, Sneaker Woman replied. *Maybe you should do that for a living—become a professional first-date whisperer.*

Denny laughed. If only Sneaker Woman knew her track record, she would know how ridiculous that suggestion was. She could barely remember her last first date, much less the last time she had made it to a second date.

Salem looked up from her bottle of perfume. "What's so funny?"

"Nothing. Just something I read." Denny vaguely pointed at her phone. She wasn't ready to tell Salem that she was still talking to the woman who had sent her an accidental text. Her sister would probably think it was strange.

When Salem continued to get ready for her date, Denny returned her attention to the phone. *So, about your sneakers question... You aren't going out with Mr. Covered-in-Hickeys again, are you?*

Sneaker Woman sent back a no with at least ten o's. *I've got some self-respect, thank you very much. I'm going out with another guy.*

The more she talked to Sneaker Woman, the more Denny admired her for putting herself out there so fearlessly. It always took Denny weeks—okay, months, if she was being honest—to work up the courage to ask a woman out, and when she finally did and the first date didn't go so well, she usually wasn't in the mood to repeat the experience anytime soon. But the same couldn't be said for Sneaker Woman, who, about a week after her last dating disaster, was getting ready to go out with someone else.

I'm not normally a serial dater, Sneaker Woman sent when Denny didn't reply right away.

I wasn't judging, honestly. More like in awe.

Well, don't be, Sneaker Woman replied. *This wasn't my idea. I hit my big three-oh last month, and my best friend—your number neighbor—gave me a six-month subscription for No More Frogs because she thinks I'm too picky and will stay single forever if left to my own devices.*

"No More Frogs?" Denny said out loud. "What the heck is that?" But she didn't want to ask to avoid coming across as clueless.

"It's an online dating service," Salem answered. "You should try it."

Denny barked out a laugh. "No, thanks. I have a feeling they are not screening their users very well."

It's an online dating service, Sneaker Woman's next message said.

I know, Denny texted back. Was there a haughty I-knew-that-all-along grin emoji?

Riiiight.

Damn, was she that transparent, even to a stranger, or was Sneaker Woman that perceptive?

Another text arrived before she could think about what to write next. *Oh shit. I have to get going, or I'll be the one showing up late. So, sneakers or no sneakers?*

Sneakers. Denny stabbed the screen decisively.

A thumbs-up appeared beneath her message. *Thanks, oh great First-Date Whisperer.*

"Do I pass muster?" Salem tugged on her top, which revealed the tiniest bit of cleavage.

Denny put her phone away and looked her up and down. "You look great. But..."

Salem shifted her weight from one foot to the other. "Yeah?"

"You're missing a pair of pink rubber boots...or yellow sneakers."

"What?"

Denny smiled. "Forget it." She pushed Salem out of the bathroom, just as the doorbell rang. "Go and have fun."

A sense of déjà vu swept over Eliza as she trudged up the stairs to her second-story apartment later that night. *Why am I doing this to myself?* She could have spent the evening at home, finishing the cockatoo earrings she was making for her boss's upcoming birthday. Instead, she had suffered through yet another date that consisted mostly of her throwing the waiter apologetic glances and trying to think of an excuse to leave early.

Wasn't dating supposed to be fun? All it had done was make her feel humiliated.

She was tempted to delete that damn No More Frogs app from her phone, but she had promised Heather to give it a chance, so she needed to stick with it for the entire six months.

Sighing, she kicked off her sneakers and stared at the footwear. "I'm starting to think you're really bad luck."

Of course, they didn't answer. The silence in her apartment engulfed her.

Maybe she should finally get a cat.

She changed into her favorite pair of yoga pants and the cozy sweater with the hole along the shoulder seam, then went into the kitchenette. When she opened the cabinet, she remembered that she had given Heather the last of the cookies and made herself a mug of cinnamon rooibos tea instead.

She settled in her easy chair, turned on the TV, and aimlessly flicked through the channels.

Oh, *Central Precinct* was still on. She put down the remote and watched Detective Linda Halliday lean across a small metal table as she interrogated a suspect, who was clearly starting to sweat.

Was her first-date whisperer watching too?

Eliza peeked at her phone. No new messages.

What did you expect? He was probably busy going about his life and wasn't interested in texting a perfect stranger. Was it weird that she kept talking to him?

Somehow, it was easier to tell him about her failed date than to talk about it with Heather—maybe because he didn't know her and didn't expect anything of her. He seemed nonjudgmental, funny, yet earnest at the same time.

Maybe I should go out with him instead. The thought made her grin. Knowing her luck when it came to dating, it would end in some kind of disaster. One of them would get food poisoning, or they wouldn't have anything to say to each other face-to-face.

No, it was safer to just keep texting...if that was what he wanted too.

He seemed like an honest guy, so if he didn't want to talk to her, he would tell her to go away, right?

Nothing about his answers indicated that he wanted to get rid of her, though. He had readily replied to each of her texts and had even answered her teasing with some jokes of his own. Maybe he was home alone in a too-silent apartment as well and would be happy with a distraction.

Before she could talk herself out of it, she opened their thread of messages and added a new one. *Is it just me, or is Linda crossing the line a little?*

She watched as the detective on TV moved her paper cup, filled to the brim with steaming hot coffee, dangerously close to the edge of the table, where it threatened to topple over into the suspect's lap.

The scene ended, and still there was no reply.

Eliza clutched her mug while she balanced the phone on her knee. Maybe he did think she was weird.

Just when she considered giving up on this awful day and calling it a night, her phone chirped.

A grin spread across her face. It was a reply from Mr. First-Date Whisperer. She put her mug down to read what he had written.

Who's Linda?

And here I thought you're a fan of Central Precinct, Eliza answered.

Ah, that Linda. I missed that part of the episode. I had to go upstairs to make sure the kid is really down for the count, not reading under the covers.

Eliza paused with her thumbs already poised to type out a reply. For some reason, she had imagined him to be just as single and unlucky in love as she was. *Oh*, she texted back. *You've got a kid?*

No. I'm keeping an eye on my niece while my sister is out.

What a decent guy! After the last two dates she had been on, it was good to see that men like him still existed. *So, how was it? Your sister's date.*

I don't know. She hasn't made it home yet.

Then her date is probably going better than mine did.

Uh-oh, he texted back, making her smile. *What happened?*

He seemed like a nice guy when we were chatting online, Eliza typed. *But when we were in the restaurant, he decided it was okay to order for me without asking me first.*

Ugh. Mr. First-Date Whisperer sent a face-palm emoji. *I'm sorry. That's really shitty.*

Why do men do stuff like that? Don't they realize how condescending that is?

I have no idea, Mr. First-Date Whisperer replied. *I'm probably the worst person to give you advice on men.*

Well, you are one, right?

So far, he had been typing as quickly as she, but now he seemed to take forever answering. Had her text offended him, or was he writing an essay about the male psyche?

But when his answer finally came, it was short. *Um, actually... no.*

No? No to what? Eliza re-read the last two lines of their conversation. Wait, what? Hastily, she scrolled back up to the face-palm emoji and studied it more closely. It wasn't the male emoji, as she had first assumed; it was the more ambiguous one that could represent a man, a woman, or a nonbinary person. She tried to remember why she had assumed he...she was a guy but couldn't remember. Groaning, she hid her hot face against the bend of her elbow. Just when she had thought her day couldn't get any worse...

Her phone chirped in her hand, making her look up.

You didn't know I'm a woman? Ms. First-Date Whisperer had written.

No. I just assumed... Sorry, I guess I jumped to conclusions. God, this was so embarrassing.

That's fine. No big deal. It's not the first time that's happened.

It wasn't the first time a stranger who had sent her an accidental text had mistaken her for a man? Before Eliza could find a polite way to ask what exactly she meant, another text bubble appeared.

Sorry, I have to go. My sister just got home and wants to tell me all about her date.

Of course, Eliza replied. For once, she was glad to finish their conversation because she didn't know what to say. She needed some time to adjust her mental image of the person she'd been talking to. *Good night.*

Good night.

Then nothing else came, as if Ms. First-Date Whisperer no longer knew how to talk to her either.

Eliza gulped down her tea, which had long since gone cold, and wiped her brow. Well, at least she hadn't made a complete fool of herself by trying to ask him...her out!

Denny and her sister sat at the dining room table, where most of their important conversations took place after Bella had gone to bed. A giant piece of cheesecake sat in front of Salem, but she hadn't even tried it yet, too busy raving about her date with Matt. She was glowing, and Denny had a feeling it wasn't an effect of the beer she had drunk at the haunted pub tour.

Salem beamed. "God, I had forgotten how much fun it is to flirt with someone."

Denny gave a noncommittal hum. "I wouldn't know." By the time she usually figured out someone was flirting with her, the poor woman had given up because she assumed Denny wasn't interested. But maybe she hadn't misread the occasional flirty undertone of Sneaker Woman's texts after all. If she had thought Denny was a man, maybe she had indeed been flirting.

"God, and the way I felt when he put his hand on the small of my back." Salem fluttered her fingers over her heart, then paused. "Do two women on a date do that?"

"Hmm?" Denny's gaze veered from where she had watched Salem excitedly wave around her fork to her face. "What?"

"Do two women guide each other inside a pub with one hand on the other's back?" Salem asked.

"Yeah, sure. Well, at least I do it. But never on a first date." Usually, Denny needed at least three dates before she felt confident enough to touch the other woman in any way.

Salem put her fork down. "What's up with you?"

"Nothing."

A frown line carved itself between Salem's brows. "You don't have reservations about me going out with Matt, do you?"

"No. It's not that, I promise. He seems like a great guy."

"Then what is it? And don't try that *nothing* bullshit on me again. You've been distracted ever since I got back."

Denny sighed. "I'm older by thirteen years. How come I sometimes feel like the baby sister?"

"Twelve years, nine months. And don't think I didn't notice you're trying to change the subject." Salem pinned her with the glare she normally reserved for Bella when she tried to get out of doing her chores.

Denny reached across the table and stole the chocolate leaf garnish off Salem's wedge of cheesecake to buy herself a few more seconds. "You remember the woman who accidentally texted me last week?"

Salem nodded.

"We, um, kinda kept texting."

"Kinda?"

Denny ignored her interruption. "And I just found out that she thought all this time I was a guy."

"Huh. Awkward."

Another sigh escaped Denny. That was what she had enjoyed most about her text conversations with Sneaker Woman: they hadn't been as awkward as her usual attempts to talk to women. But now that had changed. "Yeah." She could imagine how embarrassed she would feel if the situation had been reversed. She would want to crawl into a hole and never come out again. "She'll probably stop texting me now."

Salem studied her across the table. "And you don't want that to happen."

"No." Denny surprised herself with how fast and decisively she answered.

"Well, I guess then you'll have to be the one texting her," Salem said. "Phones work both ways, you know?"

"Smart-ass." But maybe Salem was right. So far, it had always been Sneaker Woman who had initiated a conversation. This time, it might be up to Denny to contact her. If only she could figure out what to say.

Eliza pulled out her bed that was hidden in the bottom compartment of the cabinet during the day—one of the best features of her tiny apartment. Yawning, she flicked off the light and crawled beneath the covers. Then she remembered that she had to get up at eight tomorrow to set up the booth she and Heather shared to sell their craft items at Saturday Market, so she reached for her phone and set her alarm, just in case she didn't wake up on her own.

Just as she had settled down again and tried to shut off all thoughts so she could go to sleep, her phone chirped.

Her eyes popped open, and she stared at her phone in the near darkness. For a moment, she considered ignoring it, but she knew she wouldn't be able to sleep without finding out what Ms. First-Date Whisperer had written.

If it was her. After all, other people sent text messages too.

But somehow, she knew who had contacted her. Finally, she gave up, turned the light back on, and swiped to unlock her phone.

She had been right. It was a text from Ms. First-Date Whisperer, whatever her name might be.

Look, the message said. *I don't want you to be embarrassed. It was an honest mistake.*

A glimmer of anger flared up in her. She wasn't even sure why. *Damn straight it was*, she replied. *How was I supposed to know? Since you didn't send me a picture or tell me your name.*

Um, my name is pretty gender-neutral, so it wouldn't have helped even if I had told you, Ms. First-Date Whisperer answered.

Eliza's annoyance vanished as fast as it had appeared. *Maybe we should do it anyway,* she typed back. *Exchange names. I mean, if we keep texting, I'll need a name to put in my contacts.*

It surprised her how strong the urge to know was, but she decided to follow her gut. With a tight grip on her phone, she waited for the answer.

Sneaker Woman wanted to keep texting! Denny flopped onto her bed and pumped her fist. Yes!

Another text arrived. *So? Want to tell me your name?*

Denny stopped in the middle of her little celebration and dropped her fist to the bed. Slowly, she raised her hand back up to answer. *What, and ruin the mystery?*

You're really not going to tell me your name?

Denny hesitated. Not because Sneaker Woman was a stranger and she didn't trust her with personal information but because real-life Denny was awkward and didn't know what to say to women. The nameless person Sneaker Woman had been talking to didn't seem to have that problem. She bantered back and forth as if it were the most normal thing in the world. Denny wanted to remain that person a little while longer. *Not right now. If that's okay.*

All right. But what do I put in my contacts, then? Senior citizen?

Don't you dare!

Sneaker Woman sent a grandma-with-silver-hair-and-glasses emoji. *Yep, that sounds good. It could be SC for short.*

If you call me that, I'll have to come up with a mean nickname for you too, Denny replied.

Like what? Queen of Disastrous Dates? Is that what you have me saved as in your phone?

Denny chuckled. *No. I've been calling you Sneaker Woman.*

Cute, Sneaker Woman replied. *I admit I kind of like it.*

As much as I would like to take the credit for your nickname, it was my niece, Bella, who came up with it.

She knows we're texting?

She was with me when you sent the photos, Denny typed back. *She thought the sneakers with the skirt were cute too, btw.*

Seems good taste runs in the family. Sneaker Woman added a winking smiley face.

Laughter burst from Denny's chest. There it was—that snarky banter she had come to associate with Sneaker Woman. It was good to get it back.

Chapter 4

THE NEXT MORNING, ELIZA LEANED across her display of colorful polymer clay earrings, figurines, and miniature animals lounging on rocks to watch the other crafters, artists, and the people strolling along the booths. People-watching was one of her favorite things to do while selling her crafts at Saturday Market.

Well, that and taking in the cherry blossoms in full bloom and the yummy scents surrounding her. Indian spices mingled with the aroma of artisan caramels, coconut almonds, and cheese pupusas from the nearby Guatemalan food cart. The twang of a busker's guitar, laughter, and the murmur of conversation drowned out the sound of traffic along the Waterfront Park.

The familiar white noise made her even more sleepy than she already was. She took a sip of her chai tea, but all the caffeine in the world couldn't fully wake her up today. She yawned for the fifth time in as many minutes.

Heather bumped her with her shoulder, nearly making Eliza spill her tea. "What's up with you? Are my earbud holder tacos and I boring you?" She lovingly traced her latest scrap leather creation with her fingertip.

"No," Eliza said. "I love how you made them look like real tacos. I just stayed up too late last night."

"Ooh, I forgot! You went on another date last night, didn't you?" Heather turned to face her more fully. "How was it? If you stayed out late, it must have been great." Her eyes widened. "Wait, you didn't go home with him, did you?"

"Shh!" Eliza glanced left and right while hiding behind her travel mug.

Leanne, who sold sea glass jewelry and suncatchers in the stall next to them, was arranging several pendants at the edge of her booth closest to theirs and trying hard not to appear as if she was listening in on their conversation.

"No, of course I didn't," Eliza whispered. "You know I don't sleep with guys on the first date."

Heather waggled her shapely eyebrows. "Did he try?"

Eliza emphatically shook her head. "By the time we said good night, even he realized things weren't going well, so thankfully, he didn't try to kiss me."

"Ugh. Another total flop?"

"Yeah. I'm beginning to think online dating isn't for me."

Heather shook her finger at her. "Oh, no, no, no. You're not getting out of our deal, Eliza Harrison. Two dates is not a pattern. All good things come in threes, right?"

Eliza eyed her over the rim of her travel mug. "If you have that much trust in the magic of online dating, why aren't you going on as many dates as me? You dating more was part of the deal, remember?"

"I am. But I'm never going to get as many people right-swiping me as you do. There are fewer lesbians than straight guys on most online dating platforms. But I'm chatting with women all the time, and if I find one that I seem to click with, I'll go out with her. I just usually take more time getting to know them online first. It helps me filter out the weirdos, the people who don't want to go out with a trans woman, and the chicks who are hung up on their exes."

Eliza rearranged Heather's leather bracelets at the front of the table. "Hmm. Maybe I should do the same. But with my dates, their weirdness only seems to come out once we meet in person."

Heather took a sip of her coffee. "I won't pretend No More Frogs is perfect. Despite the name, I admit you might have to kiss a few more frogs before you find your Prince Charming. But where else are you supposed to meet men if not online?"

"Hey, it's not like I sit at home all week. I leave the house every day, you know?"

"To go to work—for two lesbians. Not a lot of workplace romance going on; you have to admit that."

Eliza chuckled into her tea as she remembered walking in on Austen and Dee exchanging a sweet kiss in the storage room yesterday. "Oh, there's plenty of workplace romance going on."

"I'm not talking about your bosses. I meant for you."

Eliza tilted her head in reluctant acknowledgment. "I don't care. I love my job, and I'm happy with my life the way it is."

"I'm not saying you're sobbing into your pillow every night. But just think about how much happier you'd be if you could share all of this," Heather waved her hand in a gesture that included the entire market and the city beyond, "with someone special."

After less than five hours of sleep, Eliza wasn't in the mood to go down that road, so she took refuge in their familiar teasing. "I'm sharing it with you. Are you saying you aren't special?"

Heather straightened to her full six-foot-one height. "Of course I am. But you declared yourself not interested in my designer girls," she cupped her breasts, "or my feminine charms, so..."

Eliza peeked at Leanne, who gave her an embarrassed grin at being caught eavesdropping and held out her bag of cinnamon cashews.

"No, thanks," Eliza said.

"To the cashews or the breasts?" Heather smirked.

"Both." Eliza gave her a gentle shove, even though she couldn't help laughing. "Now stop badgering me before I'm fully awake."

Heather reached for her own travel mug, then paused. "Wait, if you weren't out late with the guy from No More Frogs, what kept you up?"

Damn. Eliza cursed herself for even mentioning that she'd stayed up too late. While Heather was her best friend and knew pretty much everything about her, she wasn't sure she was ready to share her new acquaintance. Something about their tentative friendship made her want to keep it to herself a little longer. But, of course, refusing to answer would have been silly. "Um, remember your number neighbor?"

"The one you sent your outfit pictures to? Of course!" Heather frowned. "He's not bothering you, is he?"

"No." In a murmur, Eliza added, "If anything, it was the other way around. I kept sending texts after that accidental text snafu."

Heather gave her a friendly little slap to the shoulder. "Now I get it!"

"Get what?"

"Why you don't want to keep going out with the guys from No More Frogs. You want to date him—your Mr. Wrong Number!"

Eliza grinned. "No, thanks, that would be more up your alley."

"Mine?" Heather touched her own chest with a look of confusion. "You know I don't date men."

"Good for you, honey," an elderly lady who was admiring one of Eliza's corgi figurines said.

Eliza sold it to her for half of the usual price, just for that remark. "Yeah, well, she isn't," she said to Heather while she wrapped the little dog in tissue paper.

"Isn't dating men? Who?" Heather's gaze went to the elderly lady, who held out her hand in a not-me gesture, put the corgi in her purse, and continued on to Leanne's booth. "Weren't we just talking about Mr. Wrong Number?"

"It's *Ms.* Wrong Number," Eliza said. "That's what I'm trying to tell you. She's not a man."

Heather burst out laughing and slapped her thigh. "Oh my God, you only found that out now? Didn't her name tip you off?"

"We haven't exchanged names yet." That might have seemed strange, considering that they had kept texting until three o'clock in the morning, but she had a feeling Whisperer—that was the name she had ended up putting in her contacts—had a good reason for not revealing her name, and she respected that, even though she was curious.

"Huh. Then how did you find out?"

"She sent me a nude," Eliza said with her most deadpan face.

For a moment, Heather's expression resembled that of a cartoon character with its eyes bulging out of its head. "For real?" She waved her fingers at Eliza. "Show me!"

"Jeez, I'm kidding, you perv! She didn't send me a picture, much less a nude. Hmm, maybe I should talk her into it," Eliza mused out loud. It would only be fair. After all, Whisperer had received two photos from her, while she still had no clue what the other woman looked like.

"Now who's the pervert?" Heather shot back.

Eliza rolled her eyes up at the white tent stretching over their craft goods. "I'm talking about an all-clothes-on photo, not a nude."

Heather stuck out her bottom lip in a show of disappointment. "Damn."

A young couple stopped in front of their booth. "Oh, these are cute!" The woman carefully touched a tiny cat curled up on top of a rock. "You wouldn't happen to have a fox one, would you?"

"I had one, but I think I sold it. Let me check." Eliza bent over the box in the back of the tent, glad to have escaped Heather's interrogation for now.

On Friday evening of the next week, Denny took another sip of her microbrew and glanced at her watch. It was midnight—that meant it was socially acceptable to finally get out of there, wasn't it?

Julie and two other colleagues from work had dragged her to their favorite bar and dance club, not taking no for an answer when Denny had tried to refuse.

The mix of funk and soul music the DJ played downstairs was nice enough, but the small dance floor was packed, and the low ceiling of the dim, cavelike basement made her feel claustrophobic, so she had escaped to the upper floor of the two-level establishment.

The upstairs bar section of the club was spacious, letting her breathe more freely. With paintings from local artists lining two walls, it looked more like an art gallery—except for the pool tables and the pinball machines toward the back.

She managed to snag a small table in a corner and slouched down in the worn vinyl booth, hoping no one would find her here and try to drag her back downstairs.

At least the burgers were great, and so were the garlic fries. Maybe there was something to be said for being single. She could eat all the garlic fries she wanted. She nursed her beer while she dipped the last fry into the malt vinegar mayo and watched the game being played at the pool table closest to her.

A cute redhead cleared the table like a real pool shark. Finally, she sank the eight ball and pumped her fist. When she looked up, her gaze met Denny's, and she winked at her, probably mistaking her for a man in the low light.

Denny slid lower in the booth and glanced down at her plate, even though it was empty now.

God, she hoped the redhead wouldn't come over.

She snorted and poked her chubby middle. *Like she would be interested in you.* But she didn't want to take a chance, so she tried to appear busy by fumbling her phone from her pocket.

Sneaker Woman was probably asleep, but she could still text her and say hi, right? She'd find the message when she woke up tomorrow. Maybe it would even make her smile.

Denny opened the messages app and tried to think of something to say but drew a blank. Suddenly, she felt as tongue-tied as if she had to talk to her in person. *Cut it out,* she told herself. *You're not awkward Denny Jacobs to her. You're her fun text buddy. Just say something. Anything.*

She sent the first thing that came to mind: *Hey, how are you?*

Denny grimaced. "Really original," she mumbled to herself.

But she wasn't trying to impress Sneaker Woman, was she? No need to act all suave since Sneaker Woman was straight anyway.

Just as she was about to slip the phone back into her pocket, it lit up with a reply. *Hey, Whisperer, why are you awake? Isn't it past your bedtime?*

Great. She already had a reputation for going to bed at roughly the same time as a first-grader. *Why are YOU awake?* she texted back. *Didn't you say you have to get up early most Saturdays?*

Because you texted me and my phone dinged.

Oh shit. Really?

No, just kidding, Sneaker Woman replied, making Denny blow out a long breath. *I'm up making a fox figurine a customer requested last week.*

Wow, you're an artist? Denny studied the artwork covering every nook and cranny in the bar. Was any of her work on display here? But she couldn't even be sure Sneaker Woman lived in Portland. Her area code covered several counties in northwestern Oregon, all the way up to Astoria and down to Salem.

Not sure I'd call it that, Sneaker Woman answered. *It's just a hobby, but I enjoy it. I make figurines, jewelry, and other little trinkets out of polymer clay and then paint on the details with acrylics.*

That sounds cool, Denny typed. She wanted to ask for a photo of the little fox or other things Sneaker Woman had made, but she couldn't request a picture without showing her something in return, could she?

Before she could decide, another text appeared. *Wow, we really are party animals, aren't we? It's a Friday night, and the extent of our social lives is sitting at home, texting each other.*

Speak for yourself, Denny texted back. *I'll have you know I'm out and about, socializing.* After looking at the empty booth across from her, she added, *Well, kind of.*

Kind of? How exactly does this kind-of-socializing work?

My friend Julie dragged me to this bar/dance club.

And you're sitting in a corner, texting me? Sneaker Woman sent a salsa-dancing emoji in a red dress and high heels. *Go shake your booty and have some fun!*

Fun? Denny shivered. *Being trapped in a crush of sweaty bodies, with strangers grinding into me, is not my idea of fun.* She surprised herself by admitting it to Sneaker Woman, but then again, she was a forty-one-year-old woman, not a teenager needing to appear cool...right? *I'll leave that to all the twenty-somethings here.*

Got it, Senior Citizen.

Denny ignored that nickname. She liked the other nickname Sneaker Woman had given her—Whisperer—much better. *What about you? Do you go out clubbing?* She wasn't one to ask a lot of questions, but she found herself curious to learn more about Sneaker Woman.

Maybe once in a blue moon. Not really my thing either. Although... with the right partner, grinding can be fun.

Heat shot up Denny's body and into her cheeks. God, this woman made her flush without ever having been in the same room! Good thing they were texting, so Sneaker Woman couldn't hear how squeaky her voice would have sounded if she had tried to speak. *So you're not out there, cutting a rug either, but you call me Senior Citizen?*

Well, how else am I supposed to address you since you won't tell me your name? Sneaker Woman asked. *Or have you changed your mind about that?*

Denny sent back a nervously grimacing emoji.

Sneaker Woman answered with a turkey leg, which Denny spontaneously countered with a flamingo.

That led to several minutes of trying to outdo each other in finding the most ridiculous emojis. The competition ended when Sneaker Woman sent a weirdly pixelated purple blob.

What is that? Denny asked.

Isn't it obvious? It's an alien monster.

Denny eyed the blob again. *What?*

I looked it up on Emojipedia.

You just made that up. There's no such thing as Emojipedia.

No. I pinkie-swear. Sneaker Woman added the call-me emoji—a hand with its pinkie extended. *It exists.*

Pinkie-swear? Denny grinned. How cute was that? And her creative use of emojis was pretty cute too. Denny appreciated a woman who hadn't lost her playfulness and was a little silly every now and then.

Just as she was about to send a teasing reply, someone cleared their throat not even a yard away.

Denny jumped and hit her knee on the table.

When she glanced up, Julie stood in front of her, flushed from dancing. She pressed a G&T to her cheek and gave Denny a reproachful look. "Hey!" She raised her voice over the clacking of the pool balls, the music from the loudspeakers, and the din of conversation. "I've been looking for you all over! Have you been up here all this time?"

"Um, I was hungry." Denny flipped her phone over, even though she told herself she had nothing to hide.

Unfortunately, that move drew Julie's attention to the phone. "Who do you keep texting every chance you get? You've been doing it at work too."

Denny bit back the "no one" on the tip of her tongue. Sneaker Woman wouldn't hear it, but it still felt wrong to act as if she were someone of no consequence. "I've been texting with this woman who—"

"Ooh, a woman!" Julie slapped her shoulder.

Denny stared at her. The teasing twinkle in Julie's eyes was unmistakable, even in the low light. "You know I'm gay?" While she wasn't in the closet by any means, she had never talked about her sexual orientation with Julie. She'd been single for most of the time she'd worked at the Grocery Port, so she'd had no reason to mention it. She also wasn't sure how comfortable Julie was with having a lesbian friend.

Her upbringing had probably been very different from Denny's. She had met Julie's parents several times when they dropped off bánh su kem and other Vietnamese pastries for the entire staff. They seemed like nice people, yet she got the feeling they were pretty conservative, so she wasn't sure how LGBT-friendly the Ngos were.

Julie waved a hand at her, indicating Denny's short Ruby-Rose-on-a-bad-day haircut, her button-down shirt, and her baggy men's jeans. "I might be stereotyping, but...hello?"

Denny gazed down at herself, then back up into Julie's face, which sported an amused grin. "Oh."

"Don't worry." Chuckling, Julie patted her arm. "I'm not freaking out. So if that's why you aren't downstairs with the rest of us, getting your groove on..."

"No, that's not it. I'm just not a good dancer." If there was one thing more awkward than her trying to flirt with a woman, it was her attempts at dancing.

"You think I am? Have you seen me? No one cares as long as you're having fun." Julie tried to pull her up from the table, but Denny withdrew her hand and shook her head.

The mere thought of dancing in front of all these people made her break out in a sweat. Julie and her friends were all confident, beautiful, and feminine. She would stick out like a sore thumb. "No, thanks. Dancing is not my thing. I think I'll head home now."

"Come on! It's barely even..." Julie pushed back her sleeve, but she wasn't wearing a watch. "...whatever o'clock."

"It's after midnight," Denny said. Gosh, she really felt like a senior citizen.

Julie sighed. "All right. See you Monday, then." She waved in the direction of the cell phone. "Tell your girlfriend hi."

"She's not my—"

But Julie had already turned and was striding away.

"—girlfriend," Denny called after her.

Julie disappeared in the crowd in front of the bar.

Denny groaned, flipped her phone back around, and scrolled up to read the texts she had missed.

The first was a screenshot of a website, proving Emojipedia really existed.

Then, when Denny had dropped out of the conversation, Sneaker Woman had typed: *Hello? You still there? Should I assume*

I exhausted you with my superior emojiing skills, or have you gone dancing after all?

Sorry, Denny typed hastily, hoping Sneaker Woman hadn't given up on waiting for an answer. *No dancing. My friend just came looking for me.* She didn't know how to explain the conversation with Julie, so she didn't even try.

No answer came.

Damn. Sneaker Woman had probably finished her little fox and gone to bed.

Sighing, Denny made her way to the door and then down the street to where she had parked her dyke mobile, as Salem called her eleven-year-old Subaru Outback. As she climbed behind the wheel, her phone dinged. She nearly dropped it in her haste to read Sneaker Woman's message.

No problem. I was just getting ready for bed.

An image of Sneaker Woman in a sexy satin nightie with spaghetti straps flashed through Denny's mind, then she firmly shoved it away. The woman was straight and out of her league, and thoughts like that would only make her self-conscious any time they talked. *Sleep tight,* she typed back. *I'm heading home too.*

Talk to you tomorrow. Drive carefully.

Denny smiled as she put the phone onto the passenger seat and started the engine. Apparently, Sneaker Woman was now taking it for granted they would be talking every day—and that was more than fine with her.

Chapter 5

ON THURSDAY OF THE FOLLOWING week, Eliza slid another cactus wood snowflake onto the red-and-green-striped sisal rope.

Making ornaments for their bird-safe Christmas tree in late April felt weird, but since they handmade each of their products, they had to get an early start to have enough for the holiday season.

She tied off the rope and tugged to see if it would hold up to some rough treatment from strong beaks. Yes, that should work. She gave a triumphant smile.

Her job in the tiny company wasn't making her rich, but it filled her with satisfaction, and that was more important to her than all the money in the world. She got to use her creativity and work with her hands while giving customers a toy for their pets they didn't have to worry about.

She set the string of snowflakes aside and glanced at her watch.

The apple tree branches she had hand-stripped and scrubbed with an antibacterial solution should be dry by now, so she could sand the edges. But that would have to wait until after her lunch break.

Instead of grabbing something from one of the Third Avenue food carts, which were just a five-minute walk from the office, she had brought a sandwich every day this week so she could spend a few minutes chatting with Whisperer.

Either they coincidentally took their lunch break around the same time, or Whisperer had adjusted to her mealtimes.

She cleared a corner of her worktable and sat with her sandwich in one hand and her cell phone in the other.

Oops. Apparently, she was late for their unofficial lunch meeting. Whisperer had already sent her a *Hi, how are you?* ten minutes ago. The shy greeting always made her smile.

Sorry for not answering sooner, Eliza replied. *I was testing out a new toy.*

The bubble with the three dots appeared but vanished a second later, as if Whisperer had deleted what she had written. Finally, a simple *Oh* popped up on the screen.

Eliza burst out laughing. *Not that kind of toy, pervert.* Playfully calling her a pervert reminded her of her interactions with Heather, but at the same time, talking to Whisperer felt entirely different.

Well, of course it felt different. After all, Heather had been her best friend for five years, while she and Whisperer had only been texting for three weeks.

I didn't... I wasn't thinking that, Whisperer replied.

Suuuure. Eliza still had no idea what Whisperer looked like, but she would bet her paycheck she was sporting a blush.

So, what's for lunch? Whisperer asked.

Eliza chuckled at the transparent attempt to change the subject. She took mercy on her, snapped a photo of her turkey-avocado-radish sandwich, and sent it. *You?*

Mine isn't nearly as healthy as yours. A picture of a cupcake decorated with gummy bears appeared on Eliza's screen.

Gummy bears? On a cupcake?

Yep. Lunch of champions, Whisperer replied. After a few moments, she added, *My niece remembered it was her turn to bring cupcakes to school right before bedtime last night, and this was all we had in the house to decorate them with.*

It's kind of cute, Eliza said.

Like pairing a dressy skirt with sneakers?

Exactly.

There was a short pause, and Eliza sensed what was coming.

So, Whisperer finally typed, *you test toys for a living?*

Grinning, Eliza simply answered: *Yes.* It was fun to make Whisperer work for it.

Like dolls and fire trucks?

More like sola crepe balls and nut cages, Eliza typed back.

I have no idea what you just said.

Eliza took a big bite of her sandwich before she answered, *I work for a small company that makes toys for parrots and other pet birds.*

Wow, how cool! Do you like it?

Love it! Eliza added several hearts for emphasis. *We handmake most of our toys, so I get to play with craft stuff all day.*

Sounds wonderful, Whisperer replied instantly. *How long have you been doing that?*

I've been doing it full-time for only a month. The company is still pretty new.

What were you doing before? Whisperer asked. *If you don't mind me asking.*

So far, it had mostly been Eliza asking the questions and keeping the conversation going whenever they talked, and Eliza had a feeling it wasn't lack of interest but more a lack of confidence that held Whisperer back. It was good to see her asking some questions of her own.

I don't mind at all, Eliza replied. *I worked all kinds of jobs while selling some of my stuff at craft fairs and teaching craft workshops on the side. That's how my bosses and I met—they fell in love with a flying-owl mobile I made and asked if I could make something similar with bird-safe materials. They hired me to work for them part-time in January and then full-time three months later. Boy, was I happy to give up my job as a barista!*

You were a barista? Can you do those milk foam ferns, hearts, and stuff?

Yeah, but not very well. I wasn't the greatest barista. Heck, I don't even like coffee!

Whisperer sent several bulging-eyes emojis. *You. Don't. Like. Coffee?*

Let me guess. This is where you tell me we can't be friends. As soon as Eliza had typed it, she paused. Friends. Was that what they were becoming? They didn't even know each other's names. Finally, she shrugged and sent the text anyway because it felt right.

Close call, Whisperer answered. *But I'll let it slide because I can empathize. Not with not liking coffee. But I used to be the world's worst waitress.*

An image of a woman in a cute waitress apron flashed through Eliza's mind, and not for the first time, she wondered what Whisperer looked like. *What made you so bad at it? Don't tell me you don't like food!*

Ha! No. I like it a little too much. Being in the kitchen might have suited me better. But being outgoing and talkative to charm guests wasn't my thing. I didn't make enough tips to keep a mouse alive, much less two women and a child.

Was she referring to herself, her sister, and her niece? Why was it on Whisperer to earn enough to keep them all alive? Eliza hesitated to ask. That veered into personal territory, and she didn't want to make her uncomfortable. Finally, she decided on a less personal question: *So what are you doing for a living now?*

Nothing as cool as what you do. Whisperer seemed to hesitate for a moment, then a second sentence followed. *I'm a cashier at a supermarket.* She didn't give Eliza time to comment on her job before she asked, *So that bird toy company…where's it located?*

A smile tugged on Eliza's lips. *Are you trying to find out where I live?*

Maybe?

I thought you wanted us to stay anonymous?

Well, yes, but unless you live in a tiny town, you'll still be anonymous.

Eliza hadn't been the one insisting on anonymity, so she had no problem replying, *Okay. I'll answer your question if you answer one of mine.*

I'm in Portland, Whisperer typed back. *I live in Lents.*

So they were living in the same city. Eliza liked that. *Me too. In Portland, I mean. Not in Lents. But that wasn't what I was going to ask.*

Oh.

Eliza ate the rest of her sandwich and stared at the screen. She knew what she wanted to ask—the same question she had contemplated earlier: Was Whisperer living with her sister and niece? And if she was, why? But now she was familiar with the natural rhythm of Whisperer's texts and what the little pauses meant, so she could tell she was wary.

Here's my question, Eliza typed. *What's your favorite gummy bear flavor?*

Whisperer took a while to answer. Either she had to taste all the gummy bears on her cupcake to decide, or the question had startled her. She had probably expected a different question. Finally, the text bubble popped up. *Green.*

Did you know they're strawberry flavored? Eliza asked.

I thought that was the red ones?

Nope. Those are raspberry.

OMG, Whisperer typed back. *My entire life has been a lie!*

Eliza burst out laughing.

A knock on the door prevented her from answering.

Eliza shot off a quick message to Whisperer, telling her she had to get back to work, then called, "Yes?"

The door to her office swung open, and Dee stuck her head in. "Hey, I'm making a donut run. Are you in the mood for anything in particular?"

Eliza bit back a grin. When she had first started working at Feathered Friends, she had tried to deal with Austen—the warmer, friendlier of her bosses—as much as she could because Dee came across like a prickly ice queen. However, it hadn't taken long for her to discover Dee was tough but fair...and a total marshmallow when it came to her partner, including spoiling her with her favorite donuts at least once a week.

"If they have any with gummy bears, one of those would be great."

Dee raised one eyebrow.

Why could everyone but her do that?

"Gummy bears?" Dee repeated. "On a donut?"

"Yes," Eliza said with a straight face. "Lunch of champions."

"Right." Dee walked off, shaking her head and mumbling something under her breath.

Eliza went back to work with a smile.

That evening after her shift, Denny lay stretched out on the couch with her printout, memorizing the PLU codes for the seasonal fruits and veggies. She paused at strawberries. Instead of the four-digit number, the first thing that came to mind was green gummy bears.

"4248," Denny firmly told herself. "Focus."

Salem looked up from her phone, which she was using to read a romance novel. "Yellow bell pepper."

"No. That's 4689."

"Ah. I knew it was something with a four, though."

Denny laughed. "Most of the conventionally grown produce starts with a four. Don't quit your day job."

"Not planning to." Salem's smile let Denny know she was thinking of one particular perk of her job: getting to see Matt every day.

It was nice to see her sister so happy and smitten but also a little weird—maybe because it had been so long since Denny had been infatuated with anyone that she hardly remembered how it felt.

When Salem continued reading, Denny went back to memorizing the PLU numbers. But now that she thought about gummy bears and her earlier conversation with Sneaker Woman, her code sheet no longer held her attention.

With a sigh, she gave in, reached for her phone, and typed into the messages app, *Hi, how was work?*

It didn't take long for an answer to arrive. *Good. My boss got me a marshmallow donut.*

Denny wrinkled her nose. *And you consider that good?*

Hey, no judgment from someone who had a gummy bear cupcake for lunch! Besides, I only got the marshmallow donut because she couldn't find a gummy bear one.

Okay, okay. Denny smiled at the thought of Sneaker Woman sending her boss out for a gummy bear donut. Then she sobered. *Earlier, when we were talking at lunch...*

Yeah?

Denny pushed her glasses higher on her nose. *That wasn't what you really wanted to ask, was it?*

No. Usually, Sneaker Woman was the talkative one, but now she left it at this one word.

Denny knew she could do the same. Sneaker Woman wasn't the type to pressure her into talking about herself if she didn't want to. She seemed to have a sixth sense for when to back off. But Denny found she wasn't reluctant to answer anymore. Maybe it was the fact they still didn't even know each other's names that made it easier, or maybe because she'd had the upper hand at the beginning of their acquaintance, with Sneaker Woman accidentally texting her. Or maybe Sneaker Woman was just easy to talk to.

Whatever it was, Denny took a steadying breath and typed, *You can ask.*

Okay. But if you don't want to answer once you hear my question, you don't have to, Sneaker Woman replied. *I was wondering... Earlier, you sounded like... Do you live with your sister and your niece?*

That was her question? Denny exhaled. She wasn't sure what she had expected. Likely, she had made it into a big deal in her mind when it wasn't. *Yes. Or maybe it would be more accurate to say they live with me since I lived here first. But now we both pay half of the rent for the townhouse in Lents. My sister got pregnant when she was seventeen, and when she told our parents, they kicked her out.*

This time, it took a while for Sneaker Woman to answer, as if she had to process that first. *I'm sorry. That must have been tough. How old were you?*

About as old as you are now. I'm a lot older than my sister.

Oh yeah. I keep forgetting you're a senior citizen.

The gentle ribbing loosened some of the tension in Denny's shoulders. *Seriously, I'm almost thirteen years older.*

Wow, Sneaker Woman texted back. *That IS a large age gap!*

Yeah. My parents were eighteen when they had me. Denny again surprised herself with how much personal information she revealed.

And yet they kicked your sister out when they found out she was pregnant at seventeen?

Pretty hypocritical, right? Denny sighed. *At least our age gap turned out to be a good thing because by the time she was seventeen, I had my own place and could take her in and help with the baby.*

True. It's great you were in a position to do that. I bet you're an awesome aunt.

Denny shrugged even though Sneaker Woman couldn't see it. *My niece doesn't complain too much.*

How old is she now?

Nearly eleven going on twenty-five, Denny replied.

Sneaker Woman sent a row of laughing-so-hard-it-makes-you-cry emojis. That seemed to be a favorite of hers. *I know what you mean. My nephew and two of my nieces are that age too.*

Denny pursed her lips to form a soundless whistle. Three preteens in the same house? She couldn't imagine. *Oh wow. Do you see them regularly?*

Yes, I do. The whole clan still lives in and around Portland. I see them all the time, but I had to put my foot down, or I'd see them a little too often.

Too often? Was there such a thing as seeing family too often?

I know that sounds strange, Sneaker Woman replied. *I love them all to death, but I'm the baby of the family, so when I first moved out, it was a struggle to keep them from stopping by every day to check on me. They needed to learn that I'm a grown-up and want to have my own life.*

Denny couldn't imagine that happening in her own family. Her parents had been too self-absorbed to check up on their daughters all the time, even back when they had still been in touch. Mostly, that was how Denny had preferred it, but every once in a while, she would have appreciated a little more interest. *So you were the youngest. Bet you were spoiled.*

Terribly. Sneaker Woman added a princess emoji. *But actually, my parents were pretty good at giving me limits and rules too, so I think I avoided turning into a brat. How about you? Are you the typical super responsible, bossy firstborn? Assuming you are the firstborn.*

I am. I'm pretty responsible, but my sister is the bossy one. Denny grinned as she peered at her unsuspecting sister.

Probably comes with being a mom, Sneaker Woman answered.

I'm not so sure about that. My mother wasn't bossy. She worked in a call center, and when she was home, she didn't talk much at all. Denny's finger hovered over the little arrow that would send the text she'd just written. She rarely volunteered information about her family and didn't like talking about her parents, but Sneaker Woman kept the tone of the conversation so lighthearted that her usual tension didn't rise. With a shrug, she tapped the send arrow.

Oh. I'm so sorry.

Denny eyed Sneaker Woman's last message. Why was she sorry? *Is not having a bossy mother considered a bad thing?*

No, but you said your mother WASN'T bossy, so I thought...

Oh, no, she's alive and kicking. At least last I heard. Denny clutched the phone more tightly as the old bitterness crept up in her. *I haven't seen her or my father since the day they kicked my sister out.*

It took several moments before Sneaker Woman responded. *They cut off contact with both of you? Just like that?*

Yep. My sister sent them a photo when my niece was born, but they never responded.

Wow, Sneaker Woman answered after a while. *I don't know what to say except for: I'm so sorry.*

Denny cleared her throat to get rid of the lump that had lodged there.

Salem stopped reading and looked at her over the top of her cell phone. "You okay?"

"Yeah. I'm fine." Denny fought the urge to clear her throat again.

But Salem didn't return her attention to her e-book this time. She continued to study her.

"Do you ever miss Mom and Dad?" Denny asked quietly.

Salem dropped her phone onto her lap. "Honestly? No. I'm not sure I ever had much to miss."

Denny nodded. She knew exactly what her sister meant. All her mother had wanted was to be left alone, and her father had been unable to leave his job as a corrections officer at the gate.

"Was it ever different?" Salem asked. "When you were little?"

Denny thought about it for a moment. "Yeah. I mean, they probably wouldn't have won a Parent of the Year Award even back then, but I remember a time when Mom actually tried to listen and when Dad didn't assume everyone was lying to him all the time."

"When did it all change?"

"I don't know. I guess it was a slow process. At first, I thought it was me."

"You?" Salem gave her an incredulous look.

Denny shuffled the code sheet still lying on her lap. "They didn't know what to do with me."

Salem still stared blankly.

"You know." Denny gestured at her short hair, the hoodie, and the pair of men's sweatpants she wore.

"Oh, Denny. It wasn't you." Salem's voice cracked. "I couldn't have been more of a girlie girl, and I was still just an afterthought to them."

Denny sighed. "We sure didn't win the parental lottery, did we?"

"Nope. But we did pretty well in the sister lottery department."

"Sure did."

They smiled at each other across the coffee table.

The buzzing of Denny's phone interrupted the comfortable silence.

"Are you still talking to Sandal Girl?" Salem asked.

"Sneaker Woman. And yes, I am."

"Good thing you have a phone plan with unlimited texts." Salem studied her. "Are you...? You're not telling her about Mom and Dad, are you?"

Denny bit her lip. She hadn't considered how her sister would feel about that. "Um, a little. Does that bother you?"

"Heck, no! I spilled my guts to poor Matt on our first date. I just didn't think you were the type to do that."

"I'm not." Denny glanced at her phone, then back at Salem. "At least not usually."

Salem tilted her head. "Hmm."

"What's that supposed to mean?"

"Nothing." With a grin, Salem went back to her reading.

Denny lowered her gaze to her phone.

You okay? Sneaker Woman had asked a couple of minutes ago, followed by a line of question marks.

I'm fine, Denny answered, and this time, she meant it.

Chapter 6

EARLY THE NEXT EVENING, ELIZA shook her head at her fellow Portlanders. A guy in shorts and a short-sleeved button-up stepped onto the bar's rooftop terrace, where she was waiting for Heather. Typical. The minute the sun came out from behind the clouds—which didn't happen often in April—Portlanders wore shorts and pretended it was summer, even if the temperature was in the low fifties.

Well, she wasn't much better, sitting on the windy rooftop perched high above the city just because it was the first time the sun had come out all week. Admittedly, if it weren't for the heat lamps and the firepits in the middle of the tables, she would be freezing her ass off.

Her phone chirped.

With a smile, she dug it out of her bag, eager to hear how Whisperer was doing.

But it wasn't her. The text was from Heather.

So sorry! I'm going to be late. My bus had an impromptu inspection, so I had to pick it up from the garage, and then I started talking to one of the mechanics and forgot the time...

Eliza pictured her elegant best friend deep in conversation with a burly, oil-smeared mechanic. The mental image made her laugh. But then again, Heather checked the tire pressure, the fluid levels, the air compressor, and all the other parts of her bus every day, so she could hold her own when talking shop with a mechanic.

Don't worry about it, Eliza texted back. *I'm enjoying the view while sipping my cocktail.* She took in the stunning view of downtown Portland, the Hawthorne Bridge, and the Cascades in the distance.

Next one's on me, Heather replied. *See you in ten minutes. Fifteen tops.*

Before Eliza could put her phone away, it chirped again.

This time, the text was from Whisperer. *Hi, how are you?*

The signature greeting made her smile. *I'm being passionate from miles away.*

There was a short pause, then all Whisperer typed was, *Uh, okay.*

Eliza laughed out loud, not caring that the people at the tables to her left and right were glancing over. *Don't worry. That's not code for sexting you.* Of course it wasn't. After all, Whisperer was a woman.

I didn't think so, Whisperer replied. *I assumed either your autocorrect was acting up, or it's a millennial thing.*

Neither. It's a cocktail thing. She nudged the exotic flower floating on her golden-hued cocktail aside and took a sip. The sweet yet tangy aroma of passion fruit, lemon, and brandy washed over her tongue.

Sorry, I still don't get it, Whisperer texted.

Eliza took a photo of her drink and sent it, along with, *It's the name of my cocktail. Passionate from Miles Away.*

Oh. Wait. If you're having a cocktail... Am I interrupting a date or something?

No, Eliza replied quickly. *Heather and I are meeting up for an after-work cocktail, but she's running late.*

So, no date this weekend? Whisperer asked.

An amused smile tugged on Eliza's lips. *Are you waiting for the next episode of Eliza's Horrible Dating Adventures?* A second before hitting send, she realized she was about to reveal her name, so she quickly backspaced and instead wrote, *Sneaker Woman's Horrible Dating Adventures?*

No, Whisperer replied. *I admit you always make me laugh when you recount your dates, but I'm keeping my fingers crossed for an episode of Sneaker Woman's Wonderful Dating Adventures.*

What a sweetheart. Most of the time, Eliza laughed about it when a date went wrong, but deep down, a part of her felt inadequate, as if there was something wrong with her and that was why she couldn't find a decent guy. She was grateful Whisperer didn't make fun of her, even in a good-natured way. *Doesn't look like there'll be an episode of that in the near future.*

No promising candidates at all?

Well, there was one that seemed nice. We exchanged a few messages via the app.

But?

But then he sent me a dick pic. Eliza fished the flower from her drink and took a big gulp. The pisco burned on its way down, making her cough. *So I said to hell with dating and decided on a girls' night out instead.*

What a dick! No pun intended. Guys really do that?

Eliza plucked a petal from the flower. *Not all of them, but it's not the first time that's happened. Don't tell me no one's ever done that to you?*

Um, no, can't say I ever had that particular problem with a date.

Wow, Eliza typed. *Either you're much better at picking the right guys to go out with, or you've found a dating site far superior to No More Frogs. Tell me where to find those guys!*

It took unusually long before Whisperer's next text popped up. *Sorry, can't help you with that. I don't date guys.*

Didn't date guys? Eliza repeated it slowly to herself. What did she—? Then her brain finally seemed to kick in. *Oh. You mean... you're gay?*

Yes, Whisperer replied. *Is that a problem for you?*

Eliza nearly dropped her phone in her haste to assure her. She didn't want Whisperer to worry about her candid disclosure, even for a second. *No! Not at all. My best friend is gay.* The moment she had sent the message, she groaned and slapped her forehead.

That was what all the homophobic people said to prove they weren't homophobic. For some reason, Whisperer's revelation had thrown her, and she didn't understand why. *Um, can we please pretend I didn't just say that?*

Say what? Whisperer added an innocently whistling emoji.

Eliza wiped imaginary droplets of sweat off her brow. *So, dick pics aside, do you think dating women is different from dating men?*

Oh yeah. Women are always on time, they never monopolize the conversation, and they never show up with hickeys on their necks or mention one of their exes, even in passing.

Really? Eliza asked.

No.

Eliza laughed, mostly at herself. *You had me there for a second. But I guess it depends on the person, not the gender.*

I guess so. Not that I'd know from personal experience since I've never dated a guy.

Before Eliza could continue the conversation, the doors to the bar's terrace swished open. Heather dashed out, still in her work jeans, sneakers, and the company-issued blue button-down. "Sorry, sorry," she called over the space between them.

Eliza shot off a final text to Whisperer, telling her she had to go, before greeting Heather with a welcoming smile. "No problem. Whisperer kept me company."

Heather slid onto a chair across from her and studied her with a curious gaze. "What do the two of you talk about all the time?"

"Dating women," Eliza said with a chuckle.

Heather pulled Eliza's cocktail glass to her side of the table, leaned over, and sniffed it as if she suspected Eliza was drinking something very potent.

Laughing, Eliza snatched the glass away from her.

"You aren't extending your search parameters on No More Frogs to the fairer sex, are you?"

"No. Whisperer was just enlightening me to the fact that women can be as bad a date as men."

"I could have told you that. In fact, I did tell you that." Heather signaled one of the waiters and ordered a Lonely Hearts Club and some chickpea fries. Once they both had their drinks, Heather pulled the heart-shaped strawberry from the cocktail stick and gazed at Eliza from under half-lowered lashes while she popped the piece of fruit into her mouth and chewed. "So," she wiped her fingers on the cocktail napkin, "is she married, happily partnered, living with three bossy cats, what?"

Eliza shrugged. "I don't know about the cats, but she's living with her bossy sister. And she's single."

"If she's dating women, maybe you should set us up," Heather said.

A droplet of water hit Eliza's nose. Then another. Before she could say another word, the sky opened up, and it started to rain—not the lazy drizzle Portland got most of the time, but big, pelting drops.

They grabbed their drinks and fled inside to the lounge.

"Shit." Heather shook her wet locks. "Guess that's a sign. Someone up there doesn't want me to date your mysterious friend." She peered through the floor-to-ceiling window. "Doesn't look like it's letting up. Did you bring an umbrella?"

Eliza gave her a why-are-you-even-asking-me-that look. "That's a rhetorical question, isn't it?"

"So that's a no."

"I'm a good Portlander," Eliza answered. "Of course it's a no. An umbrella wouldn't do me much good on my bike anyway."

"You don't need to take your bike home. I've got my car, so you can ride with me."

Eliza shook her head. "It'll let up by the time we leave."

When they stepped out of the lobby of the hotel the bar belonged to, the rain had slowed, but not stopped. Eliza insisted on taking her bicycle home anyway. Their apartment building was only five minutes from here, and even if she got wet, she could take a hot shower as soon as she got home.

She whizzed up Jefferson Street as fast as the poor visibility and wet streets allowed. Her jeans stuck to her thighs, making it hard to pedal. She slowed for a pedestrian who ran across the street and stepped into the bike lane without seeing her. Drops of rain clung to her face and eyelashes, blurring her vision.

She made it across Broadway without the light turning red. *Yes! Almost home.*

As she pedaled past the Oregon Historical Society, a driver in an SUV parked along the street opened the driver's side door into the bike lane.

"Shit!" Her brakes squealed as she clutched both at the same time. Her tires skidded across the wet asphalt, and then the front tire hit the door, and she was tossed from the bike.

Chapter 7

Sweat trickled down Denny's back as she heaved a box of beans onto the shelf, then placed a box of canned tomatoes next to it. By the time she had unloaded the entire six-foot pallet of canned goods, her shirt stuck to her torso. Restocking was backbreaking work, and she would have to ice her aching wrists and forearms tonight. Still, she preferred this task to running the register—especially today.

At least while clearing the pallets, she had no time to glance at her watch and wonder if Sneaker Woman had texted.

She pulled the empty pallet back into the stockroom, then went to the break room to guzzle down some water.

While there, she couldn't resist opening her locker and sneaking a peek at her phone.

Nothing. She still hadn't gotten a response—not last night, not this morning, and not during lunch.

What was up with Sneaker Woman? She hadn't received a word from her since their exchange about dating women last night.

Denny had gone over their conversation about a hundred times. Had she said something wrong? All she could think of was that she had told her she was gay. But Sneaker Woman had seemed fine with it.

Sure, Denny had met plenty of people who seemed fine with it at first...until it turned out they weren't. Denny didn't want to believe Sneaker Woman might be one of them. Her refreshing nonjudgmental attitude was one of the things Denny liked about her.

But if Sneaker Woman was so nonjudgmental, why had her phone stayed silent all day? Usually, she was in touch with at least half a dozen texts, funny memes, or unexpected observations by now. She hadn't mentioned any special plans for today, and it was a Saturday, so she should be home, even if she had gone out to sell some of her earrings, figurines, and other handcrafted items at the market.

With a grunt, Denny tossed her phone back into the locker.

"Hey, Denny." Julie stuck her head into the room. "The electric pallet jack isn't working. Can you come take a look?"

"Me?" Denny sent her an incredulous stare. "Do I look like a pallet jack mechanic or something? Just because I'm butch doesn't mean I love power tools and can fix everything that's broken!"

Julie held out both hands. "Whoa! A simple no would have been enough. What's up with you today? You've been as cheery as a porcupine with hemorrhoids all day."

The colorful comparison broke through Denny's mood and elicited a tired smile. "Sorry, I..." She ran a hand through her hair, not sure how to explain. "I'll come take a look. Maybe I can fix it." With one regretful gaze back, she closed her locker.

A low buzz drifted through the metal.

Sneaker Woman! Denny threw the locker door open so fast it bounced back and nearly hit her fingers. She snatched the phone and unlocked.

"Wow," Julie said from the door, "whoever that is really has you wrapped around their little finger!"

Denny ignored her and opened the messages app.

Damn. Her shoulders slumped. It wasn't Sneaker Woman. The message was from an unknown number.

She opened it anyway, just not as eagerly.

Hey, Whisperer. It's me—Sneaker Woman.

Denny wouldn't have needed that clarification since no one else called her Whisperer. Her heartbeat picked up, but she kept her response casual, as if she hadn't been waiting for a text all day. *Hi. New phone?*

No, not yet. I stole my mom's.

Why would she need to do that? Denny frowned. *I didn't know you had plans to see your family this weekend.*

I didn't. The entire clan descended on me to make sure I'm fine. After a short pause, a second text popped up. *I had a little accident on my way home last night.*

What? Denny's heartbeat thudded in her ears.

Julie cleared her throat and tapped her wristwatch. "The pallet jack is waiting."

"Give me a minute," Denny said, more sharply than intended. "This is important. I think something happened to Snea... my friend." Her fingers flew over the tiny letters as she tapped out, *What happened?* At least half a dozen graphic scenarios shot through her mind, leaving her queasy.

I was riding my bike home from the bar, and some guy opened the door of his SUV right in front of me. With the wet street, I couldn't stop or swerve out of the way in time, so I had an intimate encounter with the door.

Denny slumped against the locker as her knees weakened. Her fingers shook as she typed a reply. *OMG! Are you okay?*

Yeah, I'm fine. Just a few scrapes and bruises. Luckily, my bike's front tire took the brunt of the impact. My phone is toast too. It fell from my pocket when I got tossed from my bike, and now the screen is cracked. Thankfully, I know your number by heart now.

Why was Sneaker Woman talking about her phone? Denny was worried about her, not the damn phone! *What did the doctor say?*

I haven't seen one, Sneaker Woman replied. *Nothing they can do about scrapes and bruises.*

That reply did nothing to ease Denny's concern. *You should go to the ER. Get checked out. You could have a concussion or something.*

I didn't even hit my head. I wasn't going full speed when I hit the door, I just hadn't come to a complete stop because the asphalt was wet.

Still, Denny answered.

I'm fine. My dad and one of my sisters are nurses, my brother's a physician assistant, and my other sister is a paramedic. They all insisted on checking me out, and the diagnosis is unanimous. I'll live to see another day—unless my mom catches me up and about when she thinks I should be on the couch with an ice pack.

Denny's white-knuckled grip on the phone loosened. Sneaker Woman was fine, and she had contacted her, which meant she was fine with Denny's sexual orientation. *Don't worry. I won't rat you out.*

Uh, good to know because I don't think I'd be up for anything like that, especially right now.

Was it just her, or was that reply a little off? She wished she could check on Sneaker Woman, but she didn't even know her name, much less where she lived. *Are you sure you're okay?*

Yeah. But I discovered that it hurts to laugh. Read what you've just written.

Denny scrolled up.

Don't worry. I won't eat you out, her text said.

Heat flamed up her neck and flooded her cheeks. She had been so distracted by her concern for Sneaker Woman that she hadn't paid attention to what she was typing. *That's not what I wrote! Damn autocorrect! RAT! I won't rat you out. God, kill me now!*

Um, didn't we just talk about that? Sneaker Woman sent a row of crying-laughing emojis.

About what? Killing her? Denny re-read her last message. Dammit! Autocorrect had corrected what she had typed to, *God, kiss me now!*

KILL me now! Autocorrect changed it to *kiss* again, but this time, she caught it before sending the message and changed it back.

Sneaker Woman sent more laughing emojis. *Sorry, I'm not up to killing or kissing anyone right now.*

Denny's face still burned, but at least she had cheered Sneaker Woman up. She peeked at Julie, who waited by the door.

"Is your friend okay?" Julie asked.

"Yeah. More or less." Denny still wasn't fully convinced Sneaker Woman wasn't downplaying her injuries. *Listen, I have to get back to work, but there's something I need to know first.*

I really am fine, Sneaker Woman replied. *Promise.*

Good, but that's not it. Denny slid her glasses higher up on her nose. *I'd like to know your name.*

Sneaker Woman didn't reply for several seconds.

Denny held her breath. In the more than three weeks since they had been texting each other, she had been the one to insist on not exchanging names, but now the need to know was overwhelming.

Eliza, Sneaker Woman finally answered. *Eliza Harrison. I'm not giving you my middle name, because my mother's already used it on me fifty-four times in the last hour.*

Denny mentally repeated the name to herself. Eliza. That name fit her. *Nice to meet you, Eliza. Sort of.*

Likewise, Eliza replied.

Denny paused, knowing she needed to go but not wanting to.

Whisperer? Hey, you still there? Eliza asked. *Don't think you can leave without telling me your name.*

It's Denny Jacobs, she answered.

Denny? Not Jenny? That's not your autocorrect taking over again, is it?

No, Denny replied. *It's short for Denver.*

Denver?

Long story. Denny glanced at Julie, who tapped her foot. *I'll tell you next time I speak with you.*

Only once she had already sent off the message did she realize that autocorrect had changed *speak* to *sleep.*

Fucking autocorrect! Why did it have its technological mind in the gutter when she was exchanging texts with Eliza of all people? The person who had invented that thing should burn in hell.

But maybe it was her own fault. In the beginning, she had always re-read what she had written before sending, but over the last few weeks, she had become less careful when texting with Eliza.

"Denny!" Julie drew out her name as if it had eight syllables. "The boss is going to kill us—if I don't kill you first!"

Talk later, Denny typed. She caught a glimpse of several laughing emojis Sneaker Woman...Eliza had sent, then tossed her phone into the locker, shut it, and hurried after Julie.

Well, they said laughter was the best medicine, so at least her embarrassing autocorrect snafus should speed up the healing process.

Eliza clutched her ribs and gasped for breath. She was laughing so hard, she struggled to type a goodbye.

Her mother rushed from the kitchenette and perched on the edge of the couch. "Oh God, honey! Are you in pain! Want me to call your dad or a doctor or...?" She looked around for her phone and found it in Eliza's hand.

"No, no, I'm fine." Eliza reined in her laughter and handed the phone back. "Something my friend said just made me laugh, and that hurts like he...heck."

Her mother leaned over her and brushed aside a strand of hair that had tumbled onto Eliza's face. "How do you feel?"

Eliza gave her a crooked grin. "Like I've been hit by a truck...or an SUV, to be exact."

"Don't joke about it. That could have ended badly."

"But it didn't, Mom. No use focusing on the negative."

A knock came at the door, then Heather used her key to let herself in. She'd been checking in on her every hour since Eliza had returned to their apartment building with a bike that looked like a pretzel last night. "Hey, how are you doing?"

"I'm fine," Eliza said. "Could everyone please stop acting like I'm at death's door?"

Heather studied the floor as if the bamboo had formed new, fascinating patterns overnight. "I feel really bad that I let you ride your bike home in the rain."

Eliza's mother got up from the couch and gave Heather a hug. "It's not your fault, honey. I could never make that one," she pointed at Eliza, "do anything she didn't want to do, even when she was three years old."

The sight of their warm embrace made Eliza smile, and she forgot her annoyance at their overprotectiveness. She was so grateful her mother—her entire family—had practically adopted Heather into the clan. Heather's parents barely acknowledged her existence since she had transitioned, and while Eliza knew her family couldn't replace the one Heather had been born into, she hoped it helped at least a little.

After a moment, Heather freed herself and squeezed into the same spot Eliza's mother had been in before, on the edge of the sofa. A wrinkle formed on Heather's otherwise smooth brow as she studied her. "Is there anything I can get you?"

"Another Passionate from Miles Away?" Eliza answered with a hopeful look.

Heather firmly shook her head. "I don't think that's a good idea, just in case you do have a concussion."

"Spoilsport."

"Anything else?" Heather asked.

One thing came to mind immediately. "I need a new phone."

Heather jumped up, managing not to hit her knee on the coffee table. "Be right back."

Eliza grabbed hold of her friend's shirt before she could rush from the room. The sudden movement made pain shoot through her bruised body, but she held on. "Wait! I didn't mean for you to go buy me one."

A snort escaped Heather. "How much money do you think school bus drivers make? I'm getting you my old one. It's not fancy, but it still works. You can use it to text your mystery woman until you get a new one."

A warm flush washed over Eliza. "It's not like I'm texting only her. If I don't check in and assure the rest of the family that I'm fine at least once an hour, they'll show up on my doorstep with an ambulance." Softly, she added, "Besides, her name is Denny. Not Mystery Woman."

"Denny." Heather smacked her lips as if tasting the name.

"It's short for Denver, not Danielle," Eliza added.

Heather tilted her head. "So did your near-death experience finally convince her to tell you her name?"

Eliza rolled her eyes toward the high ceiling. "Jeez, it's a couple of scrapes and bruises, not a near-death experience!"

"But it did get her to tell you her name," Heather said.

"Yes, it did." Eliza couldn't wait to hear how she had ended up with a name like Denver. But first, Heather had to get her a phone. "Shoo. Phone. Now."

Laughing, Heather walked backward to the door. "I'm going, I'm going."

When the door clicked shut behind her, Eliza turned her attention toward her mother, who had been unusually quiet during the past few minutes. "You can leave too, Mom. I'm fine on my own. I know you have to finish the illustrations for the *Bailey the Boar* book."

"I will in a minute," her mother murmured, gazing at her phone. She looked up and studied Eliza with a carefully neutral expression. "New friend?" She held up the phone.

Eliza hesitated for a second before nodding. It might seem strange to call someone a friend even though they had never met, but Whisperer...Denny had become an important part of her day. It had been strange to wake up this morning without finding a message waiting for her or being able to check in with her.

"If she's more than a friend, you could tell me; you know that, right?" her mother said quietly.

Eliza nearly rolled off the couch. She tried to sit up without putting pressure on her many bruises. "Why would you think that?"

Her mother gestured at the phone.

"Mom! You're not supposed to read my messages!"

"I didn't mean to, but they were on my phone and the messages app was still open...and she said something about, um, sleeping with you."

"She didn't," Eliza said quickly. "Not really. She said 'speak with me' or something like that, and autocorrect changed it." At least her mom hadn't scrolled farther to read the message about eating her out.

"Oh."

Eliza eyed her mother. "You know, I can't tell if you're relieved or disappointed that I'm not sleeping with her."

"Maybe a little of both." Her mother chuckled. "You know I'm a hopeless romantic. I just want you to find someone—not necessarily a woman, but if it was..." She shrugged. "I'd be fine with that."

A wave of love and gratitude swept over Eliza. She had to swallow the lump in her throat before she could speak. "Have I told you lately how much I love you?"

"Yes—earlier, when I sent your dad and your siblings away." Her mother laughed, but her eyes were damp.

"Then I'll say it again. But please don't start waiting for a daughter-in-law, okay? If you ever get one, it'll be because Ryan and Nichole are finally tying the knot, not because I'm marrying a woman."

Heather let herself back into the apartment. She stopped two steps in, phone in hand, and gave Eliza a wide-eyed look. "Marrying a woman? Is there something you want to tell me?"

Eliza buried her face in her hands and groaned into her palms. "God, you two are too much."

The next day, Denny had a rare Sunday off, so she lounged in bed until she heard Bella come downstairs and start rooting through the cupboards for something to eat. She quickly threw back the covers, knowing she would find pieces of cereal in every nook and cranny of the kitchen for weeks if she left Bella to her own devices.

Once she had saved her niece from certain starvation by making blueberry pancakes, she settled down at the table with a stack of pancakes for herself.

She was midway through eating them when her phone buzzed.

Denny's gaze darted to the counter, then to Bella. They had a firm rule against books and screens at the table, so she couldn't get up to check her messages. Sometimes, being a role model sucked.

It was probably a text from Eliza. How was she doing this morning? Had she been able to sleep, bruised as she was?

For once, Denny finished her stack of pancakes before her niece did and then waited impatiently for Bella to eat the last bite of hers.

Just when Bella had cleared her plate, Salem came downstairs, yawning and running her hand through her sleep-tousled hair. "Yum. I thought I smelled pancakes." She stopped to kiss Bella's head, then did the same to Denny. "Thanks for letting me sleep in and for making breakfast. Can I have some too?"

Suppressing a sigh, Denny got up to make another stack. When she passed her phone, she gave it a longing look but resisted the urge to check her messages. It would have to wait a little longer.

Salem dug into her pancakes with the same gusto as Bella had. "Yeah, yeah, I know," she said, mouth half full. "Slow down and..."

"...chew your food," Bella finished for her.

It was what Denny had been telling both of them for years. But today, she remained silent.

"You're not joining in? What's up with you?" Salem put down her fork and reached across the table to feel Denny's forehead.

Denny batted her hand away. "Nothing." But she couldn't stop herself from peering at her phone again.

Salem turned to see what she was looking at.

Bella used the moment she was facing away to steal one of her pancakes.

"Now I get it," Salem said in a teasing singsong. "Waiting for a text from Sandal Girl?"

"It's Sneaker Woman, Mom." Bella swiped a piece of the stolen pancake through the maple syrup on her plate and glanced at Denny. "Or is this another girl you're texting?"

"No, it's still the same woman." Denny shook her head at her niece. "Jeez, who do you think I am? The female Casanova?"

Salem gave her a cheeky grin. "No one has ever accused you of that; that's for sure."

"Remind me again why I made breakfast for the two of you?" Denny grumbled.

"Because we're cute," they both said at the same time, then high-fived each other.

"Yeah, very cute." Denny pointed at the syrup dribbling down Salem's chin.

Salem wiped it off and gestured toward the phone with her fork. "So, what's up with the two of you?"

"Nothing's up." Denny swallowed to get rid of the sudden lump in her throat. "She was in a bike accident on Friday night. Some assho... uh, careless person opened their door right in front of her, and she smashed into it."

Salem sobered instantly. "Jesus, Denny, is she okay?"

Denny just nodded because that lump was still there.

"Why didn't you tell us sooner?"

Denny shrugged. It was the first time she'd made a new friend in ages, and that friendship felt like something to nurture and protect, not share.

Salem tilted her chair back and reached out her arm to grab Denny's phone. "Here. Call her."

"No, we're not doing that," Denny said but took the phone anyway. "We just text."

"Calling people is so 2010, Mom," Bella informed her.

Now that the phone was in her hand, Denny could no longer resist. While her sister and niece debated whether calling people was old-school, she unlocked her phone and checked her messages.

She had a text from another unknown number.

A smile crept onto Denny's face. Had Eliza kidnapped another family member's phone to contact her? It felt good knowing their growing friendship meant enough to Eliza that she would do that.

God, this thing is just one step up from a flip phone, the text said. *Oh, it's Eliza, btw.*

Denny's smile broadened. *I figured. No one else I know starts conversations in the middle, without any context or even a hello.*

Sorry. Bad habit. Eliza added a blushing emoji.

Don't apologize. I don't mind at all. Denny found it pretty endearing. *So, what "thing" are you talking about?*

I borrowed Heather's old phone. She activated it for me until I'm able to get a new one. I'm not sure I can even put apps on this thing.

Well, on the plus side, at least she can't nudge you to use No More Frogs to get another date, Denny replied.

Ooh, I like the way you think. Not that I'd go on a date with the way I look at the moment anyway.

At the mention of Eliza's injuries, Denny's teasing mood instantly disappeared. *How are you?*

Purple. Eliza sent an emoji with a toothy grin. *I'd send you a photo, but using this old thing, it would probably be too grainy to see anything. Are you working today?*

No. Just finished making breakfast for the ungrateful masses. Denny looked up at her sister, who was watching her, while Bella painted patterns into the leftover syrup on her plate. "Nothing to see here. Why don't you two go do the dishes?"

Twin groans answered her, but they got up because the household rule stated the person who did the cooking was excused from cleaning the kitchen. That left Denny to focus on her conversation with Eliza.

So, do you have time for that long story? Eliza asked.

Long story? Denny scratched her head with her free hand.

About how you got your name.

Denny smiled. She had a feeling Eliza was like a dog with a bone—she would keep asking until she found out what she wanted to know. *My parents say they didn't have a lot of time to think of baby names. I wasn't planned, and they only found out my mother was pregnant when she was already six months along.*

Six months??? How's that even possible?

I have no idea. Apparently, her cycle has always been irregular, and she barely showed at all until the seventh month. The docs said she must be one of those women who carry the pregnancy more toward the back of their uterus.

Aww, guess you were shy, even back then.

Denny rubbed her overly warm cheek. Was her shyness obvious, even though she wasn't as tongue-tied with Eliza? *So anyway, three months apparently wasn't enough time to think of a name, so they decided to name me after the city where I was born—Denver.*

That's quite a story, Eliza texted. *So, did they find out in time when your mom was pregnant with your sister?*

They did. Salem has never been the shy type. She made her presence known early on by causing horrible morning sickness.

Salem? Let me guess... Your family moved, and she was born in Salem?

Yep, Denny typed back. *Why break with tradition, they said.*

Phew, good thing neither of you was born in Buffalo!

Denny burst out laughing. God, she loved Eliza's sense of humor.

Salem closed the dishwasher. "Looks like Sandal Girl is doing better."

"She is," Denny said without glancing up from her phone. "And it's Eliza, not Sandal Girl."

Or Fort Wayne, Eliza added.

Or Clovis, Denny shot back.

They bounced the most ridiculous town-based names back and forth until Eliza pleaded for mercy. *Okay, that's enough! Being bruised all over and laughing your ass off don't mix very well.*

Sorry. Denny hesitated, then gave herself a mental kick and sent a hugging smiley face. That's what friends did when one of them was hurting, right?

Thanks. That's a really unique naming story. But I like Denny. Your name, I mean.

Denny couldn't help beaming as if she personally had come up with that name. *Just the name? Not Denny, the person?* She paused, not yet sending the text. Was that still considered teasing? Or was she crossing the line into flirting? She'd never been great at figuring out the difference. Finally, she decided she was overthinking things and hit send.

Yeah, well, I figure Denny the person is not so bad either, Eliza sent back.

If she had been flirting, Eliza was definitely flirting back. All just in good fun, of course. It didn't mean anything. But her natural shyness didn't care whether Eliza meant it or not. It acted up anyway, leaving her clueless as to what to reply. Finally, she typed, *I've come to like it too. My name, I mean. Especially the shortened version.*

Didn't you like it as a kid?

Are you kidding? I hated it. Denny looked for an emoji that expressed her level of hatred but couldn't find one, so she decided on a puking smiley face.

Why? It's so unique.

And that's exactly why I hated it. It made me even more different from everyone else.

What made you so different other than your name? Eliza asked. *That you liked girls instead of boys?*

That too, but it was more than that. Denny hunched her shoulders. They were veering into a territory that made her feel vulnerable. She couldn't remember ever talking about it with anyone, not even with Salem—maybe especially not with Salem. With her sister, she had always been the protector, so while she shared everyday problems with Salem, baring too much of her vulnerabilities felt wrong.

Seconds ticked by, and she was overly aware she still hadn't answered. But Eliza didn't send another question, didn't pressure her, and that made it easier.

I guess I always felt like the odd one out, Denny typed. *When other kids talked to me, I never knew what to say, so I didn't have many friends. And I got teased because I was a little pudgy. Let's just say school was a miserable experience for me.*

She stared at the text she had sent. Had she really told her all that?

Now Eliza was the one who sent her a hugging emoji. *I'm sorry. Too bad we didn't go to the same school. I would have defended you.*

The mental image of Eliza in a red cape made Denny grin. With her slim body and friendly smile, Eliza looked anything but scary. *I hate to tell you, but at the time I started middle school, you were a tiny little baby.*

Hey, I was pretty scary as an infant. Just ask my mom.

Hmm, I could. Denny swiped through the collection of emojis and picked one rubbing its chin, deep in thought, as if cooking up a sinister plan. *Since I now have her phone number. I bet she could tell me some interesting stories about you as a kid.*

Nope. Nothing to tell. I was an angel. Eliza sent the smiley face with a halo.

Why do I have the feeling you were anything but?

I have no idea what you're talking about, Eliza replied.

Of course you don't. Denny grinned as she imagined Eliza as a mischievous little kid. *So now that I've told you all about my name and my childhood, what about you? How did you get your name? Let me guess... Your parents were fans of My Fair Lady?*

Ha! I wish, Eliza answered. *Okay, I'll tell you, but if you ever repeat this to anyone, I will have to kill you. Slowly. Painfully.*

Denny slid onto the edge of her chair. This should be good. *I'll protect your secret with my life. So?*

I was named after a piglet.

Denny burst out laughing. *What?*

Well, a fictional piglet. My mother illustrates children's books for a living, and a little piglet named Eliza was the main character of the first book she worked on.

Denny's laughter trickled off into a broad grin. *That's kind of cute. Was it a bestseller?*

It sold pretty well—still does, actually. I guess kids can identify with a piglet who struggles to fit in because her tail doesn't curl, like those of the other pigs.

Denny sighed. *Sounds like a book I would have loved as a kid. So, is your mom rich and famous?*

Let me repeat myself: Ha, I wish! None of my mom's illustrator friends can support themselves on children's books alone. The starving artist thing isn't just a myth for most people.

You're an artist too, aren't you? Denny asked. *What does your mother think about that?*

Well, I'm a crafter, but yeah, the financial aspects are the same. My mom was delighted when I spent my time making jewelry and cute little animal figurines as a teenager instead of partying.

That sounded as if a but would follow. Denny waited, letting Eliza tell her story in her own time.

But as I got older and chose to do just enough temp work to stay afloat so I could pursue my crafts instead of getting a "real job," I know Mom was worried. I get why, but money isn't that important to me, you know?

I get it, Denny answered. *Having a job that puts food on the table is important, but what good does it do if it feeds your stomach without nourishing your soul?*

This time, it took a while before Eliza answered. *Wow. That's beautiful. Are you sure you aren't an artist too?*

If you ever saw the bunnies I drew for my niece when she was little, you wouldn't ask that. No, Denny wasn't an artist, but she knew what it was like to work in a job she tolerated yet didn't love. If money weren't an issue, she would sit at her sewing machine all day. But as much as she enjoyed sewing, it would never pay her rent, much less enable her to help Salem and Bella.

"Earth to Denny! Hello?" Salem waved a pair of work gloves between Denny's eyes and the phone, blocking her line of sight. "Are you coming or not?"

"Coming where?" Denny had missed the entire conversation that had been going on in the dining area since she'd texted Eliza. And not just that—she'd also missed the fact that her sister was now fully dressed and looking at her expectantly.

Salem let out an exasperated sigh that sounded a lot like her daughter's when she was fed up with something the adults were doing. "We're going down to the community garden to play in the dirt for a couple of hours."

"They're planting the eggplants today," Bella added.

Denny gave her a grin. "I thought you didn't like eggplants either?"

Bella shrugged. "It's like the cook-doesn't-need-to-clean rule. If I'm planting them, I don't need to eat them."

"That's not how it works, young lady," her mother said before turning back toward Denny. "So, are you coming?"

Denny's gaze went back and forth between Salem and the phone. Normally, she liked volunteering in the community garden, but today... "Um, I think I'm going to stay and keep Eliza company while she's stuck on the couch."

"How did I know you'd say that?" Salem gave her an indulgent smile. "All right, see you later."

Denny nodded, her attention halfway back on her text conversation.

Chapter 8

NEARLY A WEEK LATER, ELIZA flopped down on her couch belly-first, grateful she no longer felt stiff all over from her many bruises. She dangled her feet in the air while she typed a quick message to Denny. *Hey, you. Eliza here. Want to be my first?*

There was no immediate reply. She knew Denny was home since she was working the opening shift this week, and that meant she was off at two. Maybe she didn't reply because she didn't recognize the new number, or she was busy helping Bella with her homework. It was amazing how well she knew Denny's schedule and little habits already.

A few moments later, her phone chimed with the tone she had assigned to text messages from Denny.

Jesus, Eliza Won't-Reveal-Her-Middle-Name Harrison! You can't send me texts like that while I'm helping Bella with her science homework. She'll think I'm...

Yes? Eliza's grin grew. Teasing Denny was so much fun.

Sexting you.

Eliza had a feeling if they'd been talking, Denny would have lowered her voice to a whisper. She sent back a shocked emoji, its eyes and mouth wide open. *Why would she think that? I was talking about you being the first person to send me a text on my brand-new phone.*

Ooh, did you get the one we were talking about?

Yep. Couldn't resist, Eliza answered. *That camera will be great for when I take photos of my jewelry and figurines to put on Etsy. But I'll have to eat potatoes and Ramen noodles all month.*

I'm not rich or anything, but if you need to borrow some money, please don't be too proud to ask, okay?

Denny's offer came without a second's hesitation. They had never met or talked on the phone, yet she was offering to lend Eliza money, even though Denny was living off a cashier's income. It touched Eliza more than she could say. *Thank you. I mean that. But I'll be fine. The guy who caused the accident will reimburse me. His car insurance is covering everything, but it might take some time for them to send me a check. In the meantime, Dee and Austen are talking about us selling some of our handmade bird toys at Saturday Market, so I'll pick up some overtime there.*

But what about your own stall? Denny asked. *Won't you lose income if you can't sell your craft items?*

Denny's concern warmed her. *I'll only be covering the Feathered Friends booth every now and then, and Heather promised to cover our stall if I keep her supplied with snickerdoodle cookies.*

Sounds like a great deal for both of you. You'll have to give me some tips on toys. Before Eliza could even think of making a joke about the toy advice remark, Denny quickly added, *Bird toys. Bella wants a pet for her birthday, and we don't think getting a dog or a bigger animal would be a good idea, so we're thinking about a budgie.*

Cool! If she gets one, you should bring her by our booth or the office, and I'll set her up with everything she needs.

Thanks, Denny answered.

She hadn't said she would actually do it. By now, it no longer surprised Eliza. Whenever she hinted at wanting to meet, Denny changed the subject. Eliza tried not to take it personally. She sensed it wasn't a lack of interest holding Denny back, but more that Denny was afraid something bad would happen if they met face-to-face. She promised herself to be patient with her.

So, what color are the bruises today? Denny asked.

Eliza peeked through the hole in the shoulder seam of her favorite sweater. *Greenish heading toward yellow. I think they'll be gone in a few days. I hope that'll finally stop my folks from checking up on me every day.*

Well, they care. I think it's nice.

Shit, how insensitive of her! Denny's parents had never shown much interest in her and had cut her out of their lives completely, and here Eliza was, complaining about her caring family. *I'm sorry. I know I really don't have anything to complain about.*

Don't worry. I get it, Denny replied. *Overprotective family members can be quite annoying, or so my niece tells me.*

Let me guess. You are the overprotective family member. Eliza hoped she would get to see Denny with her niece sometime.

Guilty as charged. Well, me and Salem both.

What did you do? Eliza asked.

We won't let her walk home from the bus by herself, and apparently, that's destroying her street cred.

Eliza chuckled, then couldn't stop laughing as Denny relayed one Bella story after another. Good thing laughing no longer hurt.

The sound of a key in the door made her look up from her phone. This time, it wasn't an overprotective family member checking on her. Heather stood in the doorway. A frown carved a vertical line between her eyebrows as she regarded Eliza. "Oh. Sorry to barge in. I wanted to borrow some sugar and thought you were already gone."

"Gone? No. My date isn't until seven."

"Uh, did you see the time?"

Eliza glanced at the top of her phone screen. It was a quarter to seven! "Shit!" How on earth had that happened? It had been barely after five when she and Denny had started to chat. She dashed to her closet, pulling her sweater over her head on the way, and reached for the first top in sight.

"No, no, not that one." Heather walked up behind her, reached across, and plucked a partially sheer top from a hanger. "This one is sexier." When Eliza raised her brows and hesitated, she added,

"To make up for you being late. Want me to text the guy while you get ready?"

"No." Eliza struggled into her skinny jeans. "I think I can still make it on time. We're meeting at the Italian place down the street. But could you text Denny and let her know what's happening? We were in the middle of a conversation, and I don't want her to think I abandoned her."

"Sure." Heather crossed the room toward the couch, where Eliza had dropped the phone. "Ooh, shiny! Is that the new phone?"

Eliza ducked into her tiny bathroom but left the door open so they could keep talking. Good thing there were no bruises on her face, because she didn't have time to apply any makeup. Some mascara and lipstick would have to do. "Yes. I'll show you the camera later. You'll love it. But for now, just text Denny, please."

Low tapping sounds drifted over. "Dear fellow lesbian," Heather said out loud. "Eliza had to leave, but now that I have you here... What are your intentions toward my best friend? Straight best friend, I might add."

"What the...?" Eliza dropped her lipstick into the sink, raced over, and tried to snatch the phone away, but Heather was faster and sidestepped her. "You did not just write that!"

"No, of course I didn't." Laughing, Heather held out the phone so Eliza could see what she had written.

Hey, Heather here. Your number neighbor. Eliza forgot she had a date, so she had to leave, but knowing her, she'll text you afterward.

Thank you for letting me know, Denny had answered, her reply more formal than how she normally responded to Eliza.

She pulled the phone free of Heather's grip before her friend really could send a message like that. It had been a joke; she knew that. But something about the text and how Heather had phrased it... *Knowing her, she'll text you afterward.* She eyed Heather, who looked back at her with a neutral expression. If she wanted to, Heather could have quite the poker face. "You're not jealous of her, are you?"

Heather laughed, and that was when Eliza knew she really was jealous. Her friend had a habit of making light of things that caused her pain, almost as if doing that would make it hurt less when others made fun of her.

"Nah." Heather waved her hand. "I know I'm your number one lesbian friend."

Eliza straightened to her full five-foot-six height to look her in the eyes. "I don't rank my friends. You know that."

"It was a joke. Come on, let's pick some sexy shoes to go with that outfit." Heather tried to walk away, but Eliza grabbed her sleeve and held on, not allowing her to break their eye contact.

"I really like Denny—and I think you'll like her too once we all get a chance to meet." She tugged on Heather's sleeve to make sure she had her full attention before continuing. "But you'll always be my favorite neighbor, my go-to for craft advice, and the person I can count on if I need a hug or a kick in the ass."

"Oh yeah. Ass-kicking is my specialty." Despite Heather's words, her voice vibrated with emotion. She gave Eliza a smile, and this time, it seemed less forced. "Never mind me. I'm being silly."

"You're being human. And I'm sorry if I made you feel neglected or insecure about our friendship."

Heather looked at her with a slight shake of her head. "God, you're so mature. Tell me again why you're single?"

"Because, according to my best friend, I'm being too picky."

"You are. You left-swiped on three perfectly nice guys this week alone. But seriously, it's not like you're neglecting me. It's just... I've never known you to spend so much time with one person. I mean, I know you have other friends, of course, but this feels different."

Eliza nodded. "It is." She thought about it for a moment, trying to pinpoint what made her friendship with Denny so different. It was hard to put her finger on it, so she settled on: "Probably because we've never met in real life. Somehow, that makes it easier to tell each other stuff."

Heather hummed her understanding and glanced at her wristwatch. "Damn. You have to get going."

Forgoing the sexy shoes Heather had suggested, Eliza shoved her feet into her yellow sneakers. She pressed a kiss to Heather's cheek, grabbed her purse and keys, and dashed to the door. "Get yourself some sugar," she called over her shoulder.

"You too." Heather's throaty laughter drifted after Eliza as she sprinted to the stairs.

Later that night, Denny was debating whether to watch another episode of *Central Precinct* or wrap up her binge-watching session for today when her phone pinged. She snatched it from her bedside table, eager to hear how Eliza's date had gone.

There was indeed a new message from Sneaker Woman. Denny made a mental note to finally change the name in her contacts.

Ice cream, brownies, or M&M's?

An indulgent smile curled Denny's lips. Only Eliza could think that was an acceptable conversation opener. *Hello to you too,* she texted back.

Eliza sent an emoji rolling its eyes. *Hi there! So, which? Ice cream, brownies, or M&M's?*

Yes please to all of them, Denny replied.

Not helping! Pick one!

Impossible. That's like asking a mother to pick her favorite child.

Houston, we have a problem, Eliza answered. *Or in this case: Denver, we have a problem. I'm at the store, I can't decide, and I'm starting to get hangry.*

Uh-oh. Can't have that. Denny thought for a moment. *How about vanilla ice cream with brownies and M&M's sprinkled on top?*

OMG, you're dangerous!

Come on, admit it. You've already put everything in your cart, haven't you?

Instead of a reply, Eliza sent a photo showing the contents of her shopping cart: vanilla ice cream, brownies, and a huge package of peanut M&M's.

Denny laughed. It was amazing to see how well she knew Eliza already, even though they had been texting for only a month. *Why are you getting hangry? Didn't your date take you to a restaurant? How was it, btw?* If Eliza needed to overload on sugar, probably not great.

Short, Eliza replied.

The date or the guy?

Both. I think I beat my personal record for shortest date ever. We didn't even make it to the main course.

What happened? Did you fake an emergency?

No, he did, Eliza answered. *At least I think it was fake. Or do dogs really get appendicitis?*

Denny scratched her head. *I have no idea. Do they even have an appendix?*

I could google it, but I think I prefer to pretend his dog was really sick and he was heartbroken at having to leave. Easier on the ego than assuming he didn't like the way I looked or found me boring.

How could anyone think Eliza was boring or not beautiful enough? *I'm starting to think there's something wrong with the male population of Portland.*

Thanks for not assuming there's something wrong with me.

Denny had a feeling the failed dates were affecting Eliza's self-esteem more than she cared to admit, so she tried to cheer her up with a joke. *Well, your eating habits are questionable, but otherwise...*

Ha! Ever heard of not throwing stones when you live in a glass house?

I'll have you know I'm eating carrots.

Carrots? Really?

Denny took a picture of the marzipan carrots Salem had bought to decorate an Easter cake, which she hadn't gotten around to making.

Carrots, my ass!

What? Denny grinned as she typed. *I never said what kind of carrots.*

Oh shit. My ice cream is starting to melt. I'd better get it home.

Denny chuckled. *Talk to you later. And enjoy your after-date ice cream.*

I'll send you a pic when I have my bowl in hand, just to be mean. Eliza added a grinning devil.

Thanks a lot. This time, Denny didn't hesitate to send back the one-finger salute emoji.

Fifteen minutes later, Denny's phone dinged again, and she wasn't surprised to see the promised picture pop up on her screen, accompanied by the words, *Yum, yum, yum. Don't let it be said that I'm not a woman of my word.*

Denny eyed the scoop of vanilla ice cream, slowly melting on top of a huge brownie. Colorful M&M's had been arranged on the ice cream to form a smiley face. Mmm, that looked good. She abandoned her carrots, climbed out of bed, and wandered into the kitchen, phone in hand.

Two minutes later, she sent back a photo of her big bowl of caramel apple pie ice cream with chocolate syrup drizzled on top. *You're such a bad influence!*

Eliza instantly replied. *Me? You were eating marzipan carrots! Besides, why are you getting after-date ice cream when you haven't suffered through a date?*

Denny took a big spoonful of her ice cream. The combined flavors of yumminess melted on her tongue. *Believe me, I've suffered through enough bad dates in my lifetime to deserve all the ice cream I can eat.*

So you haven't had any luck with online dating either?

I haven't tried it yet, Denny texted back, spoon in mouth. *Regular dating is bad enough.*

Wait? You haven't tried online dating? Not even once? Three wide-eyed emojis followed. *You do know this is the 21st century, don't you?*

Yes, I've been informed of that fact, thank you very much, Denny answered. *I just think it's too clinical. Too superficial. You know?*

Well, we met online, and our conversations are neither clinical nor superficial...are they?

Denny dropped her spoon into the bowl to answer faster. *No! Of course they aren't. But we're not dating.* A little voice in the back of her mind added: unfortunately. She silenced it. *But most people swipe right only on the hot people, not on average-looking folks. That's the superficial part I don't like.*

I'll give you that, Eliza answered. *I hate that too. So if you don't do online dating, how do you meet women?*

It was embarrassing to admit, but Denny wanted to be honest with Eliza. Their open communication, without pretenses, was what she loved about talking to Eliza, and she trusted her not to judge. *Well, mostly, I don't. I hate bars and clubs. All I do is hide out in a quiet corner and cling to my beer, half hoping and half fearing that someone will come talk to me.*

Ugh, I'm sorry. That doesn't sound like a nice time, Eliza responded. *Okay, so that's out. What about meeting women elsewhere? Something like a book club or a cooking course. Heather met her last girlfriend at a leather craft workshop.*

This topic depressed her. More ice cream was in order. Denny slid a big spoonful into her mouth. *I tried that, but I'm not great at starting a conversation and I'm even worse at flirting with women. I'm just not spontaneous or witty.*

I beg to differ, Eliza replied immediately. *You're smart, a wonderful listener, and really funny. Yesterday, during lunch, you made me laugh so hard my boss came in to check on me because she thought I was sobbing. You're great, and any woman should consider herself lucky to date you!*

No one had ever said something like that about her. Well, other than Salem, but her sister was biased and didn't count. Her cheeks burned, yet at the same time, she couldn't stop her silly grin. *Thanks, but I'm only funny when I can hide behind my phone, not in person. I freeze whenever I try to talk to a woman face-to-face.*

And the women you might be interested in never make the first move? Eliza asked.

Denny swirled her spoon through the ice cream and plopped more of it into her mouth. *I'm more on the butch side, so women often expect me to take the lead, but as I said, I'm bad at initiating conversations.*

I think you should be honest about that. Lesbians are probably not that different from straight women. I bet they're just as sick of all the game-playing and of their dates pretending to be someone they're not. I, for one, would be seriously impressed if a guy walked up to me and said: Hey, I'd really love to talk to you, but I'm shy and have no idea what to say.

Denny sighed. If only she could date someone who shared Eliza's attitude. So far, she hadn't met anyone like her. But even if she did, would she have the guts to walk up to her and say what Eliza had suggested? She thought about it while she licked chocolate syrup off her bottom lip. *That sounds good in theory, but putting all my cards on the table and confessing my insecurities to a total stranger... I can't see myself doing that.*

I get it, Eliza answered. *Maybe you should give online dating a try after all. At least you get a warm-up period and can get to know a potential date a bit before meeting them in person. I usually set up a first date pretty fast because I can judge whether there's a chance for a connection better that way, but Heather tends to exchange texts for a couple of weeks. Do you think that might help you too?*

Well, it had helped when it came to chatting with Eliza, so maybe she was right. *Maybe a little.*

Great. I'll send you an invite for No More Frogs, if you want. You get a free trial month if a member invites you. What do you think?

Denny couldn't muster any real enthusiasm for the suggestion, but Eliza wanted to help, so she didn't want to say no. *I think I need some butter pecan ice cream to go with the rest of this.*

Is that a no, go fuck yourself?

Eliza's bluntness made her smile. If only she were more like that. *No, that's an I'll think about it.*

Good enough. And don't make yourself sick with too much ice cream.

Too much ice cream? What's that?

Good point, Eliza replied. *On that note, give me a second. I think I have some Rocky Road in the back of my freezer.*

Yum. Looks like we've achieved total ice cream compatibility.

Eliza sent back the 100% emoji.

Too bad they weren't compatible when it came to more important things, such as their sexual orientation. But Eliza being straight was probably for the best. With her lack of dating skills, Denny would likely fuck up a wonderful friendship. Sighing, she stood to get a scoop of butter pecan.

Chapter 9

THE NEXT SATURDAY, DENNY HAD the early shift, so she spent the afternoon catching up on her sewing while her sister leafed through a stack of gardening catalogs. Despite the after-date ice cream and all the other snacks she kept eating with Eliza, she could still button the pants she had started last month, but the pant legs were slightly too long.

She rolled up the cuffs to the right length and inserted pins to keep them in place, which wasn't easy to do while still wearing the pants. She had just finished on one side when her phone dinged.

With the rest of the pins firmly clenched between her lips, she straightened to see how Eliza was spending her Saturday. Had she sold the dragonfly bowl at the market this morning? It had been so lovely that Denny had been tempted to buy it from her, but she'd been afraid Eliza would want to hand-deliver it, so she hadn't said anything. The thought of meeting her face-to-face was as scary as it was wonderful. She hoped it would happen one day, but she wasn't sure she was ready for it yet.

As usual, Eliza didn't ease into the conversation with a *hi* or *how are you?* Instead, her text said, *Name your three biggest turn-ons and turn-offs.*

Denny nearly swallowed her pins. She quickly pulled them from between her lips and set them on the table. *Jesus, Eliza! You almost turned me into a pincushion!*

Pincushion? Where on earth are you? At the acupuncturist?

No. Denny hesitated and glanced at her trusted Singer Heavy Duty sewing machine, which she had set up at the dining table. So far, she hadn't told anyone but her family and Julie about her hobby. Some people would probably snicker at a butch who loved to sew. But Eliza hadn't laughed when she had confessed to being too shy to talk to women. Plus she was a crafty person herself, so maybe she would understand. *I was working on a pair of pants.*

Working on? Eliza asked. *As in, you are sewing your own clothes?*

Yeah. I prefer to shop in the men's section, but those clothes aren't made for a woman's body. I don't have the money to have stuff custom-tailored, so I started to hem my jeans and then taught myself to do more complicated projects. She held her breath until Eliza texted back, which only took a few seconds.

Wow, that's so cool! Show me what you're working on!

She sounded so enthusiastic Denny no longer remembered why she had hesitated to tell her. *One sec. I need to take them off first. I was trying them on to see if I need to shorten the legs a little.*

Before she even unbuttoned the pants, Eliza's next message popped up below her own. *No! Leave them on. I want to see what you look like in your new outfit.* When Denny hesitated, she added, *You need to send me a photo of you anyway.*

Denny scratched her head. Had she missed something? *Uh, I do?*

Yeah. For the No More Frogs profile I'm going to set up for you, Eliza answered. *That's what the turn-ons and turn-offs question was all about, btw. That's one of the prompts they have you answer.*

Denny's stomach churned. *I said I'd think about it, not that I want you to set up a profile for me.*

Okay, we'll talk about No More Frogs later, but I still want to see a picture of you. I bet the new pants look awesome.

But it wasn't the pants that made Denny hesitate. After texting back and forth for five weeks, Eliza must have formed a mental image of her. She probably imagined someone who was slim and elegant, like Eliza, or way more athletic than Denny actually was, without those love handles and the extra padding on her belly.

And for some reason, everybody always seemed to assume a butch woman would automatically have small breasts, and that definitely wasn't true for her.

Come on, Denny, Eliza texted. *You've known what I look like from day one, but I still have no idea what you look like.*

Sturdy, Denny answered.

Sturdy? That's it? That's all I'm getting?

Denny sent back a shrugging emoji to buy some time while she tried to summon the courage to send her a selfie. Why the hell was this so difficult? Eliza hadn't judged Denny for her interest in sewing; she wouldn't judge her for a muffin top either. Part of her knew that, but another part still couldn't let go of that old fear.

Denny? You okay? What's going on?

Denny resisted the urge to pretend everything was fine. The last thing she wanted to do was lie to Eliza, who was quickly becoming one of her closest friends.

I'm sorry if I pressured you too much, Eliza's next message said. *I just... I'm curious. I want to know what color your eyes are and what you look like when something I texted makes you laugh. But I know you're a very private person. If you'd rather not send me a photo, that's okay.*

I want to, Denny texted back and realized it was the truth. She wanted Eliza to know her, including the way she looked.

Then what's making you hesitate?

Remember how I told you that I was teased for being chubby in school? Denny continued without waiting for a reply so she wouldn't chicken out. *Well, it wasn't just a little teasing. It was the meanest bullying you can imagine. After that experience, it took me a long time to get to a point where I didn't hate my own body.* She glanced at her breasts, belly, and hips, the areas she struggled with the most. *Making my own clothes really helped with that, but I guess I'm still not completely over it.*

I know exactly what you mean.

You do? In Denny's eyes, Eliza was perfect. She had the slim body and small breasts Denny had always envied.

Yeah. Since I'm less than blessed in the chest department, I was teased in school too.

Denny had never imagined they might have that in common.

I'm mostly over it, except for moments when I'm trying on a nice dress, and the front gapes, making me look like a prepubescent girl in her mom's clothes, Eliza texted. *Not a sexy look, trust me.*

Denny had a hard time imagining anything not looking sexy on Eliza, but she abstained from saying that.

It took me a while to find my own style and my confidence, Eliza added. *But every now and again, I have a moment where I look at another woman and catch myself envying what she has.*

Wow. Good thing they were texting, not talking, because Denny's mouth was so dry she doubted she would be able to speak.

Wow?

Yeah. Wow. I never thought you of all people would feel like that too.

Truthfully, I think most women do. Few of my female friends are completely happy with every aspect of their bodies. It's because we're so used to being judged by how we look instead of what we accomplish. After a short pause, Eliza sent another text. *Wait, what do you mean, me of all people?*

Shit. Denny couldn't tell her how beautiful she thought Eliza was, could she? What if Eliza thought it was creepy or awkward?

But Eliza had a lesbian best friend who probably paid her compliments all the time. Nothing creepy about that. She gave herself a mental kick in the pants. *Well, because you're really beautiful. Objectively speaking.*

Eliza sent back a blushing emoji. *And you're really sweet. Objectively speaking.*

There. Eliza hadn't taken offense. She even thought Denny was sweet. Denny fought a very un-butch giggle and tried to finally relax. Today, all her insecurities seemed to be raising their ugly heads at the same time.

"What's up with you?" Salem squinted at her over the top of her gardening catalog. "Are you blushing?"

Denny firmly shook her head. "No, of course not. Why would I be blushing?"

"You tell me." Salem waved at Denny's phone. "Are you talking to Sandal Girl?"

"I already told you her name is Eliza."

Salem shrugged. "I think Sandal Girl is more fun—and it's fun to tease you by calling her that. So, are you talking to her?"

"Yes, I am." Before Salem could say anything else, Denny rounded the dining table and held out the phone. "Could you take a photo of me?"

Salem gave her a knowing smile. "Ah, so that's why you're blushing. She talked you into sending her a photo!"

"I said I'm not blushing." Denny willed her cheeks to not flush again. "And she hasn't talked me into anything. Well, not really. I just think it's time to return the favor."

"That's what I've been telling you for weeks." Salem took the phone, tapped the camera icon, and aimed the lens at Denny.

Denny waved at her to lift the phone higher. "Shoot at a higher angle. I don't want to have a double chin."

"Jeez, relax. And smile."

Denny forced the corners of her mouth up into a smile, but she doubted it came across as relaxed. A casual look was hard to achieve while sucking in your belly.

"Breathe, sis," Salem said. "I don't want to end up taking a photo of your passed-out body."

Trying not to grit her teeth as her tension rose, Denny drew in a quick breath.

Salem chose that moment to tap the trigger.

Great. Denny groaned. She probably looked like a puffer fish in defense mode. But she didn't have the nerve to have Salem snap another picture, so she took the phone from her and didn't allow herself to glance at the photo as she sent it to Eliza.

The second the word *delivered* appeared beneath the picture, she dropped onto a chair. Okay, it was done. No big deal, right?

Eliza sat up on her couch and frowned at her phone.

Denny had dropped out of the conversation after she'd called her sweet. Most of the time, Eliza found her shyness simply adorable, but sometimes, it made it hard for her to judge what was okay to say and what wasn't. Had she crossed a line without meaning to?

But they had told each other things they likely hadn't told anyone else. It had been many years since Eliza had confided in anyone about her struggles with her lack of a bust as a teenager, much less admitted she sometimes still had moments when she looked at other women with envy.

She knew Denny would understand and not judge, and she hoped Denny trusted her the same way.

But now Denny wasn't responding. What did that mean?

Her phone chirped.

Eliza blew out a breath. Denny had answered. She hadn't chased her off.

And it wasn't just any reply.

"Oh my God!" Denny had sent a picture.

Eliza clutched the phone with both hands as she stared at the photo, taking in every detail of the person she had wondered about for the past month.

The first thing she noticed was Denny's smile. It was a little crooked, as if her lips were hesitant to form a grin. But fine lines around the corners of her full mouth showed she normally loved to smile.

It made Eliza grin in return.

Then her gaze veered to Denny's eyes, which looked back at her from behind dark-framed glasses that gave her a geeky Rachel Maddow vibe. Eliza dragged her fingers over the screen to enlarge the photo so she could make out their color but still wasn't sure if they were brown or had an olive tint. They, too, had fine lines around their corners that indicated Denny smiled a lot.

Her face was lightly tanned, probably from the hours she had spent in the community garden lately, helping to build the high beds. A strand of her sandy-brown hair fell onto her broad forehead. Eliza guessed it might get some blonde streaks in summer. It was cut short along the sides and back but was slightly longer on top. Did Denny run her fingers through it when she got nervous?

Eliza could see why Denny had trouble fitting into menswear. She had broad shoulders but also wide hips and full breasts, with not much definition at the waist and some softness around the middle that would probably make her a world-class hugger.

Her broad hands were pressed to the outer seams of her pants, as if she was trying not to fidget.

Her body language screamed how uncomfortable she was, yet she had bravely stood still while someone—her sister?—snapped a photo because Eliza had requested one.

God, Denny. Eliza wished she could hug her until all her insecurities melted away and that forced smile turned into a real one.

Eliza? Denny texted. *That didn't make you run, did it?*

Damn. Eliza had been so focused on the photo that she had forgotten Denny was waiting for a reaction. *You look great!* she typed.

You really think so? Denny answered. *I still need to hem the legs.*

Of course Denny assumed the compliment was meant for her clothes, as if she couldn't believe Eliza liked the way she looked— but she did. Somehow, that strong but soft body and the vulnerable expression in her eyes fit the person she had been getting to know in the past five weeks.

I'm talking about you. Although... She took in the gray chinos Denny was wearing. They were clearly a men's cut, but they didn't bunch up in the crotch or gape at the waist. They looked as if they had been made by a tailor who knew what they were doing. *The pants look great too.*

You really mean that?

Which of the two statements was she referring to? Knowing Denny, probably both, so Eliza simply answered, *Of course I do.* She watched the bubble with the three dots appear, then disappear.

Finally, Denny typed, *They've got nice, deep pockets too. Not those tiny ones women's clothes usually have.*

So Denny had chosen to take the compliment as referring to her pants, not her looks. Eliza let it go for now. *God, yes! I hate that. Are you taking orders?*

Seriously? Denny asked. *You want me to make you a pair of pants?*

Of course I'm serious! And I bet I wouldn't be the only one who'd want a pair. My crafter friends would pay good money for women's jeans with real pockets. You could make some money if you wanted.

Denny sent back a wide-eyed emoji. *Do you honestly think the stuff I sew is good enough to sell?*

Totally. If you want me to put some of your creations on Etsy, just send me a couple of photos.

Etsy, No More Frogs... Before I know it, you'll have me on TikTok and Instagram!

Eliza smiled. It was so typical of Denny to react to a compliment with a joke. *Nah. I think two new platforms at a time are enough for a senior citizen like you. Have you given No More Frogs some more thought?*

You mean in the two minutes since I last told you I'd think about it?

Yep. So? While she didn't want to pressure Denny, a sweetheart like her deserved to have someone who appreciated her.

This time, she had to wait a minute until Denny's answer came.

Okay. I'll give it a try. But if the women on No More Frogs are as bad as the men, I'm outta there.

Deal. If her own streak of bad dates didn't improve anytime soon, they could leave the dating platform together. Eliza took her laptop off the coffee table and entered the No More Frogs URL into the browser bar.

Photos of happy couples popped up on her screen, each with a man and a woman sharing a candlelight dinner, walking hand in hand, and feeding each other wedding cake. As she did any time she visited the site, she wondered whether they were real or hired models.

So, what do I need to do? Do they really want to know my turn-ons and turn-offs?

Denny sounded a bit scared, which made Eliza grin. *Yes, but that doesn't mean you have to list your sexual preferences. It's more about the must-haves and deal breakers when it comes to dating. What are you looking for in a woman?*

Someone who's honest yet kind and caring. Denny's answer came fast, as if she had spent a lot of time thinking about it. *I'd like to meet a woman who appreciates me for me, without me having to lose weight, buy a fancy car, or start a glamorous career. Someone who gets me and who laughs at my silly attempts at being funny. Oh, and she has to like my family, of course.* Denny paused before adding, *Does that sound too cheesy?*

Maybe it did a little, at least it might to other people. But Eliza knew it was exactly what Denny needed. *No, that sounds perfect.*

Phew. Anything else?

Eliza scrolled down the page on her laptop. *Yes. There are about two dozen questions total.*

Two dozen? Jeez, are they planning to write my biography?

Eliza laughed. *Stop complaining, or I'll tell your future soul mate once I meet her.*

Okay, okay. So, what's the next question?

Finish this statement: On a typical Friday night, I am...

Texting you, Denny answered.

Warmth spread through Eliza's chest, but she doubted anyone else would find that answer as endearing. *I can't write that.*

Why not? That's what you'll find me doing on a typical Friday night. Any night, really.

Because you want your profile to stand out and sound interesting, Eliza answered. *And while I think texting me should be the highlight of anyone's day, others might not share that opinion. So how about: having fun with friends?*

That doesn't stand out either, Denny replied. *But I don't want to pretend I'm someone I'm not. That will only result in women being disappointed when they actually meet me.*

Eliza slowly shook her head. *You know what? The better I get to know you, the less I understand how that could ever happen.*

Denny didn't answer for a full minute or two. When a message arrived, it was a blushing emoji. *Um, thanks. Okay, next?*

Smiling, Eliza scrolled to the next question. *Your three best adulting skills. And don't say helping me pick after-date snacks.*

Bummer. There goes my fabulous adulting skill number one.

A chuckle rose up Eliza's chest. Filling out Denny's profile was way more fun than filling out her own had been.

It had taken three hours to complete Denny's profile, mostly because they had bantered back and forth and kept getting sidetracked discussing each of the questions and exchanging stories about their lives.

Eliza didn't mind at all because it had revealed interesting insights into Denny and had given them a chance to get to know each other better.

Finally, they reached the end of the questionnaire.

What do I do now? Denny asked.

Go to bed, Eliza answered. *It's nearly eleven, and if I'm not mistaken, you have to work tomorrow.*

No, I mean, yes, I do, but... What happens now that we've set up my profile?

You could look at other people's profiles, and if anyone sounds interesting, you could send her a message, Eliza typed.

Or I could just wait to see if someone messages me, right?

Oh, Denny. Eliza shook her head but smiled at the same time. *Yes, you could do that.*

Okay, great. Thanks so much for helping me. Still can't believe you talked me into this.

You're welcome. Just name your firstborn after me, and I'll consider us even.

I'm forty-one, Denny replied. *I don't think kids are in the cards for me. But we could name Bella's budgie after you, if she gets one.*

Eliza imagined Denny's niece talking to the budgie. "Why did you poop all over my homework? Bad bird, Eliza." She grimaced and typed, *Don't you dare.*

Denny sent a grinning devil emoji. *We'll see. But first, I need some sleep, or I won't like you at all when my alarm goes off tomorrow morning.*

Sleep tight.

You too. Talk tomorrow.

They exchanged hugging emojis—a relatively new thing—and then her phone went silent.

Eliza considered reading for a while or catching up on the new season of *Central Precinct* but then decided to go to bed too. She trudged to the bathroom.

Her phone pinged.

With her toothbrush in one cheek, she crossed her studio apartment. It wasn't the first time one of them had picked up the conversation after they had said good night. In fact, most nights, they said goodbye at least three times before they really stopped texting each other one last thing they wanted to say.

But just as she reached the phone, she realized it hadn't been the chirp associated with Denny's texts.

She unlocked the screen.

It was a text from Heather. *You awake?*

Yes. What's up?

No answer came. With the phone in one hand and the toothbrush in the other, she wandered back to the bathroom.

Less than a minute later, a key was shoved into the lock, and Heather burst into the apartment as if the building were on fire.

Eliza nearly swallowed a mouthful of toothpaste. She spat it out. "Heather! Are you trying to give me a heart attack? What are you doing here?"

"Look what I found!" Heather held out her phone. "It's her!"

"Who? What?" Eliza rinsed her mouth and dried her face, blinking water from her lashes.

"Butch Auntie! I told you about her, remember? The one who was at the bus stop covered in ketchup one day."

Eliza remembered that story. "What about her?"

"She's on No More Frogs! Look!" Heather thrust the phone at her.

Eliza took it and glanced at the small screen.

Denny's photo—the one she had uploaded to No More Frogs a few hours ago—stared back at her. "Wait. This is Butch Auntie?" She slapped her forehead. Of course! Hadn't Heather even mentioned the name of Butch Auntie's niece once or twice? There probably weren't many kids named Bella with a butch aunt in Portland.

Heather's locks bounced as she nodded firmly. "I'm pretty sure it's her. I mean, her handle is Shy_in_Portland, not Butch Auntie, and she looks different in her profile photo, all dressed up. When she picks up Bella, she's usually wearing baggy jeans and a faded T-shirt or a cashier's uniform. But I'm sure it's her."

"It is," Eliza murmured, still staring at the phone. God, the world really was a small place, wasn't it?

"What? You mean, you know her too?"

"Yeah. This is Denny."

"Denny? Butch Auntie is your Denny?"

"Well, she's not exactly mine, but...yeah. This is her. I just helped her set up her profile. How on earth did you find it so fast?"

Heather shrugged. "I was making a wet-molded leather pouch and scrolling through No More Frogs while I waited for it to dry. That's when I saw her photo."

They dropped onto the couch and stared at each other. "Wow," they said at the same time.

Heather scrolled through Denny's profile and smiled at some of the answers. "So she's single and looking for love, huh?"

Eliza nodded.

"Do you think it would be a bad idea for me to send her a message? I know I shouldn't mix work and my private life, but there aren't many single lesbians—especially not lesbians my bestie has already vetted for me—and she is kind of cute. Maybe a little too introverted for me, but you know what they say about the quiet ones... They usually turn out to be tigers in bed. Roar!" Heather formed a claw with her hand and playfully swiped the air.

Eliza elbowed her in the ribs. "You read her profile, right? She's looking for a serious relationship, not a roll in the hay."

Heather let her claw-shaped hand drop to her lap. "Hey, no need to get defensive. I was just kidding. What happened to your sense of humor?"

"Sorry, I..." She knew how hard dating was for Denny, and that was probably why she was a bit overprotective. But she couldn't violate Denny's trust by explaining that to Heather.

Heather studied her. "So you think it's a bad idea?"

"I didn't say that." It wasn't a bad idea, was it? At least she was reasonably sure Denny wasn't a transphobic asshole who would hurt Heather, and she knew Heather wouldn't make fun of Denny for her extra pounds or being shy. Total win-win situation, right?

Then why wasn't she enthusiastically nudging Heather to contact Denny right away? She'd have to examine the kernel of unease that had taken root deep inside her gut—later.

"Okay," Heather said. "It's too late to make any decisions anyway. I'll take counsel with my pillow for a night or two, maybe talk it through with Benedita to see if she thinks it could get me into trouble with the school."

"Yeah, that sounds reasonable."

"All right. Sorry for bursting in so late. Sweet dreams." Heather gave her a one-armed squeeze before getting up and walking to the door, where she turned one last time and pointed back at Eliza. "By the way, you've got toothpaste on your chin."

The door clicked shut, leaving Eliza to stare after her and rub her chin.

Two of her worlds were colliding unexpectedly, and it sent her head spinning in a way she couldn't quite explain.

Chapter 10

THE NEXT FRIDAY, DENNY'S BOSS let her leave early to get her wrist looked at.

The pain had started on Monday, but with her physically demanding job, a few aches were nothing out of the ordinary, so she had ignored them. Usually, they went away if she iced the affected area and got enough rest on her day off.

But this time, the pain had gotten worse instead of disappearing.

She'd tried to tough it out because it was inventory day; they needed all hands on deck. But by midday, the pain was so bad that she winced any time she had to lift a heavy box while restocking. Running the register wasn't any better. Every flick of her wrist made her grimace—and that wasn't how her boss wanted her to greet customers. Without her dominant hand, she was pretty much useless at her job.

Finally, she admitted defeat and told her boss.

She had hoped the doc would pull some minor miracle out of his bag of medical tricks, maybe give her an injection that would enable her to go right back to work, but he was apparently all out of miracles. Instead, he prescribed regular icing, ibuprofen, a brace, and a few days off work.

Thankfully, she worked for a company with a great benefits package, including plenty of paid sick days.

Denny slammed the car door closed with her hip and trudged to their townhouse, cradling her arm to her chest. Unlocking the front door was a struggle with her left hand. She fought to get a better grip. Jeez, why were there so many keys on her key chain?

When she got the door open, she found herself face-to-face with Salem, who stood inches away, swinging a metal shoehorn like a baseball bat. "Christ, Denny! You scared me half to death! I thought you were a burglar!"

"So you were trying to chase off a potentially armed criminal with a shoehorn?"

Salem shrugged. "I grabbed whatever was nearby. It was either the shoehorn or your old sneakers. Hmm, come to think of it, they might have made a better weapon because they smell like—" Her eyes widened as she stared at the brace on Denny's arm. "What happened?"

"Overuse and old age," Denny grumbled. "That's what happened. Apparently, tendonitis is common in my line of work, especially once you're over forty."

"Come on, old woman. Let's get you inside." Salem gripped Denny's elbow and guided her into the house as if she were ninety and couldn't walk without support.

"Watch your tongue. This old woman is still spry enough to do this." Denny gave her a light sideways kick to the ass.

"Ouch." Salem theatrically rubbed her behind. "Are you also spry enough to cook? It's just the two of us tonight. Bella is having a sleepover at Kaylee's."

Denny tossed her keys onto the counter, marched to the freezer, and pulled out two tubs of ice cream. "Dinner is served." No need to be a role model when her niece wasn't there, and after the day she'd had, she deserved all the ice cream she could eat.

Salem burst out laughing.

"What?" Denny gave her an innocent look. "The doc said to ice the arm."

"I'm sure he meant from the outside."

Denny pulled an ice pack from the freezer and wrapped it in a dish towel. "Doing it from the outside and the inside can't hurt. Grab a couple of spoons."

They settled down on the couch with their ice cream containers, and Salem picked a rom-com for them to watch.

Denny would never admit it, but she enjoyed a good romantic comedy as much as her sister did. Not tonight, though. She couldn't focus on the predictable plot, and sitting still seemed like a chore. After a while, she took the ice pack off her wrist and tossed it onto the coffee table.

She kept glancing at the clock. Was Eliza still at home, or had she left for her date with that IT guy from the No More Frogs app? She had exchanged messages with him all week, and with each message Eliza had forwarded her, Denny had liked him less. But she wasn't able to say why.

Usually, Eliza checked in with Denny before she went on a date, but today, Denny hadn't heard from her since lunch.

"Stop tapping your foot." Salem reached over from her end of the couch and slapped her thigh.

"Hey! You're hitting the injured person? That's against doctor's orders!"

"The doctor also said for you to rest, not to tap your foot at two hundred beats a minute," Salem answered.

"He said to rest my arm. My feet are fine, so I can tap them all I want," Denny grumbled.

Salem sent her a glare. "Not while I'm trying to watch a movie. If you're not in the mood, go do something else."

But since she couldn't do much without her right arm, sewing was out.

Hanging out with Eliza wasn't an option either. Even if she hadn't left for her date, she was probably busy getting ready for it, carefully doing her makeup and choosing what to wear.

In Denny's opinion, IT Guy didn't deserve that much consideration. He'd probably turn out to be another dud. There was something soothing about that thought, and that deepened Denny's frown. She would be happy for Eliza if she managed to find a nice guy, wouldn't she?

Salem stretched her foot across the cushion between them and poked her thigh. "What's up with you?"

Denny let out a long sigh. "Nothing. Just restless and bored, I guess."

"Why don't you text Eliza, see if she wants to chat?"

Denny managed not to grimace. "Can't. She's got a date tonight."

Salem paused the movie to focus her full attention on Denny.

The scrutiny made Denny squirm. "What?"

"Is that the reason you're pricklier than a porcupine with its quills at full mast?"

"Why does everyone keep comparing me to a porcupine?"

"Aha!" Salem triumphantly pointed the remote control at her. "You're evading the question. So that's a yes."

Denny looked away to settle her right arm onto a pillow. "No, it's not. Why would I be grumpy just because Eliza has a date?"

Salem poked her with her toes again. "Because you have a crush the size of the Wells Fargo Center on her."

Denny's stomach spiraled like a figure skater. Her hands went cold, even though she had taken the ice off. "Bullshit." The word echoed back at her in the silence, making her very aware that it lacked conviction. "I don't have a..." Her voice became quieter with every word until she trailed off. "Shit." She tried to rub her face and nearly whacked herself in the eye with her brace.

"Hey." Salem placed her feet on Denny's lap and scratched her thigh with her toes. "That's not so bad. Just a crush, right? You're not, like, falling in love with her, are you?"

"No!" *Take a deep breath. Now another.* "No," she repeated more calmly, "of course not. I haven't even met her, remember? It's just a silly crush. Completely harmless. It'll go away if I ignore it, and by the time we meet face-to-face for the first time, I'll have my head on straight. So to speak."

God, was that why she had been so hesitant to meet Eliza in person? She had attributed it to her shyness around new people, but then why was her hesitancy increasing the more she got to know Eliza? Deep down, she must have known she was starting to like Eliza in a way that wasn't entirely platonic.

"Too bad," Salem said. "You're really cute when you're crushing on someone. Your ears get all red any time you text her."

Denny couldn't help touching one of her ears with her left hand. "No, they don't. You're making that up."

The cha-chung sound she had assigned to Eliza's texts interrupted her protests.

"Ha! Works like a charm! Your ears are turning red."

Denny wanted to deny it, but she felt the heat in her ears. Great. If she ever met Eliza in person, she'd have to wear a hat.

"Aren't you going to answer?" Salem asked. "You're not going to ignore her now that you've admitted your crush, are you?"

"No, of course not." Denny knew she was responsible for her own feelings; she wouldn't punish Eliza for them. She could do this, right? All she had to do was to act normally and wait out this crush so she wouldn't fuck up a wonderful friendship. She tickled Salem's toes until she removed her feet from Denny's lap so she could steady the phone against her thigh.

Sneakers and skirt, or do I break with tradition? Eliza's text said.

Sneakers, Denny answered, awkwardly tapping at the keys with her left hand. *If the date isn't going well, at least you can sprint out of there.*

Good thinking! Thanks, Eliza replied. *So, what about your own dating life? Any news from the No More Frogs front?*

Truth be told, Denny hadn't opened the dating app since Tuesday or Wednesday. *Nope. No one's profile jumped out at me.* She had skimmed a few profiles of local women, but then she'd gotten distracted. Yeah, by searching for Eliza's profile and poring over every word of it! Shit, Salem was right. She really had a gigantic crush.

And no one's contacted you either? Eliza asked.

I haven't checked in a while, but I don't think so, Denny typed back. *You didn't expect them to be lining up at my virtual door, did you?*

Um, well, I had a feeling someone would contact you soon.

That made one of them. Still, Eliza's confidence in her ability to attract women felt good.

So you don't have plans for tonight? Eliza asked. *Wait. It's inventory day, isn't it?*

Eliza's familiarity with her schedule was nice. It made her feel as if her everyday life mattered. *Yeah, it is, but this time, I won't be there for the counting-stock fun. I'm out sick.*

What? You're sick, and you're only mentioning it now?

Denny ducked her head. *I'm sorry. I didn't mean to keep it from you, but I'm usually more the suffer-in-silence type. Plus I didn't want to bother you when there's nothing you can do about it.*

You don't know that. I make a mean chicken soup.

The image of Eliza showing up on her doorstep with a huge pot of soup made Denny smile. *I'm not sick-sick. I don't think your chicken soup would do much good for tendonitis.*

You've got tendonitis? Eliza asked. *How did that happen?*

The doc said it's from too many repetitive movements of my wrist.

Oh, really? Looks like we desperately need to find you a girlfriend! Eliza added a bunch of crying-laughing emojis.

A flush of heat swept up Denny's neck.

"Are you sure it's just a little crush?" Salem commented from her end of the couch. "Now it's not only your ears that have turned red. You look like a fire hydrant all over."

"Don't you have something better to do than watch me? Like finish your movie?"

Salem grinned broadly. "No. You're much more entertaining than Rebel Wilson and Liam Hemsworth."

"Thanks, I guess." Denny returned her attention to her conversation with Eliza. *The overuse is from sitting at the register, scanning stuff all day, and from lifting heavy stock, not from...that!*

God, you're so much fun to tease! Eliza typed back. *But seriously, what did the doctor say? You'll be fine, right?*

Yeah. I just need to take it easy, ice it every now and then, and wear a brace for a week. That's why I'm texting at the speed of an arthritic turtle, in case you were wondering.

God, Denny! You should have told me! You should stop texting and rest your arm.

Denny made a face, probably the one resembling her niece when she learned they'd be having zucchini for dinner. *Don't want to,* she replied.

Her phone rang in her hand, making her jump.

She glanced at the screen to see who was calling.

Shit, it was Eliza!

Her heart leaped into her throat and clattered there like a bird trying to break free. No, no, no! What was Eliza doing? She wasn't ready for this. What was she supposed to say? What if she said something wrong, something that gave away her crush and made things awkward between them?

"Pick up," Salem said.

"No! It's Eliza, and I—"

The phone stopped ringing.

Relief and regret warred within Denny, and she wasn't sure what won out. She lowered her gaze to the screen as a message popped up.

Not in the mood to talk? Eliza asked, followed by a sad face. *I thought it would be easier on your wrist, but if you're not up for it...*

Regret won the wrestling match, helped along by a heavy dose of guilt. The last thing she wanted was to make Eliza think she didn't want to talk to her. But there was only one way to undo that: she needed to call her back.

Denny sucked air into her oxygen-starved lungs. Okay, she could do this. She was a mature woman of forty-one...well, mostly mature woman. It was just a phone call with a friend.

A friend she had a major crush on.

Her fingers trembled as she tapped the screen a few times, then she pressed the phone to her ear.

While the phone rang, Salem got up from the couch, patted Denny's shoulder, and left the room, giving her some privacy.

The ringing stopped, and the call connected.

Denny said the first thing that came to mind. "Uh, hi. It's me. Denny."

A chuckle drifted through the phone, gentle as a Portland drizzle, not hard and mocking at all. "I know. Hi, Denny. It's so good to finally hear your voice."

Wow. That voice. It was warm and melodious, as she had imagined, and the way Eliza said her name set off tingles everywhere.

"Denny? You still there?"

Great. She sat, phone clutched to her ear, listening to Eliza's voice with her mouth gaping open. Thank God Eliza hadn't FaceTimed her! "Uh, yeah. Still here. Sorry I didn't pick up when you called. I, uh... Like I said, that brace is making me slow as a turtle."

"Liar." Eliza's tone was still warm and slightly amused. "You do know there's no need to pretend with me, don't you?"

Denny hung her head. "Yeah. I know that. I just..."

"Don't worry. I get it. Would it help if I do the talking and you just ooh and aah in all the right places?"

Denny laughed, and a part of her tension receded from her body as if she had been submerged in a bubble bath. "How do I know what the right places are?"

"Why don't we assume I'm a brilliant and fascinating conversationalist, so any time I pause to draw a breath would be the right place."

"Ooh," Denny said, followed by, "Aah."

Eliza's laughter burst through the phone. "See? There was no need to worry at all. You've got this conversation thing down pat already!"

They were both silent for several seconds. With anyone else, Denny would have feverishly tried to think of something to say, but to her surprise, she found it wasn't an awkward silence at all. She smiled against the phone, and she had a feeling Eliza was doing the same.

"So," she said after a while, "when's your date with what's-his-name?"

"His name is Ben...or SongBoy77. We agreed to meet for drinks and karaoke at the Voicebox at eight."

Denny glanced at her wristwatch again. It was a few minutes after seven. Damn. Just when she was finally starting to relax and enjoy talking to Eliza, she had to let her go. "Then shouldn't you get going? You're not riding your bike, are you?" Images of Eliza smashing into another car sliced through her mind, making her shudder.

"No."

"Good. Riding your bike after dark isn't safe." She tried to ignore the fact that it might mean SongBoy77 would drive her home, walk her to her door, and kiss her good night. Would Eliza kiss him back?

"No, I meant, I don't have to get going."

"Uh, you don't? Why not?"

"Because when you told me you're sick, I sent him a text, asking him to meet tomorrow instead. You kept me company when I was bruised and couch-bound; now it's my turn."

Aww. Denny's hands warmed. In fact, her entire body, starting with her chest area, was warming up. She knew she should tell Eliza she didn't have to stay home because of her, but for once, she wanted to be a tiny bit selfish. "Thanks," she said quietly.

"No need to thank me. Actually, Ben should be thanking you for giving his ears a reprieve."

Now it was Denny's turn to say, "Liar." With a voice as pleasant as Eliza's, there was no way her singing was that bad.

Eliza chuckled. "Okay, I admit I haven't managed to make anyone's ears bleed yet. What about you? Are you a karaoke champ?"

"Hell, no! Me going on stage, singing in front of a bunch of strangers?" She shuddered.

"Ah, right. But maybe you'd enjoy it without an audience. I've got a karaoke game on my Xbox," Eliza said. "We should play it sometime."

The casual mention of them getting together made Denny tense up with a complex mix of longing and dread. She swallowed heavily. "You've got to give me some time to practice my singing before that."

"Take all the time you need." Eliza's voice got even warmer, if that was possible.

They both knew singing practice wasn't the real reason Denny needed more time, but Denny was fine with Eliza knowing—as long as she didn't sense what the biggest reason was: Denny was hoping to get over her crush before meeting her.

Yeah, fat chance of that happening, a little voice in the back of her mind whispered as Eliza regaled her with the story of a customer who had called Feathered Friends this week to complain about getting his finger stuck in a finger trap they sold stuffed with nuts.

Why did Eliza have to be so funny on top of being kind and genuine?

Chapter 11

THE NEXT EVENING, SONGBOY77 A.K.A. Ben bowed with a flourish, as if he had just delivered a Grammy Award–worthy performance, and jumped from the stage. Admittedly, his singing was pretty good. Too bad the same couldn't be said about their date.

With an Elvis-like swagger, he strode back toward their table. "That was great, wasn't it?"

Eliza stared at him. *How about some modesty, buddy?* She much preferred Denny's adorable shyness to his bravado. "Uh, yeah."

Sweat dripped off his receding hairline and barely missed her virgin piña colada as he leaned down and reached for her.

What the hell? Was he trying to kiss her? Eliza pushed her chair back, away from him, and jumped up. "Would you excuse me for a minute?" She nodded toward the restrooms.

"Sure. I'll be here, missing you."

Eliza didn't know what to say to that, so she squeezed past him in the crowded bar and fled to the ladies' room. The door hadn't even closed behind her when she had her phone to her ear. "Looks like the sneakers will get a workout tonight," she said as soon as Denny answered.

"That bad?" Denny asked without missing a beat.

"It didn't get off to a good start. I didn't recognize him when he walked in. He looked fifteen years older than his profile pic and not nearly as hot," Eliza answered. "No biggie, I figured. I'm open to dating an older guy."

Denny coughed.

Eliza paused in her monologue. "You okay? You're not getting sick on top of the tendonitis, are you?"

"No, no, I'm fine. Go on."

"Anyway, I'd like to believe I'm not so superficial that I would reject a guy just because he's going bald and has a flat butt."

"You checked out his butt?"

Eliza leaned against the sink and put on a new coat of lipstick. "Of course. You don't? Are you more of a breast woman?"

A stranger joined Eliza at the sink and sent her a curious look, but Eliza ignored her.

"Um..." Denny cleared her throat, and Eliza grinned as she imagined her flushing a bright pink. "I mean, I would be lying if I said I don't notice when a woman has a nice butt or a nice, uh, bust, but believe it or not, I'm more of a smile-and-eyes woman."

Eliza sighed. Why couldn't her dates share that attitude? Ben had stared at her chest with obvious disappointment within two minutes of meeting her. But then again, she had noticed his flat butt too.

"But we aren't talking about me," Denny continued. "You were about to tell me about Flat Butt Boy. Is he a contender for the coveted Worst-Eliza-Date-Ever Award?"

"He's getting there. We're at Voicebox, right? So he climbed up on stage and, in front of the entire crowd, dedicated a song to me."

"And you think that's bad?" Denny sounded puzzled. "Seems kind of nice to me."

"It might have been...if he hadn't called me his girlfriend not even ten minutes after first meeting me!" Eliza caught the wide-eyed gaze of the girl next to her. "And I think he just tried to kiss me."

Denny was silent for a moment, then burst out, "What a creep! Do you need me to come get you?"

Warmth flowed through Eliza, like the first sunshine after the long, rainy Portland winter. She knew Denny was still fighting to overcome her shyness and work up the courage to meet in person. It meant the world to her that Denny would offer to come get her despite her own insecurities. "Thanks, Denny. But that won't be necessary. I borrowed Heather's car. Now all I need is to make up some kind of emergency, and I'll be out of here."

"I'm on it," Denny said with determination. "One emergency coming up in, say, five minutes?"

"Phew! Super-Denny to the rescue! Thanks."

Denny chuckled. "If you're going to call me that, you'd better send me a red cape."

"Ooh, and one of those tight spandex costumes too?" Eliza grinned as she imagined Denny in a miniskirt or a strapless breastplate. No, that so wasn't Denny, even though a skimpy outfit like that would reveal the strong shoulders, sturdy legs, and cuddly curves she suspected were hiding beneath Denny's pants and shirt.

Denny huffed. "Ew. No, thanks. Butch superheroines have a different dress code. Besides, how am I supposed to rescue damsels in distress while having to worry about my boobs popping out?"

A giggle rose up Eliza's chest. "True. Okay, you get to choose your own superhero outfit."

The door swung closed behind the girl eavesdropping on Eliza's conversation, and she realized she had been hiding out in the restroom for too long. "I'd better get back to the table. Five minutes?"

"Five minutes," Denny said.

They ended the call without either of them saying goodbye.

Eliza glanced into the mirror once more, swiped a strand of hair behind her ear, then walked back outside.

"There you are. For a minute, I thought you had climbed out the bathroom window," Ben said with a laugh as she joined him at the table.

Darn. Why hadn't she considered that? Eliza managed a weak laugh.

"So, do you want me to do another song, or are you ready to get out of here?" he asked. "I thought we could go to my place."

She couldn't help staring at him. They hadn't exchanged more than a few polite sentences all night. He couldn't seriously think she would sleep with him!

He laughed. "Not for what you're thinking. Although I could probably be talked into that if you try hard enough." He winked at her. "I just thought you'd like to meet my folks."

Words failed her. He wanted her to meet his parents...on their first date? And apparently, he still lived at home.

Thankfully, her phone rang before she was forced to tell him what she thought of that idea. "I'm so sorry. I have to take that. It's my roommate." She tapped the green button before he said, "Go ahead."

The first thing she heard was a low, drawn-out moan that vibrated through her entire body. "Denny? Is that you? Are you all right?" For a second, she really was worried. Was this the emergency Denny had planned to fake, or was it real?

"Y-yes." Denny panted like a dog in a hot car. "I think my water just broke."

"Your water just broke?" Eliza didn't have to fake her amazement. She hadn't expected that excuse.

More panting drifted through the phone, paired with little gasps. "The babies are coming!"

"Babies?" Eliza repeated. Plural? She bit back a laugh. Apparently, Denny thought one baby wasn't enough of a reason to run out on a date.

"Triplets," Denny answered. "At least. Get your ass to the hospital now!"

"Which hospital?"

"St. Immaculate Conception."

A burst of laughter threatened to break free. Quickly, Eliza pressed her fist to her mouth and pretended to stifle an alarmed gasp. She peeked at Ben to see if he bought it.

He stared back at her with wide eyes and mouthed, "Babies?"

She nodded and held up three fingers. "Okay, just keep breathing."

"Not planning to stop anytime soon," Denny quipped.

Eliza bit her lip to stop a grin from forming. "I'll be there as fast as I can." She hung up before Denny could say anything else to make her laugh.

"Your roommate is pregnant with triplets? Wow, cool." Ben lifted his beer in a toast.

For a moment, Eliza felt bad. Maybe she should have just told him there was no spark for her there instead of faking a triplet emergency.

"Did I mention that multiples run in my family too? And we don't do small babies either. Nine pounds, five ounces." He proudly tapped his chest. "Just to give you fair warning." He didn't laugh or even grin, as if them having kids together was a foregone conclusion.

Eliza's flash of guilt vanished as fast as it had arrived. "Sorry. I have to get to the hospital. I'm her birth partner."

"Yeah, of course."

Before he could try to kiss her, she grabbed her purse and made her escape.

On her way to the car, she called Denny. "Oh my God." She clutched her ribs with her free hand and allowed her laughter to bubble up. "When you fake an emergency, you really go all out!"

"Just quoting my sister when she was in labor with Bella," Denny said. "She was convinced it was either triplets or an alien."

"Oh, did she give birth at St. Immaculate Conception too?" Eliza paused in front of Heather's car and pressed the key fob to unlock the door. "I nearly bit through my lip trying not to laugh when you said that!"

Denny grinned. "Well, at least you had fun on a date for a change."

Eliza's laughter gentled to a soft smile as a wave of affection swept through her. She hadn't laughed so much on a date in a long time. Why couldn't the guys she dated be more like Denny—fun, sweet, and easy to talk to? "Yeah, I did."

"Are you in the car?"

Eliza slid behind the wheel. "Mm-hmm."

"Okay, we'd better hang up. No talking or texting while you drive," Denny said. "But let me know when you're home safe and sound."

"Will do." Eliza put the seat belt on but didn't start the car yet. "Denny?"

"Yes?"

"Thanks for being my spandex-free superheroine."

"Anytime."

Eliza dangled the car key in front of Heather. "Here's your baby back, safe and sound." The word *baby* reminded her of Denny's fake triplet emergency, eliciting a smile.

Heather took the key and playfully clutched her chest. "Oh my! Is that Eliza Harrison, smiling after a date? Come in and tell me all about it!" Without waiting for a reply, she took hold of Eliza's hand and pulled her across the doorstep, into her apartment, and to the couch. "How was it? Did you have fun?"

"Well, if you consider being invited home to meet the parents and being warned that big babies run in the family fun..."

Heather's lips twitched as if she didn't know whether to laugh or to frown. "On the first date? You're kidding me!"

"Nope. I swear!"

"Where do you keep finding these guys?" Heather asked with a shake of her head.

Eliza poked her. "On the dating app you talked me into using."

Heather walked to her kitchenette and poured them both a glass of red wine. "So, if the guy was a weirdo, why are you in such a smiley mood?"

"Oh, just something Denny did to allow me to escape."

Heather sat next to her, handed over one of the wineglasses, and studied her over the rim of her own. "Um, speaking of Denny... I did it!"

"Did what?"

"I sent her a message through No More Frogs."

Eliza clutched her glass. A week had passed since they had last talked about it, so she had assumed Heather had given up on that idea. "Oh."

"She hasn't mentioned it?" Heather asked.

"No. I think she hasn't checked her No More Frogs messages for most of the week."

"I hoped that's what's going on, and not that she ran screaming when she found out we know each other." Heather tilted her head and studied Eliza. "It's not going to be weird for you, is it?"

"No, why would it be weird?"

"Because you look"—Heather squinted—"worried."

Eliza stared into the depths of her red wine, then glanced back up. "I just don't want either of you to get hurt."

Heather paused mid-sip. "You think Denny would hurt me?"

"No! God, no. Denny is the kindest, sweetest person you can imagine. I'm sure she'll treat you like a queen."

"Then what's the problem? Surely you don't think I'd hurt her, do you?"

"Of course I don't." What was the problem? Eliza couldn't tell where that feeling of unease came from, but it had lingered since Heather had first mentioned wanting to ask Denny out. Was she worried that they wouldn't get along—or maybe that they *would* get along, become a couple, and then no longer have time for her? "Sorry. It's nothing. I think I've developed some kind of dating paranoia."

Heather chuckled. "Dating paranoia?"

"Yeah. Like suddenly, I can't imagine a date going well. Your little app messed me up for life."

"I hope not!" Heather pretended to bite her manicured nails. "I'm counting on being the bridesmaid who seduces all the other bridesmaids at your wedding."

"Good to know my potential wedding features so prominently in your love life. You do know that my sisters would be your fellow bridesmaids, don't you?"

Heather shuddered. "Ugh. No offense. Your sisters are cute, but I consider you the sister I never had, so that would be almost incestuous. I think I'll stick to No More Frogs dates."

Which led them back to Heather asking Denny out. "So, what did you write in your message to her?"

"Ha! Like she won't read you the whole thing word for word as soon as she—"

Eliza's phone chirped, announcing a text from Denny.

"See?" Heather smirked. "That probably means she finally saw my message and wants your take on it."

Eliza fought the urge to check her phone right away. Instead, she wagged a finger at Heather. "I'm warning you. If you two get together, then have a messy breakup three months later and never want to talk to each other again, tough luck! You'll have to find a way to get along because I'm not giving up my friendship with either of you."

Heather waved her hand. "Don't worry. We're lesbians. We always stay friends with our exes. It's in the handbook."

"Good. Because she's going to be one of my bridesmaids too."

"Ooh!" Heather bounced up and down, somehow managing not to spill her red wine. "So I do have chances to sleep with a bridesmaid after all!"

Eliza reached over to poke her again—and promptly managed to slosh wine all over her favorite pair of jeans. "Damn. I'd better soak this." With several big gulps, she finished the remainder. "Thanks again for lending me your car."

"Mi coche es tu coche."

Heather walked her to the door, where they exchanged a quick hug.

Then Eliza jogged over to her own apartment, in a hurry to soak her jeans—and, if she was being honest with herself, to read Denny's text.

She kicked the door closed behind her and unbuttoned her jeans with one hand while opening her messages app with the other.

There was indeed a text from Denny waiting for her. *OMG! Someone on No More Frogs sent me a message! What do I do?*

The panicked text made her smile but also drove home the point of how vulnerable Denny was. God, she hoped this wouldn't backfire.

Denny paced her room with the phone tightly clutched in one hand. Eliza had sent her a message saying she'd made it home fifteen minutes ago. Why wasn't she answering?

Instead of emitting the usual cha-chung announcing a text from Eliza, her phone rang. Eliza's name flashed across the screen.

Apparently, that was their normal modus operandi regarding communication now.

Denny was fine with that. She quickly tapped the accept button. "Did you see my text?" This time, it was she who started the conversation in the middle, without saying hello. "I got a message from a woman on No More Frogs! What do I do?"

"First, you take a deep breath," Eliza answered. "It's a harmless message, not a crocodile leaping at you."

Denny forced herself to stop her pacing and take a series of calming breaths. "Right. No reptiles with sharp teeth around." She chuckled, but it still sounded nervous to her own ears. "Sorry for freaking out. I just..."

"No need to apologize or explain. I get it."

And Denny sensed she really did. Eliza got her. That feeling settled over her like the superheroine cape she had requested earlier, making her feel just as invincible. She flopped onto her bed. "Thank you."

"No thanks needed either," Eliza said. Water splashed in the background.

"Where are you?" Denny asked. "Is it raining? I thought you were home."

"I am. I'm soaking my jeans."

Eliza continued talking, saying something about red wine, but the words didn't register. Denny's brain was busy picturing Eliza standing at the sink in just the sheer blouse she sometimes wore on dates and a pair of panties.

Stop it, she told herself, but her imagination had other ideas and showed her a close-up of Eliza's smooth legs. She pressed her pillow to her face, hoping the cotton would cool her cheeks. Finally, she shook off the mental image just in time to hear Eliza's question.

"Have you read it?"

Denny pulled the pillow from her face. "Read what?"

"The message, of course."

"No. I was waiting for you." Did that make her sound like a coward? Well, if it did, she didn't care. She trusted that Eliza wouldn't judge her.

"Okay, let's do it together," Eliza said. "I think I, um, might have to explain a thing or two."

About how to send a message back? That should be pretty self-explanatory, right? Denny pulled out her laptop so she could keep talking to Eliza while she logged in to her profile. The message from BodaciousJedi still sat in her No More Frogs in-box.

She opened it with a click. "I'm going to read it to you. Let me know what you think. So, BodaciousJedi says: Hi, Denny. Before we get to the usual icebreaker chitchat, I— Wait!" Denny's gaze flew back up to the top of the message, and a tremor of alarm went through her. "She called me Denny, not Shy_in_Portland! I thought you said the platform only shows other users my handle, not my real name! How does she—?"

"Denny, wait. Let me explain. Or maybe just read the rest of the message."

What the hell was going on? Denny forced herself to calm down and keep reading. "Before we get to the usual icebreaker chitchat, I have to tell you that we already know each other. Well, kind of." She stopped reading and sucked in a breath. "You... This isn't...?"

"This isn't what?" Eliza asked.

Denny shook her head. For a second, she had thought the message was from Eliza. But that was impossible. Eliza was straight and not interested in someone like her. Why would she send her a message through a dating app? "Nothing." She continued to read, hoping it would distract Eliza from asking again. "While I'd like to think I'm pretty bodacious in real life too, I'm not a Jedi. I'm a school bus driver. In fact, I'm your niece's school bus driver."

The phone nearly slid from Denny's grasp. "What the...?" She clicked on BodaciousJedi's icon, which took her to her profile page. The photo at the top showed a blonde woman in a yellow summer dress, sticking out her tongue at whoever had taken the photo. With the lightsaber in her hands, she looked like a geeky version of Marilyn Monroe.

Denny clicked on the photo to enlarge it.

It was indeed Ms. Burkhart, Bella's school bus driver. "Oh my God! You won't believe this! She's the woman I nearly asked out the day we first exchanged texts!"

"Um, you did?"

"Yeah. Salem tried to talk me into it, but I, um, chickened out at the last moment." Denny couldn't stop shaking her head. "What a strange coincidence that we'd both be on No More Frogs."

"Don't freak out, but it's not a coincidence."

For the very first time, she and Eliza didn't seem to be speaking the same language. "What do you mean?"

"She's the one who told me about No More Frogs, and I nudged you to use it, so...not really a coincidence. At least not that part."

"She told you...? Wait, you mean you know Ms. Burkhart?"

"Yeah. Her first name is Heather."

"H-Heather? Wait, you mean...your Heather is Ms. Burkhart?" Denny moved the phone away from her ear and stared at it, then stared at her laptop and the message. A few words jumped out at her: *Number neighbor. Heather. Eliza's friend.* The bed seemed to rotate around her as if she'd had a few too many beers.

"Denny? Denny?" Eliza's muffled voice came from the phone.

Denny moved it back to her ear. "Still here. I think. Wow. What are the chances?"

"Well, there are six hundred thousand people in Portland and about fifty kids on Heather's bus. If I had paid better attention in math, I could tell you exactly what the chances are."

Grasping mathematical formulas was beyond Denny's capability right now. Her head was still spinning. "How long have you known?"

"Just since Heather found your profile on No More Frogs last Saturday. I would have told you, but I figured it was up to Heather to do that."

Both were silent for several moments.

"You're not angry with me, are you?" Eliza sounded uncharacteristically timid.

"No, I just... It feels like someone is playing a prolonged April Fools' Day prank on me."

"No prank, I swear," Eliza said. "Just one of life's strange coincidences. Like me sending a text message to a stranger—and ending up with a friend. This isn't going to interfere with our friendship, is it?"

Denny sat up. "No. It was just a bit of a shock. But I'm over it now. I think. How did Heather take it?"

"She was stunned, but only for a second. There's not much that could throw Heather for a loop," Eliza said. "But she nearly gave me a heart attack when she burst into my apartment to show me Butch Auntie's profile."

"Butch Auntie?"

"I hope that doesn't offend you," Eliza said. "Heather couldn't figure out an inconspicuous way to ask Bella for your name, so that's what she called you."

"I am butch, so why would that offend me?" Denny paused. "So...does that mean she wanted to ask Bella about me? Like, she noticed me?"

"Oh yeah. I don't want to break any confidences, but yes, she did notice you. Didn't she say so in her message?"

Denny slid her glasses higher up on her nose. "Um, I didn't read past her big reveal." She pulled the laptop closer and read the rest of the message.

The last paragraph said: *So, if all this hasn't sent you screaming for the hills, never to be heard of again, would you be interested in going out with me sometime? If you are, give me a call. I think you've got my number. No pun intended. It's the same as yours, just with a nine at the end.*

"She asked me out," Denny said out loud.

"Will you? Go out with her, I mean."

Was she imagining things, or did Eliza sound hesitant? Probably just wishful thinking, right? It wasn't as if she was jealous. "I guess so."

"You don't sound very enthusiastic," Eliza said.

"No, no, it's not that. I mean, I wanted to ask her out six weeks ago, so...of course I'm enthusiastic." That wasn't a complete lie, more of an exaggeration. Maybe Denny would have been more eager two months ago, but now...

She clicked over to Eliza's profile, which she had added to her favorites, and stared at the photo of Eliza doubled over, laughing, as her chestnut-brown hair flew everywhere. God, she was hopeless.

And that was why going out with Heather was a good idea. Dating another woman would help her get over that silly crush.

"Great," Eliza said. "That's really great."

"Yeah."

For once, silence stretched between them until Eliza said quietly, "Um, I have a favor to ask."

"Anything," Denny said without a moment's hesitation. "What is it? If you're worried that I'll be a total douchebag toward Heather..."

"No, that's not it. I know you couldn't be a douchebag, even if your life depended on it. It's got nothing to do with Heather."

"What is it, then?"

"Okay, this will probably sound silly, but..."

When Eliza hesitated, Denny's heartbeat picked up. She scolded herself. This wasn't one of the rom-coms she watched with Salem.

Eliza wasn't about to confess a crush on her. But her heart didn't listen. It continued to pound, each heartbeat vibrating in her ears, nearly drowning out what Eliza said next.

"Um, do you think we—you and I—could meet first? Before you and Heather do."

Good thing Denny was already sitting because her bones and muscles melted into a puddle of goo. "God, yes." She mentally slapped her forehead, cleared her throat, and tried to sound more casual. "I'd like that."

"I know it's silly and probably makes me sound like the spoiled youngest child who wants to keep her friend to herself, but..."

"I said I'd like that, in case you missed my reply." A grin tugged on Denny's lips. It was nice to have Eliza be the one who rambled on for once—and it was nice how important this was to her.

Eliza's mouth snapped shut audibly in the middle of what she'd been saying. "Oh. Are you sure? I know you weren't quite ready to—"

"I'm sure," Denny said. "I mean, it's a first get-together between friends, not a date, right? So no reason to be nervous." And if she kept telling herself that a thousand times a day, she might believe it by the time they met.

"Right. No reason at all." Eliza's breathing reverberated through the phone. "So...when and where?"

Denny's mind scurried in a hundred different directions at once, but none of her ideas were special enough. *Not a date,* she firmly repeated to herself. But that didn't make meeting Eliza in person any less special. "You pick."

"The Rose Festival opens next Friday," Eliza said. "I don't know if you're fine with a bit of a crowd, but if you are... Would you like to go down to the waterfront, then watch the fireworks with me?"

Denny bit back a sigh. "Sounds perfect."

A beautiful fireworks display on the waterfront, lights reflecting off the shimmering river, and the crowd around them forcing them to lean close to talk. She grimaced. Yeah, that sounded like the perfect meeting place to get over her crush.

"Eliza Louise Harrison," she muttered, staring at her reflection in the mirror above the sink, "what the hell was that?"

Why had she asked Denny to meet her first? Despite her jokes about having been terribly spoiled as a child, she wasn't an entitled brat. That "I became friends with her first, so I should get to meet her first" attitude so wasn't her.

But then why was she behaving like a jealous teenager? If she didn't know any better, she'd think she had a crush on Denny.

She chuckled, then stopped abruptly. No, that couldn't be... could it?

Eliza stared at her flushed cheeks in the mirror. That was just from gulping down the red wine too fast, right?

She splashed some water onto her face, then looked back up into her own eyes.

Okay, time to be straight with herself. She smiled at her mental choice of words. By tomorrow morning, the red-wine flush would be gone, but she knew without a doubt she'd still want to be the first to meet Denny.

Maybe she did have a girl crush on her.

So what? No big deal. It happened, even to straight women. Denny was so incredibly sweet; who wouldn't develop a crush on her?

Next week, they would finally meet, and while she had no doubt she would find Denny just as adorable in person, there would, of course, be no physical attraction.

Her crush would mature into a deep friendship, and maybe one day, she would be the bridesmaid looking for a hookup at Denny and Heather's wedding.

Okay, she probably wouldn't, since she wasn't the hookup type. But she hoped the friendship part of her prediction would come true, and she and Denny would be in each other's lives for many years to come.

Chapter 12

THE SIX DAYS LEADING UP to the Rose Festival passed in a blur—way too fast and incredibly slowly at the same time.

Denny's nervousness grew with every hour that brought her closer to meeting Eliza. She wasn't half as nervous regarding her date with Heather, which they had set up for the weekend after she met with Eliza.

Maybe it was a good thing she was still off work. She was so distracted she probably would have handed back the wrong amount of change to customers or accidentally locked herself in the cooler room.

At four o'clock on Friday afternoon, Denny pulled outfit after outfit from her closet, trying to decide what to wear.

Should she wear the gray chinos? They might be overkill for the festival, but Eliza had thought she looked great in them when she had shared the photo.

You're not trying to impress her, she firmly told herself. *This is not a date.*

But she reached for the chinos anyway. Nothing wrong with wanting to look good for a friend, right?

She studied her choice of shirts.

The weather had turned warmer, and the sun peeked out from behind the clouds. Maybe something with short sleeves would make sense. She didn't want to be sweaty before she even arrived.

Finally, she decided on the baby-blue, short-sleeved button-up Salem had given her for her last birthday. Once she had the shirt on, she ran a hand over the fabric to make sure her breasts didn't strain it. The last thing she needed was to pop a button.

She turned sideways in front of her mirrored closet door, sucked in her belly, and craned her neck to study her butt. *What are you doing? She's not going to check out your butt!*

Denny untucked the shirt, then shook her head and tucked it back in. Her gaze went to her arms, usually one of her best features. But even after a week off work, small cuts and scratches from the boxes she handled still covered her forearms. Jeez, she looked as if she'd had a run-in with an aggressive cat! Should she wear a long-sleeved shirt after all?

Before she could decide, the door to her room opened, and Salem stuck her head in. "Hey, why does your bathroom smell like a perfume store?"

Denny froze. Oh no. Had she put on too much cologne? She sniffed herself. Yeah, she had overdone it a little, but it would dissipate by the time she got downtown.

"Oh, I see. First-date jitters." Salem stepped inside with an indulgent grin.

"It's not a date," Denny repeated her mantra. "I'm meeting Eliza."

"Yeah, you mentioned that a time or two...hundred." Salem flopped down amid the clothes on Denny's bed.

"Careful! Don't wrinkle that shirt! I might want to wear it." Denny pulled out the red chambray shirt from under her sister.

Salem tilted her head. "Why? The one you have on looks great."

"Really?" Denny tapped her arms. "Even with all the scratches?"

"Jeez, Denny! Didn't you say Eliza makes bird toys for a living? Don't you think she has a nick or two?"

She hadn't thought of that. Well, that solved the shirt problem. Denny turned back toward the mirror and smoothed her hand over the back of her head, trying to tame her cowlick.

Salem hopped off the bed and stepped up behind her, studying Denny's face in the mirror. Finally, she caught Denny's hand and pulled her around. "Stop worrying so much. I guarantee she'll like you, scratches, cowlick, and all."

"I know it's silly. I just..." Denny gestured as she tried in vain to find the right words to explain.

"I know." Salem wrapped her arms around her in an encouraging hug.

Denny hugged her back, even as she protested, "Don't—"

"Wrinkle the shirt, I know." Salem gave her another squeeze, then let go.

Bella shoved the door open and walked in with total disregard of the sisterly bonding she was interrupting. "Ew. Why does it smell like a perfume bottle exploded in here?"

Christ, was it that bad? Denny sniffed herself again.

"Your aunt is meeting Eliza at the festival," Salem said.

"Awesome, can I come?" Bella directed pleading puppy-dog eyes at Denny, who stood frozen.

"Not today," Salem said.

Bella's bottom lip quivered the way it had when she'd been a toddler being denied another cookie. "Please!" She glanced back and forth between them. "All my friends are going too."

For once, Denny wasn't tempted to give in. "I'll take you tomorrow, if you still want to go."

"But I want to meet Sneaker Woman too, and she's not going to be there tomorrow."

No way. Wanting her to meet the family was what had made Eliza run from SongBoy77. Denny wouldn't make the same mistake. "You will get to meet her, but not today."

Bella folded her arms across her chest. "When then?" A smile chased the pout off her face. "Oh! I've got a genius idea! She can come to my birthday party!"

Denny wasn't so sure Eliza would consider hanging out at a kid's birthday party a genius idea. "I'll ask her if I get a chance. But right now I've got to get going, or I'll be late."

They had agreed to meet by the entrance at six. That gave them nearly four hours to explore the festival, check out the carnival rides, and sample the food at various booths before the fireworks display.

Four hours. Denny swallowed. What would they be talking about for that long? Would there be awkward silences? Would Eliza grow bored spending so much time with her?

She tried to tell herself it wouldn't be any different from talking on the phone, but she knew it was a lie.

After one last glance at her reflection, she decided the cowlick was as tame as it was going to get. She grabbed her wallet and favorite jacket and walked to the door.

"Good luck," Salem called after her.

"Thanks," Denny called back.

The last thing she heard before the front door closed after her was Bella asking, "Why does she need luck if she's only meeting Sneaker Woman?"

Her niece had no idea. For Denny, there was no such thing as *only Sneaker Woman.*

Eliza had been on four dates with four different guys in the past seven weeks, but her hands had always been steady when she had applied some makeup and mascara. Now, she was jittery, as if she'd chugged a gallon of coffee.

She paused with the mascara brush raised halfway to her lashes. Why did she even need makeup and mascara? It was supposed to be a fun evening at the festival with a friend—a friend who would like her the way she was, no makeup needed.

After hesitating for a moment, she turned on the water and scrubbed her face clean.

No need to try on half the contents of her closet either, even though the urge to do so was strong. Normally, she would have narrowed it down to her top two or three choices and then sent Denny the selfies to pick for her.

Not today. She didn't allow herself to obsess over the decision as she picked her second-favorite pair of skinny jeans—black, so if she spilled anything on them, it wouldn't show as much—and a short-sleeved, formfitting sweater that emphasized her slim waist.

Oh yeah, you're not obsessing over your outfit at all. She mentally chastised herself.

At least her choice of shoes was easy. She put on the yellow sneakers with a smile, grabbed her jacket and purse, and locked the door behind her.

Unlike Denny, she didn't live far from the waterfront. She hoped a brisk walk would allow her to get rid of her nervous energy.

As she walked up Park Avenue, she wondered how Denny was doing. Was she nervous too?

It's Denny. Of course she was nervous—Denny always was when she was meeting new people, while Eliza usually wasn't. They were far from strangers, though, and maybe that was what made Eliza as nervous as she was excited. When meeting new people, she wasn't usually invested in the outcome. If they got along, great. But if they had nothing to talk about, it wasn't a big deal.

This time, however, it mattered. If that connection she felt to Denny whenever they texted or talked on the phone wasn't there in person, she would lose a close friend, not just fail to make a new one.

She took a right onto Yamhill Street without focusing on where she was going. The Ferris wheel rising over the waterfront guided her in the right direction.

As she approached the park, a light rain began to fall.

Eliza peered at the sky. Of course. Rain on the opening day of the Rose Festival was practically a tradition. Couldn't the weather gods have made an exception this year?

Loud music from a stage drifted over, mingling with the screams and laughter from the people on various carnival rides.

It was the first day of the festival, so people crowded around the entrance. Some of them—probably tourists—carried umbrellas, blocking Eliza's line of sight.

Would she be able to make Denny out in the crowd? Would she even recognize her right away, or would Denny, like some of her dates from No More Frogs, look nothing like her photo?

She pulled her phone from her purse and texted Denny. *What are you wearing?*

Once she had sent the message, she realized it sounded like a clumsy attempt at a sexting session. *I mean, are you wearing anything that stands out so I can spot you more easily?* she added. *It's pretty crowded.*

Are you here already? Denny texted back immediately.

Yes.

Me too, Denny answered.

With shaky fingers, Eliza texted, *Where are you?*

A text bubble with the same question from Denny popped up beneath hers.

Main entrance, both replied at the same time.

Eliza dropped her phone into her purse without paying attention to where exactly it ended up. She had never considered her five-foot-six height short, but now she wished she were taller as she hopped up and down in an attempt to see over the people around her.

A guy ahead of her gave her a funny look, probably trying to figure out what the heck she was doing, but she didn't care. All her senses focused on scanning the area for a glimpse of Denny.

A group of teenagers shoved their way inside, and the crowd parted.

As if guided by a magnet, Eliza's gaze zeroed in on a figure standing next to the ticket booth.

Denny.

A smile formed on Eliza's lips as she took her in.

Her short hair was tousled, as if she had run her hands through it repeatedly, and she kept reaching up to adjust her glasses. She hadn't bothered to pull up the collar of her worn, chocolate-brown leather jacket. Had she even noticed the rain?

Eliza took one step toward her.

As if sensing her approach, Denny looked toward her.

Their gazes connected.

Eliza's steps faltered, but at the same time, she felt like rushing toward her to engulf her in a bear hug. She had to remind herself it might not be the best idea.

But then Denny walked toward her, and the timid smile on her handsome face broadened more with every step she took.

To hell with a more polite greeting. Eliza jogged the last few yards between them and launched herself into Denny's arms.

Denny's pulse pounded as if she had run a mile at full speed instead of standing around for the past twenty minutes because she'd been early. When she caught sight of Eliza, her heart thrummed even faster, yet at the same time, a strange calm overcame her.

She no longer heard the music or the laughter of the people around them. All worries about her cowlick and her love handles fled from her mind as Eliza sprinted toward her.

Denny's arms rose by pure instinct, and she caught Eliza as if she'd done it a million times before. They were the same height, even though she had always imagined herself to be taller. Despite their different builds, their bodies fit like two pieces of a puzzle. Denny tightened her hold and breathed in Eliza's light, floral scent, with a touch of something smoky. *Gentle, gentle,* she reminded herself.

But Eliza wrapped her arms around her and hugged her back just as strongly.

Denny had no idea how much time had passed when she became aware of rain dripping down her collar and someone jostling her. Quickly, she let go and took a step back. "Sorry, I'm wet." Damn, that sounded wrong. "Uh, I mean, it's raining."

A smile curved Eliza's lips.

Jesus, those lips. Having lips that sensuous should be illegal. Denny forced herself to look into Eliza's eyes. Not that they were that much safer because they were the warmest brown she had ever seen.

"It's Portland," Eliza said. "Of course it's raining."

Denny continued to drink her in. The photos hadn't been able to capture how vibrant Eliza really was. In a denim jacket and a pair of skinny jeans that emphasized her slim hips, she managed to look equally graceful and down-to-earth. *Shit.* She stared at Eliza, not saying a thing! "It's so nice to finally meet you," she squeaked.

"You too." Unless she was imagining it, Eliza was staring too. "You look exactly like your photo."

Denny slid her glasses higher up on her nose. "Is that good or bad?" She hadn't meant to ask, but apparently, when it came to Eliza, her filters were nonexistent.

"Good," Eliza said. "Very good."

They gazed at each other for several seconds until Denny couldn't stand it anymore. "Uh, shall we?" She gestured toward the entrance. "I already got us tickets."

"Oh, thanks. Then the food is on me."

Denny stuffed her hands into her jacket pockets, not knowing what to do with them, as they entered the festival grounds and strolled along the white tents. "You're wearing the infamous sneakers." She pointed at Eliza's footwear.

"Of course." Eliza smiled that devastating smile again. "I don't think I'll be forced to make a quick escape today, but I have to live up to my nickname."

The time when she had called Eliza "Sneaker Woman" seemed like a lifetime ago, not a short few months.

"So, are you ready for the three Fs?" Eliza asked as they veered right to make room for a person in a clown costume taking photos with a little girl.

"Three Fs?"

"Food. Fun. Fireworks." Eliza ticked them off on her fingers.

Denny nodded. She'd been too nervous to eat anything since breakfast, and by now, she couldn't tell if her stomach fluttered because she was nervous or because she was starving.

The sugary scent of cotton candy mingled with the aroma of chili cheese fries and corn dogs. Eliza stuck her nose in the air and sniffed like a coyote catching the scent of its favorite prey.

Did she have to be so adorable?

"Don't let me eat too much. I want to try at least one of the rides, and I can't if I'm stuffed to the gills." Eliza dug in her purse and pulled out her wallet. "What are you in the mood for?"

Denny studied the various food booths. "I'm not sure yet. What are you getting?"

"A corn dog," Eliza said without hesitation. "It's been an annual tradition ever since my parents took me to the Rose Festival for the first time as a kid—well, minus the year my oldest sister convinced me they're made of dogs."

Laughter bubbled up, chasing off most of Denny's nerves. "That's just mean."

"Don't tell me you never did anything like that to your sister."

Denny shook her head. "Never. I'm too nice to play mean tricks on my baby sister."

Eliza eyed her skeptically. "Is that what she would tell me?"

"Well, if you don't believe me, you can ask her. Bella asked me to invite you to her birthday party next weekend. I said I would. It was the only way to convince her to stay home instead of coming to the festival with us, but I know spending the afternoon with a dozen giggly preteens might not be your idea of a fun Saturday, so don't feel obliged to come." Great. Now she was babbling. Denny snapped her mouth shut.

"I'd love to come." Eliza emanated such sincerity even Denny didn't wonder whether she was just being polite.

They smiled at each other before getting in line for a corn dog.

"Want me to get you one too?" Eliza asked.

"No, thanks. I'm thinking of getting an elephant ear. Wait. Let me guess. Your sister told you they were made of elephants."

Eliza laughed. "It was my brother who told me that, but I was a year older and wiser, so I didn't fall for it."

Once they each had their chosen food, they ducked beneath a tent, out of the drizzle, and shared like old friends. It was strange to feel as if she had known Eliza for years, yet at the same time not be able to shake the impression they were on a first date, no matter how often she told herself it wasn't one. She couldn't stop looking at Eliza, drinking in every little detail.

Unlike most of the women Denny had gone out with, Eliza wasn't shy about digging in. She finished the biggest corn dog Denny had ever seen, then stole the last bite of Denny's elephant ear and unashamedly licked a dusting of cinnamon off her fingers.

Damn, why did she have to look so sexy doing that? Denny averted her gaze.

They strolled along the booths, taking in the goods and games. Whenever their shoulders brushed, Denny's entire body blazed with awareness.

"Hi, Eliza," a guy selling airbrush hoodies and T-shirts called from his booth.

A woman sketching a caricature version of a customer waved a greeting too.

Eliza waved back and exchanged a few words with them but didn't stop to talk to them for long.

"Wow," Denny said after it happened the third time. "Did you forget to tell me you're a local celebrity or something?"

"God, no. The craft people in the area just tend to know each other."

Denny doubted other craft people would be greeted so enthusiastically, but she couldn't blame them for wanting to catch Eliza's attention.

The Ferris wheel loomed in front of them. They walked beneath the Morrison Bridge, which marked the start of the carnival portion of the festival.

Children and a few adults spun on a swing carousel to their right while various games promised stuffed animals and other prizes to their left.

"Want to try your luck at one of these?" Eliza gestured toward the games.

"Yeah, bring your girlfriend over here and try to win her a teddy bear, sir," the man in the basketball toss booth called over to them. "If you sink three out of five, you can pick whatever prize you want."

Denny gritted her teeth. It wasn't the first time she'd been mistaken for a man, even though she wasn't sure how anyone could miss her breasts. She resisted the urge to pull up her jacket collar to hide her blush and peeked at Eliza. How would she react to being called Denny's girlfriend?

Eliza looked back at her, probably waiting to see if she would correct the guy's assumption about her gender. When Denny didn't, she shrugged and pointed at the hoop. "Want to try?"

Denny would have loved to win a giant teddy bear or another prize for Eliza, but that was what couples did on dates, wasn't it? She held up her right hand to show Eliza the brace sticking out of her jacket sleeve. "I think I'm out of commission."

At the sound of her voice, the guy stared at her. "Oh, sorry, ma'am. I—"

She waved him off. All she wanted was to move on.

But Eliza seemed unfazed and not in a hurry. She eyed the hoop and the stuffed animals hanging behind it. "Then I'll win you a prize."

Denny hadn't expected that. No one had ever tried to win her a stuffed animal. "You don't have to do that. It could end up costing more than buying it in a store."

Eliza didn't listen. She was already handing over some money. The basketball looked huge in her delicate hands. She took up position behind the line spray-painted on the ground. Her stance wasn't exactly NBA-approved, but Denny knew better than to break her concentration by trying to correct her. In the end, winning a prize didn't matter. The important thing was Eliza having fun—and that seemed to be the case.

Her eyes flashed with determination, and she laughed as she gave a hop and let go of the ball.

It sailed through the air in a wide arc—and went through the hoop with a soft *whoosh*.

Denny knew she was staring, slack-jawed, but she didn't care. "What was that?"

"Luck," Eliza said, but the little grin skirting her lips gave her away. She received another ball and took up a stance behind the line.

Her foot positioning would have made an NBA player shiver with disgust, but to Denny, her slim body was poetry in motion as she tossed the ball again.

This time, she wasn't surprised as it swished through the net without touching the rim.

"Uh-oh," the guy in the booth said. "I think you brought me a hustler."

Eliza smiled, then sank the ball a third time. Her attempt to look casual lasted all of one second before she cheered and engulfed Denny in a celebratory hug.

Once again, Denny had her arms around her before she became fully aware of it. She told herself to politely pat Eliza's back and step away to a safe distance, but her body had different ideas. The way Eliza felt against her was impossible to resist. She held her close for a second, then, aware of her thudding heartbeat, let go.

"Looks like *she* won *you* a prize," the guy said to Denny. "Which one do you want?"

Dazed, Denny stared at the rows of stuffed animals. "Um, you pick one," she said to Eliza.

Eliza stepped next to her, so close their shoulders brushed and her perfume teased Denny's nose. "Hmm, how about...this one?" She pointed at a foot-long orange dragon.

The guy took it from its perch. His gaze flickered to Denny before he pressed it into Eliza's hands.

"Um, it's got an underbite," Denny said.

Eliza ran one finger along the tooth sticking from the dragon's mouth in a gesture so tender that goose bumps rushed across Denny's skin. "So? It's cute."

"Guess we'll take it," Denny told the guy.

As they continued on, Eliza held out the dragon. "Here."

"Uh..."

"What?" Eliza asked with a grin. "Is carrying a stuffed animal destroying your street cred?" She gave Denny a nudge with her elbow. "Be grateful I didn't pick a pink bunny."

Denny took the dragon from her. It was kind of cute. "My street cred is nonexistent anyway. Thank you."

"You're very welcome."

"So," Denny glanced back over her shoulder at the hoop shot, "how did you do that?"

"I've always been good with my hands," Eliza said with an impish grin.

Denny tried hard to not imagine what else Eliza's hands might be good at.

"Telling me scary things about the food wasn't all my siblings did when we went to any of the festivals. They taught me all the little tricks," Eliza said. "They hang the hoop at an angle, so you have to shoot accordingly."

"No wonder I wasted thirty bucks on the hoops when I tried to win Bella Olaf, the snowman plush from *Frozen*, two years ago!"

Eliza gave her a grin and a wink. "Stick with me, and I'll teach you all the tricks."

God, this woman would be the death of her!

The powdered sugar melted on Eliza's tongue as she popped the last chunk of the funnel cake they shared into her mouth. "Yum, so good."

Denny hummed her agreement. She, however, appeared to have gotten more powdered sugar on herself than in her stomach. Her beautiful brown leather jacket was sprinkled with white dots.

Eliza itched to wipe it off. *Are you out of your mind?* Most of the powdered sugar had ended up on Denny's ample chest. No way would Eliza help clean that up. Deep down, she knew it was an excuse to see if the well-worn leather jacket was as soft as it looked anyway.

Once Denny was done, she held up her sticky fingers and then pointed at her chest. "Eating funnel cake without making a mess is clearly an art form neither of us has mastered."

Eliza glanced down. Oops. Her own jacket hadn't fared any better.

They grabbed a handful of paper napkins from the funnel cake stand and cleaned themselves up.

"Where to now?" Denny asked once they were presentable.

Eliza noticed that she'd let her make most of the decisions tonight. What a nice change of pace from the guys she'd gone out with! She wondered if Denny was like this with her dates too.

They strolled past the bumper cars, and Eliza pointed at a huge Viking ship swinging back and forth like a pendulum. Serpent heads snarled at them from the ship's bow and stern. "How about this? Unless it goes upside down. That's where I draw the line. I don't want the funnel cake to make a reappearance."

"Don't worry," Denny said. "It goes pretty high, but not upside down."

"You've tried it before?"

Denny nodded. "You haven't? I thought you were the Rose Festival pro between the two of us."

"I think this is pretty much the only ride I've never tried." Eliza glanced at the brace peeking out beneath Denny's jacket sleeve. "Is it okay to do with your arm?"

"Sure. I'll be back at work on Monday, lifting forty-pound banana boxes, so braving the high seas should be fine."

"Great. But let me hold on to him for you." Eliza pointed at the stuffed dragon in Denny's grip.

"Her," Denny said as she handed it over. "I think Ms. Underbite is a girl."

So she had named it already, after pretending she didn't really want it. Eliza held back a grin. Denny was a lot like the little dragon—tough on the outside, but a total softie on the inside.

Before she could comment, Denny led the way toward the ticket booth.

Luckily, the line wasn't too long. Within a few minutes, they climbed the metal steps to the ship.

Most of the rows were still empty, so Eliza hesitated, unsure where to sit.

"Let's take the last row," Denny said. "It goes up the highest."

So there was a bit of a daredevil in her after all. Eliza grinned.

With a soft touch to the small of her back, Denny guided her toward the stern, making sure she didn't slip on the wet metal.

When a guy she went out with touched her like that, it often made her weak in the knees—at least if it was a man she was attracted to. Apparently, her body was on autopilot, because now it reacted exactly the same. The spot where Denny's hand rested heated up until she thought Denny would feel it. When they reached the last row and Denny took her hand away, Eliza wasn't sure whether she was disappointed or relieved.

"Wait," Denny said before Eliza could slide onto the yellow bench seat.

The rain had stopped a few minutes ago, but the seat was still wet. Denny took off her jacket and put it on the bench for them to sit on.

Aww, what a gentle…um, woman. Eliza studied the short-sleeved button-up Denny wore beneath. Once the ship started moving, it might get too windy in the last row. "Won't you get cold?"

Denny laughed. "No, I'm really warm."

Yeah, me too, Eliza thought.

The rows in front of them filled while they took a seat next to each other. The leather jacket beneath Eliza was still warm from Denny's body. The lap bar lowered, locking them into place shoulder to shoulder, with their thighs softly brushing. Even through her denim jacket, Eliza felt the heat emanating from Denny.

Or was it coming off her own body? What the hell was going on? She might be the first person to die from a heatstroke on a rainy spring day in Portland.

It took her several seconds to realize the ride had started up. The Viking ship quickly picked up speed. It swung higher and higher, giving them a view of the waterfront, the river, and the high-rise buildings to the east.

"Put your hands up!" someone in the row ahead shouted.

Eliza looked at Denny. Should they?

Denny met her gaze and shrugged, then lifted her hands in the air.

Eliza let go of the lap bar too, still clutching the stuffed dragon with one hand.

They grinned at each other like two daring Vikings about to set off on an exciting new adventure.

Instead of enjoying the view from high over the waterfront, Eliza couldn't take her eyes off Denny.

The wind blew Denny's short hair back from her face, revealing her flushed cheeks, and her hazel eyes sparkled with excitement.

The stern of the ship soared up again, higher than before. At the apex of the swing, they hung suspended for what seemed like a timeless moment.

A sensation of weightlessness gripped Eliza, as if she were floating in space.

Her stomach dropped. A piercing sound—half scream, half laugh—burst from her chest. She gripped Ms. Underbite more firmly and latched on to the bar with her free hand. Her fingers tangled with Denny's, who had grabbed hold of it too.

They clung to each other, laughing, caught between giddy joy and sheer panic.

Then the ship swooped back down, and Eliza could momentarily breathe, only to be swung back up and experience that moment of zero gravity again.

Minutes later, the ship came to a halt. The lap bar rose, and they stumbled down the metal stairs on unsteady legs, holding on to each other.

"Oh my God!" Eliza pointed at the ship. "That looked so tame from down there."

"Boy, I think I'm getting too old for rides like this," Denny said with a laugh. "For a second there, I felt like my heart had stopped!"

Eliza had experienced the same sensation but didn't want to admit it. She nudged Denny with her shoulder. "Don't play the senior citizen card. You're forty-one, not eighty-one." In fact, now that they had finally met in person, their eleven-year age gap didn't seem to matter at all.

Denny slipped back into her jacket, and as they continued their stroll across the park, Eliza handed back the stuffed dragon, finally allowed herself to give in to the urge, and slid her hand onto the bend of Denny's arm. Her head still spun, but at least she found the answer to one of the many questions ricocheting through her mind: Denny's jacket was still damp, but the chocolate-colored leather felt as soft as it looked.

They left the loud music and the crowd behind and strolled along the esplanade, away from the noise and the many people who knew Eliza and wanted a word with her.

The sun had dipped beneath the horizon some time ago, and darkness had fallen. With the illuminated Ferris wheel and the twinkling festival lights in the background, the stroll along the waterfront was ridiculously romantic.

And that soft, warm hand on her arm... Denny peered at it every now and then. Was Eliza aware of what she was doing? Well, for her, it was probably something she did with all of her female friends. She couldn't know the simple touch made Denny tingle all over.

She held her left arm—the one Eliza was holding on to—very still, afraid Eliza would pull away should she do something to make her aware of it.

A middle-aged couple passed them and gave them curious looks. Maybe they realized Denny wasn't a man.

Whatever they were thinking, Eliza didn't seem to care. She left her hand where it was.

Bang!

The first firework exploded, making both of them flinch.

Was it time for the fireworks display to start already? Denny was tempted to glance at her wristwatch, but that would have required her to move the arm Eliza held on to, and she didn't want to end their contact. How could four hours have flown by so fast? That never happened to Denny when she spent time with a new person.

"Is it ten already?" Eliza asked. "How did that happen?"

"I have no idea."

Music played from loudspeakers, and more fireworks rose high up over the river. One large rocket exploded into a shower of silver rain, then changed to a dark red before cascading toward the ground and fading into the night.

"Wow," Eliza whispered, her upturned face bathed in the glow of the last red sparkles. "Did you see that one? That was beautiful."

Denny gazed at her. "Yeah."

They watched the rest of the fireworks in companionable silence, interrupted only by the music and the "oohs" and "aahs" from Eliza and the rest of the crowd.

With one last burst of color, it was over.

They cheered along with the other people staring at the sky over the waterfront.

Eliza pulled her hand from the bend of Denny's arm to clap.

Denny shivered as that spot on her arm went cold. She tucked Ms. Underbite beneath her arm and shoved her fists into the pockets of her jacket.

"What now?" Eliza turned toward her and gave her a questioning look.

Denny shuffled her feet. "You have to work tomorrow, right?"

"Yeah. Austen and I are covering the Feathered Friends booth at Saturday Market."

"Then I should probably catch the next train home." Denny gestured in the direction of the nearest train stop. "I knew parking would be horrible downtown, so I took the MAX."

"I'll walk you to the MAX stop," Eliza said.

"No, I'll walk you home."

Eliza laughed and shook her head at her. "Let's compromise, or we'll still be here at sunrise, discussing who gets to walk whom."

Denny could think of worse things than spending the night like that. *Stop! God, you're a fool!* "All right. Let's walk to the MAX stop closest to your apartment."

They turned their backs on the waterfront and strolled along Salmon Street, their steps perfectly in sync. Eliza didn't put her hand back on her arm, but every now and then, their shoulders or arms brushed as they walked.

It took only a few minutes to reach the MAX stop at the corner of Sixth and Madison, a few blocks from Eliza's apartment. One glance at the TriMet app on Denny's phone showed her train was only one minute out. She wasn't ready for their evening to end, but at the same time, she was grateful to escape and get some time alone to sort out her feelings.

As the train approached, Denny thought she saw the same mix of conflicted emotions on Eliza's face, but then Eliza smiled and stepped forward, right into Denny's personal space. She wrapped both arms around her and held her tightly.

Denny hugged her back with the stuffed dragon in one hand and the other pressed gently to Eliza's back.

Other people veered around them to get on the train, which had slid to a stop a few yards away.

Reluctantly, Denny let go.

"Call me about Bella's birthday party," Eliza said as Denny walked backward to the train. "I want to get her a gift."

"Will do. Thank you for a great evening—and for Ms. Underbite." Denny lifted the stuffed animal.

Eliza nodded and waved.

Denny was the last one through the doors. She dropped onto an empty seat.

As the train carried her away, she waved and hugged the plush dragon to her chest, where she could still feel Eliza's body against her own. Shit. She was screwed.

She had spent a total of five hours with Eliza, and already, the harmless crush she'd had on Eliza before felt like so much more.

Chapter 13

THE NEXT AFTERNOON, ELIZA RUMMAGED through one of the boxes they had brought to Saturday Market. Aha! There it was. Proudly, she held out the requested sola ball to Austen. They had put the ball into a cupcake wrapper, with a candle-shaped piece of sola sticking out of it. The cute bird toy didn't really resemble the basketball from last night, but Eliza still found herself transported back to the basketball toss booth.

The open admiration on Denny's face when Eliza had sunk three shots was burned into her memory, as were the hugs they had shared and so many other moments from last night.

Austen cleared her throat, wrenching her out of her thoughts before she could relive Denny's hug goodbye for the five hundredth time. "I said sola sticks, not sola ball."

"Oops. Sorry." Hurriedly, Eliza kneeled a second time and dug in another box for the bag of sola sticks.

When she handed it over, Austen studied her. "I think we need a break. We've been working pretty much nonstop since we set up the booth this morning. How about some tea for you and a coffee for me?"

"That would be great." Letting her boss think she was merely in need of some caffeine was easier than explaining what was really going on. Not that she could explain it, even if she tried.

She hadn't slept for more than a couple of hours last night, and it wasn't the excitement of the festival or the sugar rush from the funnel cake keeping her up.

With Austen's coffee order and a ten-dollar bill, she made her way to the panini booth that, according to Austen, sold the best coffee at Saturday Market. While she waited her turn to order, she tried to sort through her jumbled thoughts and emotions.

Last night had been a surprise; that much she knew. Not so much Denny herself. She was exactly the sweet and shy, yet fun person Eliza had expected.

It was her own reaction to Denny that surprised her.

If she'd been out with a man last night, there wouldn't be any confusion. She would know exactly what she had felt: attraction, plain and simple.

But was this really so different? The emotions weren't, just the person causing them—and that was what confused her. If she were attracted to women, wouldn't she have noticed before last night? She was thirty years old, with a wide and diverse circle of acquaintances. She had met a lot of interesting, beautiful women. But while her artistic side could easily admit they were good-looking or even gorgeous, she knew without a doubt she hadn't been attracted to any of them.

None of them had made her feel warm all over from a gentle touch on her back, and none had made her want to walk them all the way to Lents so she could spend more time with them.

Only Denny.

She couldn't deny there was something about her that made Eliza's heart beat faster. But what was it? Had her subconscious latched on to Denny's more masculine-presenting side, reacting to it as if she were a man?

But that didn't ring true either. There had been no doubt in her mind, even for a second, that she'd been with a woman last night. If anything, it was that mix of strength, chivalry, gentleness, and caring that drew her to Denny.

The person in line behind her cleared their throat when Eliza failed to step forward.

Quickly, she ordered a latte for Austen, a Ceylon tea for herself, and a coffee with just enough cream to turn it from black to a dark tan color, which she paid for with her own money. She would drop that off at Heather's booth on her way back, as a thank-you for covering their stall today.

When Heather saw her coming, she held out her hands as if she were receiving a lifesaving cure. "Gimme, gimme, gimme!" She snatched the coffee from Eliza's hand and took a big sip without bothering to check if it was too hot. "Oh my God! Marry me!"

Their stall neighbor Leanne looked up from one of her sea glass pendants. "She's not interested in feminine charms, remember?"

Eliza quickly raised the paper cup to her lips to hide behind it. God, she had to get a grip. Just because she found herself attracted to Denny didn't mean she was interested in feminine charms per se, right?

Heather playfully tossed her blonde hair over one shoulder. "Her loss." She took another sip of her coffee. "Speaking of feminine charms or females I want to charm me... How are things with Denny?"

Eliza nearly choked on a sip of tea. "Sorry." She coughed and gasped for breath. "Went down the wrong pipe. Um, why are you asking?"

"She and I, we exchanged a few messages this week, and she seems nice, but... I don't know. She's pretty slow to open up. Is she always that reserved?"

Eliza remembered the way Denny had engulfed her in a bear hug, her unrestrained laughter when Eliza had told her about the tricks her siblings had played on her, and the look of the wind in her hair on the Viking ship. No, there had been nothing reserved about Denny last night. "Um, I wouldn't say reserved. She's just a little shy. Give her some time, okay?"

Heather nodded. "I'm a patient woman."

"I'd better get going," Eliza said before Heather could ask about her evening with Denny. "My boss is waiting for her coffee."

"And we know she's not a patient woman. Hot as hell," Heather made a sizzling sound, "but not patient."

"Not that boss. Austen and I are covering the booth. Dee is meeting with a local pet supply store owner, so stop salivating."

Heather pretended to dry her chin with her sleeve.

Eliza shook her head at her. Admittedly, Dee was gorgeous. Her long, black hair, intense gray eyes, and high cheekbones made heads turn wherever she went. But while Eliza thought she was beautiful, she had never been attracted to her. Apparently, whatever newfound appreciation for feminine charms she had, it was limited to Denny.

"Talk to you later." She lifted her cup in a quick wave to Heather before making her way back to the Feathered Friends booth.

The market had become busier in the afternoon, so she had to weave around people.

As Eliza approached, a customer paused in front of their booth, checking out a macaw swing.

Eliza nearly dropped both of the cups she carried. Was she imagining things, seeing Denny everywhere, in addition to the flashbacks to last night?

But there was no mistaking that chocolate-brown leather jacket or that cute cowlick sticking up at the back of her head. It was Denny.

Eliza's heart beat faster. She quickened her steps, not wanting to miss a minute with her. She squeezed through the tiny gap between their booth and the neighboring stall and slid behind the table. Without looking at her, she thrust the cup of coffee at Austen. Her gaze took in Denny.

"Hi." The olive color in Denny's hazel eyes seemed to lighten as she smiled at her across the table.

"Hi. What are you doing here? I thought you'd be at the waterfront with Bella." Eliza was very aware of Austen eyeing both of them with interest, probably wondering how they knew each other.

Denny pushed her glasses higher on her nose. "I was. I snuck away while Salem was trying to win a dragon for Bella. She took one look at Ms. Underbite and decided she needed one for herself." An affectionate smile deepened the fine lines around her eyes. "She's at that age where she thinks stuffed animals are the cutest thing ever one minute and is declaring herself too old for them the next."

"If she liked the dragon so much, why didn't you give her yours?" Eliza asked.

Denny pressed a hand to her chest and gave her a faux horrified look. "Give her Ms. Underbite? Can't do that. She was a gift and a reminder of a wonderful evening."

Their gazes tangled until Eliza had to glance away.

God, did Denny have to be so sweet? No woman, not even the straightest one in the world, would be left unaffected. Eliza peeked at Austen, who looked curious but not as if she were swooning over Denny. Maybe Denny's appeal affected only single women.

"So..." Denny tried to slide her glasses higher up on her nose, but they were as high as they would go. She quickly lowered her hand and waved at the items spread out on the table. "What toys can you recommend?" Her cheeks flushed. "Uh, bird toys, of course."

Eliza studied her more closely. She had been so busy dealing with her own emotions that she hadn't stopped to think about how Denny felt. Was she making Denny as nervous as Denny made her? Or was it just her natural shyness around people?

When Eliza failed to answer, Austen stepped closer to the table. "Depends. What kind of bird do you have? The toys that work for big birds are not always suitable for the little ones and vice versa."

Denny blinked as if only now remembering that she and Eliza weren't alone. She swiveled to face Austen. "I'm getting my niece a budgie for her birthday. We're total beginners when it comes to birds, so anything you think would work for a budgie."

Austen held up toys, talking about budgie swings, climbing ropes, and chewable balsa kabobs, but Eliza only heard half of what she said. She was too busy watching Denny's hands as she jingled a rattan ball with a bell and tugged on a rope. Had her crushes on guys ever been this distracting? She didn't think so.

After some deliberation and an extended discussion with Austen, Denny got three different toys and a recommendation for where to get the bird and a cage.

"Want me to hang on to the toys and bring them to Bella's party so you don't accidentally spoil the surprise?" Eliza asked.

Denny slid her wallet into her back pocket. "That would be great. Thank you."

"No problem," Eliza said. "Is it okay if I give Bella a six-month subscription for our Beak Box? It includes a fun toy plus a month's supply of different freeze-dried, organic veggies and fruits she can feed her budgie."

A tiny wrinkle dug itself between Denny's brows. "Are you sure it's not too expensive?"

"Nah. My bosses are very generous." Eliza grinned at Austen. "I'll finally get to take advantage of my employee discount."

"Okay. If you're sure you're not spending too much money, I bet Bella would love it." Denny stuffed her hands into her pockets and moved to the side as another customer checked out the bird toys.

Clearly, it was time to say goodbye. Too bad there was a huge table between them. Or maybe that was a good thing. Eliza wasn't sure how she'd react to another one of those awesome Denny hugs, and she didn't want to try in front of her boss.

Denny shuffled her feet. "So, guess I'll see you at the party next week. Want me to pick you up?"

"I can take the MAX," Eliza said.

"No. I'll come get you."

"Okay."

They looked at each other in silence.

"You know, if you two want to grab a bite to eat, I'm fine covering the booth for a while," Austen said.

Eliza's first impulse was to jump at the chance to spend more time with Denny, but she hesitated. Maybe she needed to get her head on straight—pun intended—first. She didn't want to give false signals and play with her feelings, whatever they might be.

Before she could decide on an answer, Denny shook her head. "I'd love to, but I'd better get back to the festival before my sister loses all our money—or wins us a herd of dragons. Knowing Salem, either could happen."

Eliza laughed. "I can't wait to meet her and Bella."

"I can't wait either." Denny pulled her hand from her jacket pocket and lifted it in a goodbye gesture that included Austen too. "Thanks again and have a great sales day." Then she turned and walked away.

Eliza shifted her weight forward, peeking over the table to watch her.

Denny walked slowly but with long strides, hands in her pockets, and a hint of a swagger to her shoulders instead of a sway in her hips.

When she disappeared in the crowd, Eliza forced herself to go back to work. She pulled out a box from beneath the table to replace the budgie swing Denny had bought. When she looked up, Austen smiled at her. "Uh, what? Wrong toy again?"

"No. Dee would kill me for making a comment like this to an employee, but, well, I'd like to think I'm a friend as much as an employer."

"You are," Eliza answered. "Feel free to say whatever you want to say."

Austen hesitated for another second. "I didn't know you were dating women. Well, one woman." She pointed in the direction Denny had disappeared in.

Eliza clutched the budgie swing. "Uh, I'm not."

"Oh. Sorry." Austen chuckled and gave her an impish look. "Guess that's why Dee insists on not commenting on our employees' private lives. I didn't mean to—"

"It's okay. I don't mind talking to you about my private life—not that I have much of one—and I certainly don't mind anyone assuming I date women. Nothing wrong with that, right?"

"No," Austen said with an absentminded grin that told Eliza she was thinking of her own girlfriend, "nothing wrong with that at all. But...you're not." It sounded like a question.

"I'm not."

"That's too bad." Austen laughed. "Your friend is cute."

"She is." Eliza had no problem admitting it or even that she was attracted to her. But that didn't mean she wanted to act on that attraction, right? Admiring another woman's handsome face or her cuddly, yet strong body was a far cry from dating her, sleeping with her, or starting a serious relationship.

She didn't want to lead Denny on and end up hurting her—provided Denny was even interested in her—so she would enjoy Denny's company as a friend and wait until these confusing new feelings faded away.

Austen gave her another curious look, but this time, she didn't comment or ask further questions, and Eliza didn't encourage her to.

Chapter 14

THE NEXT FRIDAY, IT WAS Salem who perched on the edge of the tub and watched Denny get ready for her date. The role reversal made Denny even more uncomfortable than she already was.

"Remember Spike?" Salem asked.

Denny put some gel in her hair to tame her cowlick. "Yeah, of course. He was my only sibling for many years, until you came along."

"Are you comparing me to an old bulldog with a drooling problem?"

"No. There's no competition." Denny paused, then added, "Spike was way cuter."

Salem threw a loofah at her but hit the toothbrush cup instead.

Denny caught it before it could topple over. "Why are you asking about Spike?"

"Because that expression on your face," Salem pointed at her in the mirror, "is exactly how Spike used to look when we took him to the vet."

Denny sighed and gave up on her hair. She turned and leaned against the sink. "I'm not so sure about tonight."

"Why the sudden reluctance?" Salem asked. "You wanted to ask her out back in April, remember?"

"Well, strictly speaking, *you* wanted me to ask her out."

"So you only agreed to do it to get me to shut up and weren't interested in Ms. Burkhart...Heather at all?"

Denny gazed at her still-bare feet. "No, I'm not saying that, but..."

"But you weren't hung up on Eliza back then," Salem finished the sentence for her.

Her sister's candid words made her clutch the edge of the sink behind her. "I'm not hung up on her," she mumbled, barely glancing up from a close appraisal of her toenails.

Salem gave her an oh-please-stop-kidding-yourself look.

"I'm not," Denny repeated but could hear the lack of conviction in her voice.

"Well, then going out with Heather shouldn't be a problem, right?"

"It's not." Denny sprayed some cologne on her neck and wrists. "I'm going, see?"

Bella stuck her head through the open bathroom door. "Are we going somewhere?"

"No, just your aunt. She's got a date." Salem drew out the last word in a singsong.

Bella didn't wrinkle her nose, as she usually did at the mention of dating. Instead, she looked interested. "With Eliza?"

"No," Denny and Salem said in unison.

"She's straight," Denny added while her sister said, "Your aunt is much too old for her."

"Hey!" Denny threw the loofah back at her and hit her square in the face. Too bad she hadn't soaked it in water before throwing it.

"Why?" Bella studied Denny as if she were counting every wrinkle on her face. "It's not like you're super old."

Denny snorted. "Thanks, I think."

"She's just saying that to get a bigger birthday present," Salem said.

Bella grinned and gave Denny a hopeful look. "Is it working?"

"Guess you'll have to wait until tomorrow to find out." Denny glanced at her reflection in the mirror one last time, then left the bathroom to get her shoes. For a second, she considered putting on sneakers.

No, she told herself. Sneakers were Eliza's thing, and she was going out with Heather.

Eliza's best friend. Denny raked her fingers through her hair. *Ugh.* Why on earth had she thought this was a good idea?

Eliza lay sprawled on her belly across Heather's bed, her bare feet up in the air and her hands framing her face as she watched her get ready for her date with Denny. Her stomach churned. Why, oh why had she encouraged the two of them to go out with each other?

Heather slipped her sheath dress over her head and shimmied it down her slim hips and athletic thighs. "Can you zip me up?"

"Sure." Eliza got up, moved Heather's hair out of the way, and pulled up the zipper.

"How do I look?" Heather gave a playful twirl, but the expression in her eyes was serious, maybe even anxious.

Eliza ran her gaze over the red sheath dress. It looked stunning on Heather's tall frame and dipped low in the front, showing off her cleavage in a way Eliza never could. Her gut twisted at the thought of Denny catching a glimpse of Heather's black lace bra—or, if the date went well, more than a glimpse.

"Uh-oh. You think it's too much, right?" Heather tugged on the front of the dress. "Be honest."

Eliza attempted to tamp down her conflicted emotions to reassure her friend. When they had first gotten to know each other, it had taken her a while to see behind the armor of confidence Heather wore, but now she knew it protected her vulnerable core. "No. It's perfect."

"Really?"

"Really," Eliza said, trying her best to sound lighthearted and positive. "You look beautiful."

Heather studied her carefully. "What is it, then? Something is giving you a stomachache, and if it's not the dress..."

Shit. She needed to get herself together. Dating was hard enough for both of her friends, and she was making it even harder on them with her own confusion. Eliza forced a smile. "It's nothing. I'm just a little nervous, I guess."

"You?" Heather laughed. "I'm the one going out on a date, and yet you're the one who's nervous?"

"It's silly, I know. I just worry." Eliza couldn't even say what was worrying her more—that the date might go badly or that it might go really well. "Remember that you might have to carry most of the conversation, at least at first. But please don't make her feel self-conscious about it, okay?"

"Jeez, Eliza, you know me. I'm not a jerk."

"I didn't mean it like that. I'm being ridiculous." Eliza flopped back down on the bed. "Just ignore my nervous-mom-on-prom-night routine." Of course, her concerns weren't motherly at all, but she couldn't tell Heather that.

Heather sat next to her on the edge of the bed, careful not to wrinkle her dress. A slow grin spread over her face. "Now I get it! You're jealous!"

A cold prickle slithered up Eliza's spine and fanned over her scalp, followed by a wash of heat. "W-what? No! I just..."

Heather slung one arm around her and shook her gently, as if to get her out of panic mode. "There's no need for that. Even if Denny and I end up together, I'll always make time for you, and I'm sure she will too. To quote a wise woman: you'll always be my favorite neighbor, my go-to for craft advice, and the person I can rely on to give me a hug or a kick in the ass when I need it."

Eliza slumped against her. *Oh, thank God.* Heather thought she was afraid she'd lose her best friend's attention. She had no clue what was really going on with her. And how could she? Eliza had no clue what was going on either. She had decided she didn't want to act on whatever attraction to Denny she felt, and that should have been the end of it. So why did she feel almost physically sick at the thought of Denny guiding Heather with one hand on her back and possibly kissing her at the end of the evening?

"So, crisis averted?" Heather pulled back to study her again.

Eliza nodded. She couldn't tell her it wasn't that kind of jealousy.

"Good." Heather tugged her up from the bed. "Then come help me pick out a pair of earrings."

As Eliza followed her to the dresser, she wondered how she would make it through this evening. Was it too early for a glass of wine?

Denny hadn't been on a date this awkward in a long time—okay, she hadn't been on any date in a long time, period. As if being rusty wasn't enough, she kept thinking of Eliza, wondering what she was doing and whether Heather would tell her about their date.

Not that there was much to tell since they didn't have much to say to each other.

It didn't help that the waitress gave Denny dirty looks, clearly not approving of her suit and tie. Denny felt Heather's gaze on her, and the thought of what she must think of her made Denny sweat. God, what a total failure.

The waitress set their plates in front of them and prepared to march away without another word.

"Actually," Heather spoke up, stopping her. "Could we get these to go? Oh, and throw in some disposable cutlery, please."

Damn. Denny had known it was bad, but not so bad that Heather didn't even want to stay through dinner. "I'm sorry. I—"

Heather slid her hand on top of hers. "Not your fault. Some people just aren't cut out to work in the hospitality sector," she said loudly enough for the waitress to hear.

Denny stared at her, then at the hand on top of her own. Heather's hands were smooth and manicured, but a few nicks graced her fingers, like Eliza's. *God, stop thinking about her, asshole!* It wasn't fair to Heather, who was turning out to be awesome.

When the waitress brought their boxed-up food, Denny insisted on paying.

Heather grabbed the bag. "Let's get out of here."

They walked out side by side, and Denny realized how tall Heather was. She looked shorter behind the big wheel of the school bus. But she wasn't wearing her uniform tonight. She was stunning in a red dress revealing a tasteful bit of cleavage and with only a hint of makeup that made it appear as if she wasn't wearing any.

"I'm sorry," Denny said again as they stepped onto the sidewalk. "I'm not usually..." She stopped herself. If nothing else, she owed Heather that bit of honesty. "Okay, truth be told, I am usually this much of an awkward dork. First dates make me nervous."

"Yeah, me too."

Denny stared at her. "Really?" Was Heather just saying that to make her feel better? "You seem so confident."

Heather shrugged her slim but toned shoulders. "I just hide it better than most, I guess. But deep down, I'm petrified any time I go on a first date."

Denny hadn't expected that, nor had she expected Heather to openly admit it and make herself that vulnerable. She gave her an astonished look.

"There's always that inner debate," Heather added. "Do I tell her or wait until the second date?"

"Tell her what?" Denny asked.

Heather paused at an intersection and made eye contact. "That I'm trans."

Now Denny felt even more like an asshole. She didn't want her to think she was rejecting her for who she was when the true reason was her hopeless infatuation with Heather's best friend. She really liked Heather, but a smile from her didn't leave her breathless the way Eliza's smiles did. Since she couldn't tell her that, she struggled to find the right words. Finally, she said, "Thank you for telling me."

Heather gave her a nod. The pedestrian light switched to *walk*, and she pointed toward the South Park Blocks. "You up for a picnic?"

"I'd love that."

Within minutes, they were sitting on the lawn beneath an old oak, with Denny's suit jacket serving as a blanket. They passed the containers back and forth, sharing Denny's chicken fettuccine alfredo and the smoked salmon ravioli Heather had ordered.

With every forkful, Denny relaxed more. Maybe it was because they had left the stuffy restaurant with its homophobic waitress or maybe because they had both admitted to being nervous—or maybe because this improvised picnic felt more like hanging out with a friend than the romantic setting in the restaurant.

"You didn't seem surprised." Heather pointed to the corner where she had told Denny she was trans. "So you read my No More Frogs profile."

Denny swallowed a bite of salmon ravioli. "No. I only took a quick look at your profile picture but didn't read any of your answers to the questions. I thought it would be nicer to get to know you in person." She pierced a piece of chicken with her fork. "I saw the pin you wore for Transgender Awareness Week. Not that cis people can't wear a trans awareness pin, of course. It didn't matter to me one way or the other."

"Oh." Heather lightly slapped her own forehead and laughed. "And here I thought it was such an inconspicuous little pin no one would notice—unless, of course, they were staring at my breasts."

The piece of chicken Denny was chewing nearly went down the wrong pipe. "I-I didn't!" she rasped out.

"God, you're so much fun to tease."

They ate their food in companionable silence for a few moments. The soft strains of a violin drifted over from somewhere in the park.

Denny peeked at Heather, who seemed entirely comfortable sitting propped up against the oak tree in her elegant dress. "Okay, maybe I was looking a little," she said with a sheepish grin.

Heather chuckled, clearly not offended at all.

"So," Denny said when her cheeks had taken on a more normal temperature, "how did you end up driving a school bus?"

The sun had long since set by the time they left the park and strolled toward Heather's apartment in the Cultural District.

Heather pointed at a red brick building with wrought-iron fire escapes. "This is me."

Denny glanced up at the four-story building. Warm lights shone out of some windows, and she wondered if one of them was Eliza's. Was she home, or had she gone on a date too?

"I really enjoyed tonight," Heather said.

Denny tore her gaze away from the windows and looked into Heather's eyes. "Me too."

Silence stretched between them as they paused in front of the wooden double doors leading into the building.

Denny stuffed her hands into her pockets in an attempt not to fidget. *Oh God, please don't let her ask me up—or expect me to kiss her!* She had enjoyed their time together and didn't want to hurt Heather, but the only woman she wanted to kiss was probably upstairs, in one of the apartments next to Heather's. Damn, Salem was right. She was totally hung up on Eliza and shouldn't have gone on this date. Now she felt like an ass for putting Heather through it. She deserved better than to be a distraction from the woman Denny couldn't have.

Heather clutched the strap of her purse with both hands, clearly expecting Denny to say or do something.

"So, should we..." Denny pointed back and forth between them.

"Um..." Heather lifted both eyebrows.

"Go out," Denny said so quickly the words ran into each other. "Should we go out again sometime?"

Heather looked at her for a while. "I'd love to have dinner with you again, but to tell you the truth, I'd rather do it as friends."

"Oh yeah, sure, totally. I mean, I'd love to do that."

Heather let go of her purse strap and playfully backhanded her across the shoulder. "Don't sound so relieved."

"I'm not! You're great, really. You're beautiful and funny, but..." Denny's gaze went to the illuminated windows again. *You're not Eliza.* She bit her lip—hard. *Shit.* She was screwed. So very screwed.

"There's no spark," Heather finished the sentence for her.

Denny nodded. "Well, there was definitely a friend spark, but..."

Heather leaned down and kissed her cheek. "I appreciate your honesty, and I agree. I'd love to have you as a friend, so stay in touch, okay?"

"I will," Denny said without hesitation.

When Heather unlocked the double doors and disappeared into the building, Denny rocked back on the heels of her Oxfords. *Damn.* She had hoped she and Heather would connect in a way that would make her stop thinking about Eliza. Instead, with the date now behind her, all she could think about on her way home was that she'd see Eliza tomorrow.

"God, what are you—a stalker?" Eliza groused out loud. But she couldn't help herself. Every couple of minutes, she paused the movie she was watching and listened for the rumble of the elevator or footsteps coming down the hall toward Heather's apartment.

Would Heather return alone, or would she ask Denny up for a glass of wine?

Oh shit, what if Denny stayed for more than the wine, and she ran into her tomorrow morning? Would she be able to pretend everything was fine while her friends reveled in their postcoital bliss?

A wave of nausea swept up her belly. Of all the women in the world, why was her best friend going out with the one woman she...?

Eliza froze. *The one woman I...what?*

The elevator doors swished open, and steps came down the landing.

Eliza jumped up and raced to the door, nearly falling on her ass as her sock-covered feet slid out from under her. She caught herself on the doorknob and peered through the frosted glass panel in her front door.

A single figure came toward her.

She opened the door an inch. If it was Mr. Drayton, her neighbor to the other side, returning from a walk with his toy poodle, he'd get a glimpse of her nightwear—which consisted of a pair of panties and an old, long T-shirt.

But it was unmistakably Heather walking past her.

Eliza stuck her hand out the door and waved. "Heather!"

Heather backtracked and peeked through the gap. "Oh, hey, you still up?"

Eliza nodded. "Watching a movie." Truth be told, she wasn't sure what she'd been watching. "Want to come in?" She tried to sound casual.

Heather laughed and pushed the door open. "Don't pretend you're not bursting with curiosity about my date! You're the worst actress I know."

Eliza dug her fingernails into her palm. If only Heather knew. She led her into the apartment, sat cross-legged on the couch, and flicked off the TV to give Heather her full attention. "So? How was it?"

"Can I have a glass of wine or some water before you start the interrogation?" Heather asked. "I'm parched."

"Didn't you have anything to drink with dinner?"

"Not a drop. Long story."

Eliza jumped up and set a new speed record for opening a bottle of wine and filling two glasses. Her nerves were taut like the steel cables of an elevator, and every extra second she had to wait ticked by with painful slowness.

As Eliza pressed a glass of red into her hand, Heather blinked. "Wow. That's prompt service. The waitress at the Italian place could learn a thing or two from you."

Eliza wasn't interested in the waitress. "How did it go? What was she wearing? Was she nervous? Will you go out again? Did she...kiss you?"

Heather burst out laughing. "Jeez, what's with the twenty questions?"

"Come on. Tell me."

Heather swirled her red wine with a slow smile. "Let's see... Okay; a suit and tie; hell, yes; not the way you're thinking; no."

Eliza's head spun. She had blurted out her questions so fast that now she wasn't able to pair them with Heather's answers. "Why don't you start at the beginning? And don't leave anything out!"

"Well, the beginning was pretty uneventful. She kept her gaze on the menu as if that thing had hypnotized her, and by the time the waitress brought our food, she had said maybe two sentences to me."

Oh no. Poor Denny. A restaurant setting wasn't a great choice for her. Eliza wanted to suggest a different activity for the next date, but the words refused to come. Hearing about Heather and Denny's first date was hard enough; she didn't want to suggest a second one. "What happened then? Did she relax a little?"

"Not in the restaurant. The waitress kept glaring at her as if Denny had ordered a plate full of cute kittens."

"Why would she do that?" Denny was always well-mannered and respectful. Why would anyone treat her like that?

Heather gave her a duh look. "Well, because of the way Denny looks."

Eliza frowned. A mental image of Denny formed in her mind's eye. Lately, that happened at the drop of a hat. She could easily picture the baby-blue button-up she had worn at the festival, the fabric stretching over her strong arms and generous breasts. The color of the shirt made the adorable flush on her cheeks stand out even more any time she blushed. "What's wrong with the way she looks?"

Heather put her wineglass down and hugged her. "Don't ever change."

Eliza returned the hug, then pulled back to study Heather with a shake of her head. "Seriously. I don't get it."

"Because you're not a homophobic asshole whose ideas of how a woman should look and dress are from around 1740."

Eliza stared at her. A wave of anger and fierce protectiveness bubbled up from deep inside of her until she felt as if steam would pour out of her ears any second. "What an ass! Did you stab her with your fork?"

"Believe me, I considered it."

They both took a gulp of wine at the same time.

"What did Denny do?" Eliza asked.

"Not much. She stayed polite and pretended not to notice, although I'm sure she would have preferred to either storm out or crawl under the table and hide."

Eliza emptied her wineglass with several gulps. It clanked as she set it on the coffee table with too much force.

Heather leaned forward and tilted her head to study her. "This is really upsetting you, isn't it?"

"Of course!" The words burst out of Eliza. She took a moment to compose herself before she continued. "Any of my friends being treated like that makes me so angry I could spit nails." *Yeah, just tell yourself that.* She would get angry if any other friend had been treated that way, but deep down, she knew it being centered around Denny fanned the flames of her anger even higher.

"Don't worry." Heather patted Eliza's knee. "The evening got decidedly better when we got our dinners to go and got out of there—without leaving a tip."

"Yeah?" On the one hand, Eliza was happy to hear that, but on the other hand, she wasn't sure how much better she wanted their date to get.

"Yeah. We went to the park and had a picnic, with someone playing the violin in the background."

"Sounds, um, romantic," Eliza said around the lump in her throat.

Heather shrugged. "It could have been, with the right person."

Eliza's inner bristles rose. "What's that supposed to mean?"

"Whoa!" Heather lifted both hands and chuckled nervously. "Should I be worried about you using a fork on me?"

Eliza dug her nails into her palm to get a grip. God, her emotions were all over the place tonight.

"Look, I think Denny is really nice," Heather said, her tone soft. "Once she relaxed, I had a great time with her, and you were right about her treating me like a queen. I don't regret going out with her at all."

What she wasn't saying hung in the air between them.

"But?" Eliza prompted.

"But there just wasn't any chemistry. She isn't my type, and I don't think I'm hers either."

What was Denny's type? Would she ever be interested in a woman like Eliza? But hadn't she decided her attraction to Denny was most likely a fluke, so acting on it would only hurt Denny and their friendship?

"Hey, don't worry." Heather leaned over and gave her another hug. "We mutually decided we're better off as friends. No hurt feelings."

Eliza squeezed back and nodded. Yeah. Better off as friends. That was true for her and Denny too, right?

Heather emptied her glass and got up. "And now you'll have to excuse me. As sexy as this dress is, I can't wait to get out of it and slip into my favorite hoodie."

When the door clicked shut behind her, Eliza sank onto the couch, pressed a pillow onto her face, and groaned into it.

Chapter 15

THE NEXT MORNING, DENNY PRESSED the phone to her ear and her nose to the windowpane as she stared outside. "Shit, shit, shit, shit, shit!"

It took forever for Eliza to pick up. "Yes?"

"Rain! Eliza, it's raining! What do we do?"

"Um, Denny, is that you?"

Even in her panicked state, Eliza's voice—huskier than usual—sent goose bumps up her arms. Then a realization washed over her, and she froze. Her gaze darted to her wristwatch, then outside, to where gray clouds blocked out the rising sun. "Shit, shit, shit," she repeated today's mantra. It was six o'clock on a Saturday morning. "I woke you up, didn't I? I'm so sorry."

"It's fine." Eliza sounded more awake now. "I'd have to get up soon anyway to get ready for Saturday Market. What's going on? Are you all right?"

"Yes. No. It's raining! Rain with a capital R, not just a little drizzle!"

It took a while for Eliza to answer, as if she had gotten up and glanced out the window. "Looks like it."

"It wasn't supposed to be raining! I watched the weather reports like a hawk this week, and they predicted sunshine all weekend!" Denny paced around her room. "Salem and I planned a scavenger hunt for Bella and her friends, but can you imagine half a dozen tween girls trudging through the rain? The clues will get soaked, and they'll want to go home within five minutes!"

"Is there a plan B?" Eliza asked.

"I suggested taking them bowling, but Salem says Bella's best friend did that for her birthday, so apparently, that means it's out." Denny sighed. "We need something cool that hasn't been done before. Something they won't consider babyish but that isn't too mature either. Plus our budget is super modest, so it needs to be something that doesn't break the bank and—"

"Denny?" Eliza's voice, warm and calm, broke through Denny's panic.

"Yes?"

"I've got this. Unless you need to run it by your sister first."

"No," Denny said. "We take turns planning Bella's birthday party, and this year, it's my turn. But you've got Saturday Market. You don't have time for—"

"Do you trust me?"

Denny flopped onto her bed. "I do," she said without hesitation.

"Do you have the food part covered?"

"Yeah. I figured I could help them make their own individual pizzas."

"Great," Eliza said. "You worry about the food; I'll take care of the entertainment. I have an idea, and I promise it's something fun yet inexpensive."

It was tempting. But could she really ask that of Eliza? "What about Saturday Market?"

"I planned to leave early anyway so I could come to Bella's party. Heather already agreed to cover our stall, and if I bribe her with a pepperoni pizza, I'm sure she'll agree to cover it an hour or two earlier."

For the first time since she had opened her eyes and seen the rain outside, Denny could breathe without hyperventilating. "Thank you, thank you. God, I could kiss you!"

Silence filtered through the phone.

Denny gripped the phone with one hand and slapped her forehead with the other. *She's straight, remember? No kissing, dammit!* "Not, uh, literally, of course."

"Of course," Eliza repeated with a nervous giggle. "Can you come pick me up an hour earlier so I can set up my secret entertainment program?"

"Yeah, no problem."

"I'll text you the address."

"Not necessary," Denny said. "I walked Heather home yesterday, so I know where you live."

"Oh! Right."

Another moment of silence stretched between them. Denny was used to awkward silences when interacting with other people, but between her and Eliza, this was something new, and she didn't quite know what to make of it.

"So," Eliza finally said, her tone careful, "you and Heather…"

"There is no me and Heather. I mean, not in a couples way. She was great, though. I can see why you consider her your best friend."

"Good. I mean, I'm glad you hit it off. As friends." Eliza mumbled something incomprehensible, talking to herself. "Listen, I'd better get going. I need to count my stones."

"Count your stones?" Denny repeated.

"You'll see." With that mysterious answer, she ended the call.

Denny dropped the phone onto her chest and glanced at her watch again. Okay, she had six hours to decorate the living room, pick up Bella's gift, and think of a way to interact with Eliza without giving away her growing feelings. Unfortunately, two of these things were easier to accomplish than the third.

Eliza leaned back in the passenger seat of Denny's battered Subaru Outback and watched as Denny safely navigated them across Ross Island Bridge. She bit back a grin. Denny kept both hands on the wheel, and her expression was one of total focus—as if she were transporting precious cargo.

"What?" Denny asked without taking her eyes off the road.

"Nothing. Just thinking." She'd done a lot of that lately but wasn't yet sure of the outcome.

"About what?"

"Oh, just that you must be the world's best aunt." Eliza smiled as, predictably, Denny blushed. "Seriously, you're going to great lengths for your niece. I love that."

Denny slowed as they approached a red light on the other side of the bridge. "I just want to make sure she has a wonderful birthday. She's a great kid, but she hasn't always had it easy, you know? Growing up without a dad or any grandparents..."

Eliza couldn't imagine what that might be like for any of them. She reached over and gently squeezed Denny's thigh an inch above the knee.

The Subaru screeched to an abrupt stop at the light. Denny stared at the hand on her leg.

Eliza quickly withdrew it. "Sorry, I..."

"No, no, it's fine." Denny's face turned a vivid shade of scarlet that matched the red chambray shirt she wore. "You just took me by surprise."

I know the feeling. The need to touch Denny, to comfort her, had taken her by surprise too. She folded her hands in her lap, determined to keep them to herself.

As the light turned green, Denny accelerated across the intersection.

"So," Eliza said as the silence in the car lasted a little too long, "did Bella like her present?"

Denny's tense features relaxed into a laugh. "Like? She loved it! I have a feeling if we let her, she'd take the bird to bed with her tonight! When I left, she was putting together a list of possible names, so prepare to be questioned about your favorites."

"I might not be the best person to ask for naming advice."

"Ooh, I sense a story there!" Denny switched off the soft music as if she didn't want to miss a word.

"My family had a chug when I was growing up."

"A what?"

"A chug," Eliza repeated. "A mix between a pug and a Chihuahua."

Denny gave her a sidelong glance. "You made that up."

Eliza laughed. "No, I swear, they exist. Anyway, when we adopted our chug, my parents allowed me to name him. I thought about it for days because I wanted him to have the perfect name. In the meantime, he destroyed my mom's favorite pair of shoes, licked the couch all over, and tore up my sister's homework—which the teacher, of course, didn't believe."

"So, what did you name him? Bandit?"

Eliza caught herself just in time before she could reach over and pat Denny's arm. What was up with that need to touch her? She shoved her hands beneath her thighs. "No. I named him Toast."

Denny furrowed her brow. "Toast?"

"Yep. Because that was the sentence my parents and siblings said to him most often: 'You are toast!'"

Denny's laughter—deep, rich, and unrestrained—boomed through the car, making Eliza smile in response. She loved these moments in which Denny forgot her self-consciousness.

They entertained each other with stories about their childhoods, and before Eliza knew it, Denny took a left onto a quiet side street in Lents and pulled into the driveway of a gray two-story townhouse. "I know it's not the most beautiful neighborhood, but it's affordable, and the neighbors are great," Denny said.

This time, Eliza gave in to her need to touch Denny and laid a reassuring hand on her forearm. "It looks really nice."

Since it was still raining, Denny threw her jacket over the box with Eliza's supplies and the bird toy gifts Eliza had kept and wrapped for her, and they jogged to the front door.

Denny unlocked it, cradling the box to her chest, and held the door open for Eliza.

"Thanks." Eliza stepped inside, out of the rain, and looked around.

A short hallway connected to a dining area that was decorated with balloons, streamers, and a colorful *Happy Birthday* banner. In the open kitchen, a sliding glass door revealed glimpses of a tiny, fenced-in backyard. To her left, a set of stairs led to the upper floor. The place had a lived-in, cozy look.

"Salem's and Bella's bedrooms are upstairs," Denny said as she closed the door behind them. "Mine is on this level, and I have my own bathroom too."

"Nice." For an introvert like Denny, having some space to herself was probably essential.

A racket on the stairs announced Bella's arrival. "Mom," she hollered over her shoulder. "They're here!" Then, on the last few steps, she slowed down, and Eliza thought she caught a hint of her aunt's shyness in the tween's hazel eyes.

Denny wrapped one arm around her niece's shoulders and pulled her against her side.

The protective gesture made Eliza melt inside.

"This is Bella—the birthday girl." The pride in Denny's voice was unmistakable, as was the resemblance between them. Bella's hair was longer, reaching halfway down her back, but the color was the same sandy brown as Denny's. "Bella, this is my friend Eliza."

Eliza smiled warmly at the girl. "Hi. Happy birthday."

More steps sounded on the stairs, then a woman of about Eliza's age joined them. She was taller and leaner than Denny, but Eliza would have recognized her as Denny's sister anywhere. With her hazel eyes, she looked like the femme version of Denny.

"Hey there. You must be Eliza." She took Eliza's hand in a firm grip and shook it enthusiastically. "I'm Salem. It's great to finally meet you. I've heard so much about you."

"Really?" Eliza sent a curious gaze over to Denny. "What did she tell you?"

Denny flushed to the roots of her carefully styled hair. "Uh, shouldn't we get this set up?" She nodded at the box in her arms.

"Not much to set up," Eliza said. "Just put it all on a table somewhere, and maybe spread some newspapers on the table."

Denny didn't have to be asked twice. She carried the box into the dining area, with Bella hot on her heels, jumping up and down so she could peek inside the box.

Eliza stayed behind with Salem.

"I can't thank you enough for saving Bella's party," Salem said. "Please tell me how much you spent so I can repay you."

"That's not necessary. I had all of this lying around, and I hear Denny's going to pay me in pizza."

"A woman who accepts pizza as a currency!" Salem wrapped one arm loosely around her and led her into the dining area. "I like you already."

Denny looked up from where she was putting the bottles of brush-on sealer on the table. The olive-green of her eyes seemed to light up from within as she smiled at them.

Eliza grinned back, glad Denny's family seemed to like her. Not that she had thought otherwise since she got along well with most people she met. But Denny's sister and niece were important parts of her life, so their opinion of her was important to Eliza too.

"This is so awesome." Bella held up several paint pens. "Mom, look! She brought stuff for painting rocks."

"That's not all I brought." Eliza walked up to the table, pulled the envelope with the Beak Box subscription from her purse, and held it out to Bella. "Just a little something that I thought you could use now that you have a new pet."

Bella went wide-eyed. "Wow. Thank you." She took the envelope from Eliza's hand as carefully as a cat taking a treat from a stranger, but then her demeanor changed, and she eagerly ripped it open.

"Don't you want to wait until your friends—?"

But Bella was already pulling the card from the envelope, so her mother fell silent and shrugged at Eliza. "Guess not."

"It's a subscription for bird toys and snacks! I'll get a surprise box with fun stuff every month. And look!" Bella held up a card with a green budgie on the front and the words *Have a birdtastic birthday* for everyone to see. "The bird on the card looks exactly like mine!"

"That's fantastic. I mean, birdtastic." Salem turned from her daughter to Eliza. "I wanted a card like that but couldn't find one. Where did you get it?"

"I had my mom make it. She illustrates children's books for a living."

Salem regarded her with a shake of her head. "Amazing. You really went all out for a stranger's birthday. Seems Denny wasn't exaggerating about how great you are after all."

Had Denny really said that? Eliza peered at her.

"Um, Bella, why don't you leave the rest of the gifts for later and show Eliza your new friend before your guests arrive?" Denny asked. Almost beneath her breath, she added, "While I kill your mother and find a place to dispose of her body."

Chuckling, Eliza followed Bella upstairs. It was going to be an interesting afternoon.

The scent of sizzling cheese and tomato sauce wafted through the house, but that wasn't what drew Denny to the kitchen. She leaned against the counter and peered at the dining table, where the craft party was in full swing.

Bella and her friends paid careful attention while Eliza showed them how to paint the rocks.

Her shiny chestnut hair tumbled from behind her ear as she shook one of the paint pens. She brushed it back with an absentminded swipe of her slender hand and then laughed at something one of the girls said.

God, she was beautiful. Watching her made Denny light-headed.

When Salem joined her in the kitchen, Denny looked away and tried to control her expression.

Salem leaned against the counter next to her. "She's great with the girls. I'm impressed. I've never seen half a dozen tweens pay this close attention to someone." Laughing, Salem gestured toward the table. "Or you, for that matter."

Denny scowled at her. "I'm keeping an eye on the pizza."

"Yeah, the pizza. That's what you're watching. Sure."

"Stop it, Salem." Denny drew her sister's name out the way she had when Salem had been a little girl getting into all kinds of mischief. "I know you think this is funny, but my friendship with Eliza is not a laughing matter to me, okay?"

Salem sobered and put her hand on Denny's arm. "I'm not making fun of—"

"Mom! Aunt Denny!" Bella called. "Look! I did one of Kiwi." She held up her stone. The green-and-yellow bird she had painted on it was easily recognizable as Kiwi, the budgie she had finally named with Eliza's help earlier. "Try one. This is fun."

Denny and Salem glanced at each other, then Salem patted Denny's arm. "Let's talk later," she said quietly before joining Eliza and the girls at the table.

"Aunt Denny, you too!"

Denny took a hesitant step toward the table. "Uh, there's no room." Every inch of the table was covered with newspapers, stones, paint pens, and different varnishes, and the girls sat shoulder to shoulder.

Eliza maneuvered a stool into the tiny space between her and Bella and pulled Denny down on it. "There's always room for one more, as my mom used to say." She put a stone in front of Denny and fanned out a handful of paint pens. "Here. Try it."

They sat so close, her body heat seemed to engulf Denny, making her own temperature skyrocket. When she reached for one of the pens, their knees brushed. It took all of Denny's willpower to stop her eyes from fluttering shut. She hoped her voice wasn't too husky as she said, "I have no idea what to put on the stone. What did you do?"

"Well, since we started out as text buddies, I thought I'd do a custom emoji." Eliza slid one of the stones on the table closer so Denny could study it.

Even with something as simple as an emoji, Eliza's artistic talent was obvious. The smiling yellow face looked back at her from behind black-rimmed glasses, and a light flush dusted its cheeks.

"Why is it a custom emoji?" Denny asked.

"Um, because this one," Eliza pointed at the stone she had shown her, "is a Denny emoji." She averted her gaze.

Denny stared at her. "You turned me into an emoji? So, what does the Denny emoji mean?"

"It's a very versatile emoji. It can mean all sorts of things."

"Oh, really?"

Eliza peeked up and nodded. "It's a fact."

They looked into each other's eyes, and the few inches of space between them seemed to vibrate with something Denny couldn't name.

"Hey, you two." Salem waved at them from across the table. "You're hogging the yellow marker. Can you throw it over to me?"

Denny forced her attention away from Eliza. "Sorry, sis. I need the yellow." She snatched it up from the table. "I'm making an Eliza emoji."

It turned out that rock painting wasn't as easy as it seemed. Or maybe it was, and it was only Eliza's closeness that made her hand unsteady as she drew a yellow face onto her stone. She hadn't waited long enough before drawing its eyes and mouth, so the yellow and black had mixed a little, making her features blurry. At least the emoji's hair looked great. After she had applied two coats of the gloss varnish, it was as shiny as Eliza's hair.

Eliza leaned closer to study the rock.

How could she smell so wonderful after spending hours entertaining a horde of kids? Denny discreetly inhaled more of her signature scent.

"My eyes look a bit blurry," Eliza said.

Her warm breath washed over Denny's cheek. A shiver went through Denny, and she clenched her jaw so she wouldn't let out a moan. "It's the Eliza-before-her-morning-tea emoji," she said, struggling to sound normal.

Eliza laughed. "Ah, that explains it. But why are her lips blurry too?"

Denny's gaze darted to Eliza's lips. If she were Superwoman, those lips would be her kryptonite. She bit back the first reply that came to mind: because they'd been thoroughly kissed. "Um, smudged lipstick, I guess."

"Hmm, I see." Eliza tapped those sensuous lips, deep in thought. "So, what does the Eliza emoji mean?"

Everything. Denny clamped her teeth around her bottom lip so she wouldn't say it out loud. She searched for something nice, yet innocent to say, but everything her overstimulated brain came up with sounded like a poem by a lovesick teenager.

The oven timer going off made her drop the Eliza emoji. It clattered onto the table.

"Pizza!" Bella and her friends cheered and rushed into the kitchen.

"Saved by the bell," Salem murmured as she followed them.

Within seconds, Eliza and Denny were the only ones left at the table. Though there was now plenty of space, neither of them backed away from the other. Denny sat rooted to the spot by Eliza's gaze, afraid to move and do something foolish. Her heart drummed against her ribs so loudly she was sure Eliza could hear it. She felt the urge to say something and interrupt this strange trance they were in, but she had no idea what they'd been talking about. "Uh, thank you," she got out. She waved her hand across the table. "For everything."

Eliza gave her a warm smile, but her gaze was intense and still holding Denny's. "Any time." She lightly touched Denny's arm.

Since Denny had rolled up the sleeves of her shirt earlier, Eliza's fingers connected with her skin, and every cell in Denny's body was aware of the touch.

They sat like that for a moment.

"Who's got the artichoke hearts and spinach ones?" Bella called.

Eliza let go of Denny's arm and looked away.

"Me," they both said at the same time, then glanced at each other again.

"I'll get them." As Eliza hurried to the kitchen, Denny clutched the edge of the table and let out a shuddery breath. *Holy hell.*

When the doorbell rang, Taylor scrunched up her nose. "Oh no, I think that's my dad."

Other than Addison and Kaylee, who would stay for a sleepover, she was the last of Bella's friends to be picked up.

The birthday party was winding down, and Eliza found herself as reluctant to say goodbye as the girls.

In true Portland fashion, the rain had stopped shortly after the pizza was gone, so they had gone outside to hide some of the painted rocks for people to find. Seeing the girls so excited about their creations had been fun, but her favorite part of the day had been watching Denny interact with her family. The affectionate teasing between them had made her burst out laughing more than once.

They all seemed so familiar to her that it was hard to believe she'd met Salem and Bella only five hours ago.

As the door closed behind Taylor and her father, Eliza got up. "I think this is my cue to leave too." She looked at Denny. "If you've got the time to drive me home."

Denny stood with obvious reluctance and rolled down her shirtsleeves. "Yeah, sure."

Bella glanced up from Denny's laptop, where she was scouring the Feathered Friends website with her friends. "Already? But it's the weekend. Can't you stay for the sleepover?"

"Um..." Eliza hadn't expected an invitation like that.

Salem put her hand on her daughter's shoulder. "Where would she sleep, honey? I don't think anyone over eighteen wants to sleep on a bedroll on the floor."

"She could sleep with you or Aunt Denny," Bella said.

The button from Denny's shirtsleeve ricocheted through the dining area and skidded to a stop in front of the dishwasher.

Eliza's heart beat faster. What was going on with her? It was a perfectly innocent remark. She had shared a room—even a bed—with other female friends before, so why did the thought of sharing with Denny make her heart race? She had assumed her little crush would fade away after she spent more time with Denny, but instead, the opposite seemed to be happening.

Denny was as red-faced as Eliza felt. "That's not a good idea. Uh, I mean, you promised Heather to bring her pizza, right?"

"Yeah. Right." Eliza sent Bella an apologetic look. "My friend covered our stall at Saturday Market by herself so I could spend the day with you."

Bella nodded. "Yeah, I guess she deserves some pizza. Maybe next time."

Eliza smiled, glad that Bella fully expected there to be a next time. She hoped to spend more time with Denny and her family too—and maybe introduce her to her own. *Jeez, what am I thinking?*

Now she was like SongBoy77, who had wanted her to meet his family on the first date. Some of her friends, even people she had known for years, had yet to meet her family, and it had never seemed important to her. But with Denny, everything was different, and she still couldn't wrap her head around *how* different it was.

She got hugs from Salem and, to her surprise, from Bella too.

Denny held out Eliza's jacket for her, and she slid her arms through the sleeves with a murmured "thanks," very aware of Denny's closeness and her hand brushing against her neck. Goose bumps skittered across her skin. Wow, this was wild. She couldn't remember reacting like this to anyone, man or woman.

Salem, Bella, and her friends followed them outside and waved as they climbed into Denny's car.

They drove in silence for several minutes. For the very first time, Eliza didn't know what to say to Denny. Should she tell her about the new feelings she was experiencing, maybe ask her if she felt drawn to her in the same way? But even if Denny did feel the same, where would that leave them?

With a guy, the next steps would be obvious—a date or two, a kiss or two... She stopped her thoughts before they could veer into more R-rated territory. Was she ready to go out with Denny, not as friends, but as a couple, for the world to see? Was she ready to kiss her? Because if she wasn't, she had no business saying anything. Denny deserved better than a confused straight woman who didn't know what she wanted.

Denny braked at a red light and peered at her. "You okay?"

"Oh. Yeah. Just tired, I guess."

Denny laughed.

The sound filled Eliza with warmth.

"Yeah," Denny answered as the light turned green and she accelerated across the intersection, "spending the day with half a dozen tweens can do that to you."

"Nah. They were wonderful, especially Bella. She reminds me a lot of you." Eliza snapped her mouth shut. Crap. She'd basically just told Denny that she was wonderful in a roundabout. Oh well. She was, and it was okay to tell her, wasn't it?

"I get that a lot. People often think she's mine, not Salem's." Pride infused Denny's voice. "But as much as I love her, I'm kinda glad she's not. Pregnancy and labor..." She shook herself. "No, thanks."

"Oh, I don't know." Eliza grinned. "You could deliver at St. Immaculate Conception."

They both burst out laughing, and most of the tension and awkwardness between them dissipated.

Conversation flowed easily the rest of the way, and it seemed like only minutes later when Denny pulled up to the curb in front of Eliza's apartment building.

Denny jumped out and got the box of craft supplies out of the back.

They stood on the sidewalk, Denny cradling the box, Eliza holding the container with Heather's pizza.

"Want me to help you get it all upstairs?" Denny asked.

Eliza shook her head. "No, I'm fine. I don't want you to get a ticket for parking here." She placed the pizza on top of the box, took both from Denny, and balanced them against her chest.

Now relieved of her burden, Denny slid her hands into the pockets of her baggy jeans. "Thanks again for everything. You really were a lifesaver."

"Like I said, any time. It was fun."

They both shuffled their feet.

Eliza didn't want to just say goodbye and walk away. She wanted one of those wonderful Denny hugs. But the sidewalk was still damp from the earlier rain, so if she put the box down, it would get soaked.

"All right, then. I'd better get going." Denny pulled one hand out of her pocket and adjusted her glasses. "Salem might need help herding the girls to bed." But despite her words, she didn't move toward the driver's side.

To hell with the box. There was nothing in there that couldn't take a little dampness. Eliza put the box down, stepped over it, and held out her arms to offer a hug.

Denny bridged the remaining space between them so fast, as if she'd been longing for a hug too.

Eliza sank against her, clutching her back with both hands. Being cuddled against Denny's body, firm in some places and soft in others, made her head spin. The fresh, sporty scent of Denny's cologne teased her nose. Eliza pressed her cheek to the soft leather jacket and inhaled deeply. *Mmm.* Men's cologne had never smelled so good on anyone else.

God, this felt... She struggled to describe it, even to herself. Earlier, when they'd been painting rocks and she had touched Denny's arm, she had felt the same. But that wasn't why this experience seemed familiar; she just couldn't put her finger on it. Her brain was focused on feeling, not analyzing.

Denny tightened her arms around her, then, with a sigh that ruffled Eliza's hair, let go and stepped back. "I, um..." She pointed at the Subaru.

Eliza nodded, her mouth too dry to speak.

When Denny rounded the car to get to the driver's side, she missed the curb, stumbled, and flailed to keep her balance.

Eliza's heart pounded faster, this time with worry. "You okay?"

"Yeah, I'm fine." Denny flushed a deeper pink than her cheeks already were and clambered behind the wheel.

They waved at each other through the window.

Denny started the engine, and within seconds, the Subaru got smaller and smaller until it disappeared in the distance.

Eliza stood without moving for a while longer before she bent and picked up the box with the pizza container perched on top. She cradled both to her chest the way she had clutched Denny to her earlier. The scent of Denny's cologne lingered around her, and she hoped it wouldn't fade anytime soon.

When she stepped into the elevator and let it carry her upstairs, a realization slammed into her. That was why that feeling seemed so familiar! Wrapped in Denny's arms, she felt the way she had on the Viking ship, in that moment of weightlessness as the ship reached its highest point—elated and giddy, wanting to laugh and scream out of sheer joy, but scared at the same time.

Now the question was: Did she want to get off the ship or hang on for the ride?

Salem collapsed onto the couch next to Denny as if every bone in her body had vaporized and weakly gestured upstairs toward Bella's room. "Phew! I thought they would never stop giggling and go to sleep!"

Denny wiggled her bare toes on the coffee table. She had felt less exhausted after running the register all day, but it wasn't just from keeping up with a bunch of tweens on a sugar rush. Mostly, it was from trying to keep a tight grip on her emotions whenever Eliza was near. "How did you finally manage to get them to quiet down?"

"I told Bella all that noise would upset Kiwi, and I'd have to take him downstairs if they didn't go to sleep."

The name Eliza had suggested made Denny grin. What was it with Eliza and food-related pet names?

Salem eyed her. "What's that smile for?"

"Can't I be in a good mood after throwing a successful party for my favorite niece?" Denny asked. "It was a success, wasn't it?"

"Are you kidding? Bella loved it—especially getting to show off her aunt's cool, artsy friend!"

Denny's smile widened. Eliza had been a big hit with the girls. "You liked her too, right?"

"Of course. Although..."

Denny turned her head and narrowed her eyes at her sister, ready to defend Eliza. "Although...what?"

"Although not as much as you do." Salem flashed a grin.

"Salem..." Denny lowered her voice to a warning growl.

Salem held up a hand. "Let me just say one thing, and then I'll be quiet."

"That would be a first," Denny muttered.

"I'd kick you for that remark, but I'm too tired. Anyway, I watched the two of you together, and forgive me for saying so, but that didn't look like an unrequited crush to me."

Denny wanted to deny it, but then she stopped herself. This was Salem, her sister. If she couldn't confide in her, who else could she talk to? "Okay, I admit it. I think I left crush territory behind, probably before I even met her." She let her head fall back against the couch. "It makes no sense because I've known her for two months and only met her three times, but... God, I'm so drawn to her! And it's not just because she's so damn beautiful and so nice and so...everything. I'm trying hard to be reasonable, but my heart refuses to listen." She hesitated and peeked at Salem before quietly adding, "I think if I'm not careful, I could really fall for her."

"No shit, Sherlock," Salem muttered.

Denny slid her feet off the coffee table to face her more fully. "Look, I know what you're going to say. And you're right. Pinning my heart on a straight woman—and one who's more than ten years younger too—is committing emotional hara-kiri. I know that. But you don't need to worry. I'll get over it." She sighed. "Somehow. Eventually."

"That's not what I wanted to say."

"No?"

"No," Salem said. "I meant it didn't look like your more-than-a-crush was entirely unrequited."

Denny stared at her. A flutter spread through her belly, and she couldn't tell what it was or even if it was pleasant or unpleasant. It felt like a complicated mix of both. She wanted so much to believe her sister and cling to her words with every fiber in her body, but at the same time, she wanted to curl into a ball and protect herself. "Don't do that, Salem. Don't get my hopes up. I know Eliza likes me, but to her, I'm just a friend."

"Sure, like Matt was just a friend to me before we started dating."

"There's one important difference between Matt and Eliza." Denny held up one finger.

A grin crept across Salem's face. "Eliza shaves her legs?"

Denny scowled at her. "I'm serious. Matt is interested in women; Eliza isn't. She's straight."

"Well, I know a thing or two about being straight. But let me tell you, if I ever found myself looking at another woman the way she looked at you today..." Salem tilted her head. "I'd start to second-guess that label."

Denny pulled her legs up on the couch and hugged them to her chest. But it didn't matter how forcefully she pressed her knees to her chest, she couldn't drive back the kernel of hope. "Great. Now you've done it. Thanks so much, sis. Now I'll scrutinize every little touch, every look, everything she says, hoping it means she likes me back as more than a friend. That goddamn hope is worse than being sure she'll never see me that way."

"Why don't you cut to the chase and ask her?"

"Ask her?" Denny's arms dropped from her legs as she stared at her sister.

Salem shrugged. "Why not? You two talk for hours every day. I've heard you tell her stuff I barely even knew. So why not bite the bullet and ask her if she thinks she could ever feel something other than friendship for you?"

"Oh no." Denny shook her head so hard that spots of light danced before her eyes. "I could never do that. If you're wrong, that'll make things awkward between us. Her friendship means too much to me to risk that."

"Chicken."

Denny pulled a pillow from beneath herself and threw it at her.

Salem threw it back, and the pillow fight was on.

Denny eagerly lost herself in the physical activity and tried to channel all her anxiety into it.

After a minute or two, Salem held up both hands. "Uncle, uncle!"

"I'm not your uncle." Denny hit her with the pillow again. "I'm your sister."

"Okay, then, sister, sister." Salem waved an imaginary white flag.

Denny lowered the pillow and flopped back onto the couch. If only she could wrestle her feelings for Eliza into submission as easily.

Chapter 16

ON THE LIST OF THINGS Eliza never thought she would google, *how do I know if I'm bisexual* definitely made the top three. But here she was, spending the Sunday after Bella's party reading articles on sexual fluidity and taking a quiz to determine her sexual orientation.

Instead of helping, the questions left her more confused than ever. "I would kiss a woman," she read one of the questions out loud. Her gaze flickered back and forth between the two options, *true* or *false*.

But it wasn't as black-and-white for her. If asked in the abstract, her instinct was to click *false*. She didn't want to kiss just any woman. What about kissing Denny, though?

She imagined them saying goodbye with a hug, as they had yesterday, but instead of letting go and walking to her car, Denny pulled her closer and tenderly cradled her face in her broad hands. Eliza could almost feel her warm breath on her lips as Denny's face came closer. Her heart pounded a rapid staccato, and her gaze zeroed in on Denny until all she saw was her soft-looking lips.

Just as their mouths were about to meet, a knock and the sound of a key in the lock wrenched her back to reality.

Eliza flinched and slapped her laptop closed.

Heather swung the door open and waved an empty Tupperware container. "Pizza for breakfast is the best! If you talk to Denny before I do, please tell her thanks."

The mere mention of Denny's name made Eliza feel like a teenager caught watching porn.

Heather sat on the couch next to her and gave her a curious look. "What's up with you?"

"Nothing. Just a little tired." While Eliza wanted to talk about it with someone, she wasn't sure she was ready. Besides, maybe Heather wouldn't be the best person, since she'd gone on a date with Denny. She didn't want things between them to become awkward.

Heather continued to study her. "Wild party yesterday? You disappeared so fast that I didn't even have time to ask when you dropped off the pizza."

"Well, I wouldn't call a craft party for an eleven-year-old 'wild'..."

"Yeah, if that's the highlight on your social calendar, you're doing something wrong. But don't worry. I've got you covered. Your social life is about to get much more exciting. I found the perfect guy for you!" Heather held out her phone like a celebrity presenting the card with the name of an Oscar winner.

Reluctantly, Eliza glanced at the screen, but when she recognized the No More Frogs app, she didn't accept the phone. "You know what? I think I'm going to take some time off from going out with guys." She bit her lip. Going out with *anyone*. That was what she'd meant, right? Or would she really consider dating Denny, provided she was interested?

"Come on. I've got a good feeling about this one. He's a metalsmith. Think about the beautiful jewelry you two could make together." Heather nudged her with her shoulder and winked. "And the beautiful babies. Look. He's hot...for a guy."

When Heather held the phone under her nose, Eliza took a closer look. A handsome man in his mid-thirties flashed his white teeth in a winsome smile. "Yeah, I guess he's pretty cute."

"Pretty cute?" Heather echoed. "He looks like that guy from *The Witcher*. You know, the one who also played Superman."

Eliza studied his photo more closely. With his dark hair, light eyes, and the dimple in his chin, he did resemble Henry Cavill a little.

"He sounds like a nice guy too," Heather added. She read his profile out loud until Eliza lifted both hands in a gesture of surrender.

"Okay, okay. I'll send Henry a message and see if he wants to have coffee or something. Happy now?"

Heather leaned back on the couch and folded her hands over her pizza-filled belly. "Very."

Eliza peeked at the closed laptop, where the sexual orientation quiz was waiting for her. She wouldn't finish it. An online test was silly; she knew that. Maybe going on a date with a guy was actually a better idea to help her clarify her feelings.

But if it was such a good idea, why did it feel so wrong?

The next Saturday, Eliza didn't have to help out at the Feathered Friends stall, so she volunteered to cover her and Heather's booth by herself, as a thank-you to Heather for stepping in twice in a row. After she had spent most of the week in a haze, the familiar hustle and bustle of the market soothed her soul.

She had been so distracted at work yesterday that she had accidentally squirted an entire bottle of Elmer's Wood Glue onto her worktable!

What had made her week even weirder was that she and Denny hadn't talked much, and when they had, they danced around each other instead of talking openly. Could Denny tell something was going on with her? Was she giving Eliza space to work it out? Or was she backing away from their friendship?

Eliza rearranged the pendants and octopus penholders in front of her for the twentieth time. The bow tie pendant made her smile as it reminded her of Denny. Lately, everything reminded her of Denny.

Even a person standing in line at the nearby kettle corn booth instantly made her think of Denny. Same brown leather jacket, same strong shoulders, same shapely behind.

Eliza tore her gaze away from the stranger. Jeez, when had she become so familiar with how Denny's ass looked?

Thankfully, a customer who was interested in a pair of rose-shaped earrings distracted her.

She wrapped up the earrings on a small table at the back of the booth. When she turned back around, a familiar face peeked around the waiting customer.

"Hi." Bella gave a wave and brushed her long hair behind her ear in a shy gesture that once again reminded Eliza of Denny.

"Bella! Hi. What are you doing here?"

"Mom had to work, so Aunt Denny took me to watch the Rose Parade earlier, and I talked her into making a stop at the market so I could get a foraging cup for Kiwi." Bella pointed in the direction of the Feathered Friends stall. When the customer put the earrings in her purse and left, Bella stepped closer. "Now she's stuck in line, getting kettle corn."

Eliza's gaze flew to the kettle corn booth. So it hadn't been her imagination playing tricks on her after all.

Loaded down with several bags, Denny made her way over. She wore a gray Henley shirt tucked into baggy jeans, and her leather jacket was casually slung over her shoulder. "Hi."

Eliza's mouth went dry, and she smacked her lips before she could speak. "Hi."

They smiled at each other. God, it was good to see Denny. It felt much longer than a week since they had last seen each other.

"Yum. That smells so good." Bella leaned closer to her aunt.

Eliza found herself leaning across the table too, but the scent that caught her attention wasn't the caramel kettle corn; it was Denny's cologne.

"I brought you one too." Denny held out one of the bags. "In case you didn't get to eat."

"I had a ham-and-cheese empanada earlier, but who can resist kettle corn?" Eliza reached across the table and took the offered bag.

Their fingers brushed, and a whoosh of warmth spread through her belly.

"Wow. Did you make this?"

Bella's question reminded Eliza they weren't alone. She followed the direction of Bella's gaze.

The girl was looking at one of her handcrafted journals. Eliza made the 3D covers from polymer clay and then glued them to the front of notebooks. The one that had caught Bella's attention depicted two dragons, one a bluish green, the other a dark purple with a golden sheen. They were wrapped around each other and touching noses.

Eliza nodded. "Yes, that's one of mine."

"It's so awesome." Bella turned to Denny. "Isn't it?"

"Yeah, it really is." Denny's voice was as soft as her touch as she trailed her fingertips over the scaly tail of the purple dragon.

A shiver worked its way through Eliza's body. God, these reactions were getting out of control.

Bella peered at her from under her bangs. "Would you teach me how to do a budgie one?"

"Um, Bella, you can't just—"

"I'd love to," Eliza said before Denny could finish her protest.

"Awesome! Hey, I see Kaylee and her mom over there. Can I go say hi?" Bella was gone before Denny finished nodding.

Denny shook her head with an indulgent grin. "Oh, to have that kind of energy again."

Eliza grinned at her. "Are you having a senior citizen moment?"

Denny shrugged, then resettled her jacket over her shoulder. "Thanks for being so great with her and agreeing to teach her."

"Are you kidding? She's wonderful, so it's not a hardship at all. Maybe I could bring my nieces and my nephew, and we could all do it together."

"I'd love that." Denny looked at the dragon journal, then back up at Eliza. "Are you staying until five today?"

Eliza glanced at her watch, amazed to see it was after two. "No, I'll pack up in a few minutes."

"Great." Denny gave her a shy smile. "If you don't have any plans for the rest of the day, do you want to come watch the dragon boat races with Bella and me?"

Damn. Eliza could think of nothing more perfect than spending the rest of her Saturday with Denny. For a moment, she was tempted to text Jared and cancel their date. But he'd seemed nice in all the messages they had exchanged this week and didn't deserve her skipping out at the last minute. "I'm sorry. Normally, I'd love to, but I can't. I, uh, I'm meeting someone for coffee at five, and I need to go home and get changed before that."

"Oh. No problem. I hope you have a good time." Denny smiled, but it didn't light up the olive-green part of her eyes.

They both looked at Bella, who was still talking to her friend, while silence stretched between them.

"So," Denny finally said, "coffee with someone. Is it a date?"

Eliza slid the dragon journal an inch to the right. "Um, yes." Why did admitting it make her feel so guilty? Quickly, she added, "It was Heather's idea. She thinks she found the perfect guy for me. But knowing my luck, he'll be another candidate for the Worst-Date-Eliza-Has-Ever-Had Award."

"Well, if you need someone to rescue you, let me know."

"Oh, so you can fake having quadruplets this time?"

This time, Denny's smile reached her eyes. "Nah. I'll think of something else. Can't have you getting bored with my rescue efforts."

Bella came back over. "Kaylee and her mom are going to watch the dragon boat races too. Can we go with them?"

"Sure," Denny said. "Tell them I'll be there in a minute."

After a quick wave and a "bye, Eliza," Bella ran off.

Denny shifted the pile of kettle corn bags cradled in her left arm. "Even if you don't need to be rescued, text me when you make it back from your date safe and sound, okay?"

The concern for her well-being left a warm feeling in the pit of Eliza's stomach. "Will do. Have fun at the dragon boat races."

"Thanks." Denny lingered in front of the booth for a few seconds longer, then sighed. "I'd better get going. See you soon."

"See ya." Eliza watched her leave, taking in the familiar way Denny walked, from the shoulders, not the hips. Every instinct urged her to run after her and say that she had changed her mind and would come with them after all, but she reined in that desire. After all, she had a date with, according to Heather, the hottest guy on No More Frogs to look forward to.

Her date with Jared started with a pleasant surprise: he actually looked like his profile picture.

Several female patrons of the coffee shop turned their heads to watch as he strode past. He stopped in front of the corner table she had picked and smiled at her with his toothpaste-commercial teeth. "Hi, I'm Jared. You must be Eliza."

"I am. Nice to meet you."

His gaze didn't flicker to her breasts as she stood, and he didn't try for a kiss on the cheek but greeted her with a short, not too tight hug. His cologne reminded her of Denny's.

Oh, no, no, no. This date was meant to confirm her attraction to guys, not make her think about Denny.

Jared got them hot beverages—asking for her preference instead of deciding for her—and then they settled at the table to get to know each other.

Eliza had picked a coffee shop instead of a restaurant so she could make a quick escape should things not go well. But as she finished her third mug of hibiscus tea, she realized the sun was sinking toward the horizon outside.

They had chatted about metalwork and movies and had bonded over their less than stellar experiences as baristas, with no awkward pauses or one of them monopolizing the conversation.

This time, she wouldn't be returning home with a funny story about her horrible date to tell Denny.

Gosh, there you go again, thinking about her. Here she was, sitting across the table from a funny, smart, and good-looking guy, and yet her thoughts kept returning to Denny.

When they finally left the coffee shop, Jared lightly rested his hand on the small of her back as he escorted her to the door. His touch felt nice, not patronizing. But the tingle she had expected was absent. No zero-gravity sensations set in and made her feel as if she were back on the Viking ship.

Oh God. He checked every item on her list of traits she wanted in a man, and yet...nothing. He didn't set off any of the reactions Denny's closeness caused. What did that mean?

He walked her to the corner, where they'd have to part ways since he had parked his car in a different direction from her apartment.

"Nice shoes." He pointed at her yellow sneakers as they walked.

"Thanks," she said. "I consider them my lucky first-date charm, but they haven't worked very well so far."

They reached the corner and turned to face each other.

"I hope they did today," he said. "I, for one, had a great time. Especially when you told that story about the woman who brought her pet iguana to the coffee shop." His stunningly blue eyes twinkled as he laughed.

"And I wasn't even exaggerating," Eliza said.

"That's what made it so funny." He searched her eyes. "So, do you want to go out again sometime? We could catch that movie you mentioned next weekend."

His charming grin should have made the answer a no-brainer.

But for Eliza, her answer was about more than this one date. It was a decision that felt monumental, as if it would influence the rest of her life. Maybe it would.

This time, it was Heather who lay in wait like a stalker, waiting for Eliza to make it home from her date. When Eliza trudged up the stairs, Heather's door opened, and she pulled her into the apartment. "Finally! I was starting to get worried. A coffee date doesn't normally last five hours!"

"I took a long walk through the park afterward." Eliza had thought it would help clear her head, but she still hadn't fully processed what was happening. "Sorry I forgot to call."

"You're forgiven—if you tell me every little detail." Heather closed the door behind her. "How was it? Did he really look like Henry Cavill? Was he nice? Did he ask for a second date?"

Eliza ducked her head as the questions rained down on her like hail. "Wine," she said firmly. A glass of red might help her make it through this conversation.

Heather opened a bottle of malbec and poured them each a glass. She pressed one into Eliza's hands and waved her down onto the couch. "So?"

Once they had taken a seat next to each other, Eliza started with the easiest answer. "He did look like Henry Cavill, dimpled chin and all."

"He doesn't, by any chance, have a sister, does he?" Heather let out a dreamy sigh. "Or maybe a female cousin?"

"I have no idea. We didn't talk about our families." While they had chatted easily, the conversation hadn't touched on anything deep or emotional the way it had with Denny from day one.

"So he wasn't a big talker? Lots of awkward silences?"

"No, not at all. We talked the entire time and laughed a lot."

Heather narrowed her eyes at her. "But?"

Eliza swirled the wine and watched the little streams run back down the insides of the glass. "No but. He seemed like a great guy, and I had a good time for a change."

"Phew." Heather pressed her free hand to her chest. "Finally! I was starting to feel guilty for making you go out with all those douchebags. Good to know No More Frogs isn't a total fail. So, where are you going for the second date? He did ask you out again, didn't he?"

"Yeah, he asked."

Heather waved her fingers in an out-with-it gesture. "Why do I have to drag every single word out of you? If I had just returned from a great date, you'd have to gag me to make me shut up about it. What's going on?"

Eliza put her wineglass down. She couldn't delay it any longer. "I'm not going to see him again."

"What?" With a clank, Heather's wineglass ended up on the coffee table next to Eliza's. "Why not?"

"He was great, but there wasn't any special connection." Not the kind she'd had with Denny pretty much from the start. Denny always made her feel seen and understood, while at the same time sending her into a tailspin of emotions.

"Special connection?" Heather snatched up her glass and took a gulp of wine. "Eliza, I love you to death, but are you sure you should approach first dates with such unrealistic expectations? I mean, you go on dates to *create* that connection; you can't expect it to be there from the start."

"You decided after the first date that you and Denny wouldn't work out as a couple. How's that different?"

Heather swished her wine around in a circle. "Hmm. Maybe you're right. It's just that you've been on more first dates than I have, but you always come to the same no-spark conclusion. I don't want you to end up alone because you're looking for an ideal that might not exist."

Eliza reached for her wineglass too, more for something to hold on to than because she wanted to take a sip. "It exists," she whispered.

"Since when are you such a romantic?"

"Since..." Eliza bit her lip before the rest of the sentence could slip out. *Since meeting Denny.* "Um, for a while now. I know you think I have impossibly high standards, but I just... I want it all." *And I want it with Denny.* The thought was so clear, so final that she sank against the back of the couch, needing the support. *Holy mackerel.*

Heather slid closer on the couch and wrapped one arm around her. "And you deserve it all. Please don't think I want you to settle for less."

"I know."

They sat like that for a few minutes, leaning against each other and sipping wine.

"More wine?" Heather asked when they had emptied their glasses.

Eliza hesitated. Should she stay and, with the help of some liquid courage, spill her guts to Heather? On the one hand, she longed to tell her best friend and get some advice, but on the other hand, shouldn't she talk to Denny first? They always talked about everything, and she hoped this wouldn't be the exception, no matter if Denny felt the same or not.

A chirp from her phone, announcing a text from Denny, made the decision for her.

"No, thanks. I should, uh…"

"Go tell Denny about your date," Heather finished for her.

"Um, yeah. Something like that." Eliza stood and carried the wineglasses to the sink. Her legs felt unsteady, but she knew it wasn't from the malbec. The thought of talking to Denny and confessing her confusing feelings made her struggle to breathe normally.

Heather followed her to the door. "You okay?"

Eliza didn't want to lie, but neither was she ready to tell the truth. "Kinda." She gave Heather a quick hug. "I promise to tell you later."

"All right." Heather leaned in the doorway, and Eliza felt her worried gaze following her all the way to her apartment.

She waved one last time before stepping inside. The door closed between them, and then Eliza was alone with her phone and her churning emotions.

Denny had read samples of at least ten different e-books, but none of them captured her attention beyond the first page, especially not the romance novels. All they did was make her imagine romantic scenarios involving Eliza and her date.

With a low growl, she closed her reading app and checked her messages.

Eliza still hadn't answered the *Did you make it home okay?* message Denny had sent her a few minutes ago.

She dropped her phone onto the coffee table, stretched out more fully on the couch, and covered her face with her forearm.

The sound of a key in the front door made her lift her arm.

Salem swept into the house in her above-the-knee dress and practically floated through the room. When Denny sat up to make space, she dropped onto the couch next to her, bounced twice, then kicked off her high heels.

Great. Her sister, poster child of happy daters, was home from her date, while Eliza was still out and about. That probably meant her evening was going great, and she couldn't tear herself away from the guy. Denny's stomach felt as if she had swallowed all the pins in her sewing basket. Had Eliza invited him up or gone home with him?

She rejected the thought. Eliza wasn't the type to have sex on the first date.

But why wasn't she home yet? If Eliza didn't text her within the next ten minutes, she would call to make sure she was okay.

"God." Salem let out a dreamy sigh. "That man can kiss."

Denny covered her ears with her hands. "TMI. I prefer to imagine that he drops you off with a polite handshake." Most of all, she preferred to imagine the same for Eliza and her date. The thought of some guy kissing Eliza left her nauseated.

Salem laughed. "Yep. Matt gives the best handshakes ever." She sobered and turned toward Denny more fully. "Thanks again for watching Bella. Did she give you any trouble?"

"No. Went to bed meek as a lamb."

Salem gave her a knowing look. "You bribed her with ricotta cheesecake, didn't you?"

"Yep. All is fair in war and babysitting." She had also promised Bella she would ask Eliza to come over for a journal-making session next weekend if she went to bed without complaints. But would Eliza have time for them if she hit it off with tonight's date?

"Don't let her hear you call it *babysitting*. Actually, would you mind watching her next Friday, and this time all night? Matt invited me over for—"

Denny held up both hands. "I'll watch her, but no details, please."

"I was just going to say dinner. His parents are in town, and he wants me to meet them. But yeah, I'm not ruling out an adult sleepover afterward," Salem said with a sultry grin.

Denny chose to ignore the last comment. "You're meeting his parents already? Guess it's serious, then."

Salem picked invisible lint off her dress. "You're not the only Jacobs woman who's head over heels in love."

Her words zapped through Denny with the force of an electric shock. "Whoa! I never said I'm in love!"

"You said it's more than a crush, so what else would it be? Besides, you don't have to say anything. I know you, Denny."

Shit. Denny had avoided looking at her feelings too closely so far, but she couldn't deny it. "I'm really happy for you." At least one of them had the good sense to fall in love with someone who could love her back.

"What about—?" A cha-chung from Denny's phone interrupted Salem, who laughed. "Speak of the devil."

At least it meant Eliza had made it home safe and sound. Denny snatched up her phone and checked her messages.

It was indeed a text from Eliza, saying, *Are you alone?*

Gosh, that sounded like an attempt to start sexting. She gave herself a mental slap to the head. *Get your mind out of the gutter, Jacobs.* "Uh, do you mind if I...?" She gestured at the phone, then toward her room.

"No, go ahead," Salem answered. "I'm off to bed anyway."

Denny gave her a quick hug, then hurried to her bedroom and texted back, *I am.*

Her phone immediately rang, and Eliza's name flashed across the screen.

"Hi," Denny said. "I was starting to get worried. Everything okay?"

"Yes, I'm fine," Eliza answered. In a whisper, she added, "More or less."

Denny's stomach folded itself into a pretzel. She had to draw in a breath before her lungs had enough air for her to speak. "What happened? He didn't, um, get handsy with you or anything, did he?" Because God help him if he did. Denny had never been a violent person, but images of hitting him, preferably with a baseball bat, flashed through her mind.

"No," Eliza said quickly. "Nothing like that. He was actually nice."

Denny's knees felt as if she'd just done a hundred squats, so she dropped onto the bed. "Yeah? You don't sound very sure."

"No, he really was. I liked him."

Good thing she was sitting. Despite her earlier fears, Denny had fully expected Eliza to recount another horrible date they would laugh about together. "Oh," was all she got out. "You did?"

"Yeah."

Denny closed her eyes. She should have known it would eventually happen. Eliza was too wonderful to not attract a good guy sooner rather than later. But where did that leave Denny? Could she make it through phone calls of Eliza reporting back from romantic dates, gushing about this guy? Could she listen to Eliza describing her growing feelings for him? Could she smile when Eliza told her they had gotten engaged?

"Denny?" Eliza asked. "You still there?"

"Yes," Denny managed to say. "I'm happy you finally had a good date." It was only partly a lie, she told herself. She did want to see

Eliza happy, and she had known from the start it wouldn't be with her.

"Um, thanks, but I didn't call to talk about Henry...uh, Jared."

"No? What did you want to talk about?"

Eliza drew in an audible breath, then let it back out. It sounded like a storm rushing through the phone. "I... I've got something to tell you. But I'd rather explain in person, if that's okay. Do you have time to meet up with me tomorrow?"

What the hell was going on? Denny wanted to know—now! But she was determined to respect Eliza's wishes and give her what she needed. "Of course," she said as calmly as possible. "When and where?"

"Maybe we could, I don't know, take a walk by the river or something," Eliza said.

"Sounds good to me. The dragon boat races are still going on tomorrow. Maybe you'd like to watch one since you missed them today."

"Um, sure, why not."

"Do you want me to ask Bella if she'd like to come?" Why the heck had she said that? Was she suddenly afraid to be alone with Eliza—or of hearing what she had to say?

"Normally, I'd love that, but do you mind if it's just us this time?" Eliza's voice was quiet, and Denny thought she heard it quiver.

Denny's pulse pounded in her throat. Not knowing why Eliza wanted them to be alone was torture. "No, that's okay. When?" She was tempted to suggest sunrise, knowing she wouldn't sleep a wink anyway.

"Is ten too early?" Eliza asked. "Or would you rather meet in the afternoon?"

No way could she wait until the afternoon to find out what Eliza had to say. "No, ten is fine."

They agreed to meet at the Salmon Street Springs, then, after a hastily whispered "sweet dreams," Eliza was gone.

Denny flopped down so she was lying across the bed and let the phone slide from her grasp. Her heart beat much too loudly, making her feel as if the entire bed was vibrating beneath her. What did Eliza have to tell her? Nothing good, of that she was sure. She had sounded way too serious for that.

Dozens of different scenarios bounced around her head. Was Eliza sick? Or sick of her company? Did she suspect Denny's more-than-friendly feelings for her? Oh God. What if she had made Eliza uncomfortable with that last tight hug they had shared?

She jumped up and started to pace. *Calm down.* That couldn't be it...could it? The hug was burned into her memory, and she had replayed it a thousand times. Eliza had held her just as tightly, had even put her head on Denny's shoulder, and hadn't seemed in a hurry to let go.

It had to be something else. But what?

She glanced at her watch and groaned. Eleven long hours and thirty-seven endless minutes to find out.

Chapter 17

GOOD THING THE SALMON STREET Springs were less than a mile from Eliza's apartment, so she could walk. If she'd had to drive, she would have crashed Heather's car at the first intersection. God, she hoped Denny would take the MAX.

But, of course, Denny had no idea what she was about to tell her...if she didn't chicken out. Was she really going to do this? Confess her attraction to another woman—to Denny?

The thought was still surreal. What if Denny didn't return her feelings? What if she did? Eliza swallowed. Both scenarios made her equally nervous.

Her heart pounded loudly, drowning out her footsteps on the sidewalk.

She wished she had talked it through with Heather. But her friend tended to sleep in on Sundays, and she had reached the fountain, so calling her now was out.

The jets of the fountain greeted her as she crossed the street.

She was half an hour early, but she hadn't been able to stay in her apartment for a minute longer.

Because of the dragon boat races, Waterfront Park was unusually busy for a Sunday morning. People headed toward the Hawthorne Bridge to watch the races, and a group of women with T-shirts bearing the Canadian flag carried big coolers.

Shit. This wasn't a great setting for a heartfelt conversation. She hadn't thought this through at all.

Despite the nervous energy buzzing through her body, she steered toward one of the benches surrounding the fountain. She didn't want to draw attention to herself by pacing in circles while she waited.

After two steps toward the bench, she stumbled to a stop and stared.

Denny sat on the bench she was heading toward. She wasn't sprawled out comfortably, enjoying the early-June sun. Her posture was rigid, with her shoulders drawn up as if expecting someone to slap her.

No, not someone. You. A wave of nausea rolled through Eliza. God, she was making a mess of things.

Their gazes found each other immediately, and Denny watched her cross the last few yards with wide eyes.

"It's not bad," Eliza blurted out as soon as she reached her. "What I have to tell you. At least I hope it's not."

"Oh." Denny's drawn-up shoulders lowered but only about an inch. "So I didn't...? I haven't, um, done anything to upset you?"

"No! God, no, Denny! Why would you think that?"

Denny scraped her shoe across the ground, and Eliza noticed she was wearing sneakers too. "I dunno."

Eliza sank onto the bench next to her. Since an elderly woman occupied the other end of the bench, they had to sit close. Their shoulders and thighs brushed, and a rush of warmth suffused her body.

What she was about to do might feel surreal, but there couldn't be any doubt that this—the way she reacted to Denny—was very real.

Denny peeked at her out of the corner of her eye. "If it's not me, what did you want to tell me?"

Eliza's gaze darted to the elderly woman who wasn't even trying to hide her eavesdropping. "Uh, could we walk a little?"

Denny jumped up as if sitting still was taxing for her too.

While they walked south and crossed beneath the Hawthorne Bridge, Denny kept throwing her questioning looks.

Sweat broke out along Eliza's back. Why hadn't she practiced what she wanted to say? *Tell her! Can't you see how anxious you're making her?*

Just as she opened her mouth to blurt out the first thing that came to mind, cheers rose, and four boats with brightly decorated dragon heads shot toward the nearby finish line with its bobbing orange buoys. The fast-paced drum beats matched the rhythm of Eliza's heart.

"Come on," Denny yelled over the excited voice of the announcer booming through loudspeakers. "Let's walk a bit farther."

They followed the dirt path parallel to the river, past the announcer booth and the busy area where the teams were lining up to check in. Their hilarious chants rose over the noise of the onlookers, distracting Eliza for a moment.

Once they had passed the dock where the dragon boats were loading and unloading, the drums and the announcer's voice faded into the distance, and it got quieter.

But instead of calming, Eliza's heart beat faster. She knew she had to tell her, yet had no idea how.

Denny stuffed her hands into her pockets and threw her sidelong glances but didn't hurry her along.

As if by an unspoken agreement, they veered away from the river and strolled along several artificial ponds in South Waterfront Garden, where they had more privacy.

Denny bent, picked something up, and held it out to Eliza.

It was a rock.

When she took it, their fingers brushed, and a thrill rippled up Eliza's arm. She tried to ignore it by studying the stone. With its smooth surface and round shape, it was perfect for rock painting. *Aww.* Even during the tensest moment between them, Denny had thought to pick up a rock for her. Eliza had never in her life considered the perfect person for her might be a woman, but here it was: that special connection she'd been looking for.

She had to take a risk and tell her. The ability to walk and talk at the same time escaped her, so she stopped in midstride.

Denny paused too. Her hazel eyes darkened with something like panic.

Eliza clutched the stone in her damp hand. She peeked from the yellow sneakers that had started it all to Denny. Okay, it was now or never. She opened her mouth without the faintest idea of what she would say.

Watching Eliza struggle with whatever she was about to say made a pang of anxiety flutter down Denny's spine. God, she wanted so much to take her hand to comfort her. But it would probably make things worse. She clenched her fists in her pockets and tried to give her a reassuring look—which wasn't easy since her panic was growing.

Eliza opened her mouth. Her jaw worked, but no words came out. She stomped her sneaker-covered foot as if giving herself a mental pep talk. Finally, she blurted, "You're a great friend."

Denny frowned. Telling her that wasn't what had made Eliza look close to a panic attack, was it? "Um, thanks. You're a wonderful friend too."

"I've never connected with anyone like this before." Eliza waved her hand back and forth between them. "Especially not this fast."

Warmth spread through Denny's chest. But before she could assure her she felt the same, Eliza held up her hand.

"Ugh. That isn't what I'm trying to say. I mean, it's all true, and I value our friendship a lot, but..."

Denny studied her intensely. She still wasn't sure where Eliza was going with this. "Um, this is starting to sound like a breakup. Well, a friendship breakup." She let out a nervous giggle. Shit. Since when did she giggle? "As if you're trying to say: I really like you, but I don't think we should be friends anymore."

"No!" Eliza rubbed her face with both hands and groaned. "No, no, that's not it at all. Quite the opposite. I think I like you...as more than a friend."

Denny stopped breathing. A weird buzzing sounded in her ears. "You..." She sucked a breath into her oxygen-starved lungs. "You didn't just say what I think you said, did you?"

Eliza nodded several times as if words escaped her.

Denny opened her mouth, but all that came out was a soft little "oh." Her brain felt like scrambled eggs and was incapable of formulating a clear thought. Emotions washed over her too fast to identify them all. Eliza liked her as more than a friend! She wanted to jump up and down, pull Eliza against her, and kiss her with all the pent-up feelings that had been growing inside her for a while.

Another part of her wanted to turn on her heel and run. She'd heard stories like that a thousand times, and each of them ended with the lesbian partner being heartbroken.

"Say something, please. W-what do you think?" Eliza asked quietly. Her dark brown eyes were wide.

Denny shoved her glasses higher up on her nose with her right hand, then adjusted them with her left. "I..." There wasn't enough air in her lungs.

"Oh God." Eliza covered her face with her hands again. "I shouldn't have assumed... Just because you're gay doesn't mean you're attracted to me."

"I am!" Denny finally found her voice. "I'm so attracted to you, it's getting hard to think of anything else when you're in the same room—even if you aren't in the same room, to be honest. I just didn't think you would ever feel the same."

The tiniest of smiles tugged on Eliza's lips. "I didn't think I would either."

"But you do?"

"Yeah."

Eliza hadn't said *I think so*. Even though this was new to her, she sounded as if she had given it a lot of thought and was sure of what she felt.

"Wow." Denny gestured toward a nearby bench. "Can we go over there? I need to sit down."

A quiet chuckle escaped Eliza. "Yeah, I feel like I'm about to fall over too."

Side by side, they walked to the bench and took a seat. Denny made sure she gave Eliza plenty of space, but Eliza didn't seem to want it. She sat close enough for Denny to feel her warmth.

Both were silent for a while.

Finally, Eliza said, "If you're attracted to me, why do you look so...I don't know...not exactly overjoyed?"

"Did you see the person hanging off the front of each dragon boat earlier?" Denny gestured toward the river. "The ones who were supposed to grab the flag to win the race for their team?"

Eliza nodded.

"That's kind of how I feel," Denny said. "Totally eager and feeling like I'm inches away from the best prize of my life, but also like I'm too damn close to falling overboard and getting hurt."

"That's the last thing I want to do. Hurt you, I mean." Eliza slid closer and grabbed her hand. Then she froze.

Denny held her hand loosely, letting her make the decision as to whether she wanted to pull away. Her heart beat so rapidly that she was sure Eliza felt it through her fingertips.

After a moment, Eliza linked their fingers and squeezed.

A lungful of air whooshed from Denny's chest. She returned the gentle pressure, and only now could she enjoy the feeling of holding Eliza's hand. She'd had hot kisses and even great sex several times in her life, but right now, she was convinced this was the most wonderful sensation she had ever experienced. She studied their intertwined fingers. While they were about the same height, Eliza's hand was more delicate than hers, and Denny cradled it gently.

Eliza cleared her throat. "That's why I haven't said anything so far—to avoid hurting you." Her voice sounded hoarse, as if she wasn't unaffected by the feel of Denny's hand either. "I wanted to make sure it wasn't a fluke."

Denny blinked as she processed that information. "So you've felt this way for some time?" she rasped out. When Eliza nodded, she asked, "How long?"

A hint of pink dusted Eliza's cheeks and made her look even more beautiful. "Pretty much from the first time we met in person. Maybe even before that. But when you hugged me hello that day at the festival, I think part of me knew then; I just didn't understand what I was feeling." She looked Denny in the eyes, and Denny was blown away by how honest she was and how vulnerable she was making herself. "You?"

Denny mentally went over all the little moments and snippets of conversation they had shared, some in person, some on the phone, and some via text. In hindsight, her feelings had left the friendship zone very quickly. "I think it was when you sent me a picture of you in a skirt and these." She gently nudged Eliza's sneaker with her foot. Even that little touch made her body tingle.

Eliza's eyes widened, then she laughed. "Uh, Denny, that was on the very first day, in the very first text I sent you."

Denny shrugged. "Yep. That's when it all started."

Eliza waggled her feet back and forth and studied the canary-yellow sneakers. "I guess they really are lucky."

Denny studied her face, her eyes, and that little smile playing around her sensuous lips. "You sound so calm, now that we've admitted our feelings. Isn't this freaking you out?"

Eliza tilted her head as if she had to think about it before she answered, "Not really."

Well, that makes one of us. Denny tightened her grip on Eliza's hand. "Have you...have you felt like this before? For a woman?"

"No." Eliza vehemently shook her head. "I mean, I always thought women were beautiful, but this surprised the hell out of me." She opened her eyes almost comically wide. "I never considered that I could be anything but straight. But I come from a very liberal family, and I have LGBT+ friends, so it's not like I'm worried about being damned to purgatory for all eternity if I kiss another woman."

Did that mean Eliza wanted to kiss her? Denny's gaze darted to Eliza's lips. They looked so soft and— *Stop it. Don't scare her away by rushing this.* She forced her gaze up to Eliza's eyes. "That's, uh, good. Really good."

"I'm not saying I have this all figured out or that I won't have a couple of freak-out moments. I have so many unanswered questions, and I don't even know where to start." Eliza pressed her free hand to her temple as if to push them back.

Denny gently trailed her thumb over Eliza's index finger. "If I can answer any of them, let me know."

"Thanks. I will."

Silence fell, interrupted only by the wind rustling through the tall grasses surrounding them and the distant sounds of the dragon boat races.

Denny peered across the blooming garden at the Marquam Bridge, following its arc across the river. She tried hard not to put any pressure on Eliza, but she had to know. "So, where do we go from here?"

"I'm not sure exactly. I just know that I'm attracted to you, physically and emotionally, and I'm not going to let a label or my previous assumptions about myself stop me from exploring the possibility of having a relationship with you."

Eliza talking so openly about being attracted to her filled Denny with happiness, but then the word *exploring* made her wince even though she tried to suppress it.

"I didn't mean it like that," Eliza said quickly. "Please don't think I'm looking at this like it's some sort of experiment. I never want you to feel like that, okay? It's just that this is all new to me, and I don't want to pretend I know where it'll go. I just know that I want to find out. But if that's not something you can do, I understand."

Denny's yearning fought with her fears and finally wrestled them down. She knew they might raise their ugly heads again, but if Eliza could be brave for them, she was determined to risk it too. "I can do it," she said, as much to herself as to Eliza.

The tangle of their hands tightened.

Eliza swiped a strand of her shiny chestnut hair behind one ear and smiled at her. "You said to tell you whenever I have a question you might be able to answer. I think I have one."

Denny twisted on the bench to face her more fully. "You can ask me anything."

Eliza took an audible breath. "Would you like to go out with me? Not an outing between friends. I'm talking about a date."

Wow. Denny wasn't sure what question she had expected, but not this.

"Um, is it okay to ask that?" Eliza asked when Denny didn't answer immediately. "I know you said women usually expect you to take the lead because they see you as butch, but I thought maybe you don't want to be the one to do all the work all the time and…"

Denny grinned.

"Uh, what?"

"You're really cute when you start to ramble, did anyone ever tell you that?"

"No. You're the first."

Being the first woman Eliza had ever been attracted to still made Denny nervous, but maybe being the first for other things wasn't a bad thing at all.

"So?" Eliza asked. "Are you going to answer my question?"

"Yes."

"Yes, you'll answer my question, or yes, you'll go on a date with me?"

Denny laughed. "Yes to both." She gentled her teasing grin. "I'd love to go on a date with you."

"Good. I'll think of something and let you know."

Denny just nodded as her mind caught up with what was going on. They were doing this. They really were doing this! "And what now? I mean, *now* now."

"Ice cream," Eliza said decisively.

"Ice cream?"

"Yes. I think I saw some over there." Eliza waved her hand in the direction of the RiverPlace Esplanade and the stores they had passed earlier.

Chuckling, Denny stood and pulled her up with her. Apparently, the past ease between them hadn't completely vanished now they had confessed their mutual attraction. Her earlier tension fled from her shoulders. "All right. Let's get ice cream."

Chapter 18

A FEW HOURS LATER, DENNY still couldn't shake that feeling of being asleep and having the most wonderful dream as she entered the house and tossed her keys onto a side table—at least, that was what she'd aimed for. She missed by several inches, and the keys rattled to the floor.

Salem looked up from where she was slicing an avocado. "Great timing. Bella and I are making grilled cheese sandwiches. How many do you want?"

Food was the last thing on Denny's mind. Her stomach was still too jittery. "None for me, thanks. I'm not hungry."

"Did you eat with Eliza?" Salem asked.

Just the mention of Eliza's name made Denny's heart beat faster. She picked up the keys and tried for nonchalance. "Yeah, we had ice cream."

Bella abandoned the tomato she had been slicing and walked up to Denny. "Did you ask her about next weekend?"

"Next weekend?" Denny repeated, feeling as if her brain was working in slow motion.

"Yeah. You said you'd ask her if she can come over and teach me how to make a journal."

"Oh da...darn." Denny slapped her own thigh. "Sorry, Bella. I forgot. Next weekend probably won't work for that anyway because, um, we might be going out on a date."

Salem dropped the pit she had removed from another avocado. "Wait! You mean, Eliza is going on a date, and you have a date too. Not that you and she...?"

Denny knew she had the silliest grin on her face as she nodded. "We're going on a date with each other."

"I—told—you—so!" Salem pointed the tip of her knife at her and shook it with every word. "I told you the way she looks at you is"—she glanced at Bella—"not fit for underaged company."

"Pleeeeaase." Bella rolled her eyes up to the ceiling. "It's not like I didn't see it. I could totally tell."

Seriously? Denny gazed back and forth between them. Why had everyone but her seen it coming, even her eleven-year-old niece?

Bella rushed to the stairs.

"Hey, where are you going?" Salem called. "You're not done slicing the tomatoes!"

"I have to call Kaylee and tell her. Oh my God, she'll be so jealous that Eliza is practically my new aunt!"

Denny's jaw gaped halfway to her knees. By the time she snapped her mouth shut, Bella was already at the top of the stairs. "Whoa! We're going on a date, not getting married, Bella!"

Her niece didn't answer. The door to Bella's room slammed shut.

"God," Salem murmured. "Why do kids lose the ability to close doors like a normal person as soon as they turn ten?" She put the knife down, wiped her hands on a dish towel, and pulled Denny into a tight hug. "I'm so proud of you."

Denny returned the hug for a moment before stepping back. "Um, thanks, but why would you be proud of me? For going on a date with Eliza?"

"For listening to me and asking her if she could ever feel the same."

"Uh, I didn't." Denny rubbed her overly hot earlobe. "Eliza was the one who did that, not me."

Salem let out a whistle. "Damn, that took guts."

"Yeah, she's amazing." Warmth filled Denny from head to toe as she remembered the expression on Eliza's face as she had blurted it out.

Salem wrapped her arms around Denny a second time. "I'm so happy for you!"

"Thanks. But we're taking it one step at a time. Like I told Bella, it's one date, not marriage."

Salem let go and regarded her with a wrinkle between her brows. "But you want more than just one date, don't you?"

"Of course. But I can't let myself think too far ahead. So much could go wrong. I mean, what if Eliza figures out being with a woman isn't right for her after all? Or what if the age difference between us turns out to be a problem? Or—"

Salem thrust her hand out. "Let me quote what a wise woman once said to me when I got cold feet before my first date with Matt: Eliza is probably aware of everything that could go wrong, yet she cares enough to take the risk. That has to count for something."

"It does," Denny said. "But—"

"No buts, Denny. You're overthinking it. You say you're not thinking too far ahead, but that's bullshit. You totally are—but you're only thinking of all the negative things that could happen, not of things going great between you two."

Damn. Salem was right. "When did you get so smart, baby sis?"

Salem winked at her. "I had a good role model. Now come on. My sous-chef seems to have abandoned me, so I need a new one."

"I'm not sure I can be trusted with a knife right now," Denny said. "I haven't slept a wink, and my hands are still shaking."

Salem pulled her to the kitchen. "You'll survive. And if you do cut yourself, you can ask Eliza to kiss it and make it all better."

Denny ignored the flush that mental image brought. She grabbed the dish towel from the counter, twirled it a few times, and playfully snapped it across Salem's backside.

Eliza had just entered the small, wood-paneled entrance hall of her apartment building when footsteps sounded coming down the stairs and Heather came into view.

"Hey, I just knocked on your door," Heather said. "I'm going for a Yolko Ono. Want to come?"

The thought of the fried-egg sandwich made Eliza's mouth water, even though a second ago, eating had been the last thing on her mind. Her stomach answered before she could, letting out a loud growl to remind her it was past lunchtime and she hadn't eaten anything except for a scoop of ice cream.

"I'll take that as a yes." Heather laughed, wrapped one arm around her, and pulled her out of the building.

Eliza didn't protest. She wasn't sure she would be able to eat anything, despite what her belly said, but maybe she could use the opportunity to tell Heather about her and Denny. Keeping it from her best friend any longer wasn't fair. Besides, she was bursting to tell someone, and who better than Heather?

They strolled north on SW Park Avenue.

Eliza searched for the right words but came up empty. *Come on!* She had ten minutes before they reached the square—ten minutes to tell Heather so she wouldn't choke on her egg sandwich. Eliza tried to calm her rapid heartbeat. Why on earth was this so difficult? She wouldn't hesitate to tell Heather if she were dating a guy, would she? This shouldn't have been any different, but it was.

"So, what have you been up to today?" Heather asked as they passed the Portland Art Museum.

"Denny and I went down to the waterfront." The mere mention of Denny made her voice come out in a rasp. She hoped Heather wouldn't notice.

"Oh, to watch the finals of the dragon boat races?"

Eliza tilted her head in a vague nod. "That too."

"Who won?" Heather asked.

"I have no idea. I was a little distracted."

Heather waited until they had crossed a side street before she gave her a thorough once-over. "Distracted by what?"

Eliza held her breath as she said quietly, "Denny."

Heather chuckled. "Yeah, with that shy little grin, she can be a bit—" Her head jerked around. "Wait! That shy little grin wouldn't do anything for a straight woman like you. You didn't mean it like that, did you?"

Eliza glanced at her sneakers, then at Heather. "I meant it exactly like that." She held her friend's gaze. "I...I asked her out."

At the last second, Heather veered around a *park here* sign pointing at the parking lot across the street. She grabbed Eliza's arm to keep her balance and then didn't let go. "Son of a bulldog! You did not!"

"Yes, I did. I hope that's not awkward for you. I mean, since you went out with her too."

"Pah!" Heather waved her free hand. "Forget about that. We didn't have any chemistry, but the two of you...you did?"

Eliza nodded. At the next intersection, she steered them to the right.

For several steps, all Heather did was shake her head. "When you said you'd take some time off from dating guys, I didn't think you meant you'd start dating women!"

Eliza still wasn't sure if it was women in general she was attracted to or just Denny, so she simply shrugged.

Heather slapped her forehead. "Oh! So you *were* jealous when I went out with her, just not the way I imagined! Why didn't you say anything?"

"What was I supposed to say? 'No, you can't go out with her; I want her for myself.'?" She shook her head. "I wasn't ready for that."

For once, Eliza's unflappable best friend looked stunned. "And now you are?"

Was she? "I think so. Still haven't fully recovered from the surprise, though."

"So this is the first time you've been interested in a woman, right?" Heather asked.

"Jeez, what do you think? That I've been hiding it from you all these years?"

"Well, no, but in hindsight, do you think you've ever felt something for another woman and were just in denial?"

Eliza had asked herself the same question, night after night, when she had lain awake or had googled things to make sense of what she was feeling. "I don't think so." She glanced around and lowered her voice. "I mean, there were women I admired, and I stared at a lot of breasts with longing when I was younger. But that was more of an *I want to look like that* than an *I want to touch them.* At least I think that's what it was."

A sly grin spread over Heather's face. "So with Denny's boobs... which of the two is it?"

Her friend was enjoying this a bit too much. Eliza sped up as they turned left onto Sixth Avenue to escape Heather's questioning.

But with her longer legs, Heather easily kept up with her. She held on to Eliza's elbow. "Hey, you know I'm not making fun of you and what you're going through, right? Well, maybe a little." She held the thumb and index finger of her free hand half an inch apart. "But mostly, I want to make sure you're not putting yourself into a situation where you feel pressured to do something you don't want. Can you imagine being intimate with her?"

God! Eliza started to understand how Denny must feel with her tendency to blush. Her cheeks felt feverish...and so did the rest of her body as she thought about Heather's question.

She and Denny had hugged goodbye earlier, so she could easily imagine being in Denny's arms. Her imagination took the next step, showing her the same scenario—sans clothes. As soft as Denny's favorite jacket was, her skin was probably even softer, and Eliza would be able to feel that wonderful mix of strength and softness even better. Mmm, yeah, she wouldn't have a problem with that at all.

For a moment, she allowed herself to imagine touching Denny's breasts, trusting Heather's grip on her arm to prevent her from running into a streetlamp. The thought was surreal, but not repulsive at all. She was definitely interested in finding out if Denny's breasts were as soft as she imagined.

As for doing more...

Her stomach flip-flopped, and she wasn't sure if it was from desire or panic. Probably both.

"Saved by the food cart." Heather pointed at the big, yellow truck ahead.

When had they reached Pioneer Square?

Heather laughed and patted her arm. "You take a seat; I'll get the food. You want your usual, or are you trying something new food-wise too?"

"You!" Eliza gave her a friendly push but couldn't help laughing. It felt good to talk about it—and to joke about it—because it reminded her this was supposed to be a fun experience, not something to be anxious about. "I'll take my usual, please."

She took a seat on one of the two dozen steps, which formed a semicircle of red bricks in the square's center, while Heather got in line. Eliza pulled one knee to her chest, put her chin on top, and stared off across the square without registering any of the hustle and bustle.

Wow, she was dating a woman—dating Denny! Her brain hadn't had enough time to sort through all the new information and what it might mean, but telling Heather had somehow made it more real.

She zeroed in on two young women crossing the square, laughing and talking. Did she see them differently than she had before? Or what about the beautiful redhead who sat a few steps down from her? Did she find her attractive? Her fair skin and cute nose were certainly pretty, but even the straightest woman on earth would be able to see that, right?

"Here." Heather settled down next to her and held out a sandwich. "One Free-Range against the Machine with Havarti cheese and the spicy aioli, as requested."

Eliza flinched since Heather had seemed to appear out of nowhere.

"Sorry, did I startle you? You seemed very focused on..." Heather's gaze veered around and finally landed on the redhead. "Wait! Did you just check her out?" She laughed and slapped her thigh with one hand. "Oh my God, you totally did!"

"Shh!" Eliza ducked her head and waved at her to settle down. "Jeez, could you say it any louder? I did not," she lowered her voice, "check her out. I was just—"

"Comparing her to Denny?" Heather finished the sentence for her. "Trying to find out if you have a type?"

Eliza peeled back the top slice of perfectly grilled sourdough bread and pretended to check out the contents of her sandwich. Finally, she peeked at Heather. "Yeah, something like that."

Chuckling, Heather wrapped one arm around Eliza and pulled her against her side. "Hey, that's perfectly normal in your situation. You're practically going through lesbian puberty."

Eliza chuckled even as she held up her free hand. "Uh, I'm not sure that label fits me. Lesbian, I mean. Puberty fits. I do feel like a pubescent teen."

"Okay," Heather said, "not-quite-straight puberty, then."

Yeah, she supposed that description fit her well. Even though the thought still made her head spin, she couldn't call herself straight any longer.

They both took bites of their sandwiches and moaned at the same time.

The crispy bread, the fried egg, and the melted cheese formed a perfect combination with the avocado and tomato, and the spicy aioli added an extra kick.

Runny egg yolk dribbled down Eliza's chin, and she grabbed the paper napkin that came with the sandwich, while Heather managed to eat without creating a mess. It was good to know that, even at this time of change, some things stayed the same.

Heather swallowed her bite of Yolko Ono. "So what conclusion did you come to?" She gestured toward the redhead.

Eliza gave a one-shouldered shrug. "I have no idea. Do I have to come to any conclusions right now?"

"No. You've got all the time in the world to figure it out. Let me know if you need any help with that. Theoretical help, that is." Heather waggled her eyebrows. "I assume Denny will help you with the practical parts."

Eliza threw her wadded-up napkin at Heather but refused to look away from her twinkling brown eyes. "Thanks, I assume so too."

"Ooh, do tell!" Heather nudged her. "Did she kiss you?"

"No." Eliza relived the moment they had said goodbye at the MAX stop earlier. If she wasn't mistaken, Denny's gaze had darted to her lips, and for a second, she had thought Denny might kiss her, but then she had wrapped her arms around her in a tender hug. As wonderful as that embrace had been, Eliza now realized she'd wanted Denny to kiss her.

Heather took another bite, chewed it with a thoughtful expression, and then dabbed her napkin to her lips. "Honestly, I'm not surprised she didn't."

Eliza eyed her. "What do you mean?" Dating a woman seemed to come with its own rules and expectations, none of which she was familiar with.

"Remember Cindy?" Heather asked.

"Your ex?"

Heather nodded. "She'd never been with a woman before me either, so I was super careful every step of the way, making sure she was okay with what we were doing. Knowing Denny, she'll be even more careful. You might have to take the first step and kiss her."

"Oh." Eliza paused with the sandwich halfway to her mouth. In most of her relationships, she had let her partner take the lead and initiate the first kiss. But that was an outdated stereotype anyway, wasn't it? Why shouldn't she kiss Denny first? She squared her shoulders. "Yeah, well, I just might."

Heather twirled her fist in circles above her head. "Woo-hoo! You go, girl!"

With a determined nod, Eliza stuffed the rest of her sandwich into her mouth. Yeah, she would totally kiss Denny. But before that could happen, she had to come up with the perfect idea for their first date.

Chapter 19

"WE ARE CLOSING REGISTER THREE. Please head to the next available checkout." Denny turned off the light signaling her checkout was open, stood, and bit back a groan. Her knees had stiffened after hours of sitting at the register. It had been a long shift, and now she couldn't wait to clock out.

She would go on a date with Eliza in exactly—she glanced at her wristwatch—two hours and seventeen minutes. After six days of only talking on the phone, she couldn't wait to see Eliza again, but she was also more nervous about this afternoon than she had been on any date with another woman before, and that was saying something.

She pulled her cash drawer from the register and carried it into the office.

While the shift manager counted her drawer, she said hi to Julie, who was getting ready for her shift.

"Hey, Denny," Julie said. "Tanya and I are meeting up at The Goodfoot after work. Do you want to join us?"

"Um, no, thanks. I've got plans."

"Come on. I feel like we haven't really talked in forever, and spending time at your sewing machine doesn't constitute plans."

Denny shook her head. "I've got plans with someone other than my Singer. But I promise we'll catch up soon."

The shift manager finished counting, frowned, then started over again.

What on earth was taking him so long, today of all days?

Finally, he looked up and shook his head. "You're short by ten dollars."

"What?" Denny stepped closer to the desk. It had been years since she'd been off by more than a few cents, and she prided herself on that. "Are you sure?"

He gave a stern nod.

Julie walked over. "That's a first. You're always perfectly balanced. What's up with you?"

Denny bit her lip. She couldn't admit she hadn't been able to focus worth a damn because she'd been thinking about Eliza and their date all shift. Not in front of their boss. Sighing, she signed the sheet he held out to her and promised to do better in the future.

When she went to clock out, Julie rushed after her. "Oh, I get it! It's Eliza, isn't it?"

Denny froze with her card halfway to the time clock, then whirled around. "How did you know?"

"Please! You've talked about nothing but her all week! You were a regular chatterbox for once."

Denny stared at her. "I was?"

"Well, okay, maybe not exactly a chatterbox, but you did talk about her a lot. What's up with that? Are you two dating or something?"

"Yes, we are." Denny couldn't help smiling. "This afternoon is our first date."

"Oh! So that's why you bribed me with one of your sister's famous apple pies to swap shifts with you!"

Denny rubbed her nose, pushing her glasses higher. "Um, yeah."

"Exciting!" Julie held her hand out for a high five, and Denny obliged. "Where are you taking her?"

"She's taking me somewhere, but she won't say where."

Julie let out a low whistle. "So she's wearing the pants in the relationship!"

Denny lowered her head to stare her down over the rim of her glasses. "No one's wearing the pants in our relationship." Okay, that sounded as if they spent their time together naked, and that—unfortunately—was not the case. "I mean, we're equals. She's taking me out today, and I get to decide where we're going next time."

Chuckling, Julie patted her arm. "Got it. Have fun."

"Thanks." Denny clocked out and took her phone from her locker, eager to get out of there before some emergency cropped up and delayed her. As she climbed into her Subaru, her phone cha-chunged, announcing a message from Eliza.

Just seeing her name on the screen made Denny smile.

Hey, you. Are we still on for later?

Yeah, Denny typed back. *Just leaving work. I was able to swap with Julie.*

The three dots appeared, then faded away. Finally, an answer popped up. *Uh. I didn't think you'd have to go that far to get the rest of the day off!* Eliza added several crying-laughing emojis.

What was she talking about? Denny scratched her head.

More laughing smiley faces appeared on her screen, along with, *Read what you wrote.*

Autocorrect had changed what she had written to: *I was able to sleep with Julie.* She stabbed at the keys and kept an eye on the letters that appeared. *SWAP! I meant swap! I swapped shifts with Julie.*

Thank God. I admit I don't like the thought of you sleeping with someone else.

The breath of air Denny had just inhaled shuddered from her lungs. She sat in the car without moving for a few seconds. Eliza had surprised her with little comments like this several times during the last six days. Nothing earth-shattering, but it soothed her worries every time Eliza voiced her feelings so openly, confirming that she still wanted a relationship beyond friendship. Plus she had to admit Eliza being possessive was hot.

Finally, she realized she still hadn't answered and typed, *I wouldn't.* She nibbled on her bottom lip. Should she say what was on her mind, or would that be going too fast, pressuring Eliza? Oh, what the hell. She typed quickly before she could censor herself.

I'm also not dating anyone else. Just thought I'd let you know. She paused, then added, *Okay, you already know that. It's not like I've got women lining up at my door. But even if I did, I wouldn't date anyone else. That doesn't mean I'm putting any expectations on you to do the same.*

She white-knuckled the phone while she waited for the answer. God, what was she doing? Was she seriously asking Eliza to be exclusive before their first date?

Her phone rang, and Eliza's name flashed across the screen.

Denny swallowed and accepted the call. "Hi."

"Denny," Eliza said, and the way she said her name made goose bumps trail all over Denny's body, "you followed along on my dating adventures for two months. Have you ever known me to go out with a second person when I fully intended to keep dating someone?"

That sounded encouraging. But then again... "Um, as long as I've known you, you never intended to keep dating anyone beyond the first date, so how would I know?"

"Oops. You've got me there." An impish smile resonated in Eliza's voice. "Let me phrase it differently. I have never in my life dated two people at the same time, and since I fully expect us to keep dating beyond the first date..."

Denny bit back the "you do?" that wanted to slip out. Insecurities weren't sexy. Besides, Eliza's words calmed her fears, allowing her to say, "Far be it from me to convince you otherwise, but if we go out today and it doesn't feel right to you, please tell me. It would be totally okay." *Liar, liar, pants on fire.* She would not be okay if that happened, but she wanted to do right by Eliza and offer her an out if she needed it.

"That's so sweet of you to say. I know you're looking out for me, and I appreciate it. But I don't want to go on our date with that expectation—and I don't want you to do that either." Eliza's tone was warm but firm. "I want us both to expect a great time."

"I'm sure we will." Denny always had a good time with Eliza. Maybe Eliza was right, and her anxiety was completely unjustified. "Unless, of course, you drag me someplace un-fun."

Eliza's laughter reverberated through the phone. It was quickly becoming Denny's favorite sound in the world. "Nice try. Don't think I didn't notice you trying to find out where I'm taking you."

They had bantered back and forth about it every night on the phone, so by now, it was a running joke. "Can't you at least give me a hint so I can prepare?"

"Prepare?" Eliza chuckled. "Denny, it's a date, not an oral exam."

The word *oral* sent Denny's thoughts spiraling in a direction that wasn't appropriate for sitting in her car in front of her workplace. She cleared her throat. "I know. But I have to know how to dress. What do you want me to wear?"

"What's your most comfortable outfit?" Eliza asked.

"Sweatpants and an old T-shirt with a big hole in the armpit. I've patched it up like a hundred times, and Salem has wanted to throw it away about as many times, but I threatened to put toothpaste in her favorite shoes if she dares to touch my shirt."

Eliza's laughter trickled through the phone. "I have a sweater like that. I've had it since high school, and my mom said she would not let me move out with 'that thing,' so I had to smuggle it out."

Discovering little details they had in common was fun, and Denny hoped there'd be a lot more of it later. "You don't seriously want me to wear the holey shirt, do you?"

"That might be a tad too casual," Eliza answered. "Think one step up."

"Jeans and a hole-free T-shirt?"

"Perfect."

Denny never wore jeans and a T-shirt on a first date. She always dressed up to show her date she was putting in an effort. "Seriously?"

"Mm-hmm. I really like you in jeans, and that Henley shirt you wore when you took Bella to Saturday Market looked good on you too."

Was it just her imagination, or had Eliza's voice become lower and huskier? A grin spread over Denny's face. So Eliza liked the way she looked, love handles and all. The thought filled her with warmth—and relief. "You know what? Our date hasn't even begun, and I already love it."

"God, I hope so," Eliza said. "You might think it's silly."

"Now who's going in with negative expectations?"

Eliza chuckled. "Touché. Okay, you'd better get your cute behind home, or you won't make it to our date on time."

So Eliza thought her ass was cute? "On my way. See you in one hour, fifty-nine minutes, and about twenty seconds."

They said goodbye, and then Denny threw the phone onto the passenger seat and started the engine. She couldn't wait to see Eliza.

Eliza had been as calm as a contented cat in the sun all day, but half an hour before leaving the house, the first-date jitters started. She dashed to Heather's apartment and, after a sharp rap on the door, let herself in.

Heather looked up from the leather coasters she was crafting. "Uh-oh," she said when she saw Eliza's face. "Don't panic. What do you need—advice on what to wear? Or do you want me to do your makeup?"

Eliza shook her head. "I won't be wearing any."

"Clothes?" Heather laughed. "Or makeup?"

"Haha. Makeup. I want us to be ourselves. No masks. No armor. No makeup."

A low whistle pierced the sudden silence. "This is different for you, isn't it?"

"Yes," Eliza said. "That's why I need your advice."

Heather put the mallet and leather stamps aside and led her to the couch. "Shoot. Dr. Heather, lesbian dating expert, will now answer your questions."

Eliza pulled one of the throw pillows onto her lap. "Don't laugh, but what are the rules when you're going out with another woman?"

"Rules?" Heather repeated.

"Like, who pays if you're both women? And how do I act? Is there anything I should say or not say? Do I—?"

"Whoa!" Heather made a gesture with both hands as if reining in a spooked horse. "The paying thing is easy. You asked her out, so you should pay. Then, for your next date, she can get it."

That sounded like a good solution. Eliza nodded eagerly. "What else?"

"Well, otherwise, just do whatever feels right, or ask Denny what she wants. There are no rules and no preconceived roles." A gentle smile crinkled the corners of Heather's eyes. "That's the beauty of dating a woman."

Eliza inhaled and exhaled several times. No rules. That was a good thing, right? But reinventing dating from the ground up at thirty felt a little scary.

"Hey." Heather slid closer on the couch and wrapped one arm around her. "What's going on? You're not having second thoughts, are you?"

"No!" Her voice echoed through the tiny apartment, and she lowered it before continuing. "No. That's not it. I want to go out with Denny."

"But?" Heather prompted.

Eliza studied the tips of her yellow sneakers as she tried to understand what was making her freak out. "Like you said, this feels different from my other dates."

"Because she's a woman."

It was not a question, but Eliza answered anyway. "Yes." But then she thought about it for a while longer and shook her head. "No. Well, that too, but also because there's so much more at stake."

A wrinkle furrowed Heather's brow. "What do you mean?"

"When I went out with the guys from No More Frogs, I had nothing to lose. If the date went great—wonderful. But if not, I would simply say no to a second date and try my luck with someone else."

Heather gave her a knowing look. "But it's not that easy with Denny."

"No. What I feel for her was different from the start, and I don't want to mess it up and end up hurting her or losing her, even as a friend." Eliza kneaded the throw pillow with both hands.

"There's always potential for hurting each other in any relationship where you've got a lot of emotions invested. All you can do is to keep checking in with her and be honest about what you are or aren't feeling." Heather withdrew her arm from around her and pulled the pillow from her grasp. "Now stop overthinking it and go before you destroy that poor pillow—or show up late for your date."

Eliza stood and took a step toward the door but then turned back around and hugged her. "You're a great friend; have I told you that lately?"

Heather's body in her arms shook with a chuckle. "And don't you forget it when it's time to pick your bridesmaids. I bet Denny has a couple of hot lesbian friends."

Eliza lightly slapped the back of her head and let go. "Jeez, why don't you let us get through the first date before you start printing wedding invitations?"

"All right. Have fun!"

With the intention of doing just that, Eliza strode to the door.

"Eliza!" Heather called after her. "Aren't you forgetting something?"

Forgetting? Eliza couldn't think of anything. She turned and sent her a questioning look.

"If you're supposed to pick Denny up, you need these." Heather tossed her the keys to her car.

Eliza caught them. "Oops. Yeah, they might come in handy. Thanks." God, who knew dating a woman was so thoroughly distracting?

Chapter 20

ELIZA'S HANDS ON THE STEERING wheel were damp as she stopped Heather's car in front of the Jacobses' townhouse shortly before 4 p.m.

Another car was parked next to hers along the curb, and the driver—a man in his mid-thirties—got out just before she did. He probably wanted to visit someone in an adjoining townhouse.

But as Eliza locked the car, she realized that he was heading toward Denny's front door.

"Hi." Bella appeared from behind a hedge that separated the townhouse from the neighboring property and ducked behind Heather's car.

Again, Eliza was struck by how much she resembled Denny. She smiled at the girl. "Hi, Bella. Are you hiding from someone?"

Bella shrugged.

Eliza ventured a guess. "Your mom?"

"She and Matt want to take me to the zoo." Bella made a face as if the zoo ranked somewhere below the dentist on her list of favorite places to go, but Eliza had a feeling that wasn't quite the truth.

"You don't like the zoo?"

Another shrug. "It's all right, I guess. But more for little kids."

Eliza reined in a grin. "Well, then I guess I'm a little kid because I still love the zoo. They have an aviary you can enter. Last time I went, two lorikeets sat on my arm, and I got to feed them." She pulled her phone from her purse and showed Bella several snapshots of colorful parrots.

The girl's eyes lit up. "Ooh, they're cute."

"Yeah, but you know what's even cuter? Don't tell my bosses I said so, but my personal favorites don't have feathers. The sea otters are adorable." Eliza swiped through a few photos that made Bella ooh and aah.

"I guess the zoo isn't that bad," Bella said. "Too bad you and Aunt Denny can't come."

"We'll see each other when I teach you how to make a journal."

A smile lit up Bella's face. "Can we do that next Friday?"

"Sure. Let me talk to your mom first, though, and see if my nieces and nephew can come over too."

Bella nodded eagerly, but something still seemed to gnaw at her.

Eliza studied her. "You still don't seem very happy at the thought of going to the zoo."

"No, it's fine."

"But?"

Bella shoved her hands into the pockets of her shorts, again reminding Eliza of Denny. Her gaze went to the front door, which had just closed behind the guy whose car was parked next to Heather's.

Eliza put two and two together. "Ah, I see. So you like the zoo, but not Matt."

"I dunno. I don't really know him. That's why we're going to the zoo. Mom wants me to get to know him, I guess."

"But you don't want that?" Eliza asked.

"I dunno," Bella said again. "What if he only wants to talk to Mom and thinks I'm just her annoying kid? Or he tries to order me around all the time? Or he doesn't like sea otters?"

Eliza finally saw the full picture. Her heart went out to Bella. She put a hand on her shoulder. "You've been watching him from behind that hedge, haven't you?"

Bella blushed the same shade of pink as her aunt, answering the question without having to say anything.

"How long did he sit in the car before going in?"

Bella huffed. "Forever."

"You know what that means?" Eliza asked.

Bella shook her head and searched Eliza's face, apparently eager to hear the answer.

"He's just as nervous as you."

"How do you know?" Doubt and hope warred in Bella's voice.

Again Eliza swiped through her photos until she found the one she wanted. "This is my brother, Ryan." She held out the picture of Ryan with Charlotte on one arm and a lorikeet on the other. "And this," she tapped the little girl's smiling face, "is my youngest niece, Charlotte."

Bella studied the photo, then sent her a questioning look.

"I say 'niece,' and I love her just as much as my other nieces, but Charlotte isn't Ryan's biological daughter. She's really Nichole's kid, and so is her brother Landon."

"Who's Nichole?"

"My brother's girlfriend. When they first started dating, he was so worried her kids wouldn't like him."

"But they did?"

"Duh." Eliza let out a playful laugh. "He's my brother. What's not to like?"

Bella huffed, but a grin crept onto her face. She studied the photo of Ryan with Charlotte for a moment longer. "Maybe I'll like Matt."

"Only one way to find out," Eliza said softly and pointed at the house.

Bella gave a long-suffering sigh but finally nodded. "But if he doesn't like sea otters, he's out," she called over her shoulder as she marched toward the house.

Mission accomplished. Eliza slid her phone back into her purse and swallowed as her own nerves returned. She took several deep breaths before following Bella.

The door opened before they reached it. Denny stood in the doorway, and the sight of her blotted out all other thoughts.

She looked like a model for gender-neutral fashion. The dark blue jeans fit as if they were made for her—and knowing Denny's sewing skills, they probably were. A gray V-neck T-shirt was neatly tucked in, and she wore an unbuttoned black shirt over it—probably an attempt to hide the extra padding on her sides. As if Eliza cared about that! She was too busy taking in the way the T-shirt stretched over her generous breasts and strong shoulders.

Her outfit wasn't special. Eliza had been out with guys who had worn similar clothes. But right now, she was convinced no one had ever made jeans, a T-shirt, and a simple shirt look sexier. The sleeves were rolled up, revealing her strong forearms, and when Denny lifted one hand to run her fingers through her hair, Eliza realized she'd gotten a haircut. Her hair was even shorter now, bringing out the sun-bleached streaks in the sandy-brown strands, and Eliza wondered how it would feel to run her fingers through it.

Denny's cheeks had an adorable pink tint as she stared at Eliza.

Bella walked past her aunt and disappeared into the house.

"Hi." Eliza smiled and took a step toward Denny.

"Um, hi." Denny stood in the doorway as if a magnet held her there.

Apparently, it was on Eliza to take the initiative if she wanted a more intimate greeting. The air seemed to vibrate between them as she stepped closer. God, Denny smelled heavenly. That cologne deserved an award. Eliza leaned closer and brushed her lips lightly against Denny's cheek.

Mmm, Denny's skin was incredibly soft. Tiny wings fluttered low in Eliza's belly.

When she took a reluctant step back, Denny pressed one hand to her middle as if she was experiencing the same flutter. She kept staring, then a crooked smile spread over her face. "I'd really like to talk to you, but I'm shy and have no idea what to say."

For a moment, Eliza stared back. Then comprehension hit her. It was what she had advised Denny to say six weeks ago when they had talked about Denny's problems initiating a conversation with women. Back then, Denny had said she couldn't see herself confessing her insecurities to a woman on their first date, and it warmed Eliza all over that Denny had done it with her. That sweet honesty touched her more than a suave line ever could.

She took Denny's hand, which was as damp as her own. "You don't have to say anything."

Denny's grin broadened. "Right. I can just ooh and aah whenever you pause to draw a breath."

Eliza tilted her head. "Are you going to quote me all day?"

"It's a distinct possibility. You say a lot of clever things."

"Charmer." The urge to kiss Denny's cheek a second time gripped her—or, if she was being totally honest, perhaps to kiss her lips this time. But she wasn't quite there yet, so instead, she let her hand slide up to the bend of Denny's arm and gave a soft squeeze. Amazing how natural it all felt.

Salem walked up behind Denny, followed by Matt and Bella. "Hey, Eliza." Salem made the introductions, and Matt shook Eliza's hand. His grasp was firm yet gentle, and Eliza instantly liked the warm twinkle in his blue eyes. She had a feeling he might like sea otters.

"We'd better get going." Salem slid one hand into Matt's and took hold of Bella's with the other. "Matt knows one of the zookeepers, so they're letting us in while they feed the giraffes."

It was obvious that Bella tried hard to appear unimpressed, but she didn't quite pull it off.

Eliza chuckled as she watched them troop to Matt's car.

"Drive carefully, Matt," Denny called after him.

He turned and gave her an earnest nod before opening the car doors for both Salem and Bella.

"Salem is really nervous," Denny said as they walked to Heather's car.

"Oh, Salem?" Eliza smiled. "She's the one who's nervous?"

Denny ducked her head. "I didn't say she was the only one, but yes, she is. Matt is the first guy she's ever brought home to meet Bella."

"I figured. Bella seems pretty nervous too."

"She is. I tried to talk to her earlier, but I guess she could tell I was a bit overprotective, so I'm not sure how much good it did." Denny sighed. "I saw you talk to her. What did you say that made her get into the car without any drama?"

Eliza didn't want to make a big deal out of it. "I just showed her a few photos from my last visit to the zoo."

"You like the zoo?"

"Of course I do! You don't?"

"I love it." Her enthusiasm lit up Denny's hazel eyes, making her appear like a little kid. "Especially the sea otters."

Warmth spread through Eliza's chest. So Denny had passed the sea otter test without even trying.

Denny touched her fingertips to Eliza's hand, initiating contact for the first time today. "Thank you for talking to Bella. I...I really want her to be okay with the new guy in her mom's life because he seems to make Salem happy."

"She'll be fine," Eliza said. "You're a great aunt, but I wouldn't worry too much. Unless Matt turns out to be an animal-hating macho, I have a feeling they'll get along great."

Denny turned her attention from Matt's car, which disappeared down the street, to Eliza. "You're right. Let's focus on us."

Us. Eliza mentally repeated the word. It sounded wonderful.

A tug of war ensued as they struggled over who would get to open the door for the other, then Eliza gave up with a laugh and let Denny open the driver's side door for her. If this was what dating a woman was like, she liked it.

While Denny usually preferred being behind the wheel, she was glad she wasn't driving today. Eliza's outfit and the light scent of her perfume were too distracting. When she had gotten into the car, her above-the-knee skirt had slid up a little, revealing an inch or two of smooth skin. Her simple, white T-shirt with capped sleeves clung to her slim torso. She wasn't wearing makeup, and Denny was glad. In her opinion, Eliza didn't need it. Her dark eyes were incredibly expressive, even without mascara and all that other stuff, and her pink lips had a perfect curve.

Denny spent most of the twenty-minute ride downtown sneaking glances while trying not to be obvious about it.

Finally, Eliza left the interstate and drove toward the stadium.

"Are we going to a game?" Denny asked. "The Timbers are playing, aren't they?"

"They are, but that's not where we are going." Eliza reached over and patted her arm. "Patience. You'll find out in a minute." She maneuvered the car through several side streets before finally finding a parking space.

Denny rushed around the car to open the door for her. Her breath caught as Eliza climbed out. Dear God, those legs!

"Thank you." Eliza locked the car and slid her hand onto Denny's arm.

They had to walk a few blocks to get to wherever Eliza was taking her. Denny didn't mind at all. She held her head high, proud to be on a date with a woman like Eliza.

Eliza steered her toward a lot surrounded by lush greenery and shaded by large umbrellas. A sign above the gate said *beer garden.*

"You're taking me to a beer garden?" Denny asked.

"It's not just a beer garden." Eliza led her past picnic tables and benches, where people drank canned beer and played giant games such as Connect 4 and Jenga. But she didn't stop there. Behind the benches was the tiniest, cutest minigolf course Denny had ever seen.

Denny laughed. "You picked minigolf for our first date?"

Insecurity flickered across Eliza's face. "Bad idea?"

"No," Denny said quickly. "No, it's a great idea! Any activity that isn't just me sitting across a table from you, staring and trying to come up with something witty to say, is a really great idea." Once again, Denny marveled at how easy it was to be honest with Eliza, trusting that she wouldn't be judged for revealing her insecurities.

"Are you sure?" Eliza asked.

It was soothing to see she was just as nervous and uncertain as Denny felt. "One hundred percent. But I'm warning you. You don't stand much of a chance. I'm the undefeated family champion at minigolf."

"You are?" Eliza's eyes flashed with a challenge. "Did I mention that my oldest sister nearly went pro as a golfer when she was younger?"

"Uh-oh. Can I buy you a beer before you thrash me in front of all these people?" Denny gestured at the food cart, where a blackboard proclaimed no less than fifty different canned beverages, including a large selection of craft beers.

"No. I asked you out, so I'm going to buy *you* a beer." Eliza pulled her to the food cart, where she got herself a can of hard grapefruit cider, while Denny selected an IPA.

Once Eliza had paid for their beverages and the minigolf, they each picked a club and a golf ball.

The tiny course wasn't too full, probably because it was a hidden, little-known pop-up, so they didn't have to wait.

"You go first," Eliza said before Denny could gesture at her to go ahead.

"All right." Denny handed Eliza her beer, stepped onto the faux grass, and put her golf ball down. She felt Eliza's gaze on her. Was she ogling her ass? She was tempted to glance over her shoulder and find out but didn't want Eliza to feel self-conscious, so she ignored the tingle running through her and lined up her shot.

The first hole was fairly straightforward. The only challenge was a gentle bump in the middle. Without looking away from the hole, Denny swung the club and gave the ball a gentle smack.

It rolled down the lane, made it across the bump, and slid neatly into the hole.

"Yes!" Pumping her fist, Denny whirled around.

Eliza's gaze had been on her, not on the ball. Now it darted to the hole. "Hole in one!"

The admiration in Eliza's eyes made Denny stand straighter. "You can do it too. Come on. Show me what you've got." She picked up her ball and then relieved Eliza of both cans.

Eliza stepped onto the green and put her pink golf ball down in front of her sneakers. She took her time figuring out the shot, giving Denny plenty of opportunity to admire the shape of her calves...and other body parts. Then she drew back the club and gave the ball a tap.

It slowly made its way toward the bump. Halfway up, it ran out of steam, rolled back down, and ended up exactly where it had started.

Denny fought the urge to tell her she needed to hit the ball harder to make it across the bump. Butchsplaining was just as unattractive as mansplaining.

Eliza lined up the shot again.

This time, Denny didn't let herself be distracted by her calves but took in her stance. Her grip on the club was awkward, and the ball arched to the left and mowed down a bunch of potted flowers near the second hole.

"Oops." Eliza turned toward her with a sheepish grin.

"Um, didn't you say your sister nearly went pro?"

"She did. I didn't say I inherited her talent."

"So she never showed you how to play?"

"Once, when I was little," Eliza answered. "But you know, it's no fun struggling to learn something your siblings have already mastered. That's the one thing I didn't like about being the youngest. Don't get me wrong. My sisters and brother are great."

Denny sensed a *but* coming and gestured for her to go on.

"Sometimes, they were a little too great. Whatever I did, one of my sibs had already done it before—and likely better than me."

As the older sister of only one sibling, Denny had never given it much thought, but now she saw how discouraging that must have been. "Is that why you didn't go into the medical field like the rest of them?"

"I almost did. My grandfather lived with us for a couple of years before he died when I was sixteen, and I took over a lot of his care. Everyone thought I'd become a nurse too, but I knew it wasn't a good fit. If I had worked with sick people, seeing them suffer and sometimes die, it would have eaten me up inside."

Denny could easily imagine that. For someone as compassionate as Eliza, a job in health care would be tough.

"I knew I had to find something else—something that fit me, not just follow everyone else's expectations."

Denny leaned on her club and studied her. "Do you feel like you did?"

Eliza's contented smile answered before she did. "Yeah. I was struggling for a few years, going from one job to the next. But now I'm really happy with what I do. What about you?"

Usually, Denny avoided talking about her job, but with Eliza, she didn't want to hold anything back. "The pay is decent, especially for retail, and there are aspects of the job I enjoy, but..."

"It doesn't nourish your soul," Eliza finished for her.

Denny met her gaze and nodded. The wonderful feeling of being understood surrounded her like a hug.

"What does?" Eliza asked.

You, Denny wanted to say. She sucked her bottom lip between her teeth. Being around Eliza turned her into a sentimental softie, but she had to tread lightly, or she'd scare Eliza off. "Um, sewing."

Eliza put her hand over Denny's. "There's no need to be embarrassed." She brushed her fingers down the outseam of Denny's jeans, making her shiver as if she had touched her bare skin. "You're very talented. Have you ever considered doing it for a living?"

Denny shrugged. "Not really. With Salem and Bella depending on me, being self-employed is too risky. Plus I'm not sure my sewing is good enough."

"It is." Then, as if sensing that Denny was squirming with her praise, Eliza chuckled and pointed at the flowers where her golf ball had ended up. "Too bad the same can't be said about my minigolf skills."

"Want some pointers?" Denny asked.

"Yes, please. Before I kill all the greenery around here."

Denny put the two cans on an empty table nearby, leaned her club against it, and waited until Eliza had retrieved her ball before she stepped closer. "Slide your right hand around a little. You want your palm to face the hole you're aiming for."

"Like this?" Eliza asked.

"Better, but not quite there." Denny struggled to find the right words to explain. "I could show you, but..."

Eliza peered over her shoulder and gave her a questioning look. "But?"

Even though they were the same height, Eliza's arms were a bit longer, so to correct her grip on the club, she would have to step so close that her front would be pressed against Eliza's back from hip to chest. "I, um, would have to wrap my arms around you, and I don't want to make you uncomfortable."

Eliza turned fully and looked her in the eyes. "This," she pointed back and forth between them, "is new to me, and I admit I'm a little nervous. But you never, even for a second, made me uncomfortable, and that hasn't changed now that we're dating."

Her words made Denny breathe more freely. "Oh. Good."

Eliza smiled at her. "All right. Now that we cleared that up, why don't you come over here and put your arms around me?"

A laugh burst from Denny's chest. "Yes, ma'am." She walked over, each step slower than the one before. *It's a hug. Just a hug. We've hugged before. No big deal, right?*

Eliza stopped breathing as she felt and heard Denny shuffle closer. Her heart thumped fast, as if it were trying to leap out of her chest. *Calm down. You don't want to pass out on your first date.*

Denny's arms brushed her sides as she reached around her, and her soft breasts pressed against Eliza's back.

Oh my God. Eliza's stomach flip-flopped, and her knees felt wobbly. If not for Denny's fingers over hers, she would have lost her grip on the club.

Denny's arms around her trembled—or maybe it was her own limbs. Her fingers slid over Eliza's, correcting her grip. "How does that feel?" Her warm breath fanned over Eliza's jaw as she turned her head, sending little jolts through her entire body.

"G-good. Um, I mean, yeah, that's better." Eliza tried to focus on the feel of the club in her hands, but with Denny's warmth on her back and strong arms around her, minigolf was the last thing on her mind.

Denny cleared her throat. "Great. Now relax your arms."

Ha! Relax! That was easier said than done with Denny so close.

Denny guided her through the motions twice, her hips pressing against Eliza. Each time, she stopped just short of hitting the ball. "Does that give you an idea?"

"Oh yeah." That little putting lesson had given her a lot of ideas. Few of them had to do with minigolf, though. If she had ever doubted whether her body would react to Denny's touch, those doubts had just been settled once and for all.

Denny removed her arms from around Eliza and stepped back.

A shiver went through Eliza, and her back instantly felt cold despite the late-afternoon sun. *Wow.* That had been intense. *Come on. Focus.* She gently swung back the club and sent the ball down the lane with a tap.

This time, the ball made it over the bump but veered too far left. It bounced against the metal rim, ricocheted off the other side, and rolled into the hole.

Eliza stared for a moment, then let out a cheer and jumped up and down. "Yes!"

"You did it!" Denny rushed over, cheering too, and held her hand out for a high five.

Their palms connected, then lingered, and their fingers tangled.

Eliza swallowed. She couldn't believe how good Denny's broad hand felt wrapped around hers.

Both squeezed, then let go.

Eliza laughed and hoped Denny didn't notice that it sounded a little too loud and nervous. "Too bad Andy couldn't see that."

"Andy?"

"Andrea. My oldest sister."

"Ah. I'm sure she would have been very impressed." Somehow, Denny managed to keep a straight face.

Eliza lightly slapped her shoulder. "Liar."

They continued to the second hole, and since the entire course consisted of only nine holes, it didn't take them long to complete it.

The woman at the register had given them a scorecard, and Eliza kept track for both of them after each hole. They pretended to be fiercely competitive, teasing each other about missed shots, but Eliza could tell Denny cared as little about winning as she did.

Finally, Eliza managed to hit the ball over a yellow bridge and into the last hole, ending the game. She tallied the results. "Looks like you narrowly won."

"Narrowly?" Denny laughed.

"Nineteen to..." Eliza lowered her voice to an incomprehensible mumble.

Denny cupped her hand around her ear. "What was that?"

Eliza held her head up high. "Nineteen to a stellar thirty-one."

"Ah, I see. Very narrow win indeed." Denny pulled the scorecard from Eliza's fingers and put it in the back pocket of her jeans. "I'll keep this, if you don't mind. To document that narrow win."

Would she really keep it as a memento of their first date? Knowing Denny, she would. The thought made Eliza smile. "Come on. Loser buys the food."

They returned their clubs and golf balls, then walked to the food cart. There was no line, so Eliza quickly read through their menu options and ordered the orange chicken. For a moment, she debated getting another cider with her food but then decided on an apple ginger soda. She was a lightweight when it came to alcohol, and she wanted to experience every second of their first date with a clear mind, not a tipsy one.

The woman in the food cart slid the soda in front of her, then directed her gaze at Denny. "What can I get you, sir?"

Eliza couldn't believe it. This was the second time someone had mistaken Denny for a man. The better Eliza got to know Denny, the harder it was for her to understand how it happened.

Denny touched the back of her hand to Eliza's and lightly shook her head, indicating it didn't matter to her. "I'll take an apple ginger soda too and an All-American Burger—but hold the onions, please."

No onions? Didn't she like them, or was she trying to keep her breath fresh...just in case? Eliza's heartbeat picked up.

At the sound of Denny's voice, the woman did a double take. Her eyes widened. "Oh, I'm so sorry, ma'am."

Denny flashed a smile that looked tense. "It's okay."

The woman handed Denny the soda. "The food will be a minute."

With their sodas, they settled at one of the nearby picnic tables beneath a huge umbrella to wait for their food.

Denny fiddled with the tab of her can without glancing at Eliza.

"Does that bother you?" Eliza asked softly, nodding toward the food cart.

"No. Not particularly." Denny finally opened her can and looked up.

She meant what she said; Eliza could see it in her eyes. So far, she had mostly adored Denny for her shy, sweet side, but now she realized the quiet strength and bravery it took for Denny to be true to herself and dress in a way that felt right to her, risking confusion and negative reactions from people every day. Her admiration for Denny grew.

Denny searched her face. "Does it bother you?"

"Me? Why would it bother me if someone thinks I'm going out with a guy? That's what I did up to now."

Denny slid the ring of the tab onto her pinkie and turned it around and around. "Yeah, but now she knows I'm not a guy."

Eliza slid her hand over Denny's to stop the nervous fiddling. "That doesn't bother me either. I'm enjoying our date, so I don't care what people think."

The guarded look on Denny's face gave way to a smile. "I'm enjoying it too. Very much so."

Eliza returned the grin. "Despite winning only very narrowly?"

Denny chuckled. "Yeah, despite that."

The woman at the food cart waved at them, indicating that their food was ready.

Eliza reluctantly let go of Denny's hand. "Hold our spot, please. I'll get it." She walked to the cart and pulled some napkins from a dispenser.

The woman slid the burger and Eliza's orange chicken across the counter. "Enjoy your food. And sorry again about earlier. It was an honest mistake." She waved in Denny's direction. "With her boyish haircut and men's clothes."

Eliza's temples started to throb. She fought the urge to throw the food in her face. "Boyish?" she repeated, struggling to keep her voice calm.

The woman held up both hands. "Um, her hair is quite short. That's all I meant."

"And that makes it boyish?" Eliza pierced her with a narrow-eyed gaze. "Women come in all shapes and sizes and with all kinds of clothes and haircuts. Just because a woman prefers a style that has traditionally been associated with men doesn't make her boyish."

The woman blanched and took a step back. "I...I didn't mean to offend her...or you."

Eliza bit her bottom lip so hard it hurt. She inhaled and exhaled twice. Maybe she was overreacting, but she hadn't expected to encounter that attitude in such a hip place in liberal Portland. She couldn't bring herself to apologize because she meant what she'd said. Without another word, she picked up the food and marched back toward the table.

Denny watched her approach with wide eyes.

Oh shit. So she had heard. Eliza hoped she hadn't totally messed up their first date. She busied herself placing the food on the table without looking at Denny.

"What was that?" Denny pointed at the food cart.

"Sorry. I didn't mean to make a scene. Stuff like that just makes me...gah!"

"Gah?" Denny repeated, sounding amused.

Eliza peered at her. "You're not angry?"

"Stunned is more like it. I've never had anyone defend me before and certainly not with so much passion."

"Sorry." Eliza poked around the container of orange chicken with her chopsticks. "I guess I just feel passionate about people making ignorant assumptions about how a woman is supposed to look."

"Stop apologizing," Denny said. "I kind of liked it."

Eliza looked her in the eyes, and when she saw the soft twinkle, she relaxed. "Good. I would defend you anytime, but I guess I did overreact a little." She swiped a few chopped scallions off her food. "As a teenager, I was teased for the way I looked too, and what she said hit a sore spot."

"You? Why would anyone tease you? I mean, not that assholes need much of a reason, but you're so beautiful!" Denny swept her gaze over her, not lingering in any one area but including her entire body.

A tingle engulfed Eliza from head to toe but stayed mostly low in her belly. "Thank you, but not everyone shared that opinion. In high school, I was called 'boyish' more often than I could count. That's why I got so angry."

Denny gaped at her. "What? Why would anyone call you that?"

It was nice that Denny didn't think it was obvious. Eliza pointed at her chest. "Because I wore a training bra through most of high school. I've been called everything under the sun: Mosquito Bites Girl, Flattie, and—my all-time favorite—president of the Itty Bitty Titty Committee. Once, a boy I had a crush on told me he preferred a real woman with a grown-up body."

Denny clutched the table. "God, people are ignorant jerks," she said through gritted teeth. "You don't need big boobs to be a real, beautiful woman. Back in high school, I would have killed for smaller breasts like yours." More quietly, she added, "Still would."

Now it was Eliza's turn to stare. "Are you kidding? Your breasts are beautiful!" She bit her bottom lip. "Uh, I didn't mean to say that out loud, but I'm not taking it back."

Denny went as red-faced as Eliza assumed she was. "Thank you."

They peeked at each other, then a grin crept over Eliza's face. "Okay, so we've established our mutual admiration for each other's breasts. Not what I expected for my first date with a woman, but I'll take it."

Denny stared for a second, then burst out laughing. She regarded Eliza with a shake of her head. "God, you're something else." Her tone was filled with so much affection that Eliza couldn't help beaming back.

Eliza slid the burger closer to Denny's side of the table. "Come on. Let's eat and then get out of here."

The sun was starting to set by the time Eliza pulled into Denny's driveway. After they had finished their food, they'd driven to the Japanese garden and strolled along the moss-green ponds hand in hand, enjoying each other's company and the soothing patter of the waterfalls.

Eliza wasn't quite ready for their time together to end, so she shut off the engine. "I'll walk you to the door."

A smile played around Denny's lips as they got out of the car.

"What?" Eliza asked.

"Nothing." Denny put her hand on Eliza's back as they walked toward the house—a gesture that always made Eliza feel as if she was about to melt into a puddle. "Normally, I'm the one walking my date to the door."

"Lots of firsts for both of us, then." Eliza searched Denny's face. "That's not a bad thing, is it?"

"No, not for me. You?" Denny studied her so intensely that Eliza knew she was still worried about her deciding dating a woman was not for her.

Two steps from the door, Eliza turned to face Denny and caught her hand. She wanted her to see the truth of what she was about to say in her eyes. "It's a really good thing. I can't remember ever having such a wonderful first date."

Denny's tight grip on her hand loosened. "Phew. Um, I mean, me too. I had a great time." The look in her hazel eyes left no doubt about her sincerity. "So, since we both enjoyed ourselves, does that mean we're doing this again?"

Eliza bit back a grin at how adorable Denny was. "Are you asking me out on a second date?"

Denny stood taller and squared her shoulders. "Yes, I am. Would you like to go out with me next Friday?"

For a moment, Eliza was tempted to say they didn't need to wait six long days; they could do something tomorrow, but she held her tongue, knowing she needed time to process what was happening between them. "I'd lo— Wait. Darn. I can't go out with you on Friday."

Denny's face fell. "Oh." She directed her gaze to the ground at Eliza's feet. "That's okay. I didn't mean to be too clin—"

"I can't go out with you on Friday because I'll be here, teaching your niece...and you how to make a polymer clay journal," Eliza said. "I promised her earlier, provided your sister says yes."

Denny looked up, the smile back on her face. "So I'm included in your journal-making plans?"

Eliza wanted to tell her she was included in many of her plans, not just the journal-making ones, but she held back. Why did she have a need to spend more time and be more intimate with Denny? She had never been like that in any other relationship, at least not that fast. Was that why those lesbian U-Haul jokes existed? "I wouldn't dream of giving journal-making lessons without you."

"I'm in. But I'd still love to take you on a date. How about Saturday?"

Eliza nodded without consulting her calendar app. "Sounds good."

"Great."

They took the two steps to the door, where they stood facing each other.

"I'd better get inside before Salem comes looking for me. I think they're back already." But despite her words, Denny didn't move, and neither did Eliza.

They lingered, their gazes searching each other, then veering away.

Eliza wasn't sure how to say goodbye. Should she hug her or kiss her? As wonderful as Denny's tender embraces were, she longed to be kissed, but was it the right time for Denny too? She hesitated. Then Heather's words came back to her. Denny might not make the first move, even if she wanted to kiss her.

"Good night, Eliza."

The way Denny said her name sent a shiver down her spine. "Good night."

Denny reached into her pants pocket, probably to pull out her keys.

Oh, no. Eliza couldn't let her go. Not like this. She curled her hand into the fabric of Denny's shirt at her shoulder and leaned in. The scent of Denny's cologne and something that was just her teased Eliza's senses.

Denny froze, and her breathing quickened. Longing and uncertainty were etched on her face. "You don't have to do this if you don't w—"

Eliza gave a light tug on the shirt, pulling her closer, and touched her lips to Denny's.

For two thudding heartbeats, they stood like that, then Denny kissed her back. Her lips slid along Eliza's, warm and inviting. Her hand left her pocket, and she cradled Eliza's face in a gesture so tender that Eliza melted into her.

Their kiss was sweet and soft—God, so incredibly soft—a caress of lips, no tongue or wandering hands, yet it sent a hum of excitement through Eliza. She never wanted the kiss to end.

But much too soon, Denny eased her mouth away and finished in a breathless whisper, "...want to."

It took Eliza's dazed brain several seconds to piece together the sentence Denny had started before they'd kissed. "Did that feel as if I didn't want this?" She touched Denny's bottom lip with the tip of her index finger, then couldn't resist stroking it. Wow. So silky.

Denny shook her head, seemingly unable to form words. Looking deeply into Eliza's eyes, she placed one hand on her hip.

How could such a fleeting touch send ripples of sensation through her body?

Then Eliza stopped pondering that question as Denny leaned in, and this time, Denny kissed her. She captured Eliza's lips, still tenderly, but with more confidence.

Eliza ran her hands up Denny's shoulders, over her neck, and into her hair. It felt bristly and soft at the same time as she ran her fingers through it.

Denny made a helpless little groan against her mouth. Her hands—both on Eliza's hips now—flexed, but she kept them there.

Eliza became lost in the slow slide of Denny's lips over her own, featherlight at first, then with slightly more pressure. Mmm, she couldn't get over how soft and sensual Denny's lips were.

Finally, it was Eliza who broke off the kiss to catch her breath.

They stared at each other.

Slowly, as if hesitant to lose the contact, Denny dropped her hands from Eliza's hips.

Eliza immediately missed their warmth. She allowed her fingertips to caress the back of Denny's head once more before withdrawing them.

Denny's face was flushed, and her sandy-brown hair glowed like gold in the setting sun.

She looked so stunned and happy that Eliza wanted to pull her into another kiss right away, but she needed to slow down and process what was happening.

Denny's hand trembled as she reached up to touch her lips. "Damn." She laughed, a hoarse, shaky sound. "It's going to be almost impossible for me to top this date when I take you out next weekend."

A giddy chuckle started low in Eliza's chest. "I guess you'll have to find a way to recreate this experience."

"Or improve on it," Denny said with a smoldering gaze. Then, more timidly, she added, "I mean, if that's what you want."

"It is." They were still talking about kissing, right? Eliza glanced down and tugged on one of the buttons on Denny's open shirt. She struggled to voice what was on her mind, but she wanted honesty with Denny because their lack of games and pretenses had made their relationship special from the start. "But, um, to be honest, I'm not sure I'm ready for more yet."

Predictably, a blush stole onto Denny's cheeks. What Eliza hadn't expected was the happy smile on Denny's face. She had known Denny would be patient with her but had assumed she'd look a little disappointed anyway. "Um, why does that make you smile?"

"Because I'm not sure I'm ready either. *We* aren't ready." Denny's smile broadened. "And you said you're not ready *yet*."

"Oh. Yeah, I guess I did. I mean, I assume eventually, we'll—"

"No expectations, okay?" Denny said. "I want you to do only what feels right in any given moment."

God, Denny was almost too good to be true. "Well, in that case..." Eliza pulled Denny close and kissed her again.

Chapter 21

DENNY'S KEYS CLATTERED ONTO THE side table. As soon as the door had fully closed between her and Eliza, she sank against it, not trusting her legs to keep her upright. Her mind was still reeling from that last kiss—from all three of their kisses, really.

Even though they had been more tender than passionate, they had rocked her to her core.

She licked her lips, still feeling the sweet pressure of Eliza's mouth against her own, and yet she couldn't believe this was happening to her. Eliza had kissed her! And she'd said yes to a second date.

"You okay?"

Salem's voice startled her. She pushed away from the door and nodded. "Fine. Great. Wonderful."

Salem walked over and eyed her. "Then why are you breathing so hard?"

Was she? Denny touched her chest. Her heart still thudded way too fast. She could lie, pretend she had jogged to the door and that was why she was out of breath. But she didn't want to deny this magical feeling for even a second. "Eliza kissed me."

Salem let out a wolf whistle. "Hot damn! Please tell me you kissed her back."

Denny snorted. There was no way she could have kept herself from reacting to Eliza's lips on hers. "Of course I did." On shaky legs, she followed Salem to the couch.

"So," Salem said once she had plopped down next to Denny, "was the rest of the date as good as the kiss?"

"Well, that's hard to top, but...yeah." The familiarity of their previous conversations had still been there, but now an undercurrent of newness and excitement seemed to run between them too. Apparently, Eliza had enjoyed it just as much. Not even for a moment had she looked as if she wanted to be anywhere but right there, with Denny, even when the woman in the food cart had called her *boyish*. "It was the best date I've had in...well, ever."

Salem bumped Denny's knee with her own. "I'm really happy to hear that."

"Thanks. How was your date?"

"Not as exciting as yours." Salem chuckled. "Since we had a chaperone, all I got was a kiss on the cheek when Matt dropped us off."

Part of Denny's walking-on-clouds haze cleared from her mind as she went into worried-aunt mode. "How was he with Bella?"

Salem let out a dreamy sigh. "Wonderful. I found out he gave his friend the zookeeper a prized baseball he caught as a kid to bribe him into letting us into the giraffe house after hours."

Denny had to admit he seemed to be a great guy. "What about Bella? Did she warm up to him?"

"Not at first. She barely said a word and just watched Matt like he was a prisoner out on parole—until we got to the sea otters. Then it was as if someone had flipped a switch, and they chatted like best buddies." Salem laughed. "By the time we left the zoo, I was starting to feel like a third wheel."

"Wow, that's great." Denny wrapped one arm around her in a celebratory embrace.

"Mm-hmm." Salem leaned her head against Denny's shoulder and continued to smile. Then she sobered and peered up at her. "How would you feel about me inviting Matt to join us for the Pride parade next Sunday?"

Going to Pride was something they had done as a family for years, so Denny knew this was about more than inviting Matt to hang out at a fun event with them. Salem was asking her to accept him into the family. While she was happy her sister had found love, she couldn't help being sad for herself. She had been Salem's confidante and a second parent to Bella for years, and now she was about to lose those roles. A sense of loss wrapped around her heart like a fist.

Salem moved her head off Denny's shoulder to study her. "If you'd rather I didn't invite him along, that's fine. I was just thinking it might be fun."

Denny gave herself a mental kick. She hated change, but she would deal with it—for Salem's sake. "No, that's okay. Invite him."

"Are you sure?" Salem asked.

For a moment, Denny imagined herself at the parade, watching Salem, Matt, and Bella cheer and laugh with each other as the floats moved past, while she observed from the outside. But then another image superimposed itself on the first one: a slender hand slid into hers, and Eliza leaned in to her as she pointed at something that made all five of them laugh. The fist around her heart loosened its grip. "Positive. In fact, I might invite Eliza to join us too, if that's okay with you."

"Of course it is—if you think she's ready for that."

Why wouldn't Eliza be ready to watch the parade with them? She had met Salem and Bella, and since Heather was her best friend, she had probably been to Pride before. "What do you mean?"

"Bella, Matt, and I, we're going to the parade to show our support for you and the LGBT+ community," Salem said. "But Eliza is dating you, so maybe Pride has a different meaning for her now. Is she ready for that?"

Denny let her head drop against the back of the couch. "I have no idea. I don't know what kind of label she's comfortable with at this point—if any. I didn't even think about it like that."

"Maybe Eliza won't either."

But now that Denny had started to worry about it, she couldn't let it go. *Great. Way to burst my post-kiss bubble of happiness, Salem.* Sighing, she got up.

"Where are you going?" Salem called after her. "I wanted to know more about your amazing date!"

Denny headed to the stairs. "Saying good night to Bella and seeing if she wants to talk."

"Denny?"

Halfway up the stairs, Denny paused. "Yeah?"

"Thank you," Salem said quietly. "You're the best."

Denny steeled herself against the rush of emotions flooding over her. God, a few kisses from Eliza and she felt so raw as if every feeling she experienced was amplified a thousand times. "Yeah, yeah. Don't think flattery will get you the last piece of cheesecake."

"Oops. I ate that when we got home."

Denny turned and walked down a few steps until she could peek around the corner and into the living area. "You're kidding, right?"

Salem flashed her a sheepish grin. "Hey, you got a kiss good night, and I didn't."

Hmm, true. Eliza's kisses beat cheesecake any day. She gave Salem a stern big-sister look anyway and stabbed her index finger in her direction. "Next cheesecake's on you."

It was only nine thirty when Eliza got home, so she took a detour to Heather's apartment to return her car keys. If she was honest, it wasn't about the keys. Her body and mind were still buzzing with all the emotions kissing Denny had stirred up, and she needed someone to talk to.

She knocked on the door in a rapid staccato, then used her key to let herself into the apartment.

Heather sat on the couch with her feet on the coffee table, painting her toenails a pale shade of lilac. She looked up with the brush hovering over her big toe. "Um, you didn't crash my car, did you?"

"No! Of course I didn't. Why would you think that?"

Heather waved the nail polish brush. "You have a weird expression on your face."

"Do I?" Eliza resisted the urge to reach up and touch her face—or her lips.

"Mm-hmm." Heather tracked her path to the couch and kept studying her as Eliza sat next to her. "So, if my car is fine, that means your date with Denny was either a total disaster or the best thing since the invention of pizza."

"The latter." Eliza knew she probably had a dorky grin on her face, but she didn't care. "Definitely the latter."

Heather put down the nail polish. "Better than pizza? Are we talking with or without a cheese-stuffed crust?"

"Better than cheese crust *and* extra cheese."

A low whistle broke the momentary silence. "So that special connection you're always looking for... Is it there with Denny?"

Eliza didn't have to think about it. In hindsight, that connection had been there long before their first date. "Yes, it is. With all the guys from No More Frogs, I felt like I needed to put on a show to impress them—dress the right way, say the right things, you know? With Denny, I knew I could let my walls down and just be myself."

Heather pressed both hands to her chest. "That sounds wonderful."

They smiled at each other.

"It is," Eliza said. "So, now that I've found mine, we'll just have to find your frog."

"Frog?" Heather lifted one brow. "You mean my princess, right?"

Eliza firmly shook her head. "No. Princesses with flowing, golden-blonde hair, lofty castle towers, and expensive ball gowns aren't real. I think you need a perfectly imperfect frog. Someone who loves you for you, warts and all."

"Wait, now I'm the frog in your analogy?"

Eliza pinched her thigh. "No, you're the toad."

Heather squirmed out of reach. "So, speaking of frogs and princesses... Did she kiss you?"

Just the mention of it made Eliza feel warm all over. She nodded.

"Ooh. She did?" Heather slid closer on the couch.

"Well, technically, I kissed her."

"Woo-hoo." Heather bounced up and down, jostling Eliza. Then she stopped and waved her fingers at her. "Details! Give me details!"

Eliza had never been shy talking to Heather about her love life, but this was different. Not because Denny was a woman but because she was Denny. "Like you said, I don't think she would have taken the initiative, so I made the first move. I really wanted to know what it would feel like to kiss her."

"So? What did it feel like?"

How could she put into words an experience beyond description? "Soft," she said, then added, "Right. It felt right. Actually, it surprised me just *how* right it felt. Not only the kiss. All of it."

"You didn't think it would?"

"I don't know." Eliza grabbed the nail polish off the table and pulled Heather's foot into her lap to have something to do while her mind churned. "I think it's still sinking in. I mean, imagine you suddenly realized you enjoyed kissing a guy."

Heather shuddered dramatically, nearly causing Eliza to slip and paint the fleshy part of her big toe.

"Hey, keep still!"

"Then stop saying things like that," Heather answered.

Eliza nudged her foot. "Come on. Just because you aren't attracted to them doesn't mean kissing guys is gross."

"Yeah, but didn't we just agree that kissing women is so much better?"

Eliza painted the next toe, then the one after that before answering. "Kissing Denny is. But I have no idea if it's because she's a woman or because she's...well, Denny."

Heather seemed to think about it for a few seconds, then nodded. "You'll figure it out."

"I'm not sure I want to. Not if it means kissing anyone but Denny."

The sound of Heather's good-natured laughter filled the room. "Jeez, are you sure you're not a lesbian? One date and you're already committed!"

Committed... The word lodged heavily in the pit of her stomach. Was she?

Before she could think of an answer, her phone rang with Denny's ringtone. Her heartbeat picked up, and her gaze darted from Heather's half-finished toenails to her purse. "Do you mind if I...?"

"Get out of here." Heather took the nail polish from her. "And tell Denny I said hi."

"Will do. Good night." Eliza jumped up, grabbed her purse, and pulled out her phone as she rushed to the door. Inwardly, she laughed at herself. She had left Denny less than an hour ago, and yet she couldn't wait to hear her voice again.

"Hi." Denny's voice sent a tingle of pleasure through her. "It's me—Denny."

Eliza smiled, waved over her shoulder at Heather, and pulled the door closed behind her. "Hey, you. I made it home. Sorry I haven't texted yet. I dropped off the car key at Heather's. She says hi, by the way."

"Salem says hi too."

"Tell her hi back." Eliza struggled to unlock her front door with one hand, then entered her apartment. "How was her zoo date?"

"Good. But not as good as mine."

The quiet honesty in Denny's voice filled her with warmth. "I bet not as good as mine either."

For several moments, only their soft breathing filtered through the phone as they were probably both grinning like goofballs.

Eliza cleared her throat. "So, did Matt like sea otters or not?"

"Apparently, he did. He and Bella bonded over their mutual adoration for them," Denny answered. "Wait, how did you know about the sea otters?"

"Just something Bella and I talked about when I picked you up."

"You encouraged her to give him a chance, didn't you?"

"A little." Eliza crossed her studio apartment and pulled out the bed. "Was that okay?"

"Yeah, it's great."

There was something ambivalent in Denny's tone, though. "Are you sure?"

"He's good for Salem—and I think for Bella too. She hasn't had a lot of male role models in her life so far."

Eliza sensed that there was more. "But?"

"You know, I'm not sure if it's disconcerting or comforting how well you know me already."

"I vote for comforting." Eliza kicked off her sneakers and stretched out on top of the bed. "Seriously, you know you can talk to me about anything—or tell me you'd rather not talk about it. Whatever you need, okay?"

"Thanks," Denny said so quietly Eliza had to press the phone to her ear more tightly to hear her. "I think I'd like to talk about it."

Eliza lay back and waited, not hurrying her along. She had a feeling Denny didn't share her troubles very often, so it took her a while to find the right words.

"I'm mainly worried Bella might get hurt. Not physically," Denny added hurriedly. "It's just... Kids get attached so quickly, you know? My niece in particular. She might not show it sometimes, but she feels things deeply. What if she opens her heart to him, and then things don't work out between him and Salem?"

Was this really about Bella, Matt, and Salem—or was it about them? Denny was a lot like her niece; Eliza knew that. She felt things deeply too. Was she worried about things not working out between them, despite their wonderful first date?

"What if he realizes having a ready-made family isn't what he wants after all?" Denny continued.

Again, Eliza couldn't help seeing the parallels. Was Denny worried not just about Matt changing his mind but also about Eliza deciding a relationship with a woman wasn't right for her after all? "Don't you think he thought this through before he even asked Salem out?" Eliza asked. "Or does he seem like the type who jumps into relationships too fast?"

"No, I don't think so. But sometimes feelings change."

"True. Do you think Salem's feelings will change?"

"No." Denny's reply came without a second's hesitation. "If she wasn't sure about him and her feelings for him, she would never have introduced him to Bella."

"Then why assume that he'll change his mind?"

"Hmm. You got me there," Denny said. "Maybe I'm worrying for nothing."

"You worry because you care." Her big heart was one of the things she liked most about Denny. "Is that all that's worrying you, or is there something else?"

Denny's breath reverberated through the phone as she inhaled and exhaled loudly. "What if Matt doesn't change his mind?"

Eliza tried to grasp Denny's train of thought. How would that be a bad thing? "What do you mean?"

"What if things go great between them, and he asks them to move in with him?" Denny asked in a whisper.

Oh God. Was that what had Denny so worried—the fear of her family leaving her? Eliza's throat burned. Why had no one invented a phone with teleportation abilities yet? She wanted to put her arms around Denny so badly it hurt. She had half a mind to get Heather's car keys and drive back to Lents.

"I mean, that would be great, right?" Denny added in a forced upbeat tone. "I'd be happy for—"

"You don't have to do that with me, Denny."

"Do what?"

"Pretend you're fine and be strong for others all the time," Eliza said. "I know you'd be happy for them, but that doesn't mean it wouldn't hurt you. It would be a big change. God, Denny, you practically raised Bella—raised both of them, really—from what little I know about your parents."

Denny made a noise of agreement that sounded like a pained sigh.

"No one can take that away from you. If Matt is the good, sea-otter-liking guy I think he is, he won't want to. He'll know he can't replace you. I bet you'll still be the person Bella will go to when her first boyfriend breaks her heart or her mom grounds her for skipping school or joining a cult or something."

That elicited a laugh from Denny. "Bella is too down-to-earth to join a cult."

"Okay, but for everything else, she'd still come to you."

Denny sighed, but it sounded less sad. "Yeah, but she won't be living with me anymore."

Eliza barely stopped herself from promising Denny she wouldn't end up alone. God, Heather was right. She sounded like a cliché, promising to move in before they'd even had their second date! "No, but Bella is old enough to stay the night at your house on weekends. And maybe you could find a place close to them."

"Hmm. Yeah. Maybe I could." Denny was silent for a few moments.

"You just pulled out your laptop to google affordable places close to wherever Matt lives, didn't you?"

"Um, no."

"You so did!"

Denny chuckled. "Okay, okay, I did. I'm jumping the gun a little, aren't I?"

"A little."

A low thump indicated that Denny had closed the laptop. "Eliza?"

"Yeah?"

"Thank you. For understanding and for making me talk about it. I wasn't even aware of it, but I guess this has been gnawing at me for a while."

Eliza put all her warmth and affection into her voice, hoping Denny could feel it. "Totally understandable."

"So," Denny said after a pause, "would you like to meet Matt? For real, I mean, not just shaking hands in the driveway."

Meet Matt? Truth be told, he wasn't the person she wanted to spend time with, but it seemed to be important to Denny, so Eliza said, "Uh, sure."

"Damn," Denny muttered, more to herself. "That's not how... what I really wanted to ask."

What was making her so nervous all of a sudden? Eliza's fingers tightened around the phone. "What is it? You can ask me anything."

"You know I'm not a crowd person, but Salem drags me to Pride every year, and this time, she asked Matt to come—and Bella will be there too, of course—and I was wondering..." Denny sucked in a breath as if she had run out of air. "Would you like to come with us? It doesn't have to mean anything."

"Mean?" Eliza repeated, trying to keep up.

"Straight people watch the parade all the time," Denny said.

"I know. I've been to the parade with Heather at least three—" Then it hit home what Denny was trying to say. Eliza had assumed herself to be straight the last three times she had attended Pride. She had been there as a supportive ally, not as part of the LGBT+ community. Now she would be going with her girlfriend! The thought made her head spin.

"Like I said, it doesn't have to mean anything," Denny repeated, "other than you wanting to spend time with me."

That was something she was one hundred percent sure of. "I'd love to go to Pride with you."

"Yeah?"

"Yeah." It would mean they would see each other on Friday, Saturday, and Sunday next week, but she didn't feel as if that was too much at all. In fact, Friday seemed too far away.

"Heather could come with us too," Denny said. "If you usually go to Pride together, I don't want to get in the way of that and make her feel like a third wheel."

What a sweetheart! Denny always thought of everyone else. That melting feeling in Eliza's chest was starting to become familiar. "I'm sure she'd love to come. We always—" She froze with her mouth open as she remembered their annual Pride parade tradition. *Oh God.* For a few minutes, she had forgotten she wasn't the only one who accompanied Heather to Pride to show her support.

"What?" Denny asked, sounding alarmed. "If you've changed your mind, that's totally—"

"No, that's not it. But the last couple of years, we didn't go to Pride alone."

Denny chuckled. "I know. There were fifty thousand other people there too."

"Yeah. Fifty thousand people and my entire family."

The sudden silence lasted for so long that Eliza thought Denny might have dropped her phone.

"Y-your entire family?" Denny finally croaked out.

"Well, not my grandparents, aunts, uncles, or cousins. Just my parents, my siblings, and their kids and significant others. At least those who aren't working the day of the parade."

"Just your parents and your siblings," Denny repeated, sounding faint.

"I guess you'll meet them sooner than we thought." A lot sooner. Eliza couldn't keep the slight tremor from her voice, and she knew Denny would pick up on it.

"Maybe this wasn't a good idea after all," Denny said. "Let's just forget about Pride."

For a moment, Eliza was tempted to agree. Everything was happening too fast, overwhelming her. She hadn't thought about taking Denny home to meet her family yet. There was so much she needed to figure out for herself first. But if she chickened out now, Denny's fears would fester. "No," she said as firmly as she was capable of. "I want to go to Pride with you. Unless you've changed your mind."

"No. But meeting your family... That's big." Denny was silent for a few moments. "Hmm, but maybe it doesn't have to be."

"What do you mean?" Introducing Denny to her family felt huge.

"You don't have to introduce me as your, um, girlfriend or anything. I mean, we've had one date. I don't expect you to come out to your family or anything like that."

At this point, Eliza didn't even know what she'd come out as. How could she tell her family *I'm gay* or *I'm bisexual* when she hadn't figured out what being attracted to Denny meant for her sexual orientation? But at the same time, lying to her family, keeping their growing relationship a secret felt wrong. Her temples pounded as if her head was about to explode.

"I meant what I said earlier," Denny continued. "No expectations. Tell them whatever feels right for now, okay?"

Having Denny be so understanding and not pressuring her should have felt like a relief. Instead, frustration clawed at her gut, not with Denny, but with herself. Her family was liberal and open-minded. This shouldn't be such a struggle—and yet it was.

"Now tell me everything about your parents and your siblings," Denny said before Eliza could think of an answer. "Hobbies, quirks, political affiliation, favorite ice cream flavors—I need to know everything. Just because they might think I'm only a friend doesn't mean I can't try to charm their socks off."

Part of Eliza's tension fled from her as she smiled fondly. "You don't need to know a thing about them to do that. Just be yourself."

"Yeah?"

Something in Denny's voice gave Eliza pause. "Did you think I wanted you to put on an act around my family and pretend you're straight, femme, super confident, or something else you're not?"

Denny's lack of an answer spoke volumes.

"God, Denny, no. This isn't about you. It's about me. So please don't show up on Sunday in a frilly, pink dress or something, okay?"

Denny burst out laughing. "I can honestly say that thought didn't cross my mind."

"Good. Because I like you exactly the way you are. I just need some time to figure out what that means for me."

"Take all the time you need," Denny said. "Now tell me about your family."

"Only if you then tell me all about yours."

"Deal."

Eliza sat up, propped the pillow behind her back, and prepared herself for a long conversation.

Chapter 22

ON FRIDAY AFTERNOON OF THE following week, Eliza finished work early, borrowed Heather's car again, and drove to her sister's house in Happy Valley to pick up her nieces.

Ryan and Nichole's kids were sick with a stomach flu, but Britt's ten-year-old twins had enthusiastically declared their interest in joining their craft lesson.

Instead of her sister, it was their mom who opened the door.

"Hey, Mom." Eliza gave her a hug and a kiss on the cheek. "What are you doing here? Britt isn't sick too, is she?"

"Oh, no, she's fine." Her mother pulled her across the doorstep. "Nala had her kittens, and I was in the neighborhood picking up some stuff at the Grocery Port, so I thought I'd drop by and see them."

Her mother shopped at the Grocery Port? Maybe she had even gone to the one where Denny worked. Denny might have rung up her items or directed her to the milk at some point! It felt as if the universe was giving her a nudge. Should she tell her mother about Denny?

"How are you, sweetie?" Her mother wrapped one arm around her while she led her into the house. "I've barely seen you all month. Are your bosses keeping you busy?"

"No, it's not that," Eliza answered. "I mean, we're working our, um, behinds off to develop a bird-friendly Christmas tree and make enough of them in time for the holiday season, but Austen is really good at sending everyone home on time."

"That's good. What's keeping you from visiting, then?"

Okay, the universe was giving her more than a little nudge. This felt more like a kick. Maybe she should get it over with and tell her mother, who had always been her biggest ally in the family. She searched for the right words and discarded one option after another. Finally, she decided to be as direct as possible and just say it—like ripping off the Band-Aid instead of dragging it out and making it more painful than necessary. "Uh, remember Denny? The woman I was texting with after I had the bike accident?"

Crow's feet fanned out around her mother's eyes as she grinned. "The one I thought you were dating?"

Eliza tried to swallow the lump in her throat. "Um, actually, I—"

"Aunt Eliza!" Her niece Piper rushed toward them.

Damn. Her chance to talk to her mother alone was gone. Maybe the universe didn't want her mom to find out about Denny just yet after all.

"Nala had her kittens! Come look at them." Piper tugged on her hand. "We're keeping the black and the red one, but you can have one of the calicos."

Britt stepped out of the living room with Polly in tow. "Nope! We're not keeping two; your dad and I told you that. You get to pick one, and that's it."

Identical scowls settled on the twins' faces.

"The black one," Piper said.

"The red one," Polly declared at the same time.

Eliza laughed and patted Britt's shoulder. "I predict you'll keep both."

Britt grimaced. "Thanks for the support, sis."

"Hey, I'm taking the girls off your hands for the rest of the day. How's that for support?"

"Right. I knew you were my favorite sister for a reason."

"That's what she told Aunt Andy too when she took us out for ice cream last weekend," Piper stage-whispered.

Piper and Polly dragged her into the living room to look at the tiny balls of fluff.

Britt and their mom followed, and they all stood around the cat bed in the corner, where four kittens snuggled up to their mother. Their eyes were still closed and their ears folded against their heads, making them resemble little teddy bears. Their high-pitched meows made Eliza smile.

I wonder if Denny likes cats.

Her mother leaned her chin on Eliza's shoulder so she could watch the kittens too. "They're so cute when they're this little. Just like human babies. I almost wish they could stay like this forever."

"Hey, watch it, Mom," Britt said. "I'm still cute as heck."

Their mother chuckled. "No comment." She tapped Eliza's shoulder. "So, what was it that you wanted to tell me about your friend?"

Eliza's palms went damp. Should she still tell her? But that meant Britt and the girls would hear their conversation, and that seemed a little overwhelming. Okay, *a lot* overwhelming.

"Um, she and her family will be at the parade on Sunday too, so I thought we could all meet up and go together."

"Of course, honey. The more, the merrier."

That seemed to be the end of it for her mother. She had no idea Denny was more than a friend, so for her, there was nothing else to discuss.

Damn. This was so much harder than she had thought it would be.

Eliza held back a sigh. "All right, monsters." She waved at Polly and Piper to follow her. "We should go. Denny and her niece are waiting for us."

The three girls hung on Eliza's every word as she explained and demonstrated how to shape the polymer clay to create their journal covers.

From her place next to her at the table, Denny watched just as intently—not so much because of the dragonfly journal she intended to make but because she couldn't look away from Eliza.

She wore a pair of faded jeans that had been washed so many times they probably felt as soft as velvet and were now molded to the contours of her slim hips and toned legs. Her chestnut hair was swept up into a short ponytail, exposing her beautiful cheekbones and elegant neck.

God, that neck. A stray tendril had escaped the ponytail and curled around her throat. Denny imagined brushing it aside and pressing a soft kiss to Eliza's skin.

Eliza kneaded and rolled the clay, then smoothed it into place on the sheet she'd prepared earlier. She attached hind legs to the purple dragon she was making and formed spikes along its spine.

"Wow," one of the twins whispered.

"Yeah, wow," Denny repeated without looking away from Eliza's hands. She tried hard not to imagine those fingers stroking, kneading, and smoothing over something other than polymer clay.

When Eliza turned toward Denny, their knees brushed beneath the table.

A jolt traveled up Denny's leg.

"...shaper?"

Denny jerked her gaze away from Eliza's hands and directed it to her face. "Um, sorry, what?"

A grin broke the look of concentration on Eliza's face.

Was she aware of what her mere presence and the light touch of her knee were doing to Denny?

"Could you hand me the rubber shaper, please?" Eliza repeated.

"Oh, sure." Denny glanced at the assortment of tools spread out on her side of the table. "Which one is it? This one?"

At her first question, Eliza had reached out, and when Denny tried to pick up the tool she guessed to be the rubber shaper, her fingers closed over soft skin instead of cold metal.

Neither of them let go.

They froze with their thighs touching and Eliza's upper chest pressed into Denny's shoulder. Eliza had twisted and stretched past her to reach the tool, so now their faces were only inches apart.

Their gazes met and held, then Eliza's dipped to Denny's lips.

Denny stifled a moan. *God, you can't look at me like this. Not with the kids in the room.* The need to kiss her was almost like a physical ache.

The air between them seemed to flicker, shimmering like the summer haze over hot asphalt.

"Aunt Eliza!" One of the twins tapped the table as if she had tried—and failed—to get her aunt's attention for some time. "Mine looks like a sausage with claws! Help!"

The temperature in the room appeared to drop back to normal levels as Eliza turned to face her niece.

Denny sank against the back of her chair and tried to hide that she was breathing much too fast.

"Which twin is she again?" Bella whispered next to her. "Piper or Polly?"

Grateful for the distraction, Denny turned her attention to Eliza's nieces. She scratched her neck, which still felt too warm. "I have no idea," she whispered back. To her, the two girls looked identical, right down to the freckles on their noses. How could Eliza tell them apart? She knew Bella wouldn't speak up, so she said, "Okay, you two. Give me a tip. How do I tell you apart?"

The twin who had created the sausage with claws glanced up from her clay. "That's easy." She grinned. "I'm the prettier, smarter one."

Her sister snorted. "Ha! You wish!"

Eliza set the lump of clay aside to poke twin number one. It was fun to see her interact with her nieces. "Piper's the smart-ass. Polly's the quiet one."

"And how do I tell them apart when they're both quiet?" Denny asked.

Eliza and her nieces looked at each other, then gave identical shrugs. "After a while, it'll be obvious."

Denny gave her a doubtful look, but she hoped she would be in Eliza's life for a long, long time, so she would have plenty of opportunities to learn to tell them apart.

"Yours is turning out really good." Polly pointed at Bella's cover depicting a polymer clay budgie.

Bella ducked her head as a deep blush colored her cheeks, but she couldn't hide her pleased smile. "Thanks."

Eliza had shown her how to cut feathers from a sheet of polymer clay and sculpt the quill and individual barbs with a sharp-tipped tool, and Denny was proud of how focused her niece was as she worked on her bird.

"I'm trying to make it look like Kiwi, my budgie, but it might look more like Kiwi, the fruit."

Polly laughed but shook her head. "No, it looks like a budgie. Of course, I haven't seen Kiwi, so I can't say if it looks like him...or her...or not."

"Want to see him?" Bella asked.

Apparently, the newness of having a pet still hadn't worn off.

Within seconds, the two preteens abandoned their craft projects and rushed upstairs.

Piper scoffed as if she were too mature to get excited over a budgie—but then hurried after them. "Hey, wait! I want to see him too!"

For the first time since Eliza and the twins had arrived, Denny found herself alone with her. Still sitting at the table, they turned toward each other, and their knees brushed again.

There was so much Denny wanted to say, but as she looked into Eliza's dark brown eyes, words escaped her. "Hi."

Eliza smiled. "Hi." She reached up to swipe her hair behind one ear, then seemed to realize it was tied back in a ponytail and let her hand drop onto the table.

God, she's so cute. It was a relief to see she wasn't the only one who wasn't quite sure how to act and what to do. Well, she knew what she *wanted* to do, but she was still careful not to push Eliza into anything she wasn't ready for. She reached for Eliza's hand

and ran her thumb over her knuckles. *Mmm.* For someone who worked with her hands, Eliza had incredibly soft skin. She caressed Eliza's index finger.

A noticeable shiver went through Eliza.

They both glanced at their entwined hands, their gazes following the path of Denny's finger, then into each other's eyes.

"Denny..." Eliza's voice was a low, hoarse whisper. She licked her lips.

Oh Jesus. Without letting go of her hand, Denny leaned forward. Her knee bumped against the edge of Eliza's chair, but as their lips found each other, she stopped caring.

Eliza hummed into the kiss. She slid forward, her knee coming to rest between Denny's, pressed against the edge of Denny's chair. Her sculpting tool clattered onto the table as she brought up her free hand. As they continued to kiss, she slid her fingertips over Denny's jaw and then to the back of her head.

Tingles rushed down Denny's body, and she couldn't help moaning. It took all her rapidly dwindling willpower to not deepen the kiss, slip her hand beneath Eliza's T-shirt to feel her skin, and forget the world around her. "The girls," she whispered against Eliza's lips.

"Mm-hmm. I know." Eliza gently nipped Denny's bottom lip. "We should stop..."

"Yeah."

But neither tore her mouth away until rapid footsteps on the stairs announced the girls' return.

Denny's cheeks flamed along with the rest of her body as she broke the kiss, grabbed the first tool within reach, and pretended to focus on shaping the wings of her dragonfly. She avoided looking at Eliza, knowing she would flush an even brighter shade of red if she met her gaze or glanced at her lips.

Bella dropped onto her chair with a huff and tugged on Denny's T-shirt. "Piper and Polly have an iPhone, and they're only ten!"

"We're almost eleven, and it's our mom's old phone," one twin said while her sister added, "And we have to share."

"Still," Bella grumbled. "All the kids in school have one too. I'm the only one who doesn't."

Denny groaned. "Can we discuss this later, Bella?" *When I'm not in a post-kiss haze.*

"Fine." Bella grabbed her tool, then paused and regarded Denny's cover. "Your dragonfly looks weird. Like a pair of lips."

Denny stared at her project. *Shit.* She was right. The dragonfly's wings had somehow morphed into a sensuous mouth. She peered at Eliza out of the corner of her eye and whispered, "Oops."

Eliza's gaze dipped from the dragonfly to Denny's lips. The corner of her mouth twitched as if she was trying not to burst into laughter. "Well, you should have seen the first dragonfly I made. It looked like an ice cream cone with wings."

Denny jumped up. "Ice cream! Good idea." She could use something to cool herself down if she wanted to make it through this craft lesson with Eliza sitting so close.

Denny would have bought her niece an entire flock of budgies if it meant she could get another moment alone with Eliza, but it wasn't meant to be. With all three girls right next to them, kissing her goodbye wasn't in the cards.

She wrapped her arms around Eliza in a friendly hug, but when she pressed close and that wonderful mix of her light perfume and her own scent teased Denny's nose, the embrace tightened. God, she could have stayed like this forever. Denny barely resisted the urge to bury her nose against Eliza's neck.

Finally, Eliza let go and stepped back with the same obvious reluctance Denny felt. She walked backward to the car, her gaze still on Denny, and made the sign for *I'll call you.*

Denny nodded and watched her climb behind the wheel.

"Bye, Polly." Bella waved at the twin closest to her.

Huh. What do you know? Denny gave her a quick look. Apparently, Bella had learned to tell them apart.

They both waved as Eliza competently navigated out of the driveway. Once the car had disappeared down the street, they went back inside.

Bella trailed her fingertips over the budgie on her journal. "You know," she said without glancing at Denny, "you could have kissed her goodbye. I wouldn't have minded. It's not like I haven't seen people kiss before."

"Uh, thanks, but..." Denny stared at her own journal. She would never be able to look at a dragonfly again without thinking about kissing Eliza. "It's complicated."

Bella rolled her eyes in that way only someone her age could. "That's what you and Mom always say when you think I'm too young to understand something. I'm eleven, Aunt Denny." She straightened to her full four-foot eight. "I'm not a little kid."

"I know." Denny pulled out two chairs and gestured for Bella to sit next to her. "It's not that I don't think you'll understand it here." She touched Bella's temple. "But it might be hard to grasp here." She tapped her chest. "I know my heart struggles with it."

Bella studied her with the same keen focus she had directed at her craft project earlier. "Oh. Polly and Piper don't know Eliza's your girlfriend, do they?"

Denny stared at her. One second, Bella was complaining about them not getting her an iPhone, and the next, she sounded so perceptive and mature that it blew her mind. "No, they don't." Before Bella could say anything, she lifted her hand. She didn't want her niece to judge Eliza in any way. "It's not that she's ashamed of me or our relationship. It's just that this...us...being in a relationship with a woman is new for her. She hasn't told her family yet."

Bella's eyes grew wide. "They won't kick her out once she tells them, will they?"

"She doesn't live at home anymore. But even if she did, I don't think they'd do that." Denny wrapped one arm around her. It was so telling that the worst thing Bella could think of was parents kicking their child out. The wound her grandparents had left, even without ever having met her, was deep.

"I bet Polly and Piper wouldn't care whether she's with a guy or a girl. Their parents probably won't either. I mean, they gave their kids an iPhone, so they're cool, right?"

Denny chuckled. "Very subtle, Bella."

An impish grin flashed over Bella's face. "Just saying." She flicked through her journal as if the blank pages held something of interest. "So Eliza likes both girls and guys?"

Good question. Denny wished she had a definitive answer. "She liked guys in the past. Now she likes me." Once she had said it, she realized she'd had an answer after all—one that was simple and beautiful. It brought a smile to her lips.

Bella nodded thoughtfully. "I think I do too. Like boys and girls." She closed her journal and got up. "Or maybe just girls. I haven't decided yet. Boys can be kind of gross."

Mouth gaping open, Denny stared after her.

"Don't worry," Bella said over her shoulder. "I meant for later. I'm too busy for a girlfriend or a boyfriend now."

Denny's vocal cords still weren't working by the time the door to Bella's room closed with a bang.

She had no idea how long she'd been sitting there, staring toward the stairs, when a key rattled in the door and Salem swept into the house with her happy I've-spent-time-with-Matt smile and a big, white box. "Hey, sis. I brought cheesecake." She kicked the door closed with her heel and walked over. "You okay?"

Denny hesitated. Bella hadn't said it was okay to tell Salem, and she had a right to her privacy. Besides, she was only eleven, so throwing a coming-out party for her might be a bit premature. For now, it was good to know her niece wouldn't agonize over coming out as a lesbian or bisexual at some point in the future.

"I'm fine," Denny said. "Just suffering from a lack of—"

"Kisses?" Salem threw in with a grin.

"Cheesecake," Denny said. "But yeah, I would have liked some more kisses too."

Salem got them forks and plates. "If you need the house to yourself for a few hours—or an entire night, let me know, okay? Bella and I can make ourselves scarce."

If Salem continued like this, Denny's cheeks would be stained a permanent red. "Thanks, but we're not..." She took her journal and used it as a fan. "We're, um, taking things slow."

"Ah." Salem opened the cake box. "Well, in that case, you're getting the biggest piece." She plopped it onto Denny's plate, then pointed the cake server at the journal. "Is that a dragonfly? It looks like—"

Denny groaned. "Shut up and eat your cheesecake."

Chapter 23

Eliza's doorbell rang at a quarter to six the next evening. She jumped up and rushed to the bathroom to check herself in the mirror one last time. "Oh my God, she's early!"

Heather got up from where she'd been lounging on the couch. "Good thing you've been ready to go for half an hour." She didn't try to hide her amusement. "You know, I've never seen you like this when you went out with guys."

Eliza paused in her dash from the bathroom to the door. "That's because I've never felt like this with anyone." This overwhelming mix of nerves and excitement was new.

"Which is?" Heather gave her an inquisitive look.

Eliza's gaze darted to the door. "Can we talk later? I don't want to make Denny wait."

"Sure. Knowing Denny, she's down there, pacing, sweating through her suit, and adjusting her tie for the millionth time while she's waiting for you." Heather made a shooing motion. "Go. I'll lock up for you."

"Thanks." Eliza blew her a kiss, grabbed her purse, and hurried out the door. She didn't wait for the elevator but jogged down the stairs.

Denny was indeed pacing in front of the building, but she wasn't wearing the suit and tie Heather had predicted. The pair of dark blue jeans she had picked for tonight's date was quickly becoming Eliza's favorite item of clothing because Denny looked so at ease in them—well, and because they clung to her strong thighs. Her khaki short-sleeved Henley shirt brought out the olive color in her eyes.

When Denny saw her, she stopped pacing and smiled. "Hi." Her gaze traveled over the skinny jeans, the formfitting *Keep Portland Weird* T-shirt, and the yellow sneakers Eliza was wearing.

Eliza hoped the sneakers were finally working their magic and would help them have a wonderful date. But maybe they didn't need the lucky sneakers for that. She tugged on her shirt. "Is this okay? You said comfy clothes, right?"

Denny averted her gaze from the tight T-shirt. "Yeah. Sorry, I didn't mean to stare." The cutest blush ever rose up her neck. "It's just... You look beautiful."

With everyone else, Eliza might have thought they were just trying to be polite or to flatter her since she wasn't wearing anything special, but the honest, raw expression in Denny's eyes left no doubt about her sincere admiration. "Thank you. You look beautiful too."

Denny's lashes fluttered. "Uh, thanks."

Eliza studied her. Did that compliment surprise her? Or had it made her uncomfortable? "Should I have said handsome?" It hadn't occurred to her that dating a woman—especially a butch woman like Denny—might come with its own terms, but she wanted to use whatever words made her most comfortable.

"Either works, I guess." Denny's blush deepened. "As long as I look good to you."

Now Eliza was the one to blink. Did Denny still doubt that? She took a step toward her and reached for her hand. "Of course you do." The flicker of insecurity in Denny's eyes made her heart constrict. "I'm still not used to it, much less talking about it, but..." She forced herself to hold Denny's gaze. "I'm really attracted to you. I could look at you for the rest of the day, and that still wouldn't be long enough."

"Thank you," Denny said, her voice husky. "But that might be a problem. I've booked us a spot at a bar for tonight."

"A bar? I thought you didn't like bars?"

"Not just any bar. You'll see." Denny led her to her car, which she'd parked a block away. She nodded at their hands while they walked. "Is this okay?"

Denny's hand cradled hers with tenderness, as if she were holding a fragile piece of art. Her warm skin and gentle grip felt wonderful, but at the same time, Eliza was very aware she was holding a woman's hand in the middle of downtown Portland. Not that anyone paid them much attention. Still, it would take some getting used to. "Yes." She held on more tightly, determined not to care what anyone else might think. "More than okay."

After unlocking the car, Denny opened the passenger-side door for her, then closed it once Eliza had gotten in.

Eliza loved the way Denny always made her feel treasured.

Denny circled the car and slid behind the wheel. Instead of starting the engine, she looked at Eliza.

Being in an enclosed space with her felt unexpectedly intimate. Something tugged at Eliza's belly—a pull that made her lean across the middle console.

Denny seemed to feel the same pull, because she reached over and tenderly cupped Eliza's face in one hand. Her gaze dipped to Eliza's lips. "Can I...kiss you?"

God, yes! Instead of a verbal reply, Eliza closed the remaining distance between them and kissed her. Her eyes fluttered closed. She opened her mouth under Denny's, inviting her to deepen the kiss.

The tip of Denny's tongue tentatively caressed hers.

That careful first touch sent little jolts down to Eliza's belly. A moan escaped her. She clutched Denny's shoulder as the kiss deepened. The sensuous slide of Denny's warm tongue against her own made her head spin. *Mmm. More.* The damn middle console dug into her knee as she tried to get closer, and for a second, she seriously considered climbing it and crawling into Denny's lap.

Finally, Denny eased her mouth away with one final nibble of Eliza's bottom lip, then sank against the back of her seat. She kept staring at Eliza through kiss-hazed eyes.

Knowing Denny was just as affected by their kiss sent a new wave of excitement through Eliza.

"I... You... That was..." Denny cleared her throat. "Was that okay?"

A husky chuckle escaped Eliza. "God, yes. I mean, of course it was."

"Are you sure?" Denny tilted her head and studied her. "I didn't overwhelm you, did I? You look a little...I don't know...stunned."

Was it that obvious, or had Denny learned to read her so well? Eliza decided to be honest, even though it might be embarrassing. "To tell you the truth, I'm a bit surprised."

Denny's eyes widened. "You didn't think you'd like it?"

"No! I knew I would." Eliza brushed the corner of Denny's mouth with her thumb. The silky feel of her bottom lip made Eliza want to kiss her again and again. "You're a wonderful kisser."

Denny lowered her gaze for a moment. When she looked back up again, desire smoldered in her eyes. "You're a great kisser too," she rasped out.

Eliza's breathing hitched. She forced herself to keep her gaze on Denny's eyes. If she glanced at her tempting mouth, they wouldn't get any talking done.

"So, what was it that surprised you?" Denny asked.

Eliza tapped her own chest. "Me. My, um, reaction. I knew I would enjoy kissing you again, but I didn't expect to find it so..." She squirmed in the passenger seat, not ready to say it.

"So...what?" Denny prompted.

Arousing, Eliza's brain supplied. She had never known a mere kiss could have such an intense effect on her. "So, um, hot."

Now Denny was the one who looked stunned.

"Sorry," Eliza whispered. She peeked at Denny. "Was that inappropriate?"

"No! God, no!" Denny grasped her hand. "That's good! That's great! That's really, really great. To be honest, I was a little worried about that."

Eliza entwined their fingers in a clasp so perfect it still amazed her. She squeezed Denny's hand, urging her to go on.

"I wasn't sure I'd be able to..." A flush rose from Denny's neckline. "I mean, I could kinda tell you enjoyed our kisses, but I thought maybe you just enjoyed them the way you'd enjoy a professional massage or something."

"Trust me," Eliza said, her voice hoarse, "if a massage from a therapist made me feel like that, I'd start to worry."

They stared at each other. Electricity seemed to crackle in the air between them.

Then Denny shook her head as if to clear it. "Date," she said firmly. "Bar. God, you're so distracting."

"Me? You're the one who kissed me senseless!"

Denny pulled Eliza's hand over to her side of the car, gently turned it, and pressed a kiss to the inside of her wrist before letting go.

Goose bumps trailed up the sensitive skin of Eliza's forearm, then down the rest of her body. Oh yeah. No massage therapist had ever made her feel like this.

After a deep breath, Denny started the engine.

They talked about Eliza's work and Bella's latest attempts to talk her mother and Denny into getting her an iPhone. By the time Denny parked the car ten minutes later, Eliza's body temperature was back to normal.

They had to walk a few blocks to get to the bar, and Denny again reached over and took her hand.

Soon, Denny led her across the street and pointed. "This is it."

It sure wasn't the kind of bar Eliza had expected. The floor-to-ceiling windows revealed big worktables and bright lights hanging from a high ceiling with exposed pipes. Instead of rows of bottles, a shelf of paints, brushes, and colorful yarn lined one wall. *DIY BAR,* a sign above the door said, and another one announced, *Craft and drink.*

Denny paused in front of the building. "Is this okay? I thought this might be something we could both enjoy since we like to do things with our hands. Um, I mean..."

Eliza laughed. "It's perfect." A glass of red wine, crafts, and spending time with Denny... If a better combination existed, she hadn't discovered it yet. "I've done a paint-and-sip session with Heather once, but never this. Let's try it."

Denny beamed and held the door for Eliza to enter ahead of her.

A bearded guy smiled at them from behind the counter.

Denny gave him her name and said she'd reserved a spot for them—which had been a good idea. Several people were already hammering, painting, and cutting leather pieces on two of the worktables.

"Welcome," the man said. "Have you ever been here before?"

They shook their heads.

"Okay, here's how it works. First, you pick a project." He pointed at the items on the counter: coasters, a macramé plant hanger, nail-and-string artworks, bracelets, and various leather items. "Then you grab your tool bag, an apron, and a drink from the bar—and go have fun. The instructions are in the bag, but our craft tenders are around if you run into any problems."

Eliza looked at the choice of projects, then at Denny. "How about I make something for you and you make something for me?"

Denny grinned. "Sure. That's a great deal for me. I'll end up with something beautiful, while you will take home something that looks like a three-year-old made it."

Eliza gave her a gentle hip bump. "You're great at sewing. I'm sure you'll do fine with whatever project you choose." She decided on a leather wallet, while Denny picked a beaded wrap bracelet. They each got a bag full of tools and supplies, which they took to their spot at a big, butcher-paper-covered worktable.

Denny slipped the apron over her neck.

"Wait, I'll tie it for you." Eliza put her bag of tools down. When Denny turned, she tied the apron strings into a neat bow. Denny's back was warm and solid, and she fought the urge to let her hands linger.

Then they switched positions, and Denny helped with her apron. Her fingers brushed the small of Eliza's back as she tied the strings, and since Eliza had pulled her hair into a ponytail when they had entered, Denny's warm breath fanned over her bare neck.

A shiver ran through her.

"There," Denny said, her voice lower than usual.

"Thanks." Eliza craned her neck to see the blackboard above the small bar in the back. A cold drink was definitely in order.

"Tell me what you want," Denny said. "I'll get it for you. Yelp says their draft beer is great. The stout too, if you prefer something dark."

Eliza leaned closer to whisper in her ear. "Don't tell anyone, but I don't actually like beer."

Denny stared at her with comically wide eyes. "Wait! You don't like beer or coffee? How's that possible? Don't they take away your Portland Citizenship Card for those two offenses?"

Wow. Denny remembered she didn't like coffee? It had been at least two months since she had mentioned that. She was constantly amazed at how attentive Denny was. "Nah. Only for transplants like you. I was born and bred here, so they waived the requirement."

"Oh, is that how it works?" Denny's hazel eyes twinkled.

"Yep." Eliza tapped her *Keep Portland Weird* T-shirt. "My citizenship card is safe. It doesn't even matter that I don't like kombucha."

Denny let out a playful gasp. "How un-Portlandian! Good thing I didn't know that before our first date, or I might not have asked you out."

"Um, to set the record straight, so to say, *I* asked *you* out."

A young woman at the other end of their table looked up from hammering nails into a painted board.

Eliza stiffened, preparing for a frown or a derogatory comment.

Instead, the woman smiled and lifted her glass. "Their peach blossom kombucha is actually quite good."

Okay, relax and stop expecting everyone to disapprove of you dating a woman. Most people don't care, and those who do are assholes not worth wasting a single thought on. Eliza smiled back. "Good to know, thanks."

"Do you want to try it?" Denny asked.

"Maybe later. For now, could I have a glass of sangria?"

"Coming right up." Denny strode toward the bar.

Eliza's gaze followed her. She would never get sick of watching the way Denny walked.

It didn't take long for Denny to return with a glass of sangria and some kind of fizzy drink for herself. At Eliza's questioning look, she said, "Grapefruit seltzer."

"If you want a beer, I can drive," Eliza said.

"No, that's fine." A cute pinkness dusted Denny's cheeks.

Why did talking about beer make her blush? Oh! Denny avoided drinking beer so Eliza wouldn't mind kissing her good night at the end of their date! Eliza grinned to herself. Not that a little beer would have stopped her, but she appreciated how considerate Denny was.

They each settled at the table and took their tools and supplies out of their bags. Laminated sheets of instructions fell out.

With low music playing in the background, Eliza started to follow the steps. She cut out a piece of leather with an X-Acto knife and trimmed the edges. The color of the leather was perfect—it was the same chocolate brown as Denny's favorite jacket.

Since she had worked with leather in one of the workshops she had taken with Heather before, she knew she wouldn't need the entire three hours scheduled for her project. She could chat with Denny and pause to watch her all she wanted.

Denny cut off a piece of beading silk and threaded a needle. It was easy to see she had done that a thousand times before. Her sturdy fingers were amazingly nimble as she threaded beads and ran the needle over and under the leather cord in a steady pattern.

"You're so good at that," Eliza said, still watching Denny's hands. "I really would love to watch you make a pair of pants for me sometime."

"Anytime," Denny answered.

One of the craft tenders wandered over, forcing Eliza to tear her gaze away from Denny's hands. "How is it going?" he asked. "Do you need any help?"

Denny glanced up from the bracelet. "No, thanks." She rested a hand on Eliza's shoulder. "She's a crafting pro. She's got me."

He gave Eliza a respectful nod, but her attention was on Denny and the warm hand on her shoulder. *She's got me.* The words echoed through her mind. *Do I?*

"Great." He looked at Eliza's project—which hadn't gotten past the first two steps since she'd been busy watching Denny—but said nothing. "Have fun, then."

Oops. Maybe she should shift the ratio of watching Denny versus working on her own project, or she would end up with a half-finished wallet. Eliza folded the piece of leather, dampened the crease with a splash of water, and clamped it into place. "And you called *me* distracting," she muttered.

Denny threaded another turquoise bead. "Pardon me?"

"Um, I said the sangria is really distracting. I'd better limit myself to one glass while I'm working with sharp tools. I don't want to lose a finger."

Denny's gaze went to her fingers and lingered there. "No. We definitely don't want that."

The rasp in her voice sent a shiver down Eliza's body. She flicked a bit of water from the bowl on the table at her.

"Hey!" A few drops beaded on Denny's black-framed glasses.

Eliza grinned. "Just providing some help with cooling you off."

"Oh yeah?" Denny dipped her fingers into the bowl and shot a spray of water at her. "You look as if you could use some help with that too."

They flicked water back and forth until one of the craft tenders looked in their direction.

Like two kids caught misbehaving in school, they immediately pretended to be focused on their projects.

"You're getting me into trouble," Denny whispered out of the corner of her mouth. But she didn't look as if she minded at all. A glint of mischief sparked in her eyes.

Eliza loved seeing her so relaxed and unselfconscious. She had a feeling Denny had never been like this on any other date—and, truth be told, neither had she. After kissing a lot of frogs, she might just have found her prince...who was actually a princess.

Denny had to park two blocks from Eliza's building, but she didn't mind at all. In fact, she wouldn't have minded walking all the way from North Portland if she got to spend more time with Eliza.

At the front door, they paused and turned to face each other.

"So," Denny said, "how does this date compare to last week's?"

Eliza tapped her bottom lip in a thoughtful gesture, drawing Denny's gaze to her mouth. "Hmm. Hard to tell."

"Oh? Why's that?"

"I loved the DIY Bar, and I love my bracelet," Eliza trailed her fingertips over the leather bracelet with the turquoise beads wrapped around her wrist, "but I can't give this date a final score until I've had my good-night kiss."

A smile broke across Denny's face. It was wonderful to know Eliza was just as much looking forward to a kiss as she was. "Well, in the interest of getting a final score, I guess we'd better check off the kiss requirement."

Eliza hummed her approval.

They both leaned forward, and their lips came together in a kiss that was soft and tender. But then Denny angled her head and deepened the kiss, igniting the passion between them.

Eliza's low moan was the sexiest sound she'd ever heard. Her hands found Denny's hips and pulled her closer until their bodies touched from thighs to chest.

Oh sweet mother of... Now Denny was the one moaning. God, she couldn't believe how good Eliza's body felt against her own. She allowed one of her hands to caress the small of Eliza's back while she moved the other upward to play with her hair and trail along her neck.

Eliza gasped into her mouth and broke the kiss, breathing heavily. "A ten."

"Huh?" Numbers were beyond the capacity of Denny's brain right now. Every cell in her body was still focused on the sensations the kiss had sparked.

"The date," Eliza said. "It's definitely a ten."

Denny kissed the corner of her mouth because she couldn't help herself. "Yeah. It was a ten for me too. Or more like a twelve out of ten."

They stood close, their bodies touching for several moments longer, then Denny took a step back on shaky legs. She really should get going before they ended up making a spectacle of themselves in public. But tearing herself away from Eliza was getting harder and harder every time they got together.

"Do you want to come up?" Eliza's gaze was still hazy as she pointed at the front door.

Denny's mouth went dry. "Um..." A part of her wanted to say "hell, yes," but were they ready for that? Was Eliza ready, not just physically, but mentally and emotionally too?

Eliza's passionate response had been a surprise—a very welcome surprise—but Denny knew as much as she wanted to, she shouldn't move too quickly. She was starting to hope that their relationship could work out after all, and she didn't want her overeager libido to ruin it. She gave Eliza a regretful look. "I'm not sure that's a good idea."

A giggle burst from Eliza's chest. "Just to see my apartment and talk a little. *Coming up* is not code for anything. I'm just not ready for our date to end, especially since I'll be in San Francisco on a business trip with my bosses for most of next week."

"Oh." Denny's cheeks burned. "Sorry. I didn't mean to assume—"

"Trust me; you've got nothing to apologize for. My libido thinks *coming up* should be code for something—preferably for *coming*."

A heat that had nothing to do with embarrassment surged through Denny's body. *Jesus.* Eliza's suggestive comment wasn't exactly helping her to hold back.

Eliza reached for her hand. "Come on. It might be a bit too soon to sate one of our desires, but it's the perfect time to satisfy another. I didn't notice while we were busy crafting, but now I'm really getting hungry. Let's order a pizza."

"All right. But it's still my turn to pay. I need to break in my new wallet after all." Denny let herself be pulled inside the building and followed Eliza up the stairs.

Eliza unlocked a door on the second floor, flicked on the light, and then stepped aside to let Denny enter first.

Denny walked in and looked around.

Admittedly, Eliza's apartment was small, but Denny liked it instantly. With its high ceilings and a three-sided bay window, it didn't appear claustrophobic at all. A big, cream-colored easy chair and a reading lamp stood in front of the window, where Eliza had a great view of the park, and Denny could imagine her curled up with the afternoon sun lighting her face.

The worn, plum-colored couch didn't match the easy chair, but that only added to the charm of her place. A wooden coffee table was pulled close to it, as if Eliza sometimes put her feet up after a long day at work. Eliza's craftwork was everywhere: an unfinished project was strewn over the small desk in the corner, and the bookshelves sitting to both sides of the TV were crowded with cute animals on rocks and other figurines.

Comfort and warmth permeated the studio apartment.

But there was one thing missing—and in her current state, maybe that was a good thing. She turned toward Eliza and gave her a questioning look. "Bed?"

Eliza laughed, a throaty sound that moved over Denny's skin like a sensual tickle. "Didn't we just agree that 'coming up' isn't code for anything?"

"Um, what?" Still distracted by the effect of Eliza's laugh on her senses, Denny needed a few seconds to catch up with her train of thought. "No, no. I wasn't... It's just... There's no bed, and this doesn't look like a sleeper couch."

"It's not." Eliza crossed the room toward the built-in cabinet with amber panes and pulled out a huge drawer at the bottom. "I've got a pull-out bed."

"How cool is that?"

Eliza nodded and smiled. "So, do you like it?" She swept her arm in a gesture that included the entire apartment.

"I like it a lot. It's very...you."

"I like it too. If I ever win the lottery, I'd have a separate room with a big worktable, like the DIY Bar had. But for now, this suits me just fine."

Eliza's contentment with life and the sense of feeling at ease with herself, shortcomings and all, were part of what Denny liked so much about her.

"Make yourself comfortable while I call the pizza place," Eliza said. "You like artichoke hearts and spinach too, right?"

"It's my favorite."

"Great. We've achieved pizza topping compatibility, then."

Denny sat on the couch and watched Eliza move around the kitchenette to pull out glasses while she ordered their pizza. Seeing her in her home, totally relaxed, felt special.

After placing the order, Eliza put the phone down, carried the glasses over, and sat on the couch next to Denny. "Water okay? I think I have some Coke too if you'd rather—"

"No, water is fine." Denny already felt a bit buzzed with Eliza's closeness; she didn't need any caffeine on top of that. She looked around again. "How long have you lived here?"

"About five years. I moved in on one of the rare snowy days. And when I say 'snowy,' I mean more than the few flurries that usually give our fellow Portlanders heart palpitations." Eliza chuckled. "That's how I met Heather. My dad backed the moving truck into her car."

"That's a memorable first meeting; I have to give you that."

"Luckily, it was only a dent, and she was a good sport about it. Even helped me move in."

Denny was glad Eliza had a friend like that in her life. "So you've been friends ever since?"

"Pretty much. She's been really good for me, encouraging me to go out and socialize more, when I would have stayed home alone. She even dragged me to a gay bar a couple of times."

"Would you believe I've never been to one?" Denny said.

Eliza opened her eyes comically wide, the way Denny had earlier when Eliza had revealed that she didn't like beer. "You've never, ever been to a gay bar? Don't they take away your lesbian card?"

"Now that you mention it, I did get a letter from headquarters, warning me my membership might be revoked."

"Oh no." Eliza clutched her chest in such an exaggerated fashion that Denny struggled to keep her grave expression. "Is there nothing that can be done?"

"Well, they did say that they could waive the gay-bar requirement under certain conditions."

"Which are?"

Denny raised her index finger, ticking off the first point. "Going on at least three successful dates with a woman in a three-month period."

"Hmm, since even the first time we met somehow felt like a date, I think we can consider that requirement fulfilled."

Denny stared. "It felt like that to you too?"

"I didn't consciously think so at the time, but I knew it didn't feel like making a new friend."

"For me neither. I had to remind myself every ten seconds that it wasn't a date."

Eliza painted a check mark in the air with her finger. "That's a check, then. Is there another condition?"

"Sharing at least three hot kisses with an equally hot woman within a twenty-four-hour window."

"Hmm." Eliza playfully tapped her chin. "Did they say who gets to judge the required hotness of the woman?"

"Me," Denny said in a decisive tone. "Only me."

"So in your expert opinion, would I qualify?" Eliza spread her arms wide as if to invite an inspection.

Denny made a show of running her gaze over Eliza, but even if she tried, she wouldn't have been able to pretend she was an objective judge. "You're way overqualified."

"Oh yeah?"

"Mm-hmm."

Their gazes caught in an intense tangle.

Denny wasn't sure who moved first, but the distance between them shrank to a few inches.

Eliza slid her hand up Denny's shoulder and around to the back of her neck.

The way her fingers played with the short hair there made Denny's temperature skyrocket. A tug in her belly made her move even closer, and all she could think about was kissing Eliza, drinking her in with all her senses.

Just as she dipped her head to meet her lips, the doorbell rang, startling them apart.

"Jesus!" Denny's heart thumped against her ribs. "Whoever that is, can we kill them?"

"Well, it's probably the pizza, and they frown on killing the delivery person." Eliza got up and smoothed her hands down her jeans in a way that looked incredibly sexy.

Admittedly, Denny thought everything about her was sexy, including the way she breathed. "All right." She followed Eliza to the door and pulled out her new wallet. Earlier, she had swapped the contents of her old wallet into the new one, and now she smoothed her fingers over the soft, chocolate-brown leather. "They can stay alive—but only if I get a kiss later."

"Well, if it saves a life..." Eliza brushed her lips against Denny's in a promise of more to come, then swung open the door.

As the scent of melted cheese wafted up through the cardboard in Eliza's hands, her stomach gave an enthusiastic growl, but the rest of her body wasn't as happy with the interruption. Kissing Denny could quickly become addictive, and she loved their playful back-and-forth just as much.

"Did I lose all track of time, or were they extra fast?" Denny asked as Eliza carried the pizza to the coffee table.

"Maybe a little of both. They're just down the street. The pizza is from the Italian place where I had the date with that guy whose dog had appendicitis." That had been only two months ago, yet it felt like a lifetime. So much had changed since then.

Denny slid their glasses to the side so she could place the pizza on the table. "Ugh. I still don't get why he faked an emergency to get out of your date. I've never had as much fun with anyone else I've dated before. It's so wonderful how we can laugh but also talk about deep, emotional stuff, without fear of being judged."

Hearing Denny say that made Eliza go all gooey inside. She got plates and served them each a big slice of steaming pizza. "Same here. But to be fair, I'm not sure I was like that with him. That date felt so stilted, he probably thought I was the most boring person in all of Oregon."

Denny paused with the pizza halfway to her mouth. "I still think he's a fool, but you know what? I kinda love hearing that this," she used the pizza to point back and forth between them, "is different for you. Well, beyond the obvious."

"Which is?"

"Um, me being a woman."

Eliza couldn't help chuckling at herself. "Oh, that." She took a bite of the pizza. *Yum.* Melted cheese, spinach, and the lemony aftertaste of the artichoke hearts were the perfect combination.

"Yeah, that." Denny laughed too, but the expression in her eyes was serious. "Is that really not a big deal for you?"

Wasn't it? Eliza licked tomato sauce off her lip and considered it for a moment. "It kind of is and isn't at the same time."

Denny twirled her finger, indicating for her to go on as she listened attentively. Her gaze clung to Eliza's lips in the most distracting way.

"Being with you is surprisingly easy and comfortable," Eliza said.

"Comfortable?" Denny smacked her lips as if the word left a weird taste in her mouth. "That sounds like you're comparing me to an old pair of sneakers."

Eliza elbowed her. "Hey, I happen to love this old pair of sneakers." She wiggled her sneaker-covered feet.

Denny glanced at them with a fond smile and tapped Eliza's foot with her own. "Me too. But sometimes, you want to have sexy heels or good-looking Italian loafers instead of a comfy pair of sneakers."

"I didn't say comfortable is the only thing you're making me feel." Eliza's voice dipped lower. "You're like an entire closet full of shoes, ranging from flip-flops to heels."

Denny chuckled. "Leave it to a femme to come up with a shoe metaphor to describe her emotions."

"Femme?" Eliza had never thought to apply that term to herself. But then again, she had also never thought she could be anything but straight. "Is that what you think I am?"

"Well, you're not butch."

"Do I have to be one or the other?"

Denny smiled and took her hand. "No. Just be yourself."

"I am when I'm with you." God, they were really getting mushy. Eliza gave Denny's knee a playful nudge with her own. "Besides, you were the one who started the shoe metaphors, not me."

"Oops." Denny reached for another slice of pizza with her free hand but never let go of Eliza's. "So, what's the part of being with a woman that is a big deal for you?"

"Maybe not a big deal, but there are some things that'll take some getting used to. Like how people are reacting. Or how I think people will react." Eliza dabbed at a spot of tomato sauce on her plate. "I admit I still feel a little self-conscious about holding your hand or kissing you in public."

"We don't have to—"

"No." Eliza held on as Denny tried to withdraw her hand. "We have the same right to be affectionate as any other couple. I'm training myself to ignore people's reactions."

A crooked grin tugged up one corner of Denny's mouth. "Training, hmm? Well, any time you need a practice session, let me know. But seriously, thank you for being honest. I never want you to pretend you're okay with something when you're not."

Eliza sighed happily. God, she couldn't have asked for a better person to go through not-quite-straight puberty with. "I won't. Stop worrying so much."

"I can't. It matters too much." More quietly, Denny added, "You matter too much."

They looked into each other's eyes. Emotions Eliza couldn't yet name tightened her throat. "You matter to me too," she managed to get out.

Finally, Denny broke their eye contact and slid the pizza box over to her. "Pizza's getting cold."

Eliza pulled out another slice for herself but paused instead of taking a bite. There was something she needed to know first. "Can I ask you something?"

"Of course." Denny faced her with an unguarded gaze, completely open and vulnerable. "You're one of the few people who can ask me anything."

"How did you know you were gay?" Eliza asked.

Denny grinned. "The usual way."

"Which is?"

"Like many lesbians, I fell in love with my best friend when I was about...I don't know, maybe thirteen. I can't exactly pinpoint when it happened because it was such a gradual process. I just thought about her all the time. We used to have these deep, hour-long conversations, and we hugged a little too long and too often."

Images of the hugs she and Denny had shared flashed through Eliza's mind, and she remembered the conversations they'd had over the past three months. Oh yeah, she definitely identified with thirteen-year-old Denny.

Denny gazed at a spot on the wall as if a portal had opened up, allowing her to see the past. Then she turned her attention back to Eliza. "In hindsight, it should have been obvious that I was in love with her, but I assumed everyone felt that way about their best friend."

"When did you figure it out?" Eliza asked.

"When she started going out with boys. God, I was so jealous."

Eliza could identify with that too. She remembered how she had felt when Denny had gone out with Heather, and even now, Denny talking about her first crush left a hollow feeling in the pit of her stomach.

Denny covered her eyes with her free hand and peeked through her spread fingers. "I'm ashamed to admit I chained her boyfriend's bike to a tree so he'd be late meeting her."

It was a slightly mean thing to do, but Eliza couldn't help chuckling. "And then you went to the date instead of him?"

Denny dropped her hand to her lap and sighed. "No, I didn't have the guts to do that."

"So what happened?"

"Nothing. I never told her how I felt, and a year or so later, her family moved away, and we lost touch."

That was where the parallels ended. Maybe there was something to be said for realizing you were attracted to women at a later age.

Denny gave her a curious look. "Are you asking to get to know me better or to sort out your own feelings?"

"A little of both," Eliza said.

"Are you still comfortable going to the Pride parade with me tomorrow?"

"Of course." Eliza finished her slice and pushed her plate back. "Speaking of Pride... I was thinking. With the parade winding through half of downtown and fifty thousand people lining the streets, it will be pretty chaotic tomorrow morning. Does it make sense for you to drive back to Lents tonight, just to turn around in the morning and drive all the way back in that chaos?"

Denny put down the piece of crust she had been about to eat. "What are you suggesting?"

"You could stay over." Even though she had meant her suggestion in a completely innocent way, Eliza rushed to add, "I mean, on the couch. I've fallen asleep on it before, so it should be fine for a night."

Denny visibly hesitated. "I didn't bring a change of clothes."

Damn. Eliza racked her brain for a solution. The thought of sleeping with Denny—even just in the same room—was very appealing.

Denny smiled at her. "You're cute when you're trying to work out a problem. Especially with that speck of flour on your upper lip." She reached up and brushed it away with her thumb.

That magnetic pull between them instantly increased, and Eliza forgot the problem she'd been trying to solve as she stared into Denny's widened pupils.

Denny's lids lowered, hooding her eyes.

Within an instant, their mouths found each other.

God, Denny's lips were divine. Eliza closed her eyes to revel in the sensation. She tasted like tomato sauce and something uniquely Denny—something addictive. Their tongues caressed, retreated, then met again until Eliza was about to melt. Her hands roamed restlessly down Denny's back, up her sides, then down again.

Denny pressed her hand to the dip of Eliza's lower back, pulling her closer with a barely restrained urgency.

Restraint was the last thing on Eliza's mind. Her fingers itched to feel Denny's skin. She tugged the T-shirt from the back of Denny's jeans and slipped one hand beneath while clutching Denny's shoulder with the other. *Mmm.* Never had touching someone's back been such a heavenly experience.

Denny groaned. She cupped the back of Eliza's head with her free hand, pulled Eliza's bottom lip into her mouth, and nipped it gently.

A thrill of pleasure zinged through Eliza's belly. She trailed her fingertips over Denny's smooth skin, exploring the muscles along her spine until the elastic of Denny's sports bra stopped her. With a frustrated grunt, she slid her hand around and followed the arc of her ribs with her fingertips. She traced the skin just below her breasts with her thumb. God, she was so soft there, even softer than her back. On the next pass, her thumb accidentally brushed the underside of Denny's breast. *Oh my God.*

Denny sucked in a sharp breath.

Light-headed, Eliza paused and tried to let her brain catch up with what she was doing. "You okay?"

Denny laughed, a hoarse, wild sound that sent tingles through Eliza. "Shouldn't I be asking *you* that?"

"No shoulds." She was very aware of Denny's warm hand lingering on the small of her back, on the verge of slipping beneath her T-shirt. Her pulse drummed in her ears, and she felt as if she couldn't get enough air into her lungs, but she didn't want to stop. Not yet. "You can touch me too."

When Denny finally slid her hand up and caressed her bare skin, Eliza felt the touch everywhere. Denny nibbled her bottom lip again, then kissed her jaw, and finally her neck.

Eliza couldn't hold back a moan as Denny's warm lips traced down her throat, leaving goose bumps in their wake. Her entire body was sensitized, and Eliza couldn't imagine what it would feel like when Denny touched more of her. She clutched at Denny to stay upright—and found herself cradling her breast through her sports bra.

They both froze for several heartbeats.

Denny gasped out her name.

Holy shit. Holy shit. I'm touching her breast! Excitement gathered low in Eliza's belly. She didn't know whether to wrench her hand away or to caress Denny's soft breast.

Denny arched against her, pressing her breast more firmly into her hand until Eliza felt the nipple harden against her palm.

Oh wow. She squeezed softly.

Denny pressed her mouth to Eliza's neck and groaned against her skin, making her shudder.

"Hey, look what I got y—" Heather came to an abrupt halt after taking one step into the apartment. "Oh shit. I'm sorry. I didn't know you had company."

Dazed, Eliza jerked her hand from beneath Denny's T-shirt.

Denny wrenched her mouth from Eliza's neck so fast she nearly smashed her head into Eliza's nose. She pulled Eliza's T-shirt down as if to protect her modesty, while she seemed less concerned with her own.

Breathing heavily, Eliza slumped against the back of the couch. "Dammit, Heather," she grumbled.

Heather ducked her head. "Sorry. I was just so excited because I found the perfect T-shirt for you to wear to Pride. I'll show you later."

But before she could turn and flee the apartment, Denny jumped up. "That's okay. I should get going anyway."

What? No! Eliza stared at her. "Denny, wait! Didn't we just discuss you staying over?"

"Yeah, but…" Denny gestured wildly, almost knocking over her half-full glass of water. "Like I said, I didn't bring jammies or a change of clothes."

Heather snorted. "From where I'm standing, it didn't look like you'd need jammies." When Eliza pierced her with a glare, she made a zipping-my-lips motion.

Their gazes met, and the momentary panic in Denny's eyes vanished. "Next time." Her tone promised a lot more than her bringing a change of clothes.

Eliza's pulse quickened.

After a glance to Heather, Denny bent, swiped a strand of hair that had escaped Eliza's ponytail behind her ear, and kissed her tenderly. "See you tomorrow morning. Sweet dreams."

Then she was gone.

Eliza let her head fall against the couch and glowered at Heather. "That better be the most amazing shirt I've ever seen."

"I'm really sorry," Heather said again. "I didn't think you'd ask her up and jump her bones. What happened to your not-before-the-eighth-date rule?"

"I don't have a not-before-the-eighth-date rule. I've just never before wanted to ask anyone up before the eighth date." With Denny, she hadn't hesitated—partly because she felt safe with her and partly because she hadn't wanted her to leave.

Maybe Heather interrupting them had been a good thing. They had both gotten a touch out of control. That wasn't necessarily bad, but in hindsight, it scared her a little how much she wanted Denny. Heather hadn't been far off when she had compared it to going through puberty a second time. Her hormones were working overtime, not giving her head a chance to catch up.

"Hmm, if you're that eager to get your hands on her, maybe I bought the wrong T-shirt." Heather unfolded it and held it out across her chest. Against the background of the black fabric, big rainbow letters said, *I'm not a lesbian, but my girlfriend is.*

Eliza hurled one of the throw pillows at her.

Chapter 24

THE NEXT MORNING, ELIZA BUZZED around the apartment like a bee on ecstasy. The parade started at eleven, and her family wouldn't be over before ten when they would all walk to the parade together, but she'd been wide-awake at six. She wasn't even sure what was making her so jittery.

Was it the thought of Denny meeting her family? She knew without a doubt that Denny would charm them without even trying, so that probably wasn't it.

Maybe it was the parade itself. Sure, she had been to Pride before, but she'd been an ally back then, not part of the LGBT+ community. Did she really belong now? Would it be obvious to the people in the parade that she was a total newbie and had never slept with a woman before?

She stopped in the middle of her apartment. *You're being silly. People go to the parade to have a good time, not to analyze other people's sexual experiences.*

Just as her pulse had calmed, the doorbell rang, making it speed up again.

She crossed to the door and tried to guess which of her family members it might be. Probably Ryan and Nichole, who were driving over with their parents, while everyone else would take the MAX. Or maybe Andy, who was early for everything.

But it wasn't her oldest sister. Heather brushed past her, wearing her *Is it gay in here, or is it just me?* T-shirt.

Eliza closed the door. "Since when do you ring the doorbell?"

"Since I walked in on you with your hand beneath Denny's shirt last night."

Eliza had relived that experience for half of the night, and now that loop of mental images and sensations started again. Quickly, she turned away and fanned herself.

Heather chuckled. "Guess that means you liked what was under that shirt. Speaking of shirts... Why aren't you wearing the one I got you?"

Wasn't it obvious? Eliza faced her again and gave her an incredulous look. "My family still doesn't know about Denny and me, and a T-shirt slogan is not how I want them to find out."

"Oh. Of course. Guess I was so excited about your newly discovered sapphic tendencies that I didn't think about that."

Sapphic tendencies? Eliza once again wished she had the ability to arch one eyebrow the way Heather could. That term deserved it.

The doorbell rang again.

This time, it was her family. Her parents, Ryan, and Nichole arrived first, followed by Andy. Britt; her husband, Tony; and the twins came a minute later. When they all crowded into the apartment, it seemed even smaller than usual.

Her oldest sister hurried past them without stopping. "Hugs in a sec," Andy called over her shoulder. "I need the bathroom first."

"I keep telling you not to drink so much coffee," their mother said.

"Have you experienced Andy before her first coffee?" Ryan said. "Trust me, Mom, it's better for everyone if she gets her daily quota."

Andy flipped him the bird before she closed the bathroom door after her.

Chaos ensued as everyone hugged and greeted each other.

Eliza hugged her brother. "Where are the kids?"

"With their dad," Ryan said.

"Their *other* dad," Nichole added, and the two exchanged a smile.

"I would have liked an arrangement like that when the three of you were little," their father threw in. "Another guy to take over every other weekend while I went fishing."

Eliza and Britt poked him from two sides. "Hey, we were angels."

Their parents snorted in unison.

Even as Eliza laughed, she wondered how Denny would handle her big, chaotic family. Denny was a family woman too; she knew that. But with just her, Salem, and Bella in the house, she wasn't used to the whirlwind interaction of Eliza's clan.

Andy emerged from the bathroom, waving something Eliza thought was a rainbow flag. "Is there something you want to tell us, baby sis?" Andy asked in a teasing singsong.

"What do you—?" Then Eliza caught a better look at what her sister was waving around. It wasn't a flag. It was the T-shirt Heather had given her. She had dropped it onto the pile of laundry next to her bathtub, which she had meant to do after the parade. *Shit, shit, shit.*

Still laughing, Andy held up the T-shirt for everyone to see.

Their father read the slogan and scratched his head. "I don't get the joke. If a woman has a girlfriend, doesn't that make her a lesbian?"

"No, honey." Their mother patted his arm. "Bisexual women can have girlfriends too."

"And pansexual women," Britt added.

Eliza's head buzzed.

"So who's a lesbian...or bisexual?" their father asked.

"No one, Dad. Well, other than Heather, of course. I'm just teasing Eliza." Andy's gaze went back to Eliza, and her laughter stopped abruptly when she didn't join in. "Um, this isn't your T-shirt, is it?"

A vicelike pressure started in the middle of Eliza's chest. The buzzing in her ears grew louder until she could no longer make out what everyone was saying. "I..."

Heather stepped forward and pulled the shirt from Andy's grip. "No, it's mine. I got it for a friend and left it here because Eliza said she'd do laundry this weekend."

"If I had known you're now offering laundry service, I would have brought my pile too," Andy said.

The vice around Eliza's ribcage loosened. They had bought Heather's explanation. She could leave it at that until she was ready to tell them. But what exactly was she waiting for? Did she need to pick a label before she made any kind of declaration to her family? Or was she waiting until she and Denny had shared their fifth or tenth date...or made love? Would it change anything?

Her mind jumped forward to the parade, where they would meet up with Denny and her family. Could she introduce Denny as a friend even though her heart would be pounding at the sight of her? Could she keep a respectable distance between them all through the parade even though she was longing to take Denny's hand or wrap her arms around her? And, most of all, why would she deny herself all that just so her family wouldn't find out yet?

Denny was exactly the kind of person she had always looked forward to taking home and introducing to her parents and siblings. Did she really want to hide their relationship just because Denny was a woman?

The answer pierced her with sudden clarity. She wanted Denny to be involved in every aspect of her life, including her family.

On shaky legs, she walked over to Heather and took the T-shirt from her. "Actually, the shirt is mine."

A rare silence descended over her family.

"Yours?" A frown settled on Andy's tan face. "But you're not a lesbian."

Eliza clenched her fingers around the shirt. "I never said I was. That's the whole point of the shirt." She held her head up high and met her sister's gaze. "But I do have a girlfriend."

"You...what?"

"Why didn't you tell us, honey?"

"When did that happen?"

"Who is she? Heather, it's not you, is it?"

"Is she nice?"

The questions hailed down on her so fast that Eliza couldn't keep up with who wanted to know what.

One voice drowned out the rest—Andy's. "That doesn't mean you have to wear rainbow colors and join the tribe."

Eliza stared at her sister. What on earth was going on with Andy? Britt and Ryan were closer to Eliza in age, but for some reason, Andy—who was six years older—had been her favorite playmate growing up. Even now, as adults, they were closest, maybe because they were the only ones who didn't have kids. Andy had always been the cool, liberal one, even in their family—the one Eliza looked up to because she knew exactly what she wanted. "What the hell, Andy? Since when are you a homophobe?"

"What? I'm not!"

"Could have fooled me," Eliza muttered.

"I just don't want you to label yourself too fast and jump into something that might not be right for you."

Oh, great. Not that overprotective big-sister routine again. Eliza had thought they had finally left that behind. She folded her arms across her chest, pressing the shirt to her breasts like a shield. "What makes you think I am?"

For once, her usually confident sister looked at her shoes as she answered, "Experience."

"What's that supposed to mean? It's not like I have a history of jump—"

"Not your experience." Andy raised her head. "Mine. When I was in the EMT program, I thought for a while I might be gay."

"What?" several family members shouted at once.

Andy waved her hand. "It was no big deal. So I slept with a woman once. That doesn't make me a lesbian or even bi, but it took me some time to figure that out."

Eliza's jaw worked. She needed a few seconds before she could form intelligible speech. "You slept with a woman?"

"Yep."

Great. Everyone seemed to have some experience in that area; she was the only one who didn't. Eliza couldn't stop staring or keep herself from asking. "But it wasn't your cup of tea?"

Andy's gaze went to the twins. She walked over and covered Piper's ears with her hands, nodding at Britt to do the same to Polly, despite the twins' protests. "It was a good experience. Okay, to be honest, it was amazing. A woman really knows how to make another woman—"

"Lalalala," their mother said loudly. "I think I need my ears covered too. There are things a mother doesn't need to know about her offspring."

Eliza laughed along with her sister, and her tension eased.

"Okay, Mom, I'll stick to the PG part," Andy said. She took her hands off Piper's ears while Britt released Polly. "It was good, but there was something missing. That tug wasn't there."

"Tug?" Eliza asked.

"Yeah. That emotional pull. That I-want-to-share-everything-with-you, can't-spend-another-minute-without-you feeling." Andy shrugged. "In the end, it only confirmed that I'm straight."

"What makes you think it's the same for me?" Eliza asked. "That there isn't a tug for me either?"

Andy ran her gaze over her as if she were a patient whose symptoms she was trying to figure out. "Is there?"

Eliza gulped. "Yes," she managed to get out past the thickness in her throat. "I think there is. Remember what we talked about when I started to work for Feathered Friends?"

Andy nodded. "You said you felt like you'd finally found your place after struggling to find the perfect fit for so long."

"It's the same with my relationships," Eliza continued. "You've met my boyfriends. They were all great guys, and I was happy enough with them. But I never felt like: this is it. It never hurt to think I might not get to spend the rest of my life with them."

For the second time in as long as she could remember, her entire family was silent. Everyone stared at her until she squirmed beneath the attention.

"So..." Andy drew out the syllable as if she needed time to think. "This mysterious girlfriend of yours, she makes you feel like that?"

Eliza's mouth was so dry that she had to unglue her tongue before she could answer. "She does. I've been waiting for that deep connection all these years. I never expected to feel it with a woman, but I do." She swayed as she brushed aside the last layer of doubt and no longer held anything back, not even from herself. "I think I love her."

Her gaze darted from Andy to her parents, and she wasn't sure if she was waiting for them to confirm her feelings or tell her it couldn't be. She didn't even know which option would soothe the sudden spike of anxiety. For a few seconds, her family looked as shocked as Eliza felt. How on earth had love snuck up on her so fast? But now that she'd said it out loud, she knew it was true.

"Aww, honey." Her mother was the first one to rush over and engulf her in a warm hug. "I'm so happy for you. It's your friend Denny, isn't it? Why didn't you tell us sooner? I told you we'd be fine with it if you ended up with a woman."

Britt sent Eliza a commiserating smile. "God, don't you just hate it when Mom turns out to be right?"

"Whoa!" Andy raised both hands. "Mom, you knew about this?"

One arm still wrapped around Eliza, their mother turned toward Andy. "I caught them exchanging, um, sexy texts after Eliza had the accident."

"Mom! We weren't doing that! It was autocorrect!" God, could the floor please open up and swallow her whole? At least Denny wasn't there. She probably wouldn't have stopped blushing for the next three years if she'd heard that.

Their father chuckled. "Is that what they call it nowadays? Autocorrect?"

"No, really! Back then, there was nothing..." Eliza cut herself off before she could say *nothing between us* because that didn't feel right. There had been a lot between them from the very first message. "I had no idea I could feel that way about a woman—about anyone—back then."

"Well, you might not have known, but I did," their mother said. "That's why I wore this." She stepped back to present her T-shirt. It said, *Proud mom,* and the second *o* was represented by a rainbow heart.

"I thought that was for Heather because we kind of adopted her," Andy said.

"Well, it's for Heather too. I figured it could be for Heather alone until your sister was ready to tell us about her lady love."

Okay, even for her family, this was starting to feel surreal. She just hoped Denny wouldn't freak when she saw her mom's T-shirt.

"Um, speaking of..." Their father tapped his wristwatch. "I think we should go, or she'll think we stood her up."

As they all trooped to the door, Eliza shook herself out of her shock and caught Andy's arm. "Please be nice to Denny and don't try to intimidate her with your big-sister routine. I know you think you need to protect me, but I'm not a teenager anymore." Even though being around Denny made her feel like one.

"I know you're an adult." It was the first time Andy had said that so clearly. With a smile, she added, "But you're still my baby sister."

"*Younger* sister," Eliza said.

"All right. Younger sister. And that means Denny will get the 'I'm an EMT, so if you hurt her, I know how to kill you and make it look like an accident' speech, just like your boyfriends did."

"Yeah, because nothing says 'welcome to the family' better than being threatened with murder," Tony said. "She did it to me too."

"And to me," Nichole called over to them.

Andy shrugged. "Didn't chase either of you off, did it?"

Eliza could only hope it wouldn't chase Denny off either.

Denny bobbed up and down on the balls of her feet, barely resisting the urge to jump so she could see above the crowd. The person in front of them blocked her view with their rainbow top hat. She bit back a curse.

She, Salem, Matt, and Bella had arrived early to secure spots at the North Park Blocks, close to the start of the parade, but there was still no sign of Eliza and her family.

Where were they? Eliza hadn't changed her mind, had she?

Denny dismissed the thought. But what if Eliza's parents had found out their daughter was dating a woman, and now they were freaking out?

"Hey, what's with the sourpuss face, sis?" Salem poked her arm with the rainbow flag she was waving even though the parade hadn't started yet. "It's Pride! You should be beaming!"

"I will," Denny said, still scanning the crowd, "as soon as Eliza gets here, and her family doesn't immediately dislike me."

"Dislike you?" Salem echoed. "Why would they?"

Denny couldn't name a reason, other than what she looked like. But Eliza's family went to Pride to support Heather, so surely they wouldn't care that she didn't fit society's view of what a woman was supposed to look like. Still, meeting Eliza's family felt like a huge step, and she couldn't help worrying.

Then her gaze zeroed in on a familiar face in the crowd, like a searchlight honing in. All the worries that had plagued her fell away, and she couldn't help the cheesy smile that formed on her lips at the sight of Eliza walking toward her.

God, she looked incredible. Even in the mass of people surrounding her, she stood out. In jean shorts, a red tank top with spaghetti straps, and sandals, she showed off more bare skin than Denny had seen on her before.

Don't ogle her, she firmly told herself. *Whatever you do, don't ogle her in front of her family!* She forced herself to focus on Eliza's ponytail that bounced with every step, instead of letting herself admire the slender legs and the nearly bare shoulders on display.

Eliza showed less restraint. She let her gaze roam over every inch of Denny, from her trekking sandals and her khaki shorts to her navy button-up with little rainbows all over it and her sunglasses, which she had hooked to the front of her shirt.

Denny's skin heated, and it wasn't from the sun beating down on them.

Good thing Eliza's family followed behind her and couldn't see the expression on Eliza's face, or their just-friends cover would have been blown.

A rush of excitement blasted through her as Eliza returned her smile. They had seen each other last night, but even that felt like too much time apart. Their gazes never left each other until Eliza was right in front of her.

"Hi," Eliza said. Despite all the people surrounding them, there was something intimate about her greeting and the way she looked at Denny, as if Eliza saw only her. "Happy Pride!"

"Happy Pride." Denny realized she was leaning forward, her body pulled in by Eliza's closeness. Not sure how to greet her in front of her family, she searched Eliza's face for guidance. Was a hug okay?

Eliza took another step toward her, then one more, right into her personal space. She leaned in as if to kiss her.

Denny froze. She tried to signal with her eyes, but Eliza moved closer anyway. Had she forgotten her family was watching? *What—?*

Eliza slid one hand onto her waist. Then her lips—so incredibly soft and tasting faintly of vanilla ChapStick—were on hers. It was only a peck, but it lingered a few seconds too long to be a greeting between two friends.

Almost without conscious thought, Denny's arms came up, and she rested one hand at the dip of her spine. The gesture was much too familiar, but she couldn't help herself. *Shit. We're totally failing at this just-friends thing.* When she finally let go, she expected to be faced with disapproving or confused expressions.

Instead, a slim woman in her early sixties who could only be Eliza's mother walked toward her with a welcoming expression on her face. "Hello. You must be Denny. It's so nice to meet you."

Denny somehow managed not to let her mouth gape open. Had Eliza's mom missed their greeting? "Yes, I am. Nice to meet you too."

"Oh, in case there's any doubt, I'm Kathleen, Eliza's mom." She pointed at her T-shirt.

Denny had only a moment to stare at the *proud mom* slogan and the little rainbow heart before Kathleen pulled her into a hug.

Over Kathleen's shoulder, Denny sought Eliza's eyes. What the hell was going on?

Eliza answered with a shrug and an adorable smile.

When Denny escaped Kathleen's embrace, she numbly shook the hand of Eliza's father, who wore a *Hate less, love more* T-shirt.

The next to greet her was Heather.

Denny wasn't sure how to act around her. Would things be awkward between them now that she was dating Eliza, especially after Heather had walked in on their make-out session last night? But Heather bent and hugged her as if they were old friends.

Denny found herself clinging to her for a second, thankful to see her familiar face in this sea of strangers.

"Relax," Heather whispered into her ear. "The Harrisons are really cool. No one's going to come after you with a shotgun or threaten you with a Bible."

Then Heather let go, and the rest of Eliza's family descended on Denny. With each sibling, husband, and girlfriend she was introduced to, her confusion grew. What was going on? Eliza's family acted as if they knew she and Eliza were dating!

"If you hurt her, you answer to me." The last sister—a taller, older, more athletic version of Eliza—gave Denny's hand a firm shake and pierced her with a glare that would have made a mafia boss proud. "I'm Andy, by the way. Welcome to the family."

All Denny could do was stare at her.

Eliza turned toward Salem. "May I?" Without waiting for a reply, she took the rainbow flag from Salem's hand and whacked Andy's shoulder. "I told you not to do that!"

Andy's features relaxed into a grin. "Sorry. Couldn't resist."

Salem turned toward Denny. "Is this my cue to tell Eliza if she hurts you, she'll have to deal with me and my big, burly boyfriend?"

Gamely, Matt flexed his biceps. With the rainbow suspenders he wore, he didn't manage to make it appear threatening at all.

"And me!" Bella called.

Eliza waved the flag to get everyone's attention. "Guys, stop it. No one is going to hurt anyone, okay?"

Dazed, Denny watched as their families introduced themselves to each other. It was surreal to see Salem hug Heather, Eliza's mom, and even the slightly intimidating Andy.

With their families distracted, Eliza finally joined Denny. She leaned against her shoulder and wrapped one hand around her upper arm. "I'm sorry," she whispered. "I didn't mean to spring this—them—on you without warning, but..."

Denny moved her shoulder against Eliza's in a discreet caress. "It's okay."

Eliza searched her face. "Is it really?"

"Yes, of course. I just didn't think you were ready to tell them about us."

Eliza's laughter vibrated through them both. "I didn't think so either, but then Andy found the T-shirt—the one Heather gave me—and I realized I didn't want to lie. I'm proud of you...of us."

The hundreds of people surrounding them seemed to disappear as they looked into each other's eyes.

Giddiness bubbled up inside of Denny, and she felt as if she had drunk a bottle of champagne all by herself. Apparently, she'd been more worried about how Eliza's family would react than she had realized. She'd secretly been afraid that coming out as a woman who was dating another woman would be a big struggle for Eliza.

With that huge obstacle out of the way, she felt as if she could hug the entire world.

She sensed more than saw Eliza grin next to her.

"What?"

"You're beaming," Eliza said. "It seems you really love Pride."

I love you. Denny bit back the words at the last moment. *Oh my God!* Had she really just thought that—and nearly said it? It was much too soon to feel like this, wasn't it? She had always been more reserved with her feelings and never risked her heart so quickly. But Eliza had been the exception to so many rules for her from the very start. As scary as it was, she was all in, with no regrets and no holding back.

But she had to, at least for now. It was too soon to say it. She didn't want to overwhelm Eliza and pressure her into saying it back before she was ready...if she indeed felt the same.

Luckily, several of Heather's friends—some with trans flags around their shoulders and one who had died her hair blue, pink, and white—came over, setting off another round of introductions and distracting Denny.

She watched as Eliza greeted them all as if she knew them well. One of them, a redhead whose T-shirt declared them to be a *Nonbinary Badass,* said something that made Eliza laugh.

"Yes, this is her." Eliza looked at Denny with a fond smile. "KC, this is Denny, my..." She hesitated and dug her teeth into her bottom lip while her gaze searched Denny's.

Denny held her breath. Was she about to say...?

"Girlfriend," Eliza finished. Her voice went up, making it sound like a question.

Denny felt as if someone had handed her an award. "Yeah, that's me. Eliza's girlfriend." She snapped her mouth shut and held out her hand instead. "Hi, KC. Nice to meet you."

Heather's friends crowded around her to introduce themselves, and Denny's head spun as she tried to remember all the new names and faces.

Just when it became too overwhelming, Eliza pointed to the other side of the intersection, distracting everyone's attention away from Denny. "Look! I think they're about to—"

Her last word was cut off by the roar of engines as the Dykes on Bikes revved their motorcycles, ready to kick off the parade.

The sound reverberated off the buildings around them, making the windows shake. Even through her thick-soled trekking sandals, the vibrations sent a tingle through Denny's feet.

A current of excitement swept through her, raising goose bumps all along her skin.

Eliza shivered as if she felt it too, and they exchanged a long look. Getting to share this experience with Eliza made it even more special.

The rider in the front pumped her fist in the air.

Then, with a blast of their horns, they were off.

The crowd around them hollered, whistled, and cheered as the riders roared past. There were dozens of them, some leather-clad, some in bikini tops, and others bare-breasted.

"Aunt Denny, look!" Bella had to yell to be heard. Laughing, she pointed at a goggles-wearing dog riding in a rainbow-colored sidecar.

Pride offered a lot to see. After the Dykes on Bikes had passed, the first floats rounded the corner. Drag queens strutted down the street in high heels, burly guys showed off their rainbow tutus, and people in unicorn costumes waved at the crowd.

Blasting music and someone yelling through a megaphone made conversation nearly impossible, but Denny didn't need words to enjoy the experience.

Eliza squeezed her arm with every new group as she pointed out cute dogs with rainbow collars and strollers draped with *love wins* flags.

At the end of the day, Denny's arm might be bruised, but she didn't care. Pride had never been so much fun. With Eliza at her side, she didn't mind being trapped in the middle of a huge crowd, surrounded by a big group of new people.

The best part was seeing how comfortable Eliza seemed amid all the LGBT+ people. While she might still not know where exactly she fit into the community, she appeared at home in it. She cheered, danced, and sometimes sang along without the slightest fear of judgment—and nobody was judging. Her family seemed to be a lot like Eliza, accepting everyone the way they were.

Even Andy turned out not to be a hard-ass. She laughed with Heather and her friends as if she had known them for ages, and she let Bella paint a rainbow flag onto her cheek.

Another group marched past, blowing soap bubbles into the crowd.

One bubble floated over and lingered inches from Eliza, reflecting the sunlight and Eliza's face as she looked up.

Denny pulled out her phone but wasn't fast enough to capture the magical moment before the bubble touched Eliza's nose and burst.

Laughing, Eliza closed her eyes against the soapy spatter.

Denny wiped it away with the back of her fingers. When their gazes met, the three little words rose up again, this time with even more urgency. A thrill that was equal parts excitement and sheer terror coursed through her.

Eliza grinned and broke the moment by stealing Denny's Pride baseball cap and putting it on her own head.

"Hey!" Denny's protest instantly died away as Eliza repaid her with a short but heartfelt kiss. It took a second for her lips to react and move against Eliza's. She hadn't expected a second, longer kiss in public, especially not in front of her family. Her entire body vibrated, not just from the kiss, but from a rush of happiness.

"What, no fight?" Eliza asked against her lips. "You're letting me have the cap?"

Denny adjusted the cap on Eliza's head so she could still see her expressive eyes. "It looks much better on you anyway."

When the parade wrapped up two and a half hours later, Denny wasn't ready for their time together to end.

"Who's up for pizza at our place?" Salem asked.

Denny sent a grateful look her way and immediately stuck her hand up in the air.

"Me," Eliza shouted, beating even her nieces and Bella.

Heather's friends glanced at one another.

"There's a party at Tipsy's, so I think I'm out," Fiona—the woman with the blue, pink, and white hair—said.

KC nodded. "Yeah, me too."

Heather hesitated but finally told her friends, "I can never resist pizza. I'll catch up with you later."

Eliza's brother and his girlfriend had left their car in a parking garage a few blocks from the parade route. Denny gave them their address so they could drive over with Eliza's parents.

As the rest of them trooped to the nearest MAX station, Eliza reached for her hand and entwined their fingers.

Denny walked as if on clouds. This was the best day ever.

Okay, maybe apart from that make-out session yesterday.

Eliza had been afraid her big, chaotic family might be too much for Denny and her small family, but her worries had clearly been unfounded.

Her father made Salem laugh at his corny dad jokes, and her mother had managed to draw Bella out. Now the usually shy tween was gesturing with both hands as she entertained Eliza's mom and the twins with a story about something Eliza couldn't hear from the other end of the noisy table.

Denny finished the conversation she'd been having with Britt and Tony and turned to Eliza. "This is kind of nice," she said quietly, sounding surprised.

"Not too much?" Eliza asked.

"Maybe a little." Denny held her thumb and index finger a fraction of an inch apart. "But in the best of ways."

Eliza leaned her knee against Denny's. "You can recharge your introvert batteries while I'm gone."

Denny let out a sigh. "Don't remind me."

"It's just four days." But even though she looked forward to going to the Pet Products Expo with Austen and Dee and exploring San Francisco a little, she had to admit she'd miss Denny too.

"Do you want the last slice, sis?" Ryan held up the nearly empty pizza box.

"God, no. I ate too much already." Eliza held her full stomach with one hand and popped the button of her shorts with the other. "If I keep this up, my pants won't fit me anymore."

Next to her, Denny let out a groan. Her gaze lingered on the unbuttoned shorts, making a heaviness of a different kind settle in Eliza's belly, way lower than her stomach.

Salem scoffed. "Denny can fix that problem for you. She's great with her hands."

Denny crumpled her paper napkin into a ball and threw it at her. "Salem!"

"What?" Salem touched her chest, looking like innocence personified. "I was talking about your sewing skills. You could easily make Eliza a new pair of pants."

"Yeah, right."

"Well, you did promise to make me a pair with nice, deep pockets," Eliza said. "If that offer still stands, you could come over once I'm back from my business trip and take my measurements." Christ, was it just her, or did that sound as if she was inviting Denny over for so much more than a pants-making session? Images of Denny running a tape measure around her breasts flashed through her mind. *Um, Denny is going to make you a pair of pants. Why would she measure your chest?*

But the images lingered, and she didn't push them away.

Truth be told, if Denny's hands wandered a bit—or a lot—while she measured, Eliza wouldn't mind at all.

"Of course the offer still stands. If you want, I could come over after work on Friday and..." Denny's cheeks reddened.

Eliza swallowed. She would have paid good money to see the images running through Denny's mind. Were they anything like hers? They were probably more graphic because, unlike Eliza, Denny knew exactly what could happen between two women, while Eliza's experience ended at touching Denny's breast through her bra.

God, she really had to stop thinking about this since both of their families were right there.

Andy cleared her throat. "Before you go into any more detail, I think I'll head out. It was great to meet you all, but I've got a twelve-hour shift tomorrow and need to get some sleep." She looked at Heather and Eliza. "Want to catch the MAX together?"

"Yeah," Heather said. "I should catch up with my friends before I miss all the fun. Uh, not that this wasn't fun. It really was."

Denny jumped up. "I'll drive you. It's after six, so most Pride celebrations should be over, and traffic should be back to normal."

"You don't have to—"

"Thank you." Eliza raised her voice over her sister's. "We would love that, if you don't mind."

Denny grabbed her keys. "Of course I don't mind." More quietly and with an adorably shy smile, she added, "It gives me more time with you."

Eliza knew she meant it, and that warmed her all over.

"Jeez, are they always like that?" Andy asked Salem, who laughed and nodded.

"Half of the time, I think it's cute. The other half, I'm tempted to pour a bucket of cold water over their heads to get their attention."

Denny gave her sister a gentle shove. "Says the woman who barely ate any pizza because she was too busy staring into Matt's eyes."

"Ew," Bella said loudly, making everyone laugh.

They all left the house together, then headed to various cars.

Matt volunteered to drop Britt, her husband, and the twins off, while Ryan and Nichole had driven over, so they would take their parents home.

"So what did you think?" Eliza whispered as she hugged her mother.

Her mother's lips twitched into a mischievous smile. "The pizza was wonderful."

"Mom!" Eliza stopped herself from stomping her foot. "You know that's not what I'm asking. What did you think of Denny?"

Her mom's smile softened. She glanced at Denny, who was watching them with wide eyes, as if she suspected she was the topic of conversation. "She's wonderful too. I can see why you love her."

"Shh, Mom! I haven't told her yet." Eliza threw a panicked look at Denny, but thankfully, she was now talking to Britt and Tony and hadn't overheard them. "It's all still very new, but I think this is it for me."

"Well, it's clear to me that she's just as taken with you," her mother said.

Eliza hugged her more tightly. "Thank you for making this so easy."

"All we want is for you to be happy—and I think Denny makes you happy. So why wouldn't we support that?"

If only all parents were like that. Eliza knew she'd won the jackpot in that regard. "She does." Her gaze strayed to Denny again. She kissed her mother's cheek, then hugged her father and the rest of the family.

When Denny unlocked the Subaru, Andy climbed into the back seat with Heather, leaving the passenger seat for Eliza.

"That's a first," Eliza murmured as she got in. "I've never gotten to ride shotgun. Andy was always quick to claim the passenger seat because she's older and taller." She flashed Denny a grin. "I guess that's one of the perks of being your girlfriend."

Denny paused with the key halfway to the ignition. Her focused expression softened as if hearing that title still made her all gooey inside.

Heather made a honking noise. "Are we waiting for something?"

"Um, no." Denny started the car.

God, she was so adorable. Eliza couldn't help smiling.

Denny looked at her for a second and returned the smile. "What?"

"Nothing," Eliza answered. "Just had a great day. It was incredibly empowering to be around so many other queer people."

Heather leaned forward until her head was between the front seats. "*Other* queer people? So have we lured you over to the dark side?"

What? Eliza mentally played back what she had just said. Oh. Her gaze darted to Denny, who pretended to focus on driving, but Eliza knew her well enough to know she was listening to every word. She wanted to reach over and put her hand on Denny's nearly bare thigh to soothe her—and, frankly, to feel her skin—but with her sister in the car, she resisted the urge. "I'm still not sure which letter of the LGBT+ alphabet fits me best, but referring to myself as straight doesn't feel right anymore. So yeah, I guess queer will do for now."

"I think that means Denny gets a toaster oven," Andy said.

Eliza turned and gave her a questioning look. "Toaster oven?"

"Lesbian inside joke," Heather said.

Why did her sister know all the secret women-loving-women lingo, while she—the one with the girlfriend—had no idea? Eliza saw some extensive googling in her future. And maybe she should read up on how to please a woman in bed too.

The rest of the ride was over much too fast, and before Eliza was ready to say goodbye, they reached their apartment building.

Heather and Andy jumped out, probably to give them a moment alone.

"I had the best time today, and I really liked your family," Denny said. "But I have to admit I'm looking forward to Friday, when it'll be just you and me."

"God, me too." Eliza finally gave in to the urge to put her hand on Denny's leg. Mmm, her skin was so soft and warm and so...

Denny let out a groan and pressed her hand over Eliza's, stopping the movement of her fingers.

Oh shit! Eliza hadn't even noticed she'd let her hand wander halfway up her thigh. When had that happened? "Sorry, I—"

"Don't apologize." Denny's voice sounded deeper than usual. "It's just..." She nodded toward the sidewalk, where Andy and Heather stood waiting.

"Yeah." Eliza slid her hand out from under Denny's and moved it to a safer spot on her knee. "Call me later?"

"Of course. I'll tuck you in via FaceTime, like always."

The term made Eliza chuckle. "I'm not a kid who needs to be tucked in."

"I know." The husky rasp in Denny's voice sent a shiver through Eliza. "Believe me; I know. But I love tucking you in anyway."

"Mmm, me too." She loved having Denny be the last person she talked to before falling asleep. "I'll miss you while I'm gone."

Denny teasingly bumped Eliza's shoulder with her forehead. "I'm pretty sure your phone will work in San Francisco."

"Yeah, but I like it better when I know you're just a few miles away."

A knock on the side window made them both jump. Eliza's fingers flexed on Denny's knee, but she didn't let go. When she turned her head, her sister peered through the window.

"Are you coming or what?" Andy mouthed.

"Yeah, yeah, hold your horses." Eliza turned back toward Denny. Saying goodbye to her got harder every time they did it. Maybe on Friday, she wouldn't have to. The thought made her breathless. She unfastened her seat belt, leaned across the middle console, and pressed her lips to Denny's in a gentle kiss. God, so soft. She wanted to thread her fingers through Denny's hair and deepen the kiss, but she was too aware of their audience on the sidewalk, so she reluctantly pulled back. "Drive carefully."

"I will. And you call me when you make it to San Francisco." Denny's gaze followed her, even as Eliza closed the passenger door between them.

Once Denny's car had disappeared down the street, Eliza turned toward her sister and Heather.

Andy studied her with a frank look that made Eliza tense because she knew her sister had never been one to hold back. "You know, I'm used to seeing you with men."

"You make it sound like there were dozens of them!"

Andy waved her away. "That's not what I meant. Anyway, I thought seeing you with Denny would be weird."

Eliza struggled not to stiffen. It had taken some time for her to wrap her head around being attracted to a woman, so she needed to give her family time to adjust too. "Was it?"

"Strangely, no. You two look kind of natural together."

Warmth loosened Eliza's tense muscles. She couldn't help beaming. "Does that mean I have your sisterly approval?"

"Do you need it?" Andy asked. "Aren't you the one who always insists that you're no longer a kid?"

"Need it? No. But I'd like to have it."

Andy wrapped one arm around her shoulder. "You've got it." She waited a beat and then flashed a grin. "But if she hurts you, I'll still come after her with a sharp instrument."

"She won't." Eliza hoped Denny had come to the same conclusion about her.

Chapter 25

ON TUESDAY EVENING, ELIZA ENJOYED a glass of wine with her bosses in the restaurant of the hotel where the Pet Products Expo was being held. What she enjoyed even more than the wine was watching the waiter's reaction to her intense boss.

"I'll have the roasted chicken with the sweet potato gnocchi," Dee said.

"Excellent choice, ma'am."

Dee held on to the menu, thwarting the waiter's attempt to take it. "And we'll have the tapas plate, the cilantro-marinated prawns, and some pita bread to share."

The waiter clearly struggled to keep a straight face as he nodded and hurried away.

"What?" Dee said once he was gone. "I'm starving."

Austen studied her with an indulgent smile. "No wonder. You've been going nonstop since we arrived, honey."

Trying to keep up with Dee had made Eliza's head spin. Dee had them all furiously scribbling notes on their competitors' latest products and attending useful seminars, while Dee focused mostly on talking to distributors and retailers. It was only day one of the expo, and she had already collected more business cards than her card case could hold.

"Maybe you should slow down a little," Austen said. "We just wanted to dip our toes in and get a feel for the market this time, remember? And have some fun while we're here."

Dee set her strong jaw, and a fierce glint shone in her gray eyes. "Oh, I will have a lot of fun if that guy from Birdmania offers to buy us out one more time. I'll tell him exactly where he can shove his cheap bird perches."

"That's precisely what I mean. Maybe tone down your competitiveness a tad. This is our first year in business, hon. We're not out to achieve world domination."

"Yet," Dee added. Then her expression softened, and she covered Austen's hand resting on the table with her bigger one. "You are having fun, aren't you?"

Austen turned her hand beneath Dee's and entwined their fingers. "Of course."

Eliza loved their dynamic, but watching them look deeply into each other's eyes made her yearn for Denny. How was it possible to miss anyone so fiercely after only a couple of days?

"Oh, that's beautiful. Did Heather make it for you?" While Eliza had been thinking about Denny, Austen had turned her attention toward her.

Eliza glanced at where she pointed and realized she'd been playing with her wrap bracelet, tracing each bead with her fingertips. "Um, no." She knew she could leave it at that or simply say it had been a gift. But her job was a big part of her life, and so was Denny. "Actually, my girlfriend made it for me." Calling Denny that still felt surreal and wonderful in equal parts.

A broad smile spread over Austen's face. She nudged Dee with her elbow. "I told you!"

Dee held up both hands. "Leave me out of this. I'm not commenting on an employee's private life."

"Me neither," Austen said. "I'm just happy for someone I consider a friend."

"It's okay. I don't mind talking about it." A chuckle escaped Eliza. "In fact, I probably couldn't stop talking about it...about *her* even if I tried."

"It's that friend of yours who bought the budgie toys, isn't it? The one you insisted wasn't your girlfriend."

"Well, she wasn't back then." Hard to believe that had been merely a month ago. "But yes, she's the one. Her name is Denny." Saying her name made Eliza warm inside.

"Right. I should know her name by now. She's been back two or three times with her niece, probably hoping you'd be covering our stall."

Aww. Eliza hadn't known Denny had done that.

Austen grinned at her partner. "Reminds me of a certain someone who kept showing up in the lobby and the company's cafeteria at the times I was most likely to be there."

"Hey, I was Kudos's COO." Dee didn't quite pull off a haughty look. "Supervising staff was part of my job duties."

"Supervising me while I eat chocolate mousse? Uh-huh."

They bantered back and forth all through dinner, making the time fly by, but Eliza declined dessert anyway. She couldn't wait to get back to her room so she could call Denny and hear about her day.

Once she was upstairs, she didn't even get changed before she lifted the phone to her ear.

"Hi, you!" A noise indicated Denny had dropped whatever she'd been doing to focus solely on their conversation. "How was the first day?"

"Great."

"But?" Denny prompted.

Eliza kicked off her shoes and flopped onto the bed. "No but. We're learning a lot and making some great connections."

"But?" Denny said again.

How did she do that? Eliza sighed. "Um, but I'd rather be back home right now. I miss you." She huffed out a breath. "Jeez, kind of ridiculous, isn't it? It's been only two days since we last saw each other!"

"Well, if you're ridiculous, then so am I because I miss you too."

Hearing that made Eliza melt inside. She loved that Denny had no problem admitting to missing her. "It feels a little weird. In a good way," Eliza added quickly. "But this is new for me. I've never been like this in any other relationship."

"No?"

"Nope. Definitely not. Maybe because I was always eager to assert my independence." With Denny, she didn't feel that need, because she knew Denny would always respect her and let her be her own person.

Denny was silent for a moment. "Can I...? Is it okay if I ask about your previous relationships?"

"Of course it's okay." Eliza adjusted the pillow beneath her head. "What do you want to know?"

"Everything. Anything. Whatever you want to tell me."

"Okay, here's a summary: You remember what I told you about my search for a job that fit me, right?" When Denny made a sound of confirmation, she continued, "It was the same with relationships. In my twenties, I tried a lot of different jobs and, to be honest, a lot of different guys too." She realized how that might sound to Denny and quickly added, "Well, not like dozens or anything. And I didn't sleep with all of them."

"No judgment, even if you did." Denny sounded as if she meant it.

"My last relationship ended when he got a promotion that took him to London, and I realized I didn't love him enough to give up my life in Portland and go with him. That's when I, to quote Heather, became 'very picky.' I'd had enough of being in a relationship just for the sake of it. I hadn't been on a date in a year and a half, which is why Heather nudged me to give No More Frogs a try."

"Thank God she did," Denny said. "Otherwise, you wouldn't have sent that accidental text asking for outfit advice."

Eliza smiled as she thought back to that first text. "What about you? Have you ever had anyone in your life you'd move across the Atlantic for?"

"Yeah." Before Eliza could decide whether she should be jealous, Denny added, "Salem and Bella. I haven't been in a lot of relationships—just three—and only one since my sister moved in with me. My last girlfriend broke up with me after accusing me of always putting Salem and Bella first." She paused. "Maybe she was right."

"It's not a competition," Eliza said fiercely. "At least it shouldn't be. I promise I'll never make you choose between them and me."

"Thank you." Denny's voice was quiet and vulnerable.

Wow. Maybe her business trip was a good thing after all. At least it had made them talk about something that, on some level, seemed to have worried Denny. Sometimes, it still seemed easier to talk about difficult topics on the phone, maybe because that was how they had first gotten to know each other. "So there hasn't been anyone else since? Not even...you know, just for sex?"

"No. I'm not the just-for-sex type."

That answer didn't surprise Eliza.

"I've been on a couple of dates," Denny added, "but I haven't slept with anyone in an embarrassingly long time."

Now it was Eliza's turn to say: "No judgment, okay? You've got no reason to be embarrassed."

"Maybe it's not so much embarrassment as...well..."

"Nervousness?" Eliza asked when Denny didn't finish her sentence.

"A little," Denny said. "Okay, a lot. It's been five years. And please don't say it's like riding a bike."

Eliza stifled a giggle. "If it feels anything like riding a bike, you're doing it wrong."

That made both of them laugh.

Eliza smiled into the empty hotel room. She loved Denny's laughter. "You'll be fine, Denny. We'll be fine."

"What about you?" Denny asked. "Aren't you nervous at all?"

"Hell, yes! I'm so nervous I shake all over thinking about it." Admittedly, that wasn't all nerves—part of it was excitement and desire too.

Furniture creaked as if Denny had sat up in bed. "Don't be. I promise I'll communicate the entire time, and I won't touch you in any way that would make you uncomfortable."

"I know that. That's not what worries me at all. You always make me feel comfortable in all the other areas of our relationship, so I have no doubt you'll do the same when it comes to making love."

Denny was silent for a few moments. Was she thinking about what else might make Eliza nervous...or processing her use of the term *making love* instead of *having sex*? Surely, deep down, they both knew it would be so much more than sex.

"What is it, then? Are you worried about safer sex?" Denny asked. "You really don't have to be. That's the one good thing about how long it's been for me. I got tested a few years back. Everything was fine, and I haven't been with anyone since."

"Same here."

"So if you're not worried about me or about being safe, that means you're worried about your...um, performance," Denny finally said.

Her choice of words made Eliza smile. "Of course I am. After five years, you deserve someone who'll blow your socks off in bed. What if I'm an awkward klutz?"

"Then we'll be awkward klutzes together. That kind of makes me feel better."

Eliza laughed. "Glad to be of service. Denny?"

"Yeah?"

Eliza wanted to tell her again how much she missed her and that she loved her. But she didn't want to say those momentous words when there were more than six hundred miles between them. "It makes me feel better too."

"Good. We really will be okay."

"I know," Eliza said. "And if it's not perfect the first time, I read somewhere that it takes ten thousand hours of practice to achieve greatness in anything."

"Ten thousand..." Denny gasped out between bursts of laughter. "God, you'll be the death of me. But if you're committed to putting in ten thousand hours, so am I."

It felt as if she would agree to commit to so much more, but Eliza didn't hesitate. "I am." She rolled onto her side and listened to the sound of Denny's breathing. "Now tell me about your day."

Chapter 26

ON FRIDAY EVENING, DENNY RANG Eliza's doorbell. When no answer came, she rang it again and glanced at the window. Since they had talked on the phone last night, she knew Eliza had made it home safe and sound from her business trip, so why wasn't she opening the door? Had something happened to make her late?

Just when Denny reached for her phone to call her, the intercom crackled. "Yes?" Eliza's muffled voice came through the device.

"It's me, Denny."

"Come on up," Eliza said. "I'm running late and just stepped out of the shower."

Denny tried not to picture Eliza in the shower, hot, soapy water streaming down her body, but it was like trying not to think of a pink elephant. She nearly missed the moment when the door buzzed. Belatedly, she pulled it open.

She'd better take the elevator. Her hands were already damp at the thought of running her tape measure over Eliza's body, and she didn't want to be a sweaty mess by the time she reached the apartment.

When she arrived on the second floor, Eliza greeted her with a sheepish smile. "Sorry it took me a minute to open the door. I was on a cleaning spree earlier and needed a shower."

Denny scrubbed the entire house every time Eliza came over, so it was good to know it wasn't just her. When she stepped past

Eliza into the apartment, she caught a whiff of her shower gel and perfume—a heavenly combination.

Eliza's favorite jeans and a white, short-sleeved knit top clung to her still-damp skin. She looked incredible.

"Hi again." Eliza closed the door. She ran her gaze over Denny, then stepped close until her freshly showered scent engulfed Denny again. "Mmm, you smell wonderful."

"I was just thinking the same about you." Denny kicked off her sneakers and let the backpack slide to the floor so she could wrap both arms around her.

They came together in a tender, lingering kiss...and then another. Their bodies molded together, and when Eliza caressed her back and shoulders, Denny struggled to remember their plans for the evening. "Pants," she got out when they finally drew apart a few inches.

Eliza's lips curled into a smile against her own. "Is that a suggestion to take them off?"

"No!" She was determined to let Eliza make that choice, without putting any pressure on her, even though it was becoming harder to hold back. "I'll get a more accurate sizing if I measure you wearing just your underwear, but I've measured people fully clothed, and it turned out fine."

"Did you bring a tape measure?" Eliza asked.

Denny nodded and bent down to dig it out of her backpack, along with her notepad and a pen. Damn, her fingers trembled. She ducked into Eliza's tiny bathroom to wash her hands and take a minute to get herself together. *Measuring. That's all you're going to do,* she sternly reminded herself.

When she returned, Eliza had turned on the floor lamp since the sun had sunk behind the neighboring buildings and the light was fading.

Denny placed the notepad and pen onto the coffee table and unrolled the tape measure. When she turned to find the spot with the best light, the tape measure fell from her hand, and she nearly sank onto the floor next to it.

Eliza had popped the button of her jeans and slid down the zipper. Slowly, she pulled her pants down over her hips, revealing smooth legs and a pair of black panties.

With every inch the jeans lowered, Denny's body temperature shot up more. Her heartbeat drummed in her ears. *Oh. My. God!* She tried not to stare, but it was impossible.

Eliza shifted her weight. "Um, you did say this would be more accurate, right?"

Denny mentally kicked herself out of her trance and picked up the tape measure. "Yes. This looks...uh, works much better." She kept her gaze on Eliza's face and searched her eyes. "If you're comfortable with it."

"Comfortable isn't the first word that comes to mind for how I'm feeling." Eliza's chuckle sounded nervous. "But I trust you, and eventually, I'd like us to see a lot more of each other's bodies than just our bare legs."

God, how could Eliza turn her inside out without even trying? The honesty and vulnerability in Eliza's eyes blew her away, and the glint of passion made it hard not to cross the room and strip off the rest of her clothes. Denny swallowed against her dry mouth. "I'd like that too." Her voice came out in a rasp. "But this isn't a ploy to get you naked. You know that, right?"

A tender smile chased the hint of nervousness off Eliza's face. "Of course I know that. I know *you*."

"Okay. Then let's do this." Mentally, Denny added, *Before I chicken out.* She rubbed her hands together to warm them, even though they were as overheated as the rest of her body. On unsteady legs, she crossed the room toward Eliza.

Eliza licked her lips—which looked way too sexy and didn't help Denny focus on her role as a seamstress. "How do you want me?" She gestured down her body, then, as if realizing her question could be mistaken for innuendo, added, "I mean, do I just stand here?"

The last thing on Denny's mind was wanting Eliza to put on clothes, but she forced herself to say, "First, I need you to put on a pair of shoes. Whatever you want to wear most often with the pants I'm making you."

Eliza's panty-clad hip brushed Denny's as she walked past her toward the door. When she returned, she was wearing the canary-yellow sneakers.

Booming laughter burst from Denny's chest. As fond as she was of those sneakers, they didn't add to the sexiness of bare legs and high-cut panties. Maybe that was a good thing.

Eliza laughed along with her. "Yeah, I know." She shook one foot. "Hot, right?"

"On you, a pair of neon-green Crocs would look hot."

"No one looks hot in Crocs."

"You'd manage."

Their gazes caught, and the expression in Eliza's dark eyes raised Denny's body temperature even more. If they continued like this, she'd die of a heatstroke before this was over.

She tried to remember the task at hand. "All right. Stand upright but relaxed, with your feet hip-width apart, and look straight ahead."

As Eliza followed her instructions, Denny stepped closer. She flexed her fingers, not knowing where to safely put them. "Um, first, we have to find your natural waist."

Eliza glanced down at herself. "Is it hiding?"

Denny chuckled. "Kind of. The natural waist is the narrowest point of your torso. There's a trick to finding it. If you bend to the side, we can see where the crease forms."

"Do you want me to take my top off so you can see?" Eliza crossed her forearms in front of herself as if preparing to pull her knit top over her head.

Oh heavens. If she did that, Denny would either pass out or bite through her lip in an attempt to keep herself from touching Eliza the way she had wanted to for weeks. "Maybe you could just, um, pull your top up a little."

Eliza bunched the fabric together in her fists. Were her hands shaking? She slid the top up until the hem rested right below her breasts, baring a flat midriff and the sexiest belly button Denny had ever seen.

Okay, focus—on the task, not her body! Denny clutched the tape measure like a lifeline. "Thanks. Now bend over to the side." When Eliza did, Denny's gaze followed the graceful arc of her body and the way her top slid up on one side, revealing the edge of a black bra. *Crease.* She was supposed to look for the crease indicating her natural waist, not ogle other parts of her body. "Got it. Your natural waist is right...here." She laid her finger lightly against Eliza's waist.

Eliza inhaled sharply.

"Don't hold your breath, or we'll get the measurements wrong."

"Measurements. Right." Eliza exhaled. She straightened so she was no longer leaning to the side.

Denny tried to keep her gaze on the tape measure, not on Eliza's skin, as she drew it around her waist. When it was in place, she slid a finger between the tape and Eliza's body, making sure it wasn't pulled too tight. *Oh God.* Her skin was warm and soft. Sweat broke out along Denny's spine. *Twenty-seven, twenty-seven, twenty-seven.* She repeated the waist measurement like a mantra as she quickly backed away and scribbled it down.

It occurred to her that she could have put the notepad on the floor next to her, but then she wouldn't have a reason to create some much-needed distance between them so she could cool off.

Measuring Eliza's hips wasn't any easier on her libido, because she had to run the tape measure around the fullest part of her hips and the curve of her butt, but the worst—or maybe the best—was yet to come.

Denny went to the coffee table, where she'd left the notepad, and wrote down more numbers, hoping she'd be able to read them later. "Let's do crotch length next."

"Crotch length?" Eliza's laugh—low and husky—made Denny tingle all over. "Now that sounds sexy."

To Denny, every part of Eliza was sexy, no matter how much she tried to hide behind sewing terms. She held one end of the tape measure against Eliza's front at waist height. "Um, the tape needs to be looped through your legs, over your butt, to waist level in the back."

"Go ahead."

Eliza took over holding the tape against her front as Denny threaded the other end through her legs and ducked behind her to read off the number, glad to hide her flushed face for a moment.

The outseam was next. That would give her a break—or so she thought. She kneeled in front of Eliza to put her finger against the tape measure on the outside of her ankle. But she hadn't considered that this new position would bring her head level with Eliza's panties. The most erotic images ricocheted through Denny's mind—of her leaning forward, pressing a whisper of a kiss to Eliza's lower belly, and then...

She shook her head to get rid of the tempting vision. Quickly, she brought the tape down the outside of Eliza's leg. "How do you want it?" Her voice was breathless. "I mean, how long do you want the pants to be? To here?" While holding the tape measure with the other hand, she trailed one finger over the spot beneath her ankle.

Eliza had slipped her feet into the sneakers without wearing socks, and now a trail of goose bumps rose beneath Denny's finger. She nodded three times, as if her vocal cords refused to cooperate.

While Denny was already kneeling, she wrapped the tape measure around Eliza's calf, then her ankle. God, her legs were perfection. She fought the urge to run her fingers along the curve of her calf and up the back of her knee, where her skin would probably be even softer. *Numbers,* she reminded herself. *Write them down. Now.*

She fled to the coffee table and jotted down the new measurements.

But the sweet torture wasn't over yet.

"Um, your thigh is next." Denny surprised herself with the ability to form words.

Eliza slid her feet wider apart, inviting her closer without hesitation.

Denny's cheeks felt as if she were running a fever as she wound the tape measure around Eliza's upper leg. She felt Eliza's gaze on her hands, making her even hotter. "Don't glance down," Denny whispered. "Look straight ahead."

It was as much to ensure the measurements were accurate as to hide how much this affected her. She bent to read off the number where the end of the tape measure met the imprinted scale, bringing her face closer to Eliza's smooth leg. *Twenty point five.* Again, she tried to focus on the cold logic of the number, not on the warm skin beneath her hands. When she pulled the tape free, it slid along Eliza's thigh like a caress.

Eliza let out a low sound, almost a moan, sending a jolt of pleasure straight to Denny's core.

God, she was doomed. Now all she wanted was to get her to make that sound again, but that wasn't why Eliza had invited her over. *You've got this. Just one more.* "Inseam," she got out in a raspy croak.

Eliza caught her bottom lip between her teeth and nodded.

Denny knelt again—partly so she could measure all the way down to Eliza's ankle, but mostly because her legs weren't too steady. Her hands shook as she moved the tape measure as far up the inside of Eliza's thigh as she dared, right to the edge of her panties, and held it there with one finger. *Oh my God.* If she moved her finger another inch or two...

Eliza stood rigid like a mannequin. Was she even breathing?

Denny peered up at her to make sure she was okay.

Their gazes caught. Eliza's pupils were so wide that her eyes appeared black. "Denny?"

Now Denny was the one who stopped breathing. "Yeah?"

"I think we're done measuring."

"Yeah, let me just get this last—"

Eliza clutched two handfuls of Denny's shirt and pulled her up. "Kiss me."

Oh hell. Denny dropped the tape measure and gripped Eliza's hips. Their bodies and mouths collided.

Eliza tangled her hands in Denny's hair. Her lips parted on a moan that vibrated through Denny. Her bare thighs brushed Denny's as she pressed closer. The taste, scent, and feel of her flooded Denny's senses until her brain was on overload.

She gathered the quickly diminishing remainder of her self-control to pull her mouth away.

Eliza murmured a protest and nipped at her bottom lip.

Arousal flared through Denny. Her knees weakened. She clasped the small of Eliza's back, her fingers grazing the swell of her butt, and whispered against her lips, "If you want this, I think it's time to pull out your bed."

Eliza blinked, her eyes hazy. "I want it. I want you." The intensity of her gaze washed away the last of Denny's hesitation.

Hand in hand, they crossed the room and pulled out the bed. They looked down at it, then at each other.

A tiny kernel of worry still lingered deep inside of Denny. What if Eliza realized that this—loving a woman...loving *her* physically—wasn't right for her?

But under Eliza's admiring gaze, that concern melted like the tiny bits of snow Portland got in winter.

"Since you've been looking at me half naked for the past twenty minutes, how about you take off your pants too?" Eliza tugged at the top button of Denny's jeans in a gesture equally teasing and tentative.

She hadn't even touched her directly, yet a jolt of desire spiked through Denny. Her fingers trembled with a mix of nerves and arousal as she popped open the first button, then the next. After each one, she paused to peer at Eliza, who watched, transfixed. Denny worked loose the last button. She slid her jeans past her hips, stepped out of them, and pulled off her socks.

Without glancing away from Denny for even a second, Eliza kicked off the canary-yellow sneakers.

They looked at each other, both in their shirts and underwear.

Denny hesitated. Eliza had never been with a woman, so Denny knew she should take the lead and undress first, but getting naked in front of anyone—especially a woman she wanted to impress—had never been easy for her.

Eliza broke into a sweet smile. "Are we both waiting for the other to strip first?"

Denny grinned back. "Apparently."

"God, we're quite the pair, aren't we?"

"I'd like to think so." Knowing that Eliza—who was perfect in her eyes—struggled with insecurities too made it easier to tackle her own. Denny gripped the hem of her T-shirt. "Together?"

Eliza nodded and kissed her for a moment, as if to reassure them both.

They held eye contact, losing their connection for only a second as they pulled their tops up and over their heads.

Denny forgot her own state of near undress as she stared at Eliza. The sight of her small breasts nestled in black lace made her mouth go dry. *God, so sexy.* She was torn between wanting to admire the view for a while longer and wanting to take the bra off so she could get her hands—and mouth—on her.

Eliza's gaze raked over her.

Denny squirmed and pressed her arms to her sides, hoping to flatten the extra padding on her hips.

"Don't do that." Eliza stepped closer. Gently, she pushed Denny's arms aside and trailed her hands down her sides until they rested on her hips. The slow slide of her thumbs over her belly made Denny's breath catch. "I love your body."

Denny's gaze flew up. The intense expression on Eliza's face confirmed her words. "You...you do?"

"Every bit of it," Eliza said firmly. "It's beautiful. You're beautiful, inside and out."

For the first time in her life, Denny believed that someone— Eliza—meant those words. A rush of happiness swept over her with such force that she swayed.

Their lips came together for another passionate kiss, and Denny no longer cared that Eliza's hands were on her hips, where she could feel her love handles. She pressed her body against Eliza, needing her close. Her warm skin against her own made Denny light-headed, but it also made her crave more contact, more of Eliza. She broke the kiss to whisper against her skin, "I love your sexy undies, but, um, can we get rid of them?" She trailed her finger along the strap of Eliza's bra, then the edge of her panties.

A tiny shudder went through Eliza, vibrating against Denny's chest. "If we can get rid of yours too."

Denny pressed a kiss to the top of Eliza's bare shoulder and nodded. She gathered her courage and pushed her boxer shorts down her hips. There was no seductive way to take off a sports bra, so she simply pulled it up and over her head.

Eliza stood very still and let her gaze travel up Denny's body with a focus so absolute that Denny felt it like a caress. Finally, she took in Denny's breasts.

Denny would have crossed her arms over her chest, but the awe on Eliza's face was so obvious that Denny's self-consciousness melted away. Without hiding her body, she waited for Eliza to undress too.

Eliza peeled off her panties. The way she rolled them down her long legs was the hottest thing Denny had ever seen. Her breath caught in expectation as Eliza reached around herself. She fumbled with the clasp of her bra. Just as Denny considered offering her help, the hooks gave way, and the bra straps slipped down her arms. Before the bra could fall to the floor, Eliza caught it and held it clamped to her chest. Insecurity flickered in her eyes.

Denny's heart went out to her. She kissed Eliza's upper arm, where the bra strap rested. "I love everything about your body," she whispered against her skin. "Absolutely everything. Let me see you. Please."

Slowly, Eliza let go of the bra. It tumbled onto the pile of clothes on the floor, baring her to Denny's gaze—and her touch.

Eliza stood rooted to the spot for a second. The urge to cross her arms over her bare breasts was strong, but she didn't give in. There was no need to hide her body—or her insecurities—from Denny, especially since she clearly liked what she saw.

Denny looked at her with an intensity that robbed Eliza of breath. Admiration and desire mingled in her gaze.

Eliza's heart beat a rapid staccato high in her throat as she pulled back the covers. It was happening! She was about to sleep with a woman...with Denny, and she had no idea what she was doing! Oh God!

Denny cupped her face with both hands, cradling it and guiding her head so she was looking into Denny's eyes.

Everything Eliza felt—the nerves, the excitement—was reflected there, along with quiet reassurance.

"If this is too much, you can tell me any time," Denny said. "Nothing will happen tonight that you don't want."

"That's the problem." Eliza's tense lips relaxed into a smile. "I want *everything*, and I have no idea what to do and where to start."

Denny traced Eliza's smile with her thumb and returned it with a tender grin. "How about we start right here?" She eased her down onto the bed, then carefully lowered herself on top and lingered over her on one forearm. Their nipples were almost touching, and Denny's thighs tangled with hers.

At the whisper of skin against skin, Eliza sucked in a breath. How was it that Denny could make her feel so comfortable yet so out of control at the same time?

Denny hovered over her as if waiting for something—probably waiting for her to tell her it was okay to move to the next stage.

It was so much more than okay. This felt right. Eliza craved feeling her closer. She slid her hands back onto Denny's hips, mesmerized by her warm, soft curves, and gave a tug.

Denny sank onto her more fully. Their breasts pressed together, and Denny's thigh rubbed intimately against Eliza, making her gasp. At the same time, Denny's unmistakable desire coated her leg, and her rapid-fire heartbeat thrummed against Eliza's chest, thudding along with her own.

God. Oh God. Eliza couldn't help arching against her. Their bodies were so different, yet they fit together so well.

So far, Denny had always let her set the pace when it came to their physical relationship, but now she took the lead—and it was as much of a turn-on as her gentle touches.

Denny cupped Eliza's face with one hand as she kissed her forehead, her nose, her cheeks, the corner of her mouth. With each kiss, she murmured soft words against her skin, but Eliza was too dazed to make them out.

Eliza's hands roamed up and down Denny's back. A gasp escaped her as Denny trailed her lips along her jawline and nipped her earlobe.

Denny knew exactly where to touch her and how to touch her. With her mouth and her hands, she found every sensitive spot, even some Eliza hadn't known about until now. She pulled one of Eliza's hands to her mouth and trailed featherlight kisses along the inside of her wrist, then nuzzled the skin below her ear and slid her lips across her throat. With delicate nibbles, she explored the curve where her neck joined her shoulder.

Eliza let her touch wherever she wanted. She had never felt so completely open and vulnerable, yet so seen and desired. Her pulse raced beneath Denny's lips.

"Mmm, your skin is so soft," Denny whispered. Her warm breath tickled the hollow of Eliza's throat. She drew a slow, sensual path down the center of Eliza's body, then back up, avoiding her breasts for now and touching her with her fingertips only, worshipping her.

Eliza glided her nails down Denny's spine to anchor herself. Her body felt as if it was about to catch fire.

Denny traced the line of Eliza's collarbone with her hands, then her lips. "Do you know how often I dreamed about this?" Her tongue swirled in sensual patterns across her upper chest. "Being able to touch you?"

"No dream," Eliza gasped out. "This is real."

Denny shifted against her, skin sliding over skin as she moved lower. "I know it is. This is so much better than even the best of my fantasies." She layered openmouthed kisses and lazy licks across Eliza's ribs just beneath her breasts.

Heat sizzled through Eliza. She glanced down at her breasts, which looked even smaller now that she was lying down. "Really?" she got out with a gasp.

"Really." Denny rested her palm along the curve of one breast. Her gaze on Eliza's face, she caressed her breast with the gentlest of touches, then ran her thumb over the nipple, which hardened instantly.

Desire jolted through Eliza, leaving no space for doubts and worries.

Denny kissed a leisurely circle around the other nipple, then swirled her tongue around and around until her warm breath fanned over the hardened tip.

A heavy ache settled low in Eliza's belly. She dug her fingers into Denny's shoulders. "Denny..."

Denny hummed a confirmation against her nipple, then fluttered her tongue across it in a hint of a touch. After another, firmer lick, she closed her lips around it and sucked gently.

Pleasure zinged through Eliza's body, all the way down to her center. She cried out.

Denny lifted her warm mouth off her breast and searched her face. "You okay?"

Not trusting her voice, Eliza nodded. She tangled both hands in Denny's short hair and pulled her back down.

"God, so responsive," Denny whispered, her breath teasing Eliza's nipple. Then her mouth was on her again.

Denny caressed her breast, alternating between slow swipes, teasing flutters of her tongue, and gentle sucks until Eliza was a boneless, quivering mess.

Eliza rocked her hips against Denny's belly in search of more contact. She hadn't been prepared for her body's response to Denny. The hot tug of Denny's mouth on her breast made her head spin. Already, her arousal had built to a heart-pounding need. Gasping, she realized she could probably come like this.

Without lifting her mouth away, Denny rubbed her thumb over the other nipple.

Oh God, she *would* come like this.

As if sensing how close she was to spiraling out of control, Denny pulled her lips away and went back to licking circles around her nipple while she trailed her hand down Eliza's belly.

Muscles rippled beneath her touch. Every cell in Eliza's body thrummed in anticipation. Her pulse hammered in her ears, mingling with Denny's moans of enjoyment as she caressed her.

Tenderly, Denny explored the dip where Eliza's hip met her leg, sending ripples of pleasure through her.

She tried to get her breathing under control, but it was a losing battle as Denny ran her fingertips around to a spot on her inner thigh, then moved them upward in an agonizingly slow trail. "*Denny.*"

Their gazes held, connecting on a level so much deeper than just physical. This wasn't sex. This was making love. Eliza struggled to hold back the words crowding her throat, not sure if this was the right time for them.

Denny stroked along her folds, then dipped between them. She slid her finger up one side of her clit and down the other but never directly across it.

Urgent need pulsed through Eliza's body. Denny's touch was too much and not enough all at the same time. She dug one hand into Denny's shoulder while scraping her nails over the back of her thigh with the other. "Please, Denny," she whispered in a voice she nearly didn't recognize as her own. "I need you."

A throaty groan rumbled through Denny. After one last kiss to Eliza's breast, she slid up her body, igniting little fires along her skin, and found her mouth again. Her velvety tongue glided against Eliza's, and just when Eliza lost herself in the kiss, Denny mimicked the motion with her finger across Eliza's clit.

Eliza tore her mouth away to gasp for breath. Her vision blurred, and she rapidly blinked to get her eyes to focus, desperate to see Denny as she touched her so intimately.

She caressed her in long strokes, then in small, tight circles. "Does that feel good?"

Instead of an answer, Eliza writhed and trembled beneath her, completely on sensory overload. She arched into Denny's touch. "Oh! Oh, yes. More!"

"More of this?" Denny rubbed her clit again. "Or do you want me to...?" She traced her opening with one fingertip.

The sensation sizzled across Eliza's nerve endings, blotting out all thoughts. She gasped out a reply but wasn't sure what—probably "yes" or "please" or Denny's name.

Denny's eyes smoldered as she pushed into her a little, dragging a hoarse cry from Eliza's throat.

Everything in her tightened with need. Her hips bucked against Denny, urging her deeper, and she surrendered herself to the rhythm Denny set.

A tremor rippled through her. Close. So close already. Her whole world narrowed down to Denny's hands on her, her warm breath on her lips, her soft moans and whispered words.

Denny stayed with her, moving at a perfect pace. The awe and hunger in her eyes drove Eliza higher.

Pressure coiled deep within her. Her hips lost their rhythm. She dug her toes into the sheets and her fingers into Denny's butt as she pushed up to meet her thrusts one last time.

Denny slid in again and at the same time brushed across her clit with her thumb.

Eliza's mouth fell open, and she pressed it to Denny's damp neck to stifle a cry. Flashes of light burst behind her tightly closed eyelids. Pleasure pulsed outward, and her entire body went taut, then collapsed back onto the bed.

Oh wow. She drew in deep gulps of air and tried to make sense of what she'd just experienced.

Denny cupped her face with her left hand and pressed kisses to her cheeks and finally her lips. She whispered something, but Eliza's brain couldn't yet process the words.

Once their breathing had returned to normal, Denny kissed her again and slowly withdrew, sending one last ripple through Eliza. "You're so beautiful. So amazing."

"Me?" Eliza laughed shakily. "You're the amazing one. I don't know what I expected, but not...this. Every touch from you made my head spin and my body..." She looked up at Denny with an impish grin. "Well, I think you felt how my body reacted."

A groan vibrated through Denny's chest. She shifted her legs against her, and Eliza felt her wetness coating her thigh. "Yes. God, yes. The way you responded to my every touch and just let yourself go... It took my breath away."

"I can't remember ever letting go like this before." She felt so safe with Denny.

Denny gazed down at her with the expression of someone who'd just had a supernatural encounter. "Me neither. I got so lost in you, I wanted it to last forever."

"Good." The pleasure-induced fuzziness finally receded as a different kind of need took over. Eliza trailed her hands along Denny's back. A sheen of perspiration made her skin even softer to the touch. "Because we're not done yet."

Denny stared at her, eyes wide and defenseless, as she rolled onto her back. The complete trust on her face blew Eliza away.

Eliza settled onto her side next to her and raised herself onto one elbow so she could see Denny better. So much naked skin and sexy curves on display made her senses reel. "You'll have to be patient with me while I figure out how to make you as breathless as you made me."

"You've already accomplished that."

Eliza smiled and trailed her fingers over Denny's damp temple, smoothing back her disheveled hair. "I haven't even touched you yet."

"You touched me here." Denny took Eliza's hand and pressed it to her chest, over her thudding heart.

Oh. The swell of Denny's breast rested beneath her hand, warm and soft, distracting Eliza from her heartfelt words for a moment.

She leaned over her, too overcome to find the right words, so she kissed her instead.

Denny moaned into the kiss and pulled her down on top of her. Hardened nipples rubbed against Eliza's, stirring her arousal alive again.

Oh no, you don't. This was Denny's turn. With a gasp, Eliza pulled back.

Darkness had fallen while they'd made love, and now the light from the floor lamp in the corner played over the dips and curves of Denny's body, creating enticing shadows Eliza couldn't wait to explore. Sweat glistened on her skin, which was tanned on her neck, face, and limbs and creamy pale everywhere else. Eliza couldn't help staring, mesmerized by the sight of full breasts and a rounded belly she'd only seen in her imagination until now.

Before Denny could start to squirm under her gaze, Eliza slid her hand onto her hip. That spot always drew her in. She stroked her fingers along Denny's side. *Mmm, so soft.*

A shiver ran through Denny, and she inhaled sharply.

Eliza paused, acutely aware of how inexperienced she was. "Does that tickle? Or do you not like to be touched there?" She knew Denny was self-conscious about her love handles, but Eliza thought they were aptly named because she adored them.

"No, you can touch me there." Denny cleared her throat. "You can touch me everywhere."

Eliza hummed. "I will." She trailed her fingers over the curve of her belly, the smooth skin between her breasts, and along the ridge of her collarbone.

Each touch drew a reaction—goose bumps, a jump of her pulse, or a groan of approval.

Encouraged, Eliza lowered her head and added her lips and finally her tongue to the caresses. She tasted the salty skin on the side of Denny's neck, enjoying the frenzied pounding of her pulse beneath her mouth. Trying to find out what would feel good to Denny was fun. Apparently, it all felt good to her. A nibble on

Denny's earlobe elicited a gasp, and a line of kisses across her smooth shoulder caused a quiver.

So intriguing. And so incredibly soft—not only Denny's curves, but her skin too. Women's bodies were so different. But mostly, *Eliza* felt different...more open. More herself.

"You feel so good." She nuzzled the slope of Denny's breast.

Denny's chest heaved beneath her. She trailed her fingers through Eliza's hair but didn't try to urge her down.

Not that Eliza needed much urging. She studied the pleasing curves of Denny's breasts. They were ample and creamy, her nipples darker and larger than Eliza's own. Beautiful. Her mouth watered, and suddenly, she wanted nothing more than to worship them with her hands, her lips, and her tongue.

Carefully, trying not to fumble like a teenager, she trailed the back of her fingers along the outer curve of one breast.

When she looked up, Denny was watching her with hooded eyes.

Eliza flicked her gaze back and forth between Denny's face and her breasts as she cupped one of them, filling her palm with its softness. *Wow.* So nice and soft and round. She massaged it tentatively.

Denny caught her bottom lip between her teeth.

Ah, she liked that. Eliza squeezed a little more firmly. The nipple hardened against her palm, and she rubbed the pad of her thumb across it, thrilled at her ability to excite Denny. Soft moans spurred her on.

Denny shook beneath her, and the remainder of Eliza's hesitancy fled. When touching Denny with her fingers was no longer enough, she bent her head and exhaled against her nipple, causing more goose bumps to ripple across Denny's chest. Eliza tried to kiss them away but only managed to raise more.

Finally, when Denny's breathing turned shallow, Eliza lowered her mouth to her nipple and kissed it. It tightened even more against her lips. Eliza couldn't get enough. She nibbled the underside of her breast, kissed the upper slope, circled her areola with her tongue, then swiped it across the taut tip.

Denny groaned deep in her throat and writhed against her. The little noises that rose up her chest made Eliza grow bolder with every second.

She switched to the other breast, wrapped her lips around the nipple, and sucked lightly.

With a gasp, Denny cupped one hand around the back of her head and pressed her closer. She twisted restlessly beneath her, and her damp curls tickled Eliza's thigh. "Jesus, you're killing me." Her voice was thick with need. She let out a hoarse laugh. "But I'm glad you're discovering you're a breast woman."

"Hmm, I think I am. But mostly, I'm a Denny woman." Eliza placed one last kiss on her breast, then focused on smoothing her palm down Denny's quivering body. When she reached the trimmed patch of hair, her confidence wavered for a moment. Sure, Denny had the same body parts as she did, but the angle was different, and she was much too aware of how hopelessly inexperienced she was at this.

But even stronger than her insecurity was her burning need to make Denny feel good, to let her experience what she had just minutes ago.

Denny spread her legs in a silent invitation. Again, the openness and trust in her eyes made something twist in Eliza's stomach.

She trailed her fingers through Denny's damp curls. When she encountered slick heat, they both sucked in a breath. She pressed a kiss to the valley between Denny's breasts as she experimentally brushed one finger across her clit.

Denny moaned long and loudly, and the sexy noises never stopped as Eliza kept moving her finger.

Eliza's senses reeled. She loved hearing her reaction to what she was doing to her. Denny's pleasure was evident, every sensation she experienced right there on her face, in her eyes. Knowing exactly what Denny felt, what every little gasp and moan meant was a powerful turn-on. Eliza pressed her thighs together as another wave of arousal gathered low in her belly.

Denny rocked against her, making her fingers slide lower.

"Do you want me to...? Do you like penetration?"

"No," Denny gasped out.

A bang of disappointment slammed into Eliza, surprising her. It wasn't a big deal, right? She didn't always want or need it either.

"I mean, not...oh God...not usually. But now..." Denny slid her hand down Eliza's arm and closed it around her wrist.

The way she guided her was the hottest thing Eliza had ever experienced—at least until one of her fingers pressed inside. She moaned at the tight heat surrounding her.

Denny's hips thrust upward, and she let out a string of garbled words.

All Eliza could make out was "again" and "more," so she pulled her finger back, then carefully pressed in with two. As Denny's hips rose and fell against her, Eliza's uncertainty faded away, and she met her stroke for stroke.

Denny made the most erotic sounds with each thrust of her fingers. Her eyelids flickered closed, and a lovely pink flush bloomed on Denny's chest, throat, and face. She flung her head back in total abandon.

Eliza's breath caught. She loved watching her like this. Loved *her*.

"Eliza!"

She didn't know what Denny wanted her to do, but it didn't seem to matter as her body moved on instinct and seemed to hit exactly the rhythm Denny needed. As Denny arched against her higher and faster, her thigh pressed against Eliza's wetness.

Oh God! Her breath exploded out of her in a strangled moan.

The muscles of Denny's neck corded as she strained against her. She dragged open her eyes, and their gazes connected.

Pleasure pulsed in Eliza's belly. She moved her fingers faster, pressed herself harder against Denny's thigh. A roaring started in her ears.

With a shout, Denny surged up once more, then froze and shuddered. Her inner muscles pulsed around Eliza's fingers.

As Eliza watched her come, another orgasm rippled through her, taking her by surprise. She cried out and slumped onto Denny.

Denny slid her hand onto the small of her back but otherwise lay without moving, panting beneath her. Her heartbeat thundered under Eliza's ear, then slowed to a more normal rhythm.

"Wow," Eliza whispered against the damp skin of Denny's shoulder. "What was that?"

Denny's gentle laughter vibrated through her. "That," she peered up at her with a giddy expression, "is called an orgasm."

Eliza nipped her shoulder, then kissed it. "I know that, thank you very much. I just didn't think I could... Um, I mean, twice in a row is not my norm."

One hand still resting on the small of her back, Denny kissed her tenderly. "Nothing about tonight has been the norm. It's been exceptional. Extraordinary. Out of this world. Absolutely pheno—"

Eliza captured her mouth in a deep kiss before she could go through the entire thesaurus. There were better ways to spend the rest of the night, and she intended to discover them all.

Chapter 27

THE LIGHT OF THE RISING sun filtered into the studio apartment, waking Denny. She lay still and listened to Eliza's soft breathing nearby...very nearby. When she finally opened her eyes, the sight that greeted her made her smile.

Eliza was nestled in her arms, her head on the same pillow, cheek pressed to Denny's shoulder, and one leg slung across her thighs. The soft glow of the early-morning light dusted her bare shoulders with gold. She lay so close that Denny went nearly cross-eyed looking at her, but she couldn't stop.

It had to be early, probably before six, and she was still tired, yet she didn't want to go back to sleep. She wanted to experience every minute of her first morning with Eliza—hopefully, the first of many.

Last night had been incredible. Thinking about it warmed her more than the sun on her face. And she'd loved the intimacy of holding Eliza afterward just as much—skin on skin, talking softly until they both fell asleep. Never before had she felt so close to anyone.

Clearly, all her worrying had been for nothing. Once they had bared their bodies to each other, Eliza hadn't seemed uncomfortable even for a second.

Denny suppressed a chuckle so she wouldn't wake her. Nope, Eliza clearly wasn't uncomfortable with her female form at all. The fingers of her right hand were splayed over Denny's breast, cradling it. Denny had never been a big fan of her breasts—or the rest of her body for that matter—but after Eliza had gotten so much enjoyment out of them, she was starting to see them in a new light.

Eliza let out the cutest little yawn and stretched against her, sending tingles through Denny's body. She snuggled closer and pressed her face into the crook of Denny's neck. "Good morning." She sounded sleepy and very satisfied.

"Good morning." Denny drew slow circles on her back with her fingertips, trying to ease her into wakefulness. "How are you feeling?"

Eliza raised up on one elbow and gave her a smile so sweet that Denny's mind turned to mush. "Since you used up all the words in the thesaurus last night, I think I'll settle on *happy*."

Aww. The three little words that could change everything between them lingered on Denny's tongue, demanding to be spoken. Should she tell her?

Before she could come to a decision, Eliza settled back into her arms. "Denny?" she asked with her cheek on Denny's chest.

"Hmm?"

"Do you have everything you need?"

Denny slid her arms around her more tightly. "Mmm, yeah."

A chuckle escaped Eliza. "No, I meant, do you have all the measurements you need?"

Measurements? With Eliza so close and all the emotions churning through her, measurements were the last thing on Denny's mind. "Uh, I think so."

"Are you sure?" Eliza asked. "I'm not an expert, but isn't there a saying about 'measure twice, cut once' or something like that?"

"Mm-hmm. There is."

"Then maybe you should double-check my measurements. Just to make sure."

A rush of desire surged through Denny. She struggled to form words. "Is that your clever way of letting me know you aren't done with me yet?"

Eliza braced herself on her elbow again. The playful gleam in her eyes turned into a soft yet intense expression. "I don't think I'll ever be done with you."

Denny stared up at her. She barely dared to breathe, afraid what she saw reflected back in Eliza's expressive eyes might be an illusion. But she knew it wasn't. She'd felt it last night. Even before that. Saying it was scary anyway. She braced herself. It was time to put herself out there and hold nothing back. "Eliza, I—"

"I love you."

Denny's mouth snapped shut. She opened it again, but instead of the words she'd wanted to say, giddy laughter tumbled out. She pressed Eliza against her and rolled them around to pepper her face with kisses.

Eliza threaded her fingers through Denny's hair. An equally giddy chuckle vibrated through her. "Does that mean...?"

"I love you too." She kissed her softly, then longer and with more urgency. "I can't believe you said it first."

Eliza grinned at her. "I was always a fast learner."

"Oh yeah?" Her voice came out husky. "Care to prove that?"

"Anytime."

When they made love again, it was slow and intimate, with a lot of whispered "I love yous." This time, there were no hesitations, no inhibitions, no doubts. Nothing but love and passion.

Afterward, they curled around each other and fell back asleep.

Not long after Eliza had dozed off in Denny's arms, the ringing of her phone startled her awake.

What the...? Heart pounding, she sat up and glanced around with bleary eyes. Where was that damn thing? She quickly climbed out of bed so it wouldn't disturb Denny.

One more ring and she located it on the coffee table.

Heather's name flashed across the small screen. *Oh shit.* It was Saturday! And that meant Saturday Market. She swiped her finger across the device and lifted it to her ear. "I'm so, so sorry!

I overslept, but I'll be right there. Just give me..." She flicked her gaze down her well-loved body. No matter how late she was, she needed a shower before she was fit to head out into society. "Um, ten minutes. Fifteen max. I'll meet you out front."

"It's okay," Heather said. "Want me to come over and make you a big travel mug of Earl Grey?"

"No!"

Denny sat up in bed and sent her an alarmed look.

"I mean, no, thank you. I'll get something at the market." Eliza picked up her clothes and carried them toward the bathroom. Next to the bed, she stopped and touched her free hand to Denny's cheek.

"Is everything okay?" Heather asked. "You sound strange."

Eliza bit her lip. "I'm fine. I'm great. Denny, um, stayed over."

"Why didn't you say so?" Heather let out a cheer. "Get back into bed with her, and don't worry about the market. I've got it covered."

Eliza's gaze went back to her nice, warm bed, with the cuddly, naked woman in it. She hesitated. "I can't let you do this all the time. That's not fair to you."

"Eliza Louise Harrison! If you show up at our booth before eleven, I'm going to be pissed. Do you hear me?"

God, she had the most wonderful best friend on earth. "Thank you, Heather. You're the best. I owe you."

"You owe me all the details. Can't wait."

Before Eliza could protest, Heather ended the call.

Eliza plopped onto the edge of the bed. "I completely forgot about Saturday Market."

"Oh shit. Me too. After last night...and this morning, I can barely remember what day it is. Good thing I'm not working today." Denny pulled the sheet off her body and swung her legs out of bed, revealing more naked skin than Eliza's brain could handle. "You take a shower; I'm going to make you some tea and breakfast."

She had the most wonderful best friend *and* the most amazing girlfriend. Before Denny could rush off, Eliza grabbed her hand. "We don't have to hurry. Heather is covering the booth until I get there."

"Phew. She's a lifesaver. Does that mean we can go back to bed? After all, we haven't put in ten thousand hours of practice yet."

The gleam in Denny's eyes made Eliza's heartbeat quicken. It was tempting, so tempting, but she didn't want to take advantage of Heather's generosity. "Oh God, if it gets any more perfect than last night, I might never leave this apartment again. How about this? We take a shower, get dressed, have waffles for breakfast, and make some for Heather too because they're her favorite."

"Hmm." Denny stroked her chin as if giving it some thought. "Will there be kisses over breakfast?"

She was so darn cute. The urge to kiss her right then and there gripped Eliza. "That could be arranged."

"Then it's a deal. Come on!" Denny caught her hand and tugged her toward the bathroom, then paused after two steps. "Unless... When you said we should take a shower, did you mean you wanted us to take turns? We can totally do that if you'd rather shower alo—"

Eliza brushed her lips against Denny's. "Well, we're in a bit of a hurry, so showering together to save time makes sense, right?"

Denny nodded eagerly. "Total sense."

Grinning, they hurried to the bathroom.

It turned out showering together did not save time—quite the opposite. Eliza's hair was still damp when they finally wove their way around the stalls and people at Saturday Market, but she couldn't bring herself to care.

Heather tapped her watch. "It's not eleven yet, but I'll let it slide because I don't want to burst your postcoital bubble."

Leanne from the booth next to theirs glanced from Eliza to Denny, who took on the color of a chili pepper.

"Um, why don't I go get us some tea and coffee?" After a wave to Heather and a quick kiss to Eliza's cheek, Denny hurried off.

Leanne stared after her, then directed a questioning look at them.

"It turns out that my friend here is interested in feminine charms after all, just not in mine." Heather pressed her hand to her chest in a dramatic gesture.

Eliza turned from where she'd watched Denny walk away to send Heather a glare. But since she still felt as if she was floating on puffy, pink clouds, it didn't pack much heat. "And my friend over there is interested in waffles, but she's making embarrassing comments, so I'm not sure she deserves any."

"Waffles! Gimme, gimme!" Heather waggled her fingers and nearly snatched the Tupperware container from Eliza. How she managed to wolf down the first one in seconds without choking or getting powdered sugar on herself was a mystery to Eliza. Finally, she slowed down and studied Eliza. "Seriously, how are you doing with...all this?" She pointed in the direction Denny had gone.

Eliza peered at Leanne, who was thankfully distracted by a customer wanting to buy one of her suncatchers. She slid behind the table where she could talk to Heather without anyone overhearing. "I'm good. More than good. I'm happy."

Heather nodded. "You look happy. So..." She lowered her voice to a whisper. "Your sleepover... I don't really need any details, but... was it what you expected? Was it right for you?"

Instead of focusing on Heather, Eliza's gaze searched the booth where Denny stood in line. "I've never experienced anything so right in my life," she whispered back. "It was so...everything."

"Everything, hmm?" Heather's teasing grin transformed into a soft smile. She wrapped one arm around Eliza. "I'm so happy for you. I know you were a bit worried you might find yourself not all that drawn to, um, her feminine charms once the clothes came off."

"Trust me; that was not a problem." Her stomach tightened at the mere thought of getting naked with Denny and touching her bare skin. "I figured out it's not that I'm attracted to her *despite* her being a woman. Her being a woman is a big part of what draws me to her."

Heather leaned closer. "So that means you're bi?"

Eliza shrugged. "If I had to pick a label, that might come close. But frankly, I don't care. And thankfully, Denny doesn't either. I love that about her." She looked at Denny again, who was now on her way back to their booth. Even in the crowd, she found her immediately.

Denny seemed to sense her gaze and beamed at her.

"I told her that this morning, you know? That I love her. And she said she loves me too." Eliza barely resisted the impulse to jump up and down like a giddy teenager.

"Well, duh." Heather laughed. "I could have told you that. She was totally smitten with you, even back when she went on a date with me. I mean, how else would she have been able to resist me?"

Eliza stole a piece of waffle from the container since her breakfast had consisted of more kisses than food. "I have no idea. You're irresistible."

"And that's why I'm counting on seducing a bridesmaid at your wedding."

Of course, Denny reached the stall at just that moment. The paper cups of coffee and tea in her hands tilted dangerously to one side. "Um, wedding?"

Her deer-in-the-headlights expression made Eliza laugh. "Don't worry. It's an old joke between Heather and me. I'm not dragging you down the aisle anytime soon."

"Damn," Heather said. "There go my bridesmaid plans."

Denny handed her one of the paper cups. "Don't give up so fast. Who knows? Maybe one day..."

Eliza froze with her hand halfway to the cup of tea. Denny was thinking that far ahead already?

The deer-in-the-headlights look returned as did the chili-pepper color of Denny's cheeks. "Um, forget I just said that. It's way too soon to think about that."

It was. Still, the thought didn't scare Eliza or make her feel overwhelmed. "What if I don't want to forget what you just said?"

The noise of the crowd around them seemed to dim as they gazed into each other's eyes.

Denny cleared her throat. "You don't?"

"I don't." Eliza closed her fingers around the cup and Denny's hand. "I mean, we're talking about maybe one day, not going to the courthouse next week, right?"

"Right."

Heather raised her paper cup. "I'm giving it a year, tops, before you two are tying the knot."

"Heather?" Eliza said without looking away from Denny's eyes. "Shut up and eat your waffles."

With her hand cupped around her mouth, Heather leaned over to Leanne, who had finished up with her customer, and stage-whispered, "Notice how they didn't say I was wrong."

"Eat your waffles, Heather," Denny and Eliza said in unison.

Epilogue

DENNY LOWERED THE NEEDLE OF her sewing machine into the denim, then put the pressure foot down. In her mind's eye, she already saw the finished product—the way it would cling to Eliza's slim hips, make her legs look even longer, and put a smile on her face because it had real pockets.

Before she could sew a single stitch, Salem walked past the dining room table for the fifteenth time in the last hour and went to the fridge. Like the previous fourteen times, she peeked in, then closed the door without taking anything out.

Denny pulled her foot off the pedal. "What's up with you?"

Salem turned. The expression on her face was the same one she'd worn when Denny had caught her eating the cheesecake their mother had left on the counter to cool twenty years ago. "Nothing." She walked over and pointed at the half-finished jeans. "I thought you were done with the orders for today."

"Two new ones came in, but these are for Eliza." Denny caressed the fabric with her fingertips.

"Another pair? How many pants does one woman need?"

"As many as she wants," Denny said. "Besides, it's been forever since I made her a new pair. I haven't had the time since I gave notice at the Grocery Port so I could focus on Real Pockets."

Salem gave a noncommittal nod and paced back to the fridge.

Denny watched her. The last time she had seen her so restless and so picky about food had been... "Oh my God!"

Salem whirled around. "What happened? You didn't stick yourself with the needle, did you?"

"No." Denny jumped up and joined her in the kitchen. She gripped both of her sister's hands. "Salem, are you by any chance, um, pregnant?"

"What?" Salem withdrew her hands. "No! Why on earth would you think that?"

"Because you've checked the fridge like a million times, but nothing seemed to appeal to you, and the last time I saw you so restless was when you were trying to work up the courage to tell me you were pregnant."

Salem gave her a tone-it-down wave. "Shh. Stop saying that word. I'm not...you know what, and if Bella hears you say that, she'll get on my case again, like when she was five and wanted a little sister."

"So you're not...you know?"

"No."

Denny grinned at her. "Too bad. You make great kids."

Salem pierced her with a stern look, but the corners of her mouth twitched up into a smile. "I do. Well, with your help. But I think Bella is it for me."

"If it's not that, what has you as nervous as a rabbit in a kennel full of hound dogs?"

Salem peered at her fingernails, then turned her hands over to study the pads of her fingers too.

A big lump lodged in Denny's throat. So there was something Salem didn't know how to tell her. "You're not sick, are you?"

"No, I'm fine."

"Okay, then spit it out before I have a heart attack."

Salem grabbed her hand and pulled her to the couch.

Uh-oh. If she needed to sit to digest the news, it couldn't be good. Denny's knee bounced up and down. How she wished Eliza could be there to soothe her and tell her everything would be fine.

Salem covered Denny's knee with her hand, stilling it. "Well, it's been a year since Matt and I first started going out..."

"I know. It's not like I could have missed the giant bouquet of flowers he gave you for your anniversary."

Salem elbowed her in the ribs. "Hey, you're one to talk! The bouquet you gave Eliza last week made mine look tiny!"

Okay, maybe she had gone a bit overboard, but it had been the anniversary of the accidental text message that had brought Eliza into her life, so that day would forever be a reason to celebrate. "Back to the topic at hand. Matt and you."

"Things between us have been going really well, and he's great with Bella too, so..." Salem tightened her grip on Denny's knee and peeked up at her. "We're talking about moving in together."

Denny sank against the back of the couch, needing the support. "Oh." A burning sensation spread from her stomach to her chest. She struggled to get herself together. She could fall apart later, when she went over to Eliza's, but for now, she had to support her sister. "That's wonderful." It was—at least for Salem. But the thought of what it would mean for her made her nauseated.

Salem's eyes shone with happiness, yet at the same time, they swam with tears. "Part of me doesn't want to go," she whispered.

"Don't be silly." Denny nudged her roughly, holding back her own emotions. "Matt is a great guy."

"I know. He's the best, and I want to live with him, but it doesn't feel right to leave you behind." The tears clinging to the corners of Salem's eyes spilled over and ran down her cheeks. "When Mom and Dad kicked me out... I don't know what would have happened to Bella and me if not for you. You've been our rock throughout all these years, and I'll never be able to repay you for what you did for us."

Denny swallowed down her own rising tears. "You don't need to repay anything." Her voice was husky. "We're family."

"I know. And we will always be. I hope you know that." Salem reached for Denny's hand and pulled it onto her lap. "Even when we're living in separate places, I want you to be part of our lives."

"I will be; don't worry. You won't get rid of me that easily." Denny needed all her self-control not to grip her sister's hand too tightly. She knew it was time to let go. "I'll be at your new house so often that you'll want to change the locks to keep me out."

Salem snorted. "As if you could tear yourself away from Eliza long enough to hang out with us all the time."

"I'll bring her, of course."

"Sounds good to me." Salem dug into her jeans for a tissue but came up empty.

Denny reached into her own pocket and handed her a clean one. "You're wearing Real Pockets jeans, and you're still not carrying tissues?"

"I know, I know." Salem blew her nose. "What kind of mom am I?"

"A great one. You and Bella will do just fine."

Salem dropped her tissue and threw herself into Denny's arms. "Thank you. Not for the tissue. For everything," she whispered against her shoulder. "I'll miss you like hell."

"Me too." Denny pressed her lips together, afraid she'd burst into tears if she said more. "You just had to pick my PMS week to tell me, didn't you?"

"Oops, sorry." Salem chuckled shakily.

After another minute or two, Denny pulled back. "So, when will you be moving?"

"We were thinking at the end of the month, actually."

That soon? Denny fought not to let her feelings show.

"Matt is nearly finished fixing up the house his grandma left him," Salem added. "You need to come see it soon. It turned out beautifully. And the best thing about it: it's only a few blocks from here. Bella won't even have to switch schools."

Denny blew out a breath. That had been one of her concerns. Like Denny, her niece wasn't the best at handling change. "Oh, that's great."

"Yeah. For you too. You can hop over any time."

"Assuming I stay here." Denny indicated the townhouse. "Not sure I can afford the rent on my own, even now that sales at Real Pockets are picking up."

Salem nibbled her bottom lip and regarded her with a hopeful look. "Any chance Eliza might want to move in with you?"

Denny carved a pattern into the denim covering her knee with her fingernail. Getting to wake up with Eliza every day, share every morning and every evening with her would be a dream come true. But it wasn't just up to her, and so far, Eliza hadn't indicated she wanted to move in together. "I don't want to pressure her. Her independence is important to her, especially since she had to fight so hard for it with her family."

"For Christ's sake, Denny! Just ask her!"

"Hmm. Maybe I will." However, she doubted she would work up the courage to do so anytime soon. She wrapped one arm around Salem and pulled her against her side. "So, who was the brave one who asked the other to move in? You or Matt?"

Salem laughed. "Me, of course! Sometimes, I think you and Matt could be related. He's been hinting for months. Letting me and Bella pick out the tiles and the countertops for his new house and painting one of the rooms in Bella's favorite color. But every time I thought he would finally ask, he chickened out."

"Poor guy."

"Poor guy?" Salem echoed. "Poor me! If I had waited for him to get up the nerve to ask, I'd be a grandmother by then!"

"Nerves aside, I think he's a great fit for you."

"I think so too," Salem said softly.

"But there's one big drawback."

Salem furrowed her brow. "Drawback? What do you mean?"

Denny fought to keep a straight face. "If you marry him, you'll be Mrs. Kowalczyk."

Salem's hair brushed Denny's shoulder as she firmly shook her head. "Nope. He'd be Mr. Jacobs. And we're not getting married. At least not yet."

A smile tugged on Denny's lips. That was what she and Eliza had said last year, yet every day that went by made her more certain that she wanted to spend the rest of her life with her.

"Have you told Bella?" Denny asked after a while.

Salem snorted. "You think she could keep something like that from you for even a second? I was hoping you'd help me tell her."

Denny stood and pulled Salem up with her. "All right. Let's go tell her."

"Now?"

"No time like the present."

Salem pointed both of her index fingers at her. "Keep that attitude for when you head over to Eliza's later. There's a townhouse with her name on it."

Denny held her breath as Bella seemed to digest the news.

"So what do you think?" Salem asked softly.

Bella tugged on the covers of her bed. "Would we move into the new house with him?"

"Yeah. You know the big room you picked the color for?" Salem waited for Bella to confirm with a nod. "That would be yours."

Excitement flashed in Bella's eyes, but she didn't smile or say anything for a while.

When Salem opened her mouth, Denny shook her head, knowing Bella needed time to think it through and come to her own conclusion.

"I could keep going to my school, right?" Bella sounded young and vulnerable, not like the tough, mature nearly twelve-year-old she pretended to be most of the time.

"Yes, of course."

"If we're getting new furniture, can I have a loft bed? You know, one with a desk underneath."

"Sure, honey," Salem said. "If that's what you want, we'll get you one."

Bella seemed to think about it for a few seconds longer. "I guess it would be okay, then. We could all..." She paused, and her face fell. Slowly, she looked up at Denny, who stood behind Salem at the foot of the bed. "You're not coming, are you?"

"No, kiddo, I'm not." Denny struggled to keep her voice from breaking. *Don't cry. Don't fucking cry!*

Bella stared at her with a shocked expression, as if she couldn't imagine living in a house where Denny wasn't.

Quickly, Denny added, "But the new house is so close that you could spit and hit me. I promise we'll still see each other all the time. You can come over whenever you want. I'll leave your room exactly the way it is right now, and you'll always have a place here too." Assuming she somehow managed to pay the rent for the townhouse by herself...or convinced Eliza to move in with her.

Bella considered it for a moment. "Having two rooms is kind of cool. But it's still weird. Like when Kaylee's parents got divorced."

Denny chuckled and hoped it didn't sound like sobbing.

"I get why you'd think that, but I hope you know we're not moving out because your aunt and I had a fight or because we love each other—or you—any less," Salem said. From her place on the edge of the bed, she looked over her shoulder at Denny, then back at Bella. "You both know that, right?"

Denny nodded along with Bella. Of course she knew that. Hearing it soothed the raw feelings churning in her stomach anyway.

"Okay," Bella said after a while. "We can move...but only if you teach Matt to make blueberry pancakes, Aunt Denny. Mom sleeps forever on Sundays. If I wait for her to get up, I'll starve."

Salem laughed, but her voice sounded choked.

"I can do that," Denny said, half laughing and half sniffling. "Or, even better, you could sleep over on Saturdays, and we'll make pancakes together."

That seemed to cheer Bella up, maybe because it confirmed that Denny still wanted her to be a part of her life. "Deal." She held her hand up for a high five.

Denny walked around Salem and complied. Then she bent and kissed Bella's forehead. "You'll always be my favorite niece, you know that, right?"

"I'm your only nie—" Bella's head snapped around, and she stared at Salem. "I am her only niece, right? You're not pregnant or anything, are you?"

Salem tossed up both hands. "What is it with you two and thinking I'm pregnant? For the record, I am not. The next person being welcomed into the Jacobs family will be Eliza, not a baby. That is, if your aunt ever gets up the courage to propose."

Bella sat up in bed. "You totally should. Then you wouldn't be alone." While she had sounded younger than she was earlier, she now looked much older as she directed a concerned gaze at Denny. But then a grin spread over her face, and she added, "And we would have someone who cleans the kitchen after we made blueberry pancakes."

"Jeez. Such a romantic." Denny jumped at the chance to lighten the mood. "You definitely don't get that from me."

Salem got up from the edge of the bed and kissed Bella's forehead too. "We'll talk more about it tomorrow, but are you okay with what we talked about? Do you think you'll be able to sleep?"

"Can I finish the book?" Bella held up the hardcover she'd been reading. "It's still early, and I can sleep in tomorrow."

Salem eyed the remaining pages behind the bookmark. "All right. I'll look in on you later. But if the book is boring or you want to talk more, come downstairs, okay?" When Bella nodded, Salem walked to the door.

"I'm going over to Eliza's, so I'll say good night now." Denny kissed her niece's forehead again, then lingered next to the bed for a few seconds. *Come on. It's not like they're moving out tonight. She'll still be here when you get back from Eliza's tomorrow.* She forced herself to follow Salem. When she reached the door, she gazed back.

Bella hadn't opened the book to continue reading. "Aunt Denny?"

"Yeah?"

"If I don't live with you anymore," Bella dragged her finger along the covers, like a plow on a field, "can I still join you when Eliza and the twins come over for craft lessons?"

That was what had her worried? Sometimes, a tween's brain worked in mysterious ways. "Of course. I'd never think of having a craft lesson without you."

Bella wiped away the groove she'd made with her finger. "Great. Good night."

"Good night." Denny took her in for a few more seconds, then turned away and bounded down the stairs. She couldn't wait to get to Eliza's and sink into her arms, where she could finally stop reining in her emotions.

On the last step, she remembered she wasn't going to Eliza's apartment. They were meeting up with Heather at their favorite Italian restaurant.

Normally, she loved catching up with Heather and hearing the latest stories about her school bus kids, but right now, the only person she wanted to see was Eliza.

Something was going on with Denny. Eliza had sensed it as soon as she had walked into the restaurant. At first she had thought Denny had to adjust to being among people after working from home all week, but that was clearly not it.

Denny picked an artichoke heart from a slice of pizza, popped it into her mouth, and chewed it with as much enjoyment as if it were a piece of cardboard.

"You okay?" Eliza asked quietly.

Denny nodded. "I'm fine."

After nine months of spending every weekend and most evenings together, Eliza could tell an "I really am fine" from an "I'm not fine at all, but I can't talk about it at the moment"—and this was definitely the latter. The urge to find out what was wrong and to provide comfort was strong, but she knew she shouldn't push Denny now.

"So, who's going to cover our stall at the market tomorrow?" Denny asked. "Heather, is it the two of us again?"

The *our* made Eliza smile. She allowed the obvious attempt to change the topic but pulled her phone from her pocket and slid her hands beneath the table so she could text Denny under the cover of the tablecloth.

"Yeah, I think Eliza prefers hanging out with her hot boss at the Feathered Friends booth," Heather said.

Eliza snorted. "Please. I have my own hottie, and Dee doesn't even know women other than Austen exist." When Heather was distracted by the waitress asking if she wanted more wine, Eliza tapped out a text beneath the table. *What happened? Do I need to kick someone's ass? I totally can. I have my lucky sneakers on.* Without looking, she snapped a photo of her footwear and sent it to Denny.

That put a smile on Denny's face. Her hands with her phone disappeared under the tablecloth too, and a few moments later, Eliza peeked at her screen and read, *Thanks. No ass-kicking required. I'll tell you later.*

Heather regarded them across the table. "Do you two need a minute alone?"

"No." Denny put her phone back into her pocket, and Eliza followed suit. "Sorry. That was rude of us."

"You two are lucky you're stinking cute together, so I'm letting you get away with it." Heather sobered and eyed Denny with obvious concern. "But are you really okay?"

Denny lowered her gaze to her pizza. For a moment, Eliza thought she would once again claim to be fine, but Denny looked back up and studied Heather. Finally, she nodded to herself, as if deciding that Heather deserved her trust. "Kind of. My sister and Bella are moving out at the end of the month."

God, no wonder Denny was in such a daze! Eliza reached beneath the table again and took her hand.

Denny clutched her fingers gratefully.

Heather lowered her slice of pizza. "That's a big change. For all of you. Are you okay with that?"

"It'll take some getting used to, but I'll be fine." Denny clung to Eliza's hand, even as she chuckled. "Bella is the one who's struggling to adjust. She said she would only move in with Matt if I teach him how to make blueberry pancakes."

Eliza's heart ached for her. She knew Denny was laughing it off because she couldn't allow herself to feel all the sadness and anxiety over this big change. Not in public. Not with anyone but her.

Heather laughed but sent Eliza a questioning look. So she, too, sensed Denny wasn't okay, but she didn't know if she should let her get away with pretending she was.

Eliza subtly shook her head. This wasn't the time or place where Denny could take her emotional armor down and reveal her big, soft heart.

"The things that worry Bella the most are baffling. It was very important to her that she still be included in our craft lessons." Denny's smile seemed less forced, and a warm light entered her eyes as she looked at Eliza. "I think she has a crush on you. Not that I can blame her."

"Um, honey, I'm pretty sure the reason she's so eager to come to the craft lessons isn't me," Eliza answered. "I think she has a crush on Polly."

Good thing Denny hadn't been eating her pizza anyway, or she would have choked. She stared at Eliza. "What? No! She's only eleven."

"She's almost twelve. You were only a year older when you fell in love with your best friend."

Heather nodded. "Lesbian rite of passage. Been there, done that too."

Denny took a big swig of her beer. "You really think my niece might have a crush on your niece? How do you know?"

"She gets that special look in her eyes when she looks at Polly. It reminds me of how her aunt looks at me."

The stunned expression on Denny's face transformed into a tender smile. She leaned over and kissed Eliza softly. When the kiss ended a moment later, Denny gazed into her eyes and pointed at herself. "This look?"

"Yeah. That's the one I meant."

Denny smiled, and the shadows of grief lifted from her eyes.

Heather threw a piece of pizza crust across the table. "God, you two! And I thought that honeymoon phase would pass. It's cute, but I'm telling you right now if you're late to Saturday Market again, it'll take more than some waffles to make up for it."

"Jeez, it happened once," Eliza said. Her birthday last month didn't count because Heather had told her to sleep in.

Denny's blush told her she was thinking about that morning too.

Heather glanced back and forth between them and smirked. "Whatever that blush is about, I'm sure I don't want to know." She gestured at Denny's mostly untouched pizza. "But you'd better clean your plate so you can keep up with your younger lover over there."

Denny glared but then picked up a slice of pizza and took a big bite.

Two hours later, Denny clung to Eliza in the pull-out bed as she told her all the details she hadn't wanted to talk about in the restaurant. Usually, she hated crying and making herself vulnerable in front of others, but with Eliza, she felt no shame when the tears she had held back all evening finally spilled over.

Eliza cradled Denny's head against her shoulder with one hand while she drew a soothing pattern along her bare back with the other. She let Denny talk without interrupting. When Denny was done, she tenderly wiped the tears from her cheeks with the back of her hand and kissed the corners of her eyes. "It's going to be weird not having them around at first, but you'll be fine. You're not alone; you know that, right?"

Not yet trusting her voice, Denny nodded.

"You've got me and my entire family, and it's not like Salem and Bella are moving to Tibet, where you can never visit them."

"I know." Denny sighed. "I'm being a big baby."

"No, you're not," Eliza said. "They've lived with you since before Bella was born. It's a big change. I totally get that."

Eliza's understanding warmed Denny from head to toe. She rolled over, taking Eliza with her so they were lying in their favorite cuddle position, with Eliza's leg thrown across her thighs and her hand resting on Denny's breast.

"What do you think you'll miss most?" Eliza asked quietly.

Denny caressed the small of her back with her fingertips while she thought about it. "It might sound strange, but I think it'll be not waking up to Bella rooting around the kitchen for breakfast. As much as I love my sister, I'll miss Bella most."

"That makes sense. I mean, you've basically been a second parent to her. A lot of your day was scheduled around her, especially since you started working from home. More often than not, you were the one who made breakfast and dinner, and you dropped her off and picked her up from the bus."

"Even though she insisted she's—"

"—not a baby and can walk home alone," they finished the sentence together and shared a laugh.

The persistent ache making Denny's throat burn finally lessened. "After nearly twelve years, it'll be hard to get used to not being responsible for a kid, but like you said, I'll be fine. Eventually."

Eliza let out a hum of agreement, her breath fanning over Denny's shoulder, but she didn't say anything.

Denny rubbed her fingers back and forth above the dip of her waist. "You okay? You've gone very quiet."

"Just thinking."

"About what?"

Eliza lifted herself up on one hand and peered at Denny. "Um, maybe you don't have to get used to that...if you don't want to."

"Get used to what?" Denny tried to replay their conversation in her mind but still wasn't sure what Eliza meant.

Eliza nibbled her bottom lip. Her gaze veered away, then back to Denny's face. "Not being responsible for a kid."

Denny's heart slammed against her ribs. "You don't mean...?"

"I know I'm totally putting the cart before the horse, but have you ever considered having a kid of your own...of our own?"

Wow. Eliza was indeed talking about what she thought she was talking about! The thought of a toddler with Eliza's eyes or her cute smile made the burning ache in her throat flare up again. God, she wanted that, but...wasn't it too selfish? "I don't know, Eliza. I'm forty-two."

"Right." An impish grin formed on Eliza's lips. "You're a senior citizen. I keep forgetting that because the things you do to me..." A gasp escaped her. "It always feels like you're definitely in your prime."

Denny couldn't hold back a smile. "Well, I have the right motivation."

Their lips came together in a tender kiss. Then they paused, legs tangled, and stared at each other.

"Are you serious about this? You want a baby with me?" Denny whispered. "We don't even live together...unless you want to change that?"

"Do you?"

That question was far easier to answer. "Well, I love the townhouse, and I'd love to have you living there with me. I know it would mean a bit of a commute for you, and I'd totally understand if you don't want to give up this apartment. I mean, it's homey and conveniently located and right next to Heather, so..."

"You're cute when you babble." Eliza rubbed her nose against Denny's. "Yes."

"Um, thanks. I was thinking you could take the MAX to work and..." Her brain finally caught up with what Eliza had said. "Yes? Did you say yes?"

"I did. What's a bit of a commute if I get to come home to you every night?"

They kissed again, then once more.

Denny's entire body vibrated with happiness. She would get to share a home with Eliza! But that wasn't all. Eliza also wanted them to have a child together. "I mentioned thinking I was too old for kids before. But you never said anything about wanting them."

"We were talking about kids in general, not about having kids together," Eliza said. "And back then, I wasn't sure kids were part of my life plan. I mean, I never not wanted them, but—"

"Um, what?" Denny's mind was reeling. "You lost me."

"A year or so ago, I didn't feel the burning need for a child. I wasn't against the idea, but kids were more of a nice-to-have, not a must-have for me."

"I remember you running out on SongBoy77 when he mentioned wanting you to have his babies." The memory made Denny chuckle.

Eliza snorted. "Yeah, and then you got me out of that date by pretending to give birth to triplets."

"Hmm, I sense a common theme. So, what changed?"

"I fell in love with you," Eliza said with the emotional openness Denny admired so much. Her eyes shone. "As soon as I met you, it was like putting on my favorite pair of sneakers. You just fit. We fit. You're loving and loyal and so wonderful with kids. When I watch you with Bella or my nieces and nephew, I just melt." She let out a wistful sigh. "But if having a baby with me is not what you want, that's totally okay. This only works if you want it too, and if you don't, you never have to be afraid that I'll end up resenting you for it."

Denny's throat closed up, and she had to work to get the words out. "That's not what I'm afraid of."

Eliza softly stroked her hair. "What is it then?"

"I'll be..." Denny stopped herself. God, here she was, talking as if it was about to become a reality! "I *would* be in my sixties by the time the kid is out of high school."

"Hmm, I guess then I'll have to be the one to teach her or him soccer and baseball, while you do the less strenuous stuff." A teasing grin lurked at the corners of Eliza's mouth.

"You?" Denny poked her playfully. "I love you, but you're awful at anything to do with balls."

They stared at each other again, then burst out laughing.

"You're right. I guess I'm more talented in other areas." With a smoldering look, Eliza trailed her finger along the curve of Denny's breast.

A tingle zipped down Denny's body. She covered Eliza's hand with her own, not wanting to get sidetracked.

Eliza sobered and flattened her fingers against Denny's chest, directly over her hammering heart. "What's going on in that beautiful, overthinking head of yours? Honestly, if you don't want—"

"I do," Denny said in a whisper that nearly got drowned out by the roaring sound in her ears. "I want to have a baby with you." She wanted everything with Eliza—a home, a future, a family. "I'm just scared to let myself want it. What if something goes wrong?"

"Then we'll deal with it together. You took a big chance on me—a supposedly straight woman—and I took a chance on you. Maybe it's time we took a chance together."

It sounded so right and so easy when Eliza said it like that. Maybe it wouldn't always be easy, but deep down, she knew it would be right. She exhaled shakily. "Okay."

"Really?"

"Really." Now that Denny had let herself want it, she couldn't rein in the broad smile spreading over her face.

Eliza let out a squeal that probably woke up half of her neighbors. Not that Denny cared. "We're going to do this! We're really going to move in together and have a baby and...oh my God!" She kissed Denny's forehead, her cheeks, her mouth, then trailed her lips down her throat, across her breasts, and down the curve of her belly.

Denny's breath caught. Her hips arched against Eliza. "Um, what are you doing?"

Eliza grinned at her from where her lips hovered against Denny's lower belly. "Well, if you're going to be the mom responsible for teaching soccer and baseball, we have to keep you fit."

"And this is your idea of an appropriate fitness program?"

Eliza slid lower and kissed the sensitive skin at the bend of her leg. "Are you complaining?"

A moan escaped Denny. She spread her legs to encourage Eliza's touch. "Nope," she got out, already breathing faster. "Not at all."

"Good." Eliza nibbled on the inside of her thigh, making Denny writhe. "Hmm, maybe we should aim for triplets."

Denny's laughter turned into a throaty groan as she wound her fingers into Eliza's hair and forgot about triplets, fitness programs, and everything but Eliza for the rest of the night.

If you enjoyed this book, also check out Jae's workplace romance *Under a Falling Star*, the book in which Eliza's bosses meet and fall in love. Austen starts a new job as an administrative assistant. On her first day, she has an unusual run-in with the company's hot but prickly COO. As they work together, the ice quickly begins to thaw.

Other Books from Ylva Publishing

www.ylva-publishing.com

Under a Falling Star
Jae

ISBN: 978-3-95533-238-9

Length: 369 pages (91,000 words)

Falling stars are supposed to be a lucky sign, but not for Austen. Her new job as a secretary in an international games company isn't off to a good start. Her first assignment—decorating the Christmas tree in the lobby—results in a trip to the ER after Dee, the company's second-in-command, gets hit by the star-shaped tree topper.

Dee blames her instant attraction to Austen on her head wound, not the magic of the falling star. She's determined not to act on it, especially since Austen has no idea that Dee is practically her boss.

The Roommate Arrangement
Jae

ISBN: 978-3-96324-279-3

Length: 333 pages (119,000 words)

Comedian Steph hopes to finally get her big break in LA. But to afford the rent, she needs a roommate. Enter Rae, a former cop guarding her wounded soul behind a tough exterior. At first, they clash horribly, but bit by bit, Steph breaks through the walls Rae has built around her.

Falling in love is no laughing matter in this opposites-attract lesbian romance with a bit of fake relationship.

Changing the Script
Lee Winter

ISBN: 978-3-96324-296-0

Length: 317 pages (104,000 words)

LA-based indie filmmaker Alex Levitin finds herself in New Zealand to save the "worst movie ever". Things might go easier if she didn't almost run over the standoffish local cop, Sam Keegan, and if the film wasn't being sabotaged. As Alex and Sam reluctantly join forces to find the set saboteur, attraction flares.

A funny, small-town lesbian romance about clashing cultures and daring to dream.

A Roll in the Hay
Lola Keeley

ISBN: 978-3-96324-355-4

Length: 185 pages (66,000 words)

Veterinarian Tess has quit the city and her cheating girlfriend for a new life in a Scottish village. On day one, she has a run-in with stuck-up Lady Karlson who tries to boss Tess around as if she owns the whole town...which she sort of does. But could there be something more to the constant, rising tension between the warring pair?

An enemies-to-lovers lesbian romance about making your own path.

About Jae

Jae grew up amidst the vineyards of southern Germany. She spent her childhood with her nose buried in a book, earning her the nickname "professor." The writing bug bit her at the age of eleven. Since 2006, she has been writing mostly in English.

She used to work as a psychologist but gave up her day job in December 2013 to become a full-time writer and a part-time editor. As far as she's concerned, it's the best job in the world.

When she's not writing, she likes to spend her time reading, indulging her ice cream and office supply addictions, and watching way too many crime shows.

CONNECT WITH JAE
Website: www.jae-fiction.com
E-Mail: jae@jae-fiction.com

Wrong Number, Right Woman
© 2020 by Jae

ISBN: 978-3-96324-401-8

Also available as an e-book.

Published by Ylva Publishing, legal entity of Ylva Verlag, e.Kfr.
Ylva Verlag, e.Kfr.
Owner: Astrid Ohletz
Am Kirschgarten 2
65830 Kriftel
Germany

www.ylva-publishing.com

First edition: 2020

Credits
Edited by Alexa Bitsko
Cover Design and Print Layout by Streetlight Graphics

CPSIA information can be obtained
at www.ICGtesting.com
Printed in the USA
LVHW091459250321
682476LV00001B/114